BELLEVUE

BELLEVUE

A NOVEL

ROBIN COOK

G. P. PUTNAM'S SONS
NEW YORK

PUTNAM
— EST. 1838 —

G. P. PUTNAM'S SONS
Publishers Since 1838
An imprint of Penguin Random House LLC
penguinrandomhouse.com

Library of Congress Cataloging-in-Publication Data

Names: Cook, Robin, author.
Title: Bellevue: a novel / Robin Cook.
Description: New York: G. P. Putnam's Sons, 2024.
Identifiers: LCCN 2024009219 | ISBN 9780593718834 (hardcover) |
    ISBN 9780593718858 (epub)
Subjects: LCSH: Bellevue Hospital—Fiction. | Medical fiction. |
    LCGFT: Historical fiction. | Novels.
Classification: LCC PS3553.O5545 B45 2024 | DDC 813/.54—dc23/
    eng/20240229
LC record available at https://lccn.loc.gov/2024009219
p.   cm.

Printed in the United States of America
1st Printing

Book design by Patrice Sheridan

For Cameron,
My wonderful son,
"Shoot for the moon, aim for the stars!"

BELLEVUE

PROLOGUE

D r. Clarence Fuller, a forty-four-year-old psychiatrist, emerged from his Gramercy Park brownstone at exactly eight o'clock and eyed the shiny new Checker taxicab waiting for him at the curb. It was a weekday-morning ritual he'd arranged with a local cab company to convey him to work at the Bellevue Psychopathic Hospital. Although the trip was only two and a half blocks east and ten blocks north, he preferred to ride rather than walk, especially now that it was mid-November and decidedly chilly. Clarence, an avowed automobile enthusiast who prided himself on his 1947 Cadillac Series 62 convertible, knew he was looking at a brand-new 1949 Checker A2. As he opened the rear-hinged back door and climbed into the spacious interior, he greeted the uniformed driver and complimented him on the car.

"Yup," the driver responded as he put the cab in gear and pulled away from the curb, heading east on 20th Street. "Just got this beauty yesterday, and it drives like a dream."

Eyeing the two collapsed jump seats on the floor in front of him, Clarence extolled the roominess and cleanliness of the car, which the driver also acknowledged. Clarence then sat back and relaxed. Although he wasn't a particularly superstitious individual, he couldn't help but take the brand-new taxi as a positive sign for the outcome of the day. Although the mere fact of having landed a position as a psychiatric attending at the famed Bellevue Hospital was a definite feather in his professional cap, he was one of many jockeying to be the heir to Dr. Menas S. Gregory, who had run the Psychiatric Division as a fiefdom for almost thirty years. Of course, Clarence knew he had a significant leg up on the competition, since he was a fourth-generation Bellevue physician. His father, Dr. Benjamin Fuller; his grandfather Dr. Otto Fuller; and his great-grandfather Dr. Homer Fuller had all been celebrated Bellevue surgeons extending back over two centuries. Although Clarence had briefly contemplated becoming a surgeon to follow in his forebearers' footsteps, he'd decided that the mysteries of the human brain and the exciting progress being made in the field of psychiatry were much more intellectually stimulating and too much of a temptation to pass up.

In his quest to be named chief of Bellevue's Psychiatric Division, Clarence currently saw his main in-house competitor to be Dr. Lauretta Bender, who had built up the division of child psychiatry to unforeseen heights and who was now polishing her credentials with the groundbreaking use of extensive electroconvulsive therapy, even employing it on children as young as four.

At first Clarence had lamented that he couldn't see a clear way to challenge Dr. Bender, but then he'd gotten wind of something that was even more promising. The procedure was called *lobotomy* and had been developed by Portuguese neurologist Dr. António Moniz, now tipped to win the Nobel Prize for Physiology or Medicine.

Clarence, like Dr. Moniz and an American named Dr. Walter Freeman—who'd significantly simplified lobotomy by changing it from a process that required a full operating room with anesthesia into a bedside procedure—saw lobotomy as an efficacious way of emptying the packed "disturbed wards" of the country's insane asylums, including Bellevue's. At last, a rapid twenty-to-thirty-minute procedure could change most, if not all, of the institutionalized patients from shrieking and screaming lunatics who often required straitjackets into docile, childlike individuals who could be discharged home instead of being kept like caged animals.

Immediately appreciating the lobotomy's promise, Clarence had jumped on it, actively bringing the procedure to Bellevue and championing its use in an expanding variety of patients. As the numbers mounted, so did his belief that the procedure would provide a tremendous boost to his professional prestige, especially after today. At 9:00 A.M. sharp, he'd scheduled a bedside lobotomy on an eight-year-old named Charlene Wagner, a girl whose prominent parents had given up on her after years of effort and struggle with her ongoing and significant behavioral problems.

Although Dr. Bender had considered using electroconvulsive therapy on Charlene, her schedule was currently so backed up that Clarence was able to intervene by talking directly to the parents. He had immediately appreciated the girl's potential to benefit his career aspirations, since she was an otherwise healthy and photogenic child despite her outrageous conduct. Accordingly, he'd invited the press, alerted both the medical and surgical chief residents so that interns and residents could be encouraged to come and observe, and called the head of the nursing school, who promised to send a large contingent of first-year nursing students. As far as Clarence was concerned, Charlene's lobotomy was to be a newsworthy command performance that might very well tip the scales to put him solidly out front as the next Bellevue Psychiatric Division director.

Since the taxi driver had driven Clarence to work on multiple previous occasions, he knew exactly where the doctor wanted to be dropped off. The man pulled to a stop directly in front of the massive wrought iron gate on the corner of First Avenue and 30th Street. After Clarence thanked the driver and alighted from the cab, he paused as he always did when the weather permitted to gaze up at the massive, eight-story Bellevue Psychopathic Hospital. It was, in his estimation, the most impressive and physically imposing psychiatric institute in the world, as well as being probably the most famous.

Although its construction had started in the Roaring Twenties, the building wasn't completed until 1933, sixteen years previously, at the height of the Depression. Regardless of the difficult economic times, it had been constructed of expensive red brick and gray granite in a grand Italian Renaissance style with no dearth of architectural embellishments, including porticoes, niches with terra-cotta and concrete vases, pediments, and decorative cornices. Overall, despite its elaborate details, it fit very well with the main Bellevue Hospital building that had opened at the turn of the twentieth century, designed by the renowned architectural firm McKim, Mead & White. The main hospital, too, had been built of red brick and gray granite but with substantially fewer architectural flourishes.

From where Clarence was standing, he could not see his office window, as it was in the central, ten-story portion of the structure and faced south, looking out over the rest of the Bellevue Hospital buildings. Once he'd given the building the respect it deserved, Clarence pushed open the wrought iron gate and hurriedly headed for the First Avenue entranceway. Most people used either the grander 30th Street entrance or the more convenient 29th Street one, which faced the Bellevue Hospital complex. Both led to a common reception desk. Clarence preferred the lesser-used First Avenue entrance as a sign of respect, as if the building was somehow sentient, a thought that always made him smile.

As excited as he was, he didn't waste time waiting for an elevator to get up to his third-floor office but rather used the ornate Leonardo da Vinci–inspired central stairway. After a cursory hello to his scheduling secretary, Grace Carter, who handed him his day's itinerary and told him all was ready for Charlene's procedure, he disappeared into his inner sanctum. Clarence changed his suit jacket for a long white doctor's coat, better for the pictures he assumed and hoped the press would be taking, and went to his desk. Although few of the other psychiatrists on staff ever wore white coats, Clarence often did. In his opinion, the coat was more professorial and in keeping with his position as a medical academic.

From the desk's central drawer, he carefully lifted out a fancy wooden box and opened the lid. Nestled in cloth-lined depressions were two custom-made orbitoclasts, which he was going to use for the upcoming lobotomy, one for each eye. The instruments had been designed for Clarence according to the specifications dictated by Dr. Walter Freeman, who had devised the transorbital lobotomy bedside technique that Clarence now exclusively used. The stainless-steel instruments looked surprisingly like traditional ice picks, each with a ten-inch-long pointed stiletto blade. The difference was that they had rounded stainless-steel expanses on the bases of their handles, which enabled them to be struck with a mallet to drive them through the thin, bony roof of a human eye socket. Also nestled in the box in its own cloth-lined depression was a machine-tooled, stainless-steel mallet.

Satisfied that all was in order, Clarence stood up and slipped the box into one of his white coat's deep side pockets. After a quick check in the mirror behind his coat closet door to make sure his hair was in place, he headed out of his office. Again using the stairs, he ascended to the fifth floor, where he'd had Charlene Wagner moved from the locked ward for disturbed children into a private and particularly photogenic room. As he walked along the two-toned yellow-tan central corridor, passing beneath the squares of purely decorative faux ribbed vaulting that lined most of the building's hallways, he felt his excitement ratchet upward.

Entering the room, Clarence could not have been more pleased. It was crowded with nursing students in their starched, white-smocked outfits, a handful of interns and residents, and, more important, a number of reporters, some even holding large press cameras. A few flashbulbs went off, causing him to blush and wave.

Just as he expected, Charlene Wagner looked angelic in an off-white dress. Following his orders, she'd been tranquilized with Luminal that morning and was currently asleep in her bed with her blond hair splayed out to frame her cherubic features. She was tall for her age, appearing nearly prepubescent. Three impressively sized psychiatric attendants were grouped around the head of the bed, which had been pulled away from the wall. Behind them were two windows that offered a narrow view of the East River.

After handing off his box of instruments to a nurse who would see to their sterilization, Clarence cleared his throat and gave a short and concise history of the patient and an explanation for why the procedure would be beneficial to everyone, including the troubled girl. He wanted to make the affair as short as possible to emphasize the utility of lobotomy to help empty the disturbed wards of the country's mental institutions. He asked if there were any questions, but no one raised their hand.

Without more ado, Clarence took the hypodermic syringe filled with lidocaine from one of the attending nurses. While some devotees of the transorbital lobotomy used electric convulsion to render the patient unconscious, Clarence's opinion was that it wasn't necessary. He was convinced that local anesthesia was more than adequate since the interior of the human brain was devoid of sensory fibers. After a nod to the male attendants, one grasping Charlene's head to steady it and the other two holding her arms and torso, Clarence leaned forward and retracted the girl's right upper eyelid. A hefty psychiatric nurse grasped the girl's ankles.

Charlene let out a howl and a string of expletives and struggled against the restraining hands, but to no avail. With considerable adeptness, Clarence rapidly infiltrated both medial upper eyelids and then walked the needle point along the roof of both eye sockets to anesthetize those areas. The process took literally seconds. Satisfied, he handed off the syringe, waited a few beats for the lidocaine to take effect, then took up one of the orbitoclasts.

While the psychiatric attendant struggled to keep the screaming child's head motionless, Clarence raised the lid of her right eye and then pushed the point of the orbitoclast at a forty-five-degree angle into the conjunctival recess until it hit up against the boney vault of the eye socket. He then took the mallet from the assisting nurse and, with a few decisive taps, penetrated the bone, pushing the orbitoclast into the girl's brain.

Now out of breath, Charlene fell silent as Clarence advanced the orbitoclast to the five-centimeter mark. Once it was at that position, he merely pushed the handle of the instrument several inches medially and then several inches laterally, causing the instrument's flattened tip to sweep through brain tissue and effectively sever the nerve pathways between the forebrain and the midbrain.

Several flashbulbs went off, but no one said a word. Ignoring the observers, Clarence advanced the orbitoclast to the seven-centimeter mark and repeated the lateral sweeping motion before pulling the instrument out.

"The right eye is already completed," Clarence said as he handed off the first orbitoclast to the assisting nurse and took the second. "All we need to do is repeat the procedure on the left, and we are done. What should be plainly obvious is that this is a simple, straightforward, and remarkably effective procedure. Are there any questions before we continue?"

Clarence glanced around the room. No one spoke. He could see that the nursing students in particular were agog. Returning his attention to Charlene, Clarence once more began the procedure, again using the mallet and several taps to penetrate the boney roof of the left orbit. After sweeping the orbitoclast medially and laterally at five centimeters, he then advanced the instrument to the seven-centimeter mark, sweeping it medially. But when he swept it laterally, disaster struck. To his horror, a sudden pulsating jet of blood arced up alongside the orbitoclast, forming a miniature geyser and spattering a line of bright crimson dots down the front of his otherwise spotless white coat.

Shocked at this unforeseen event, Clarence reeled back as the throbbing geyser continued spraying blood, causing other people in its path to leap away from the bed. Instantly, he knew what had happened. Given the strength of the pulsating jet of blood, the orbitoclast had undoubtedly severed the anterior cerebral artery, the main blood supply to the forebrain.

Clarence was paralyzed by sheer panic and had no idea what to do as he stood there frozen in place, staring at the offending instrument still sticking out of Charlene's left eye. As the pulsating jet of blood began to lessen, he briefly considered trying to get the girl over to surgery in the main hospital. Yet his intuition nixed the idea, telling him it would be futile, since she had essentially had a massive hemorrhagic stroke. But in the middle of his confused panic, one thing that seemed clear was that this obstreperous, behaviorally outrageous, and contrary girl had managed to remain in character. Instead of helping his career, she'd probably managed to sabotage it and thereby ruin his chances of using lobotomy to become Bellevue's psychiatric chief.

CHAPTER 1

Monday, July 1, 6:15 A.M.

When Michael Fuller's phone alarm woke him with its insistent jangle, he literally leaped out of bed in a near panic while fumbling to turn the damn thing off. He'd been in the middle of a disturbing nightmare of being chased down endless yellow-tan corridors without the slightest idea of what or who was chasing him or why. All he knew was that he had been panicked out of his mind and as a result his heart was still racing.

With the back of his hand, he wiped his damp brow and took a deep breath to calm down. He'd never before experienced such a uniquely frightening dream. Certainly, he'd had his share of nightmares while growing up, but nothing like what he'd just endured. Although he'd had some minor difficulty getting to sleep the night before, due to his mixed emotions about the upcoming day, he certainly didn't expect first-day jitters to have caused such a dream.

For twenty-three-year-old Michael Fuller, this first day of July was going to be momentous, marking the beginning of a whole new chapter in his life. Today was the first day of his surgical residency at Langone Medical Center, known colloquially as NYU, and he was going to be specifically starting at the renowned Bellevue Hospital. Although he'd felt definite anticipatory excitement, he'd also experienced a measure of anxiety. Certainly more than he realized, as was clearly evidenced by the bad dream. When he'd been on duty in the hospital as a medical student, there'd always been a resident available when an emergency happened. Suddenly now he was the resident, meaning from today on, there'd be no immediate backup. He would have to handle whatever emergency he might face when he was alone in the middle of the night on the hospital's surgical ward, a circumstance that was very scary. His fear was that he wasn't ready, that medical school hadn't prepared him adequately.

But at the same time Michael felt uneasy, he also felt decidedly fortunate. As one of seven first-year NYU surgical residents, a position formerly known as an internship, he'd been chosen by chance to start at Bellevue along with another first-year resident, Andrea Intiso. Even being assigned with Andrea was a lucky twist of fate as far as he was concerned, because they were both graduates of Columbia University's historic College of Physicians and Surgeons. There, purely by chance, they'd been teamed up as medical students for their clinical pathology, physical diagnosis, and internal medicine rotations. Consequently, he knew her to be a friendly, dependable, smart, and plucky woman, and he liked her.

The other five first-year surgical residents, three men and two women, had been assigned to the various other hospitals in the sprawling NYU Langone Health complex for their first two-month rotation. Mitt, a nickname Michael had been given as a toddler and still preferred, would also be assigned to these other hospitals in due course, after his first rotation at Bellevue. For him it was akin to having won a lottery because it was Bellevue Hospital that had attracted him to apply to NYU for his residency training for two major reasons.

The first reason was its distinguished history, including three centuries of fostering many major medical advances. He knew that Bellevue Hospital had even established the very first residency in surgery way back in 1883, which was still the model for surgical training worldwide.

The second reason was personal.

Mitt descended on his paternal side from a long and impressive medical pedigree. Way back in the seventeenth century a direct ancestor of his named Samuel Fuller had been on the *Mayflower* and served as the Plymouth Colony's medical doctor. But more to the point from Mitt's perspective, he was a direct descendant of four consecutive generations of celebrated Bellevue physicians, three surgeons—the latest of whom had also done a Bellevue surgical residency—and a psychiatrist. All four of these physicians had been contemporary leaders in their fields, particularly his closest relative, Dr. Clarence Fuller, his paternal great-grandfather. Mitt had made it a point to read a number of Clarence's lauded research papers, in which he championed and helped develop methods of psychotherapy and even anticipated groundbreaking behavioral therapy.

Mitt had been impressed enough with what he'd read of Clarence's Bellevue career to consider specializing in psychiatry himself, but Mitt's father, Benjamin, a highly successful Boston-based hedge fund manager who was in secret a frustrated surgeon after deciding against medical school despite his own father's encouragement, prevailed upon Mitt to follow in the renowned footsteps of his surgical forebearers, particularly Dr. Benjamin Fuller, Mitt's father's namesake.

Mitt was the first to admit—with deserved appreciation—that his father's generous economic inducements had played an outsized role in getting Mitt to apply to medical school and then choose a surgical subspecialty at NYU Grossman School of Medicine. One of the inducements was the fully furnished and professionally decorated apartment Mitt was now occupying on the fourth floor of 326 East 30th Street, which he knew was beyond anything a first-year surgical resident could typically afford. Same with the fancy Mercedes-AMG parked in a nearby garage.

After dashing into his posh, newly renovated bathroom, Mitt lathered himself in preparation to quickly shave. As he'd learned during the first week that he'd occupied the apartment to attend his NYU residency orientation, he had to scrunch down to take advantage of the magnifying shaving mirror. It had been positioned at a height significantly lower than appropriate for Mitt's lanky six-foot-four frame.

With his coordination and considerable stature, which he'd reached at a youthful age, he'd been pressured as early as the sixth grade to play basketball. Mitt had declined and continued to do so through high school and college. He'd never appreciated what he labeled as the "marginal utility" of organized sports, much preferring to concentrate his extracurricular activities and attention on mental exercise rather than physical. His preferences leaned toward debating, playing chess, and music, particularly the piano. Ever since he could remember and maybe as early as age two, Mitt had been more cerebral than physical.

Working quickly to navigate the disposable razor around and over his angular and pale face, Mitt was conscious of the time. He was due in the fifteenth-floor surgical conference room at Bellevue Hospital at 7:30 A.M. sharp. Luckily the hospital was a mere five-minute walk away. After a quick rinse and dry, Mitt paused to study his reflection. He was worrying anew about how he was going to hold up under the stresses of being a newbie resident, especially if and when he had to face medical emergencies alone.

Although he had hardly been a polymath in high school and college, he'd done extremely well grade-wise, such that he was confident in his basic intelligence. Due to his interest in academics, Mitt had advanced more quickly than his peers and graduated high school at sixteen, college at nineteen, and medical school at twenty-three, making him the youngest of the current batch of first-year surgical residents at NYU. None of his academic accomplishments had been a surprise to his proud parents, who'd recognized Mitt's precocity from an early age.

But there was more to Mitt's intelligence than a high IQ. He wasn't sure exactly when he first became aware of the capacity, but he had a kind of precognitive ability that he secretly labeled his "sixth sense." It wasn't constant, and he had no idea how to provoke it. When he'd applied to boarding school, college, and even medical school and then surgical residency, the moment he sent off his applications, he knew he would be accepted. He'd been so confident in his belief that he'd never experienced the anxiety that all his friends did, and on all four occasions, unlike his friends, he'd only applied to one school or program, not the usual dozen or more.

Adding to this unusual precognition, Mitt had on occasion the ability to sense what people were thinking. Again, it wasn't a constant capability, and he didn't know how to encourage its manifestation other than recognizing that it required concentrated mental effort and a clear mind. Curiously enough, when he was able to predict the future or tell what someone was thinking, it was almost always accompanied by varying degrees of tactile sensations along the insides of his arms or thighs, the back of his neck, or across the front of his chest. He likened these sensations, which he called *paresthesia,* the technical term, after taking neurology in medical school, to something like the "pins and needles" he'd feel when his extremities' circulation was compromised.

In contrast to his precognitive faculty, which there was no way he could explain, he believed his ability to sense what people were thinking was probably based on an acute and unconscious sensitivity to a wide variety of idiosyncratic clues people unknowingly projected by their posture, expressions, and choice of syntax. Although the possibility that he possessed some rare psychic power had occurred to him on occasion, he'd dismissed the idea out of hand as being entirely anti-scientific. In college he had majored in math, physics, and chemistry and believed he could have pursued any one of those scientific fields if he'd been so inclined, which didn't leave a lot of room for believing in the supernatural.

Mitt had never told anyone about these special talents, not even his parents, even though as an only child he had a relationship with them that had been, and still was, particularly close. Knowing what his parents were thinking without them being aware was often to his advantage, although this was not always the case with his contemporaries. Especially during his teen years, it was usually disheartening for him to sense what girls thought of him, as it was often negative. Mitt was the first to admit that he was not a member of the "in crowd," as he was decidedly bookish, hardly a positive in the teen value system he grew up in. On the other side of the coin, he did find his unique abilities helpful in giving him a leg up with his schoolwork. Before an exam, all he had to do was talk to his teachers or professors to predict what was going to be asked, eliminating any surprises. From an early age he developed a penchant for good grades.

After brushing his short, dirty-blond hair into a semblance of order, Mitt returned to his bedroom to dress. Casting an eye on the bedside clock, he was shocked by the raucous ring of his mobile phone. Curious and mildly unnerved at who could possibly be calling so early on a Monday morning, he snatched up the device. The answer was obvious, and he should have guessed. It was his father. Clicking on the phone and holding it up to his ear, Mitt said: "What in God's name are you doing up at this hour? Are you ill?" He knew his father was an inveterate night person who usually remained in his home office until well past midnight to digest the early-morning European financial news to give him a jump on his workday.

"Ha ha," his father fake-laughed. "As if I'd miss the big day. To be truthful, I'm jealous. At the same time, I couldn't be any prouder. I hope you enjoy yourself!"

"Ditto that," his mother, Clara, voiced in the background.

"I'm not sure 'enjoy' is the right word," Mitt said. "To be honest, I'm a bit nervous." In the back of his mind, he quickly banished the thought of his nightmare. "It's an awful lot of responsibility. Going from medical student to resident is a big step, like going from day to night with no twilight." After another glance at the time, he put his phone on speaker, placed it on the top of his bureau, and continued dressing.

"You will do fine!" Benjamin said with conviction. "You excelled in medical school, so you couldn't be better prepared."

"We'll see," Mitt said noncommittally. He didn't want to get into a discussion about the deficiencies of current undergraduate medical education, which were looming in the back of his mind. "But thanks for calling. I'll let you know how the day went as soon as I can. It might not be until tomorrow. I sense I'm going to be on call tonight, but I don't know for certain. Andrea and I haven't been given our schedules, but since there are only two of us, the chances are fifty-fifty." He actually already knew he would be on call that night, but he didn't want to get into a discussion about how he knew. As for Andrea, his parents had met her at their recent medical school graduation. They also knew from a previous phone call that both she and Mitt had been assigned to Bellevue to start their residencies together.

"Our illustrious surgical ancestor Dr. Benjamin Fuller has to be tickled pink that you are following in his footsteps."

"I hope so," Mitt said. He'd thought about his ancestor on multiple occasions, including the night before. Benjamin Fuller was his most esteemed surgical forebearer, born just before the Civil War in 1860. He earned his formidable reputation at Bellevue, serving first as an intern, then a resident, and finally as an attending physician. He'd worked with the internationally famed surgeon William Halsted and also with William Welch, the father of modern pathology, until both men switched from Bellevue to the newly formed medical school at Johns Hopkins. For Mitt, it was daunting to follow such a legend, as it undoubtedly raised expectations for his performance with the powers that be. Was he up to it? Mitt had no idea, but he was soon going to find out. For him the situation was like jumping into the deep end of a pool with only a rudimentary knowledge of how to swim.

"I'm convinced you are going to become more famous than my namesake," Benjamin said as if sensing Mitt's insecurities and wanting to be supportive. "I can feel it in my bones."

"Famous or not," Mitt responded, glancing again at the time, "I have to get a move on here. I'm due at the hospital at seven thirty sharp."

"Of course," Benjamin said. "Call us when you can. Good luck!"

"Yes, good luck," Clara called out in the background.

Mitt disconnected the call and quickly ran the knot he'd made in his tie up under his chin and folded down the collar of his shirt. Donning the short white coat and white pants he'd been given during his brief orientation at NYU Grossman School of Medicine, plus the lanyard he'd been given with his hospital ID, he checked himself in the mirror. At least in his all-white outfit he looked like a surgical resident, even if he didn't feel like one.

CHAPTER 2

Although it was just after seven, the rising sun already felt distinctly warm on Mitt's face as he quickly walked east on 30th Street toward First Avenue. There was no doubt in his mind that it was going to be another summer scorcher in New York City. Yet a broiling afternoon, no matter the temperature, wasn't something he needed to worry about. He suspected that once he entered the Bellevue Hospital high-rise, he would not leave again until tomorrow. His precognition of the night before, heralded by a trace of pins and needles on his chest, had signaled that he, and not Andrea, would be on call on their first night of surgical residency.

The traffic on First Avenue was already heavy with a surging melee of cars, taxis, buses, and trucks emitting a muffled roar, and as Mitt approached the vehicular free-for-all, he felt both his excitement and anxiety rachet upward. Luckily the excitement significantly overshadowed the anxiety, which had lessened considerably following his brief chat with his parents.

Reaching First Avenue, he had to stop at the curb to wait for the traffic light to change. Looking north while he stood there, Mitt could make out most of the NYU Langone Health complex, which stretched for three entire city blocks. Turning his head and gazing to the south, he could see most of the Bellevue Hospital complex, including the dominating twenty-five-story hospital tower. Beyond that was the veterans hospital. The view in both directions justified the area being called "hospital row."

Directly in front of Mitt on the north side of 30th Street he could see the Office of Chief Medical Examiner, which he knew was a fancy title for the New York City morgue. He didn't know very much about forensic pathology, having had only a single lecture on the subject during his second year in medical school, but he knew enough about it to appreciate that the building housed the largest such institution in the world. More important, from his perspective, it had its origins—like a lot of major medical advances—at Bellevue Hospital. There was absolutely no doubt he was joining a celebrated medical community with an impressive history.

When the light changed Mitt scurried across the avenue. Reaching the safety of the curb on the east side, he stopped for a moment to gaze up at the strangely impressive building on the southeastern corner of First Avenue and 30th Street. Surrounding the sizable ten-story structure was an imposing and oddly decorative rusty wrought iron fence whose granite stanchions were topped with concrete urns. The barricade was so substantial and unique that it begged the question of whether its role was to keep people out or in.

The building itself was red brick with granite highlights and lots of curious decorative architectural details that looked particularly out of date in contemporary New York City. It was the antithesis of a typical NYC glass skyscraper. But what was most glaring about the building was that it was so obviously abandoned, save for a small portion down near the East River that Mitt knew was being used as a men's homeless shelter. The rest of the structure's enormity was empty, and had been so for more than thirty years. The windows on the granite-encased first floor were boarded up, and a small garden area in front of the two wings that faced First Avenue was entirely overgrown with weeds and vines. And like so many New York City buildings, its first floor was partially covered by scaffolding.

Mitt was well aware that he was looking at the former Bellevue Psychiatric Hospital, which had been called the Bellevue Psychopathic Hospital when it opened back in the 1930s. He was somewhat knowledgeable about the building because it was where his celebrated ancestor Dr. Clarence Fuller, who had spent most of his professional career at Bellevue, had his office. When Mitt had come for his residency interview, he'd seen the structure and had taken the time to look up its history. When the six-hundred-bed facility had opened nearly a hundred years previously, it had been the talk of the town and quickly became the most famous psychiatric hospital in the world. In many ways, it was the reason the name Bellevue had become synonymous with a mental institution rather than a comprehensive medical facility, which it had always been.

Continuing southward, Mitt walked into the cool shadow the building's looming size provided. He paused again at the wrought iron gate that was secured with a heavy chain and weighty padlock. Looking between the rusting wrought iron uprights, he gazed at the building's rather decorative entranceway, secured with its own chain and padlock. For a moment, he was transfixed; there was something remarkably sad about the portal. Mitt pondered the innumerable poor souls who had passed through to be essentially incarcerated in the building, and he found himself imagining what kind of painful stories they might tell.

At the same moment, he felt a surprising, transient surge of the tactile sensations that he normally associated with his prognostication abilities. The feelings were a particular surprise because he wasn't facing a circumstance that called for a prediction. Nor was there another human being whose thoughts he could sense because he was essentially alone facing an empty structure. A few passersby hurried behind him in both directions, but for him to sense someone's thoughts, he had to make eye contact with them, which certainly wasn't the case.

With a mystified shrug, he forced himself to pull his eyes away from the deserted building and continue on his way. Time was passing, and the last thing Mitt wanted to do was be late on his first day. Yet he couldn't resist one last quick look over his shoulder at the old Bellevue Psychiatric Hospital, wondering how the building had managed to avoid being demolished or repurposed after the last of its psychiatric patients had been transferred over to the newer high-rise. He'd read that more than a decade earlier there had been some talk of turning it into a hotel and conference center for the NYU medical center, which would be an easy conversion with its unique letter H footprint and hundreds of individual rooms, each with windows. Yet obviously it hadn't happened. Why, he had no idea. The building's continued existence as a sad, empty shell made no sense. It was a total anachronism and also an affront to its illustrious history.

CHAPTER 3

Monday, July 1, 7:11 A.M.

A long with a sizable throng of other people, Mitt entered the I. M. Pei–designed combination lobby and Ambulatory Care Pavilion of Bellevue Hospital. Although the hour was still early, the place was already hopping with a mixture of patients and staff and a smattering of homeless people. And once he was inside the expansive, multistory glass-topped vestibule, he was in for a pleasant surprise. The entire red-brick, marble, and granite façade of the previous-turn-of-the-century McKim, Mead & White–designed Bellevue Administration building had been preserved and incorporated into the interior of the 2005 structure. To get into the hospital itself, he had to walk under the original granite archway encompassing a high relief seal of the city of New York.

As he passed under the old archway, he was in for a second surprise. Mitt felt yet another unexpected flush of strange sensations on his arms, thighs, and chest that were even more pronounced than what he'd experienced a few minutes earlier, strong enough to make him stop abruptly in his tracks. Unfortunately, his sudden halt caused several hurrying people to run into him, causing a minor pedestrian pileup.

"Sorry, sorry," Mitt repeated to those he'd blocked in the relatively narrow passage. He stepped out of the way, again totally confused as to why he was experiencing such sensations when previously they'd always been associated with recognized stimuli. He looked behind him at the faces of the people coming into the hospital, as if someone might explain to him why he was experiencing what he was, but obviously that didn't happen. A few hospital staff briefly glanced in Mitt's direction as they hurried past. All had expressions he interpreted as mild irritation. In truth, he didn't have any idea why he was experiencing these sensations, and he imagined his face probably reflected his confusion. Adding to it was a vague feeling of foreboding that he also couldn't explain.

But then as quickly as the new paresthesias appeared, they disappeared. With mild bewilderment and a slight shake of his head, he rejoined the moving crowd. A few minutes later, he and a sizable group of people crammed into one of the many elevators.

The ride up took more time than Mitt had allotted because the car stopped on just about every floor. Each time, there was an uncomfortably long pause before the doors deigned to close, heightening his unease. Mitt found himself checking his watch on several occasions, as if doing so would speed things up, but it didn't.

No one spoke during the entire elevator ride. Everyone was either silently watching the floor indicator or checking their mobile phones. Finally on the fifteenth floor, several people pushed to get off along with Mitt.

Immediately upon exiting, Mitt asked one of the hurrying staff, obviously a nurse, if she knew where the surgical conference room was located. She was a middle-aged, friendly-looking Black woman whose hair was tightly cornrowed.

"I most certainly do," she said brightly. "Follow me! I'm going right by it." She waved over her shoulder as she headed out of the elevator lobby. "Are you one of the new surgical residents?" she asked, glancing back at Mitt as she walked.

"I am," he responded. "Is it so obvious?"

"Your pristine outfit," the woman said with a gleeful laugh. "It's a giveaway. Besides, it is the first day of July, and we nurses all know what that means in relation to the house staff."

"I can imagine. It's probably the most dangerous day for patients in teaching hospitals across the country."

"Ha, ha! You got that right."

"Are you a nurse on the surgical service?"

"Not officially, but I'm here today," the woman said. "I'm a floater. I like variety. One of the regular surgical nurses called in sick. I'm filling in for her." She hesitated for a moment and pointed at an unmarked, slightly ajar door. "That's the surgical conference room, and good luck with your residency. I'm sure I'll see you around." She then hurried on ahead to where the hallway opened up into an expansive but empty waiting room for one of the surgical clinics.

"Thank you," Mitt called after her as he pushed the conference room's door fully open. The room beyond was a moderate size with a spectacular view over the East River, with Brooklyn in the distance. To the left was a podium with an old-fashioned chalkboard behind it. To the right were several dozen modern student desk chairs with attached writing arms. Sitting in one of them in the first row was Andrea Intiso.

"Whoa! It's about time," Andrea called out with a tone that was humorous but tinged with a hint of relief. "I was beginning to worry

I'd be facing the day on my own." She sprang to her feet as she spoke and came toward Mitt, offering one cheek, then the other, in her inimitable style. Mitt pressed his cheeks alternately against hers while air-kissing as he'd learned to do. For him it was an unnatural gesture of affection since physical intimacy had not been part of his upbringing. Although there had been hugs here and there, more with his father than mother, there had never been much kissing or cheek pressing. But Andrea had been persistent from day one, and he'd learned to adapt. Now he appreciated the gesture.

"You're cutting this pretty damn close," she said, glancing at the time on her phone as she folded her five-foot-eleven frame back into the desk chair. "Five minutes isn't much of a cushion. Hell, I've been here chewing my nails for a good half hour already."

Andrea was slim and athletic with bobbed dark hair and very dark but bright eyes that appeared to be all pupils. She was also somewhat of a fashionista, particularly for a medical trainee. This morning, she was wearing a bright red dress that was quite striking under her white coat, especially compared with Mitt's all-white outfit. She was a quintessential first-generation Italian American with an easy smile and olive skin. Both her parents had come to America for graduate school and ended up marrying and staying in academia as tenured professors right there in New York. Andrea grew up in the city and attended Columbia undergraduate and its medical school tuition-free thanks to her parents being on the faculty.

"I didn't mean to cut it this close," Mitt admitted as he sat in the chair next to hers. "On my way here, I stopped to stare at the old psychiatric hospital on the corner. It's where one of my physician ancestors had his office. His name was Clarence Fuller."

"I remember you telling me. It's so cool you are following in your ancestors' footsteps."

"Some ways cool and some ways not so cool," Mitt said. "I'm hoping the expectations of the powers that be of the residency program aren't beyond my capabilities. Anyway, are you familiar with the building I'm talking about? It's just down the block and part of the Bellevue complex."

"Vaguely," Andrea admitted. She shrugged. "I guess I passed it on my way in. Why do you ask?"

"The place intrigues me," Mitt said. "It's an enormous empty hulk except for a small portion of it down Thirtieth Street being used as a men's homeless shelter."

"Why does the rest of it being empty bother you?"

"It just seems odd to me that a building of that size with such an interesting and illustrious history would stay empty for almost forty years, especially since New York hasn't been all that sensitive to its historical buildings—just look at the Penn Station debacle. But the psych building's location alone makes it inordinately valuable, so it sitting unused here in the middle of hospital row is a gigantic waste. I mean, why hasn't it been renovated or demolished and something built in its place? It doesn't make any sense."

"You might be right, Mitt, but facing our first day of surgical residency, we've got much more pressing concerns to think about." Andrea rolled her eyes for emphasis. Worrying about an empty psychiatry building was the last thing on her mind.

"Yeah, you're right, but I tell you, looking at the place gave me a weird feeling." Mitt was tempted to explain the paresthesia he'd experienced, knowing that she would be familiar with the term from their medical school neurology rotation, but he hesitated. He'd never said anything to anyone about having such tactile sensations on a fairly regular basis, as it would necessitate trying to explain a personal phenomenon he didn't truly understand himself. Besides, what about the similar tingling he'd felt while walking under the preserved granite archway as he'd entered the hospital proper? In many ways that episode was more curious, since the old psychiatric hospital seemed creepy enough to elicit some kind of a physical response in anyone.

"What do you mean, 'weird feeling'?"

"Sort of a crawly skin sensation. The place looks kind of scary. Maybe it's all the outdated architectural embellishments—concrete urns, entablatures, pediments. It's got a ton of that kind of antiquated decorative stuff. What I recall is that the building was built in an Italian Renaissance style, sort of like a misplaced Medici palace." Mitt laughed and nodded, pleased to make an indirect reference to Andrea's Italian heritage.

"I do remember glancing at it briefly back when I came down here for my residency interview with one of the Bellevue attendings, and it didn't remind me of a Medici palace in the slightest." Andrea again rolled her eyes, clearly thinking the association totally ridiculous.

"Well, I agree it's a stretch. I doubt it was supposed to look like a Medici palace. The idea just popped into my head. Anyway, the building is rather famous . . . or infamous. I suppose you know that a lot of celebrity types were inpatients, people like Norman Mailer and Sylvia Plath. When it was up and running, it had six hundred patient beds. That's a lot of beds and a lot of mentally compromised people. Can you imagine some of the stories its patients could tell if they were still around?"

"If they could communicate at all," Andrea said.

"Okay, I can tell you aren't all that interested," Mitt said, raising his hands in surrender and deciding to change the subject. "Tell me something else, then," he continued in a more serious tone. "When you entered the hospital this morning from the lobby by passing through the architecturally preserved archway, did you feel anything creepy?"

"That is one very weird question. What's going on with you? Are you trying to pull my chain? What on earth do you mean, 'feel anything creepy'?"

"Just that. Really! Like pins and needles or the hairs standing up on the back of your neck?"

"Are you losing it? Come on! What's gotten into you? Maybe I felt some anxiety to go along with the anxiety I felt the second I opened my eyes this morning, and the anxiety I feel right now. Is that what you mean?"

"No. Not at all. I'll tell you why I'm asking. I felt a kind of prickling sensation the moment I passed under the archway, and I was wondering if you might have had some similar sensation. It was enough for me to stop walking. I thought maybe it could have been a draft or something, but there was nothing."

Andrea eyed Mitt with a wry smile. "You are definitely starting to worry me. Are you all right?"

Mitt laughed and made a quick attitudinal about-face. "I'm fine. Truly. I'm just playing with you. I mean, we're both hyped-up, since it is our first day."

With apparent relief, Andrea followed his lead and chuckled nervously. "You are too much, but I have to admit, you did get to me. I thought you were being serious and losing it. I assure you, I haven't felt any prickling sensations, but I've certainly had my share of nerves. I'm sure you have, too."

"You got that right," Mitt said. Andrea was correct that they both had more immediate concerns. "I even had trouble falling asleep last night."

"What's your biggest worry, when all is said and done?"

"I suppose my biggest is when I try to imagine what it's going to be like tonight when I'm alone and on call and possibly facing something major, like a cardiac arrest."

"How do you know you'll be on call? Did you volunteer or have you heard something I haven't?"

"I should have said *if* I'm on call," Mitt quickly corrected. He gritted his teeth. There was no way he wanted to get into any kind of discussion about his prognostic abilities.

"If that is your only worry, you are way ahead me," Andrea said. "I'm even nervous about daytime and dealing with all the experienced nurses who know a ton more than I do about actually taking care of patients. I mean, my knowing the intricacies of the human immune system or the molecular detail of intermediate metabolism isn't going to carry much weight when it comes to handling a chest tube."

Mitt had started to agree when the door to the hall burst open and in swept the chief surgical resident, Dr. Vivek Kumar, like a minor whirlwind. Trailing along behind him at a respectful distance was a female resident. With only a brief nod in Mitt and Andrea's direction, Dr. Kumar stepped behind the podium. The second resident stood off to the side, intently eyeing Dr. Kumar, as if waiting for a cue.

CHAPTER 4

Monday, July 1, 7:30 A.M.

O kay, I'm going to make this short and then turn you over to Dr. Van Dyke here, who supervises first- and second-year residents along with our rotating third-year NYU medical students. My name is Dr. Vivek Kumar, and I am the Bellevue Hospital chief surgical resident. I assume you remember meeting me briefly during your orientation over at the medical school last week, but then again you were being introduced to a lot of people. What I want to do this morning is give you two newbies an idea of what specifically you will be facing here at Bellevue over the next two months and what's going to be required of you."

Mitt certainly remembered Dr. Kumar and had been impressed from the moment he laid eyes on him. Mitt's favorable initial assessment was now being confirmed in spades. The man, who had arrived at precisely the time specified, radiated an aura of total confidence along with a vast and almost inconceivable knowledge of medicine, particularly surgery. And now, perhaps because he was on his home turf and feudal domain, he also projected an expectation of excellence and hundred percent commitment along with a low tolerance for suboptimal performance. Mitt briefly glanced over at Andrea, wondering if she felt the same intimidating vibes.

Returning his attention to the chief resident, Mitt saw the man was of average height and inordinately handsome, with a trim silhouette and movie-star good looks. His dark complexion and particularly thick, shiny black hair were highlighted by his outfit. Kumar was dressed as the quintessential surgical resident plucked from central casting with a spotless, highly starched, and wrinkle-free white doctor's coat over sharply creased white slacks. There were a few colorful pens and a lone penlight in his breast pocket, and a stethoscope was slung casually around his neck.

"You two are about to get your first taste of the power and joys of the practice of general surgery," Dr. Kumar continued. "And from the word 'go' you will be key members of our team. Particularly at night and on weekends, one of you will be the first line of defense for any problems with our in-house surgical patients, both on the surgical wards and in the intensive care units. Of course, you will have the support and backup of on-call second- and third-year residents, who have consultation access to us fourth- and fifth-year residents, along with our talented attending staff, but you will be called first to analyze the situation and decide how to proceed."

Mitt again looked briefly at Andrea, and this time she returned the glance. The choice of the initial comments by the chief resident served to fan both their anxieties, especially his mention of intensive care units. Everyone, including medical students, knew that the ICU was where the most critical patients, those with sophisticated and potentially life-threatening needs, were located. For Mitt and Andrea to face such situations at this point in their training seemed beyond their capabilities.

"Starting this morning you will be assigned specific patients who are either in surgery or scheduled for today. These patients will officially be yours to follow closely and manage with the support of more senior residents and the attending surgeon. Also, today you will be assigned patients scheduled for admission and surgery tomorrow. These people will also be your patients. What that means is that you will do the admission workup, prepare them for their surgery, assist at their surgery, and then manage their postoperative course. Each day at morning rounds, which start at six thirty sharp in this room, you will have already examined each of your patients and be in a position to present their conditions to the entire team. Are there any questions so far?"

Mitt's anxieties ratcheted upward, and he glanced yet again at Andrea, who nervously returned the look.

Dr. Kumar paused, staring back at the newbies. When neither gave any indication they wanted to speak, he continued. "This all might sound like a lot of work, and for good reason. It will be. But there's more. A weekly three-hour protected educational block must be respected, meaning besides your clinical responsibilities, you will be required to attend our SCORE lecture series, which our senior residents present in conjunction with the appropriate attending surgeons. Additionally, you will also be expected to attend Thursday grand rounds, provided your surgery schedule permits, as well as various departmental conferences, including most particularly the Mortality and Morbidity Conference. On top of that, you will be expected to spend time in our simulation center, particularly to gain familiarity with laparoscopic instruments and techniques.

"What you are hopefully gaining from my remarks this morning is the clear understanding that you are here at Bellevue primarily to learn, and we want to make absolutely sure that happens. Any questions at this point?"

Both Mitt and Andrea were too intimidated to ask questions, and both unconsciously settled more deeply into their respective seats to avoid calling attention to themselves. At the same time, Mitt knew that there was a conflict between learning and service, particularly during the first year of residency. First-year residents were, when all was said and done, remarkably cheap labor and had been historically abused as such. The year was, in reality, exactly the same as what used to be called "internship." When the abuses that interns had suffered became common knowledge, the name changed but the demands didn't.

"Okay," Dr. Kumar said. "I'm glad we are on the same page. Still, there's one more important issue I want to raise. Our program here at Bellevue respects the Accreditation Council for Graduate Medical Education, or ACGME, decision on resident work hours. We are serious about adhering to the limit of 'eighty hours per week over a four-week stretch.' You will hear more about this issue from Dr. Van Dyke. That's it! How about now? Any questions for me?"

Mitt and Andrea didn't dare to breathe lest any movement might draw unwanted attention.

"Okay," Dr. Kumar said with a brief hand clap followed by a gesture toward Dr. Gloria Van Dyke. "Now I'll turn this over to one of our talented third-year residents. She will be filling you in on some of the necessary details and getting you started on your journey." With a final nod toward the two first-year tyros and then to Dr. Van Dyke, he briskly exited the room.

"All right, I'll also be quick," Dr. Van Dyke said. A strikingly athletic young woman dressed in scrubs under a white doctor's coat, she stepped behind the vacated podium and projected a confidence nearly equal to the chief resident's, suggesting she was a dutiful understudy. In Mitt's mind, it underlined something he'd already garnered as a medical student about the field of general surgery. It was based on a very hierarchical system that had changed little over its hundred-and-fifty-year history. Those on the lowest rungs of the ladder, like he and Andrea, had to be bullied or somehow cowed to earn entrance into the "club."

"First and foremost," Dr. Van Dyke said, "please make certain your cell phones are hooked up with the hospital communication system. For the nurses and me to be able to get ahold of you at all times is obviously of prime importance. And as recent medical school graduates, I'm going to assume you are more aware than I was that it is essential to enter everything you do and even think into our electronic health record or EHR. Do I have that right?"

Both Mitt and Andrea nodded. Establishing their connectivity had been one of the first things they had done, and they'd been fully indoctrinated into the demands of the EHR.

Dr. Van Dyke then pulled a couple keys from her pocket and held them up. "I have keys here for the two on-call rooms you will be using and which I will be showing you shortly. It's vitally important that these rooms be locked at all times. I imagine you both have heard of the Dr. Kathryn Hinnant tragedy."

Mitt and Andrea nodded. A bit more than thirty years previously a vagrant who'd actually been living in a Bellevue Hospital mechanical room raped and killed a pathologist who was working in her isolated office on a weekend. It had had a profound effect on the institution, as it should have.

"Literally thousands of people are in and out of Bellevue on a daily basis," Dr. Van Dyke explained. "On-call rooms must always be locked."

Both Mitt and Andrea nodded.

"Also included in my tour will be our eighteen ORs, where you will be spending a significant amount of your time, the OR locker rooms, as well as the surgical inpatient wards. I'll also be quickly walking you through the ambulatory surgical areas as well as the intensive care units on the tenth floor.

"Now I'd like to follow up on Dr. Kumar's comments about ACGME rules on resident hours. It will be your job to keep track of your hours and give them to me. We do want to make certain that the program is in compliance, as we don't want to lose our accreditation." She laughed hollowly. "If that were to happen, none of us would be able to become certified by the American Board of Surgery. I don't have to explain to you what kind of disaster that would be."

Mitt nodded once again as if he were agreeing that it was appropriate for him and Andrea to be responsible for reporting their hours. He could already see that the system was designed to thwart the attempt by the ACGME to limit resident hours for the safety of patients and for the residents' health. If he, as a surgical resident, were to report—essentially complain—that he was being asked to work too many hours, he'd risk being blackballed and possibly fired. *Such is life,* he thought. But he wasn't surprised. When he'd applied for a surgical residency, he had a pretty good idea of what was involved, including very long hours and a very hierarchical, almost feudal structure.

"Okay," Dr. Van Dyke said. "Before we start our tour, are there any questions?" She left the podium and approached Mitt and Andrea, handing them both their on-call room keys.

"I have a question," Andrea said, finding her voice. "Which one of us will be on call tonight?"

"Ah, yes. Thanks for asking. Dr. Fuller will be first at bat. I went with alphabetical order to make the decision. All right, let's head out!"

Andrea turned and looked questioningly at Mitt as if to say: *How the hell did you know?*

Mitt merely shrugged.

CHAPTER 5

Mitt looked up at the institutional clock on the wall of OR #12 and could see that he'd been in the operating room for almost two hours. It was his first operation as a surgical resident, and it wasn't going as well as he would have liked for multiple reasons. He was standing on the left side of the patient along with a fourth-year resident, Dr. Geraldo Rodriguez. On the opposite side was Dr. David Washington, a physically imposing vascular surgeon. The case was an excision of an abdominal aneurysm, which was a pathological outpocketing of the main artery of the body, the aorta, in the patient's abdominal cavity below the diaphragm. The patient, Benito Suárez, was an otherwise healthy thirty-eight-year-old Hispanic male. The problem for Mitt was that he couldn't see the operative field despite forcibly gripping the handle of a retractor with both hands. Mitt's retractor was holding back the left side of Mr. Suárez's incision, including some of the patient's intestines, to expose his aorta.

Dr. Rodriguez had essentially crowded in front of Mitt, placing his right arm over Mitt's arms in his attempt to assist the surgeon, who was currently struggling to work up under the diaphragm. This meant Mitt was being pushed against the anesthesia screen and forced to face the back of Dr. Rodriguez's surgical gown—the operative site completely obstructed. All he could see was the wall clock by glancing upward, or by looking to the left past Geraldo's backside, he could see the scrub nurse on her stool and facing the instrument tray. In the opposite direction and over the anesthesia screen, he could see the anesthesiologist sitting on his wheeled stool and monitoring the patient's vital signs.

What this all meant for Mitt was that although he was physically in the operating room during what he imagined was an interesting case, there was no way he could appreciate any of the details. He had no real idea of what was going on inside the patient other than gathering that Dr. Washington was having significant technical difficulties sewing the upper portion of a graft to the patient's aorta to replace the section that had been removed. The problem had been caused by the need to remove more of the proximal aorta than expected yet keep from going into the chest cavity.

Although Mitt couldn't see her at the moment, there was another surgical resident standing to Dr. Washington's right. She was a second-year resident named Dr. Nancy Wu. Mitt had been cursorily introduced to her at the same time he'd been introduced to the others by Dr. Van Dyke, who'd accompanied Mitt when he first entered OR #12. At that time the surgery had already been underway for an hour and a half. Mitt had seen that Dr. Wu was holding a retractor similar to the one Mitt was about to be handed. She was holding back the right side of the abdominal incision.

The situation was physically uncomfortable for Mitt as well as mind-numbingly boring, even though Dr. Washington would pause on occasion to explain what he was doing. But without being able to see either Dr. Washington or the operative site, it was nearly impossible for Mitt to picture what was happening. All he could do was hold on and watch the clock's second hand as it slowly and repeatedly swept around the dial. At least the time gave him an opportunity to relive the morning.

The tour he and Andrea had been given by Dr. Van Dyke had been very helpful to quell some of their shared anxieties. Although Mitt, and Andrea to a lesser extent, had tried to break through Dr. Van Dyke's formality and her air of superiority as a third-year resident in contrast to Mitt and Andrea's lowly first-year status by offering personal information and asking personal questions, she'd resisted. For Mitt, it corroborated his impression of exactly how hierarchical surgery remained and how the system perpetuated itself.

The first thing Dr. Van Dyke had shown them was the on-call rooms, which were both simpler and nicer than Mitt had expected, especially with their modern en suite bathrooms and even showers. Encouragingly enough, there was also a resident lounge with a television, although both he and Andrea wondered if it had ever been used since the remote was nowhere to be seen.

Next they were given a short tour of the all-important staff cafeteria, which they were assured was open 24/7. With their every-other-night on-call schedule they would most likely be eating most of their meals there. From the cafeteria, they were taken to see all the surgical inpatient wards, where they met a lot of the day staff. Everyone from nurses to various aides and even housekeepers were super friendly and welcoming. Mitt was pleasantly surprised, particularly by the nurses. He'd always thought that they might resent the new residents, whom they would have to help become oriented. Mitt even tried to commit some of the day-shift nurses' names to memory but soon gave up because there were simply too many. Next, he and Andrea were shown around the surgical ambulatory clinics before heading to the ICUs on the tenth floor. There, both newbies were seriously interested in the tour, but at the same time felt cowed by the state-of-the-art technology and the precarious conditions of the patients.

The final aspect of the tour had been the OR suite, including the OR lounge and locker rooms. And then, once they'd changed into scrubs, they had been shown the operating rooms and given specific instructions on how to scrub their hands before going into surgery. After that, they'd been assigned ongoing cases, with Mitt being sent into OR #12 for the abdominal aneurysm while Andrea was to join a team doing a laparoscopic gallstone removal in OR #8.

At first Mitt thought he'd won out since the aneurysm case was far more intriguing than a mere laparoscopic gallstone removal. But after two hours, Mitt's opinion changed. Now his presence seemed more like a burden than an opportunity, underlying in real time the conflict between education and service in the hospital residency programs. After the first half hour, Mitt hadn't learned a thing. In fact, if anything, his arrival seemed to have heralded a negative change in the OR's atmosphere and hence the flow of the procedure.

When Mitt had first arrived, everyone on the OR team was busily engaged, seemingly finding contentment if not pleasure in their efforts, particularly with the understanding that they were literally saving someone's life. Having an abdominal aortic aneurysm, especially a large one with a dangerously thin wall like the current patient had, was akin to having a death sentence. At any given moment, perhaps with just a bit of exertion involving the abdominal muscles, the aneurysm could rupture, instantly causing rapid exsanguination into the abdomen and almost instantaneous death.

But then, right after Mitt had joined the group and been handed the retractor, small annoying things began to occur, eventually changing the dynamic from a contented team to a group of people on edge. First the scrub nurse handed Dr. Washington a pair of dissecting scissors that were somehow not up to his standards. With irritation, he brandished the instrument in front of the scrub nurse's face, complaining that she should have checked it, seen that it was defective, and never handed it to him. He then tossed the offending scissors over his shoulder onto the floor, evoking a negative response from the circulating nurse, who shook her head as she bent over to pick them up.

"Sorry," the scrub nurse had said, but in a tone that suggested she wasn't all that sorry. "I wasn't aware there was anything wrong with them."

"Well, you should have known," Dr. Washington had snapped.

Mitt, who'd been in the room for only a few minutes, sensed that Dr. Washington was on edge because he was having operative difficulty, which was aggravated by the supposedly defective scissors. The surgeon subsequently did explain what the difficulties were. After he'd removed the section of the aorta with the aneurysm, which had occurred prior to Mitt's arrival, he'd had to remove progressively more of the proximal aorta, meaning closer to the heart, because the vessel's wall was also visibly abnormal. "That's going to make sewing the proximal part of the graft a challenge," the surgeon had announced, which certainly had proved to be the case.

About a half hour after the scissors incident, there'd been a bit of a mix-up between the scrub nurse and Dr. Washington during the exchange of a small piece of the aorta, which the surgeon wanted

Clinical Pathology to look at and confirm it was normal enough to hold sutures. Whether this second incident was the scrub nurse's fault or the surgeon's was unclear, but the result was that the biopsy fell onto the sterile drapes that covered the patient and then onto the floor, requiring the circulating nurse to retrieve it.

"Good Lord!" Dr. Washington snapped. "What the hell? Pay attention, for Christ's sake!"

"I had my hand out for the biopsy," the nurse complained. "But you missed!"

Mitt had actually seen what had happened. The nurse did have her hand out, but as she redirected her attention to reach for the container she was going to put the biopsy in with her other hand, her outstretched hand had moved. At the same moment, Dr. Washington had prematurely looked back into the wound as he released the pressure on the forceps he'd used to pick up the piece of tissue. It was as if some nefarious spirit had willed the episode to occur.

"I'm paying full attention!" the scrub nurse said indignantly. "Are you?"

For a few tense moments, the nurse's rhetorical question hung in the air like a bank of dark clouds threatening a summer thunderstorm. Everyone in the room held their breath, tensely wondering what kind of reaction Dr. Washington would have. Mitt would later learn that the surgeon had a notoriously short fuse. But on this occasion, perhaps tempered by the challenge at hand, he chose not to say anything further and just went back to work.

The final minor episode was the strangest of all, since Mitt believed he saw it happen yet couldn't explain it like he could the others. Unable to see any of the operation and with his mind wandering, he found his vision did as well. One minute he'd be watching the clock, the next watching the scrub nurse, and the next glancing at the anesthesiologist, who seemed to be in his own world beyond the anesthesia screen.

Suddenly, in front of Mitt's eyes, a pair of forceps fell from the instrument tray, causing Dr. Washington to literally jump as they hit his arm before falling onto the drapes. "What the hell?" he bellowed as he straightened up, grasped the wayward forceps, and tossed them back onto the instrument tray, whose contents the scrub nurse was continuously adjusting to make sure she could anticipate the surgeon's needs and requests.

"What the hell are you doing?" Dr. Washington demanded, again seemingly using the minor episode to give vent to his frustrations about the case.

"I'm doing what I always do," the scrub nurse said defiantly. "I'm trying to anticipate your needs."

"I didn't ask for forceps," the surgeon snapped.

"I was loading the needle holder," the scrub nurse responded. "I didn't touch the forceps."

"Oh yeah, sure!" Dr. Washington spat. "They just jumped off the instrument tray on their own accord."

At this point in the tense exchange, Mitt tried to remember what he'd seen. At the moment of the incident, he'd been looking in the scrub nurse's direction but with unseeing eyes because his mind had been elsewhere, worrying about his first night on call. From Dr. Kumar's comments, he was going to be the first line of defense, and with the sheer number of patients involved, it would be a huge responsibility. To make matters worse, one of the patients he'd be covering was going to be Benito Suárez, whose difficult surgery he was currently experiencing but not seeing.

With a definite sense of confusion, Mitt tried to grapple with what he thought he'd seen, namely the forceps tumbling off the instrument tray on their own, which was impossible because they were bound by the same laws of gravity as everything else in the universe. He shook his head, realizing he must have conjured up the event out of a combination of his boredom and anxieties. There was no way he'd seen what he thought he'd seen, no way at all. With that decided, Mitt went back to just trying to get through the experience, keeping tension on the retractor despite his complaining muscles and letting his eyes and mind wander.

"Okay!" Dr. Washington said sometime later in an encouraging tone, pulling Mitt back to reality. "It's done! Finally, the proximal end of the graft is sutured in place. That was not easy, but it's done. Now let's move on to suture the distal end, and once we've done that, we're out of here."

"Great job!" Dr. Rodriguez said as he took a step to the left, moving out from in front of Mitt. Suddenly Mitt wasn't staring at Dr. Rodriguez's back but could see Dr. Washington, and more important, by leaning forward, he had a view into the wound. By bending a bit to the left, he could even see the sutured end of the graft up under the diaphragm.

Mitt felt Dr. Rodriguez take the retractor from him, which the fourth-year resident repositioned to expose the distal end of the transected aorta, and then, without a word, reattached Mitt's hand to the instrument's handle. For a moment, Mitt felt as if he were being treated as an insensate extension of the retractor. But then he silently criticized himself for faultfinding, because, after all, he was being afforded the opportunity to help save a person's life.

"The cut end of the aorta also looks a bit questionable to me," Dr. Rodriguez said. "What's your take, Dr. Washington?"

"I see what you mean," Dr. Washington said. He asked for a pair of forceps and scissors and snipped off a tiny piece of the vessel.

"Let's have Pathology take a quick gander at this section as well. We might have to remove more of the aorta. Let's hope it isn't defective all the way down to the renal arteries. That would change this into one hell of a marathon procedure."

This time, there was no problem with the exchange of the biopsy between the surgeon and the scrub nurse, and within minutes the circulating nurse disappeared from the OR to take it to Pathology.

While they waited for the results, Dr. Washington gave Mitt a short tutorial on the operative treatment of abdominal aneurysms, belatedly stimulating Mitt's interest in the procedure. He even talked about Dr. Valentine Mott, a celebrated Bellevue surgeon from the early nineteenth century who had been willing to operate on such abdominal aneurysms before anesthesia and antisepsis.

"The man was a Bellevue phenomenon," Dr. Washington gushed. "The speed with which he had to work because of the lack of anesthesia was truly unbelievable." With that comment, Dr. Washington glanced over the anesthesia screen to acknowledge the role the anesthesiologist played. The anesthesiologist nodded in return, happy to accept the recognition.

Dr. Valentine Mott was a historical figure whom Mitt knew something about, as Mitt's ancestor Dr. Homer Fuller had been a contemporary of Mott's at Bellevue Hospital. Mitt often thought about how technically difficult and stressful it must have been being a surgeon back then without anesthesia, considering the sheer pain the patients had to endure. In those days operative speed was crucial. He'd read that Dr. Homer Fuller had done an amputation at mid-thigh in nine seconds. On top of the speed requirement was the burden of postoperative infections. In those days as many as half of all patients operated on died of sepsis.

"The aortic wall is definitely abnormal and probably won't hold a suture," the circulating nurse announced the moment she pushed back into the OR. "A formal report will be forthcoming, but the pathologist wanted you to know ASAP."

"Oh, shit," Dr. Washington voiced, looking back into the wound with a shake of his head. "As I said, this could turn out to be one hell of a long case."

CHAPTER 6

Mitt raised his eyes to look at the wall clock and marveled at the position of the hour hand. In many ways he couldn't believe he was still on the same case. It had been close to eight hours since he'd entered OR #12. Even more impressive, Dr. Washington, Dr. Rodriguez, and Dr. Wu had been working for almost ten hours.

As a medical student Mitt had heard of exceptionally long surgical procedures, but he'd been led to believe they involved unusual cases like face transplants or the separation of conjoined twins that require the participation of multiple surgical specialties and not more routine conditions like an abdominal aneurysm. Never in his wildest imagination could he have guessed he'd be caught up in such a rite of passage on his very first case as a surgical resident. Was such an unusual, luck-of-the-draw circumstance a good omen or a bad one as far as his residency was concerned? He had no idea, and there was no way to guess. All he knew was that he was currently bored silly.

On the positive side, since the conclusion of the difficult suturing of the proximal section of the graft when his view of the operative field had been completely blocked, he'd been able to see—and thanks to Dr. Washington's explanations to understand—what was transpiring even though he wasn't contributing much. Consequently, he knew exactly why the case was dragging on for so long. It was all because the patient's aorta, at least the abdominal portion, had extensive developmental abnormalities, causing its wall to be considerably thin and friable. It was this problem that explained not only the origin of the aneurysm but also why Dr. Washington had had to remove more and more of the vessel to find a portion strong enough to hold sutures. He was doing this by taking progressive biopsies and sending them off to Clinical Pathology. Unfortunately, as this process continued, it involved sacrificing sections of the aorta with branches that provided arterial blood to various abdominal organs including the kidneys. Each of these vessels had to be separately connected to the graft, requiring a ton more suturing and lots more time.

But the technical difficulty of the surgery wasn't the only reason the case was taking so long. The tension between the surgeon and the scrub nurse had continued, underlining for Mitt how important it was that their interaction be smooth. Not long after the forceps incident, there was an awkward handoff of a needle holder. At the time, Dr. Washington reached for it without taking his eyes from the site where he intended to place the next suture, but then moved his hand. As a result, instead of the instrument being slapped into his waiting palm, it hit up against his thumb and fell onto the drapes.

Again, from Mitt's vantage point, there was blame on both sides. Dr. Washington's hand had definitely moved at the last second, but it was also true that the scrub nurse had let go of the instrument too soon in her eagerness to pick up the empty needle holder the surgeon had just dropped onto the drapes. It was like a miscue between track-and-field sprinters exchanging a baton in a relay race.

Since there was already a degree of acrimony in the air from the previous miscues and since both the surgeon and the scrub nurse were strong-willed and highly confident in their professional abilities, neither was about to accept responsibility. The result was a harangue from the surgeon followed by one from the scrub nurse followed by a pregnant pause as if a time bomb was about to go off. It took the anesthesiologist to speak up and remind everyone that, in his words, "time's a-wasting." "Come on, guys," he added. "Call a truce! We need to finish up this case."

Luckily for all concerned, 3:00 P.M. rolled around soon after, which saw a shift change, and a new scrub nurse and circulating nurse arrived to take the place of those going off duty. Dr. Washington made a point to greet the new scrub nurse as if she were a savior, immediately complimenting her on how smoothly she took over. From that point on, the atmosphere improved, and things continued apace.

Fortunately neither Mitt nor any of the other members of the surgical team had to stay in the OR continuously, as the case dragged on for hours. Everyone got to take a bathroom break, which meant leaving the OR. An hour previously, it had been Mitt's turn. When the urge to urinate had reached a critical state, he'd hesitantly brought up the subject, and Dr. Washington responded by saying: "Of course you can take a break. I was beginning to worry you weren't human." Dr. Washington laughed at his weak attempt at humor. He, Rodriguez, and Wu had all already taken their breaks.

Mitt couldn't believe how much he appreciated getting out of OR #12 even for a few minutes. And he made the best of the time. After relieving himself in the men's locker room, he paused in the surgical lounge to check his phone for messages. There were two. One from Dr. Van Dyke saying that he had been assigned three patients who were being admitted that afternoon for surgery tomorrow: Ella Thompson, age eighty-two, for an aortic valve replacement; Roberto Silva, age sixty-three, for a pancreatectomy; and Bianca Perez, age seventy-one, for a colectomy. She went on to say he would be responsible for doing their histories and physicals and presenting them briefly on rounds in the morning before scrubbing in on their surgeries.

The second text was from Andrea, asking him to give her a call when he was finished with his case. Although Mitt wasn't done with the aneurysm repair, he took the time to call her. He felt the need to complain to someone and get a bit of sympathy, and there was no one better qualified than Andrea.

"It's about time," Andrea said immediately on answering, pretending to be miffed. "Where have you been? Why haven't you called? Did you not get my text?"

"If you can believe it, I just got it now," Mitt said. "Seriously, I'm still caught in OR #12 on the same case I was initially assigned. I was just allowed out a few minutes ago to take a leak."

"Jesus," Andrea remarked. "That sounds terrible. Has it at least been interesting?"

"Not for the first couple of hours. All I was doing was holding a retractor. And to make it worse, the assisting surgeon, a fourth-year resident by the name of Geraldo Rodriguez, had to essentially step in front of me to help the surgeon, who was working up under the diaphragm. That meant I was holding the retractor under the assistant's arm, and all I could see was the back of his surgical gown. It was miserable."

"Yikes! Not fun."

"Tell me about it," Mitt agreed. "Later, after the proximal portion of the graft had been finally attached, things improved. At least I could see something, and Dr. Washington provided more explanation. He's a vascular surgeon."

"Is he good?"

"He must be to be on the staff here at Bellevue, but I don't know how to judge, to be honest. Personality-wise I'm not overly impressed. He's rather narcissistic. He and the scrub nurse practically fought on several occasions, and I kind of sided with the nurse, who wasn't about to take any crap. Anyway, the atmosphere was pretty tense for a time."

Mitt was tempted to explain more but feared it would take too long. Despite recognizing he was hardly a key figure, he felt guilty being out of the OR.

"Bummer," Andrea commented, using one of her favorite words. In her personal vocabulary it was both a noun and an adjective.

"How was your gallstone case?"

"It was fine. It was almost over by the time I arrived, so I didn't see much. The surgeon was Dr. Kevin Singleton, another fourth-year resident, who is a great teacher, inordinately personable, and really patient. The main thing I learned today was how important it's going to be to spend time in the simulation lab to get accustomed to handling the laparoscope. Let me tell you, it ain't easy, especially when you are looking at a video screen in one direction and handling an instrument in a completely different direction."

"I hadn't thought of that," Mitt said. "God! It's intimidating to think of all we have to learn."

"To say the least," Andrea said. "By the way, you've been assigned three cases to do the admission and scrub in on. Did you know?"

"Yes. I just read a text from Dr. Van Dyke. I'll get to it when I get out of the OR. Where are you now?"

"I'm on my way home. I finished admitting my three cases for tomorrow morning and couldn't think of any reason to hang around. Sorry."

"Don't be sorry," Mitt said. "I'm sure I'd do the same if the situation was in reverse."

"One thing I have to say, the floor nurses are all terrific and surprisingly helpful and understanding, knowing how little we know about actually taking care of patients."

"That's encouraging," Mitt said. "I'm sure I'm going to need some help tonight when I'm on call."

"I think you will be pleasantly surprised by the nurses' attitude. I was. I expected them to be a lot more impatient. I advise you to go around and introduce yourself to the evening nurses. I did, and I think it was a great way to break the ice, as they definitely run the show. Anyway, good luck tonight. I'll be eager to hear what it's like and how it went when I see you bright and early."

"Thanks. I'm probably going to need a degree of luck. See you in the morning."

After Mitt had disconnected the call he hesitated for a beat, wishing he, too, was on his way back to the safety of his apartment. Taking a fortifying breath, he headed for the swinging doors leading into the main portion of the operating room area.

"How are you with suturing, Dr. Fuller?" Dr. Washington called out the moment Mitt pushed through the door to OR #12 after re-scrubbing his hands and forearms.

"I haven't had much experience," Mitt admitted guiltily as he went through the process of re-gowning and re-gloving.

"It's his first day of residency," Dr. Rodriguez explained.

"Yes, Dr. Van Dyke mentioned that," Dr. Washington said. A moment later after a final check that all the suture lines of the graft were holding, he abruptly stepped back from the operating table and snapped off his surgical gloves. Looking directly at Mitt, he said: "Well, here's a perfect opportunity for you, young man, to get some experience by helping close the wound." He then added: "I trust that the three of you can somehow manage without me."

"I'm sure we can," Dr. Rodriguez said. He glanced at Dr. Wu for confirmation.

"Absolutely," Dr. Wu added on cue.

"Fine," Dr. Washington said condescendingly. "I'll be in the surgical lounge if you people run into any problems."

"I'm sure we will have no problems," Dr. Rodriguez said.

"Thank you all," Dr. Washington said as he waved over his head on his way to the door. In the next second he was gone.

A brief silence followed the surgeon's sudden departure, everyone momentarily frozen. Mitt sensed a feeling of relief on the part of all, including the anesthesiologist who'd replaced the original anesthesiologist at the same time the new nurses had come on.

"Exactly how much suturing experience have you had?" Dr. Rodriguez asked Mitt, breaking the silence.

"Just the rudiments," Mitt admitted. During his third-year surgery rotation, Mitt had attended a couple of afternoon sessions arranged to teach the medical students the basics of suturing and knot tying, but he hadn't taken the opportunity too seriously. Nor had his assigned partner. At the time he had still been debating which specialty he was going to pursue.

"Okay," Dr. Rodriguez said. "Dr. Wu and I will close the fascia with wire. After that Dr. Wu and you, Dr. Fuller, can close the sub-cutaneous layer followed by the skin. What do you guys say?"

"Sounds like a plan," Dr. Wu said with a nod.

"Sounds good to me," Mitt said. He was encouraged, thinking that maybe the day could be salvaged as a decent teaching day after all.

CHAPTER 7

M itt pushed his food tray forward on the stainless-steel railing that ran along the front of the glass-enclosed cafeteria food service line and stopped at the drink offerings. Back at the main-course selections he'd chosen meat loaf and mashed potatoes, and the aroma drifting up from his plate was making him salivate. A few hurried bites of a bagel that morning in his apartment had been the only food he'd had all day, and he was understandably starved.

The last forty minutes of his first surgical case as a resident had gone reasonably well. As planned, after Dr. Rodriguez and Dr. Wu had closed the abdomen's midline incision with wire, he and Dr. Wu had closed the subcutaneous layer with gut sutures. Dr. Wu had placed the first two, then handed the needle holder to Mitt. Self-conscious under the supervision of two more senior residents, Mitt had struggled to a degree but managed to imitate Dr. Wu's placement for his first suture as a resident. When no one said anything to make him question what he'd done, Mitt fumbled with tying the knot. With commendable patience despite the length of time the operation had been going on, Dr. Rodriguez instructed Mitt on the proper technique and how to keep tension on both ends of the suture while running down and securing the second tie.

After observing the placement of several more subcutaneous sutures, Dr. Rodriguez followed Dr. Washington's lead and left the OR. From then on, Dr. Wu watched Mitt finish with the subcutaneous level and begin the silk sutures for the skin.

"Try to roll your wrist when placing the skin sutures," Dr. Wu had suggested, and she demonstrated what she meant. "The idea is to close the skin by just having the edges come together so as not to pucker out or roll into the wound."

"I get it," Mitt had said. When he'd finished, the skin edges were just "kissing."

"Not bad," Dr. Wu had said.

When the case had finally been over, Mitt hung around at Dr. Wu's suggestion to help the nurses and the anesthesiologist move the patient onto a gurney for the trip to the Post-Anesthesia Care Unit, or PACU. By that time, the patient was awake and responding to his name and his vital signs were normal. Once in the PACU, Mitt also participated with Dr. Wu in writing the postoperative orders.

A few minutes later, while staring at his clothes hanging in his open locker, Mitt made a sudden decision not to change but rather merely to put his white coat over his scrubs. He had no idea what the evening and night would bring, but he thought he'd be more prepared in scrubs, come what may. What he was secretly hoping was that he would be able to get some rest, and he thought the scrubs could serve a dual function as pajamas as well as hospital work clothes.

When he'd finally left the operating suite, hunger pains forced him to head to the cafeteria before going around to introduce himself at the various inpatient wards as well as locate the three patients he needed to work up. No matter what, it was going to be a long night, and he definitely needed calories to face it.

"Can I help you?" the food service woman said, seeing Mitt pause before the drink selection apparatus.

"Thank you, but I'm just having trouble deciding what I want," Mitt said. The choices were legion: all manner of soft drinks, various types of milk, and sparkling and still water. Although he didn't usually drink sodas due to their overabundance of sugars, he thought a bit of caffeine in a cola might stand him in good stead as he faced his first night on call. Deciding on a diet cola, he proceeded to fill one of the large paper cups. Since the dispenser functioned so quickly, the cup brimmed before he was ready, and a small amount spilled over the top.

"Oops, sorry," Mitt said to the food service woman standing behind the counter and watching him.

"Not a problem," the woman said. "It happens all the time."

Still feeling like a klutz, Mitt lifted the overfilled cup and placed it on his tray. Letting go of the cup, he was about to push the tray on to the dessert selection when the full cup of cola tipped over, flooding his entire tray with soda, including drenching his meat loaf and mashed potatoes.

"Oh, shit!" Mitt said by reflex before remembering where he was. With a sense of shock, because this had happened although he had not yet touched the tray, he reared back with his hands raised at chest level as if he expected the tray itself to do something equally unexpected.

Having witnessed the accident, the food service woman immediately came out from behind the cafeteria counter to lend a hand. "Not a problem," the woman reiterated graciously. She used a dish towel that she had slung over her shoulder to sop up some of the cola from the brimming tray before taking it to the nearby soiled-dishes window.

Although Mitt had lowered his hands, he hadn't moved, feeling dumbstruck as his mind replayed the episode. Had he touched the tray? He must have to cause the cup to tip over, yet he was certain he hadn't. Was his mind playing tricks on him? Was his blood sugar that low from not having eaten anything for twelve hours? Even more unnerving, the incident reminded him of the curious forceps episode in the operating room.

Stepping back to get out of the way of people moving along the food line, an embarrassed Mitt watched a janitor who had appeared with a mop clean up the small amount of cola that had spilled onto the tiled floor. A moment later the food service woman pressed a clean tray into his hands and directed him back to the beginning of the cafeteria line.

The next time Mitt stepped in front of the drink dispenser with the new tray and a second serving of meat loaf and mashed potatoes, he made certain to fill the cup far short of the brim. This time he put the cup on the tray and let go of it slowly, watching it intently, ready to grab it if it showed any inclination to tip over on its own accord. As expected, it stayed perfectly upright, making him believe he must have inadvertently and unknowingly hit the previous cup. Attributing the entire episode to a combination of fatigue and hypoglycemia, he moved on to the dessert section. He wasn't a big dessert guy, but having no idea when he might eat again, he decided on a wedge of apple pie.

Picking up his tray, Mitt scanned the room. It was moderately crowded, reminding him that Bellevue Hospital was a huge operation 24/7, with a support staff of over five thousand people, including more than a thousand doctors, one of which he was for the next two months. After spotting an empty table against the far wall, he headed toward it. He wasn't being asocial. His plan was to wolf down his meal and get started on his evening's work. He was well aware that doing three admission workups would take considerable time and effort, and that job was on top of being on call. He really had no idea of what the evening's demands were going to be and whether he was up to the challenge. In short, he felt nervous as hell.

"Excuse me," a cheerful, clear voice said about twenty minutes later, halting a forkful of apple pie en route to Mitt's mouth. He looked up into a tanned oval face framed by a nimbus of remarkably curly blond hair. Her surprisingly dark eyes were bright in contrast to her hair, and her expression was cheerful but questioning. "Are you Michael Fuller?"

"I am, but I prefer Mitt."

"Fine and dandy, Mitt," the woman said agreeably. Like Mitt, she was dressed in scrubs overlaid with a doctor's white coat. She was holding a tray of food. "Mind if I join you?"

"Of course not," Mitt responded immediately. By reflex he started to get to his feet.

"Don't get up!" the woman commanded. She put her tray onto the table and took the seat across from Mitt. "My name is Madison, Madison Baker. I'm a second-year surgical resident along with Nancy Wu, who you met this morning."

"Yes, we were on a case together."

"So I heard. I also heard it went on a little longer than planned. I'm afraid you experienced a bit of trial by fire. Dr. Washington, bless his soul, isn't the easiest person to get along with."

"He and the scrub nurse weren't seeing eye to eye."

"So I also heard. Not unusual. He has a reputation for flying off the handle when things don't go smoothly and then blaming everybody but himself."

"That doesn't surprise me," Mitt said, trying to be diplomatic.

"Please," Madison said, pointing at Mitt's apple pie. "Don't let me keep you from your dessert." She then picked up her knife and fork and started to work on a pork chop on her plate. "I wanted to meet you because Dr. Van Dyke told me you were on first call tonight. I'm on call, too, so I'm your backup so to speak. We have a handful of 'sickies' sprinkled around the wards and in the ICU, so you might not get a lot of shut-eye. I hope you are prepared." She took a bite of her meat and started chewing, giving Mitt a chance to respond.

"I have three workups to do," Mitt said, more as explanation than an excuse.

"Yes, I know. But you should have time to get that done. No problem. During the early evenings, there are a lot of residents around, finishing up for the day. Same with a handful of attendings who do their hospital rounds after their office hours. If nurses have questions or problems, they turn to whomever is available. That will save you from running around doing stupid, insignificant stuff. Remember, the nurses here are an impressive group, which isn't surprising since there's been a nursing school at Bellevue for a hundred and fifty years. Anyway, are you interested in a bit of advice from someone who's just finished her first year?"

"Of course," Mitt responded. As nervous as he was, he could use all the advice he could get.

"With these admission workups, don't take the time and energy to do a full medical school workup, like finding out what disease their maternal great-grandmother died of. Do you know what I'm saying? These patients have already been worked up to the nth degree and it will all be in their electronic health record, which you will have access to. Your job is to make sure that something hasn't come up since they've last been seen in clinic that would make their imminent surgery problematic or contraindicated. For example, like they've developed a sore throat or a sudden fever, or, God forbid, you feel an enlarged liver that's not in the EHR. Do you get my drift?"

"I think so," Mitt responded. What she was saying about medical school workups rang true: All of his had literally taken hours and included very detailed medical histories.

"You can do a good admission workup in twenty minutes, a half hour tops, unless, of course, you find something abnormal and not already documented. If you do, the attending surgeon has to be called immediately and apprised."

"I think I get it," Mitt said. Her advice made a lot of sense. He was beginning to feel a modicum better about facing the night. Her confidence was encouraging. She'd obviously learned a lot in her first year of residency. Mitt could hope he'd be in a similar position a year from now.

"I also encourage you to go around and introduce yourself to the various head nurses. The more they know you as a person, the better off you'll be. You can learn a lot from the nurses. Believe me!"

"I was planning on going around introducing myself," Mitt said. "My partner, Andrea Intiso, advised the same."

"Good advice! I see you've finished your pie, so don't let me hold you up. I'm sure we'll be seeing each other during the course of the evening. I assume you have a key to one of the on-call rooms."

"I do."

"Perfect. You might not have a chance to spend too much time in it, but at least it is there. Good luck."

"Thanks," Mitt responded. He stood up and lifted his food tray. "And thanks for seeking me out and offering the advice. I appreciate it."

"You're welcome. Try to remain calm. You'll get through this."

Mitt nodded and smiled, but it was a nervous smile. His intuition was sending warning signals that he was in for a struggle, and from experience he knew his intuition was rarely wrong.

After depositing his soiled tray at the appropriate window, Mitt left the cafeteria and walked to the elevator bank. His plan was to head up to the seventeenth floor, where the surgical inpatient rooms were, meet the head nurses, then do the same on the sixteenth and fifteenth floors before heading down to the tenth, where the surgical intensive care unit was located. In the process he'd find out the location of the three patients whose histories and physicals he needed to do. Well, maybe he would skip the ICU.

When the elevator arrived, Mitt was relatively surprised to find it almost full, not with house staff and nurses but with people of all ages, from crying babies to the elderly. As he squeezed into the cab, it dawned on him that it was the middle of normal visiting hours. Thanks to the crowd, the elevator stopped on almost every floor, but by some strange coincidence, by the time it reached seventeen, he was the only passenger still in the car.

As the doors slid open, Mitt hastened off but immediately froze in his tracks as though he had collided with a brick wall. But what stopped him wasn't a physical impediment; he was assaulted by the worst and most nauseating smell he'd ever experienced. It was so bad it defied description, and he literally retched. Mitt clasped a hand to his mouth and pinched his nostrils shut to keep from vomiting. It was as if he'd been dropped into an open sewer, pungent and fecal.

Rapidly, his eyes darted around in search of the source of the revolting stench. But he saw nothing amiss. In the distance he could hear the normal sounds of a hospital. And then, as quickly as the smell had assaulted him, it dissipated as if a sudden wind had blown it away. But there was no wind.

Momentarily stunned, Mitt took in a few cleansing breaths as he continued to glance around the immediate area of the elevator lobby, still searching for an explanation. Seeing nothing abnormal, he carefully moved forward, watching where he was placing his feet lest he step in something revolting. Reaching the point of the intersecting hallways, he was able to see in three directions. The building's footprint was a huge square, with the patient areas divided into the points of a compass, 17 East, 17 North, 17 West, and 17 South. All the patient rooms were on the building's exterior, with windows, while all the support spaces were on the interior.

In every direction from where Mitt was currently standing, he could see snatches of busy, normal hospital activity with uniformed staff darting in and out of sight. He even spotted several food carts being pushed past his line of vision, announcing that it was the dinner hour in addition to visiting time. But most important, there was no explanation for the fleeting, horrid smell. None whatsoever. But as weird and revolting as it had been, at least it was gone.

For a few minutes Mitt remained where he was, struggling to make sense of what he'd experienced . . . or thought he'd experienced. Since there was no obvious source for the disgusting smell and the odor had vanished so quickly and completely, he wondered if perhaps his tired, overwrought mind had somehow managed to dream it up. Such thoughts begged the question: Was he having an olfactory hallucination? He had no idea but that was the only explanation his tired mind could conjure. He recalled the issue had come up in his medical school third-year neurology rotation. Like a host of other random facts that cluttered his brain from four years of medical school, he somehow remembered such an episode was called *phantosmia*. How he remembered, he had no idea, but he even recalled that a particularly strong phantosmia had its own name: *cacosmia*.

With a shake of his head in mild disbelief, he thought that maybe he'd had his own cacosmia. If so, it was certainly a first.

Mitt took a couple more deep breaths to fortify himself and set out eastward, down a long hallway, toward one of the nurses' stations. Each inpatient floor had two such nurses' stations, one in the east wing and one in the west. He knew it would not be difficult to find because it was literally in his path, serving half of the patients' rooms on the seventeenth floor. As he headed in its direction, he marveled at how different the new Bellevue was from the old. In the old Bellevue, of which he'd seen pictures, particularly in a terrific Bellevue Hospital history book titled *Bellevue,* which he'd read that very June, the patients were crammed cheek by jowl into large, elongated wards with beds lining both walls and common latrines. The new Bellevue had a variety of room sizes but mostly sextuplets, with a fewer number of triplets and even some singles. The predominant number, six, had been a compromise between the Bellevue Hospital administrative planning board and Medicare and Medicaid demands. Of course, the real luxury was that each room had its own bathroom, a striking innovation for a public hospital.

The nurses' station that Mitt approached was a beehive of activity. It was defined by a white laminate counter that formed an enclosure of approximately twenty-by-twenty feet. There were two entrances to this command post, which had a bank of video screens hanging from the ceiling, displaying patients' vital signs. A host of computer monitors sat on the interior wraparound desk, and every single one was currently being used by an attending physician, a resident, or a nurse. People were scurrying in and out.

It was easy for Mitt to pick out the head nurse. She was acting like a traffic cop at a busy intersection or a conductor in the middle of a symphonic performance. He approached her directly but had to wait for her to deal with several nurses and aides before she acknowl-edged him.

"Can I help you?" she asked, her rapid, commanding tone befit-ting her role. She was a sizable Black woman with a striking hairstyle of lots of short braids.

"I just wanted to introduce myself," Mitt said self-consciously. With so many staff members within earshot and such a tumult of activity, the last thing he wanted to do was draw attention to himself. "My name is Mitt Fuller. I'm a new first-year surgical resident, and I was caught in surgery all day, so I haven't met any of you evening-shift nurses."

"Well, glory be," the head nurse said, putting the backs of her hands on her hips and eyeing Mitt with surprised appreciation. "What a thoughtful gesture, Doctor. My name is Kaliyah Wilson. Everyone calls me Kay. I'm pleased to make your acquaintance. Wel-come to the team."

"Thank you," Mitt responded. "I also want to warn you and your colleagues that I'm on call tonight, my first night. I hope I'm up to your expectations, come what may. I'm a bit worried that medical school didn't train me very well in practical terms."

"You'll do fine," Kay scoffed, giving Mitt a small wave for empha-sis. "Relax! There's always a bit of adjustment, and we nurses often joke about July first being dangerous. But I like your attitude, as I'm sure others will, too."

"I also wanted to ask if perhaps Ella Thompson, Roberto Silva, or Bianca Perez are here on seventeen? They were admitted this after-noon, and they need admission histories and physicals, which I've been tasked to do."

"Nope, they're not here with us. We only had one admission to-day, and it wasn't any of those three, but I can tell you where they are." She leaned forward and typed the names into the computer directly in front of her. "Okay," she added a minute later while straightening up. "Thompson and Perez are on Fifteen East and Silva is on Fifteen West."

"Thank you," Mitt said before stepping out of the way. There were now several other people vying for her attention.

Leaving the central desk, Mitt headed back the way he'd come and then over to the west side of the building to stop in at the floor's second nurses' station, where he repeated his introduction. Again, it went as well as it had with Nurse Wilson. With the seventeenth floor taken care of, he sought out a stairway, thinking that would be the fastest way to get down to the sixteenth floor, where he intended to repeat the process of introducing himself.

A stairway was easy to find, as it was clearly marked with a red illuminated Exit sign, but before he entered, he checked to see if the door was locked from inside. It was good he checked because it indeed was locked. Had he used the stairs, Mitt would have had to go all the way down to the first floor to exit, which he was obviously loath to do. Instead, he headed back to the bank of elevators just to go down a single floor.

As he approached the elevator lobby at the end of the long hall, he braced himself in case he was assaulted by the same phantosmia he'd experienced earlier. Luckily he wasn't.

With a bit of relief, he joined a handful of visitors who were waiting for an elevator to arrive. A few of them eyed Mitt, obviously recognizing that he was one of the doctors from his white coat and scrubs. He imagined they were duly impressed, which made him feel strangely proud. At the same time, he was glad they had no idea of all the uncertainties he felt.

When he boarded the crowded elevator, he felt self-conscious pressing the sixteenth-floor button, as it seemed ridiculous to be using an elevator to go one floor. But he need not have bothered because when the doors opened on the sixteenth floor, there were a number of people waiting, meaning the elevator would have stopped anyway. Mitt had to push through them in their eagerness to board.

For a few minutes after the elevator departed, Mitt remained standing in the now-empty lobby for fear he might have to face another horrid olfactory hallucination like up on the seventeenth floor. Hesitantly he sniffed the air as he glanced around the immediate area. Only after it seemed apparent he wasn't going to be reassaulted did he allow himself a few normal deep breaths. Reassured, he then started forward, once again heading eastward to mirror what he'd just done upstairs.

As he walked, his mind jumped ahead. Assuming his sixteenth-floor visit would be as quick as the one to the seventeenth had been, he'd soon be facing his three admission histories and physicals down on the fifteenth floor. He found himself particularly thankful for Madison's suggestions. Had she not made them, he would have done medical school histories, which would have taken many, many hours. Mitt was hopeful he could get back to the on-call room for some rest before he had to face whatever it was going to be as "the first line of defense" for all the needs of all the surgical inpatients.

As Mitt approached the busy sixteenth floor east nurses' station, he found himself wondering if he was going to be lucky that night and not have to face a complicated clinical problem that he was ill-equipped to handle. Regrettably, as soon as the question formed in his mind, his precognitive abilities suggested he was not going to be lucky, and the disturbing thought was combined with a bit of his characteristic tingling. All in all, it was not an auspicious omen.

CHAPTER 8

Wearily, Mitt walked down the long hallway from the elevator bank and entered the resident on-call area. On this occasion, the lounge area was empty. When he'd passed through four hours earlier there had been a group of residents including Madison Baker relaxing in the room. He'd stopped to say hello and had been introduced to several of the internal medicine residents who were also on call. He hadn't joined them as he was tempted to do, but rather had gone into his assigned room, taken a quick shower, and tried to get some sleep.

Unfortunately, as keyed up as he'd been, he hadn't been able to fall asleep before being called to the sixteenth floor to check on a patient who had allegedly fallen out of bed.

On that mission, he'd learned that the first-year resident was required by hospital policy to examine everyone who had supposedly fallen out of bed even though most often no one had fallen out of bed at all. Instead, what normally happened was that the patient had sagged to the floor on the way to the bathroom, while in the bathroom, or on the way back to bed. This had been the case on his first such mission as well as on a second one he was just returning from at that moment. As he keyed open his on-call room door, he imagined that checking on people who were said to have fallen out of bed was going to be a common occurrence for him as the year progressed.

So far, despite his concerns, his first night on call had progressed without any major disasters or even a minor problem. He'd completed the three admission histories and physicals without an interruption. Following Madison Baker's suggestion, he'd tried to limit the history taking, but it was difficult. In contrast to his medical school experience, where he'd been encouraged to be agonizingly thorough, he had to consciously limit his delving into the patients' family histories of disease and injury. Of the three people, he'd been the most impressed by Ella Thompson, a grandmotherly eighty-two-year-old Black woman. During the course of the history, Mitt had learned she was actually a great-grandmother with fifteen great-grandchildren. Mitt had been impressed with how cavalierly she seemed to be facing open-heart surgery in the morning. She'd had heart issues since she'd had rheumatic fever as a teenager, and she told Mitt she was looking forward to having it taken care of once and for all by having her leaky mitral valve replaced.

The other two workups hadn't been as interesting or easy. Both had required translators, which made the process much more difficult. It had been Portuguese for Roberto Silva and Spanish for Bianca Perez, and both patients through the translator claimed to know next to nothing about their family's or even their own medical histories. They were also both minimally cooperative, as if resenting Mitt's efforts. Following Madison's advice, he concentrated on making sure there was no immediate contraindication for their scheduled surgery, which there didn't seem to be. Helping the process to a degree, all three had extensive medical histories in their EHRs, which included documented cardiac issues for Thompson, details about pancreatic cancer for Silva, and a long history of diverticulosis for Perez.

Following the completion of the three admission workups, Mitt had gone back to the on-call room but had been quickly called out on his first falling-out-of-bed episode. This was followed by being kept busy hour after hour with one minor problem after another, often involving a combination of dosage questions, IV issues, sleep medication requests, or demands for laxatives. He found the nurses very helpful and often apologetic at having to call him to solve such problems, which they were certainly capable of handling but couldn't because of hospital policy based on legal constraints. He was now hoping for a breather, having just dealt with his second falling-out-of-bed episode, and he hoped despite his predictive fears he could get some needed sleep.

Once inside his room, Mitt eyed the bed and then looked over at the bathroom door while feeling totally exhausted from having been on the go for some twenty hours. His momentary confusion was stemming from a debate on whether to take another quick shower. Despite his feeling rather grubby, the bed won out. Without even taking off his white coat or slipping out of his shoes, he lay down, stretching his tired legs out to the end of the bed and briefly massaging his thighs. He figured he would just relax for a few moments before getting up and at least washing his hands and face. But it didn't happen. In the next instant he was in a dreamless sleep.

When his phone rang in his pocket, Mitt bolted up into a sitting position, feeling momentarily disoriented to time, place, and person. Quickly he oriented himself to the on-call room before struggling to get the phone out of his pocket. As he answered, he noticed the time. It was 2:10, meaning he'd been asleep for maybe a half hour.

"Hello," he said. His voice was so scratchy that he had to repeat himself.

"Dr. Fuller, my name is Helena Santos. I'm a nurse assigned to your patient Benito Suárez, the abdominal aneurysm repair. He is complaining about pain."

"Okay . . ." Mitt said, trying to organize his thoughts. Knowing firsthand the extensive surgery the man had that day, he knew that his having significant pain was hardly surprising. When Mitt had gone by earlier in the evening to introduce himself to the patient and check on him, Suárez had seemed to be doing reasonably well. Mitt had managed to learn this even though there was a significant language problem. The man was Brazilian, and Mitt didn't speak Portuguese, and the man's English wasn't very good.

When checking the EHR at the time of his visit, Mitt had noticed that the patient had what Mitt assumed was adequate pain medication prescribed on a PRN basis, a Latin term for pro re nata, or as needed. There was even a setup where the patient could administer the pain medication himself via his intravenous line, with some limitations as to how often. "Do you know if he has been using his pain medication?"

"Yes, he has," Helena said. "Plus, following written orders, I was able to give him some additional pain medication if needed, which I did an hour ago. But he is again complaining, and it is way too soon for him to be given yet another dose."

"What would you have me do?" Mitt questioned, unable to think clearly in his tired state.

"You need to come and check on him," Helena stated with a hint of irritation.

"Okay," Mitt said, realizing from her tone he had little choice even though he didn't think his being there was going to provide any answers. "I'm on my way." He disconnected the call, put his legs over the side of the bed, and stood up. A wave of dizziness hit him, but it quickly passed. Going into the bathroom, he splashed cold water on his face. He stared at his image in the mirror as he dried himself off. Dark circles were prominent under his eyes, while the whites had spiderwebs of tiny red vessels. He certainly wasn't looking his best. To try to help his appearance, he pushed his hair into a semblance of order. As he did so, he wondered what he was going to look like a month from now if he appeared this bad during his first night on call.

Trying to rally his energies, he headed out of the bathroom but was still in a daze. As he passed his bed, he eyed it nostalgically. Leaving the on-call room, he made sure the door was locked behind him. By the time he got to the elevators, he felt a little better and more awake, especially after taking a few deep breaths waiting for one of the cars to arrive.

Reaching the night-darkened fifteenth floor, he stopped at the appropriate nurses' station on his way to Mr. Suárez's room. In contrast with earlier that evening when he'd done his workups, the area was peaceful, with only three nurses silently busy in front of separate monitors behind the counter. No one even looked in his direction until he called out.

"Excuse me! I'm Dr. Fuller, and I'm looking for Helena Santos. Any idea where she might be?"

"I think she's over in 1504," one of the nurses said. She was the only one of the three who looked up in Mitt's direction. "At least that's where she was a few minutes ago."

"Okay," Mitt said. "If she appears, tell her I'm down there." The nurse nodded but didn't verbally respond.

As he headed down the darkened hallway with the muffled sounds of monitoring devices emanating from various rooms, he hoped that the nurse would still be there. He was counting on her offering suggestions of what to do. Otherwise, he might have to call Madison, which he'd rather not do for something as trivial as adequate pain medication. If and when he called her, he wanted it to be about something serious. He didn't want to become known as someone who cried wolf over insignificant details.

As he reached 1504, he noticed the door was completely open and the rare single room was moderately illuminated. Entering, he could see that it wasn't from the overhead lights but rather from a reading light behind the bed that cast long shadows across the rest of the room. There was also some light coming from the open bathroom doorway.

Benito Suárez was propped up, with his torso slightly raised by pillows behind his head and shoulders. Both side rails of the bed were up. An intravenous bag was hanging from a pole attached to the head of the bed, and the tube ran down into the man's forearm. He was a stout, heavily built man in his late thirties who appeared much older. He had a ruddy complexion with short dark hair and rounded facial features that were currently pulled into a grimace of pain. Both hands were gripping the sheets on either side of his body. Save for the dressing over his abdominal incision, which was held in place with paper tape, he was naked from the waist up. A narrow tube that Mitt knew functioned as a drain snaked out from beneath the paper tape and was connected to a small clear container hanging beneath the bed. Beads of perspiration dotted the man's forehead.

Feeling nervous and inadequate but pretending otherwise, Mitt walked up to the right side of the man's bed, glancing at the drainage container as he did so. He noticed there was a small amount of bright red blood in its base, yet since the container and the connecting tube were mostly empty, he gave it little thought. He assumed the nurse on the opposite side of the bed was Helena. It had been apparent they were conversing when Mitt arrived but now both looked in his direction.

"Hello, Mr. Suárez," Mitt began. "I understand you are experiencing some discomfort." He purposefully tried to minimize the situation in hopes it would solve itself.

"*Muita dor, Doutor. Muito! Muito!*" he managed through a clenched jaw.

Mitt glanced over at Helena although he had a pretty good idea of the meaning.

"He says he has a lot of pain, Doctor," the nurse said. "Too much."

Mitt nodded in understanding. "And, just to be certain, he's had all his prescribed narcotic, correct?"

"Absolutely. As I mentioned on the phone, besides his own pain meds, I gave him an additional dose just a little more than an hour ago, but it hasn't touched him, as you can plainly see. He's not due for another dose for another three hours."

"Okay," Mitt responded, as much for himself as for the others. His mind was in high gear, trying to decide exactly what to do. Short of calling Madison, the only thing that came to mind was possibly taking a peek at the incision and maybe gently palpating the man's abdomen. At least it was something. He said as much to the patient, using gestures and very simple English, trying to ask if it would be okay.

"*Por favor faça alguma coisa, Doutor. Por favor!*" Benito managed.

"He said okay, go ahead," the nurse translated.

As gingerly as he could, Mitt began to pull the upper edges of the paper tape off Benito's abdomen, hoping not to make the man's discomfort worse. Slowly he succeeded, and eventually he was able to fold the entire dressing down toward the foot of the bed, exposing most of the sutured incision that Mitt had done under Nancy Wu's supervision. At the lower end, the drain tube issued forth, again with a tiny amount of bright red blood in its lumen but not a lot. From Mitt's perspective everything looked normal, with the "ladder-rung" sutures crossing the incision every centimeter or so. At Dr. Wu's direction they had all been snugged up but not too tight. The circulation of the tissues appeared fine.

"Do you need some gloves?" Helena questioned.

"That would be a good idea," Mitt said, embarrassed he'd not thought of it.

The nurse immediately disappeared, leaving Mitt and the patient alone in the room. Benito looked up at him with what Mitt interpreted as a pleading expression. The problem was that Mitt still had no idea what to do.

"I'm sorry you are having so much difficulty," Mitt said, feeling the need to say something while they waited for the nurse's return.

"*Eu não entendo*," Benito groaned.

"He says he doesn't understand," Helena explained as she came back into the room. She handed Mitt a package of sterile gloves. He was impressed by her speediness even though he knew this room was relatively close to the nurses' station and hence to all the supplies.

"I assumed as much," Mitt said as he tore open the package and struggled to don the gloves while maintaining their sterility. As he fumbled through the process in front of an audience, he thought that the proper technique for donning surgical gloves was yet another one of those little, practical things he should have been taught in his four years of medical school.

When he was ready, Mitt leaned over the patient and examined the sutured incision by gently palpating its edges. Everything felt normal, without any localized lumps that might suggest a hematoma or collection of blood. Then another idea occurred to him. Maybe he should press on the sides of the abdomen very carefully to get an idea of the man's intra-abdominal pressure and explore the possibility that the drain was clogged. If that had happened, he asked himself, might fluid possibly build up and cause the acute pain the man was experiencing? It seemed like a plausible idea, yet as he continued to carefully palpate, the abdomen didn't seem to be as tense as he would have expected if that were the case. On the contrary, it seemed to be as soft as normal even with the man tensing by reflex when Mitt gingerly pushed in.

Mitt straightened back up to his considerable full height. As potentially intellectually rewarding as the concept of a blocked drain had momentarily been, it now seemed out of the question. The problem was that he needed to come up with yet another theory as to what was going on to cause the man so much discomfort despite adequate narcotics.

While Mitt's mind grappled with the issue at hand, he noticed something strange. The light in the room seemed to flicker. Mitt glanced at the source, the reading light at the head of the bed. When that was clearly as steady as normal, he wondered if the origin had been inside his own exhausted brain. Remembering his earlier, very weird phantosmia, Mitt shifted his gaze to the nurse for confirmation, and she, too, appeared momentarily addled, staring at the reading light. Seeing her reaction made him change his mind; maybe there'd been a blip in the power in the entire building.

But then Mitt was distracted by a strange popping sound, diverting his attention away from both the nurse and the flickering light back down to Benito's incision. To Mitt's surprise and shock, the uppermost suture of the midline incision had opened with a pop, as if the knot had just suddenly been untied by some mysterious internal force. Before Mitt could react to this strange phenomenon, the same thing happened to the second suture and then the third. It was as though the incision was unzipping. Even more alarming, at the very same time the sutures were spontaneously untying, Benito's belly began obviously and rapidly swelling, akin to a balloon inflating.

With a reflexive urge to do something in the face of a growing catastrophe, Mitt shifted sideways to allow him to place the palms of his gloved hands along the sides of the progressively opening incision to try to push the edges together to keep further sutures from bursting open. But his effort was to no avail. The abdomen continued rapidly to swell, and the sutures continued to open, with some not untying but cutting through the skin. And now it wasn't only the skin sutures. The deeper-layer catgut sutures were audibly popping open in the interior of the wound, same with the even deeper and stronger wire sutures as the man's abdomen kept ballooning.

Before Mitt or Helena could react, the entire wound burst open with a sudden, pulsating geyser of bright red arterial blood. It came in gigantic spurts as each one of Benito's heartbeats pumped out his life's blood, drenching himself, the bed, Mitt, and even running down onto the floor.

Helena leaped backward, howled, and then disappeared from the room as Mitt continued to try ineffectually to hold the edges of the wound together, with the misguided idea that he could possibly stem the flow. In the next instant Helena and a bevy of other nurses came dashing back into the room carrying a host of sterile towels. Not sure what to do with them, Mitt grabbed them and jammed them blindly down into the gaping incision in hopes of stemming the blood loss.

He was literally up to his elbows in gore, the sleeves and front of his white coat and his scrubs soaked in bright red blood.

At least Mitt's pressure with the towels was working, or so he thought, since the blood flow significantly decreased and then appeared to stop. That was until one of the newly arrived nurses said that the patient had no blood pressure although there was a weak pulse. It was then obvious to everyone that Benito Suárez had bled out.

"What the hell are we going to do?" Helena yelled at Mitt.

Mitt stood up and pulled his blood-soaked arms out of the wound and looked blankly at Helena, as confused as ever. Before he could respond, Madison Baker came dashing into the room like a godsend. "Good God!" she voiced with a shake of her head as she confronted the scene.

All the nurses now turned to Madison as she rushed up to the bed, her eyes taking in the entire disaster. "Let me be sure: This was today's abdominal aneurysm case, correct?" she demanded.

"Yes," Helena fired back.

"Okay, cool it!" Madison ordered. Instead of barking orders as Mitt and the nurses expected, she pulled out her phone and then disappeared from the room.

For a few seconds, all the nurses and Mitt exchanged confused glances, then all but Helena and three others left. Mitt didn't know what to say or what to do until he decided to at least remove his blood-smeared surgical gloves. As soon as he did, Madison returned.

"Okay, I spoke with Geraldo Rodriguez and told him what happened. He wasn't at all surprised. He said the patient's aorta was in super-sad shape, and he was surprised they had been able to attach the graft at all. Actually, I had already heard that from Nancy Wu, so when I ran in here, I wasn't about to pull out all the stops for a full-scale resuscitation and order up an emergency surgery. Dr. Rodriguez fully agrees. Obviously, the abdominal aorta blew. Whether it was the anastomosis or another part of the aorta, we'll have to wait for the autopsy to find out. Anyway, that's all she wrote. It's now a medical examiner case. Get housekeeping up here, ladies, please, and, Mitt, you do the paperwork. Okay?"

"Okay," Mitt said, feeling shell-shocked. He didn't know what doing the paperwork required, but he was reasonably sure the nurses would fill him in. He followed Madison out into the hallway. Helena and the three other nurses stayed back in the room, starting the cleanup. Mitt took off his blood-soaked coat and balled it up with the bloodiest parts on the inside.

"How long were you in the patient's room before the shit hit the fan?" Madison questioned en route to the nurses' station. To his surprise her tone was remarkably normal, similar to how she'd sounded down in the cafeteria.

"Not long," Mitt said, finding his voice with some difficulty. He felt traumatized.

"Why didn't you call me immediately?" Madison continued to question him matter-of-factly. "Why did you wait? Hell, that must have been a horrendous experience for you. More trial by fire, I'd have to say."

"I was trying to handle it myself," Mitt admitted sheepishly. "I suppose I should have called you. I don't know why I didn't. I'm afraid it is all a steep learning curve. I just wish I was better prepared, for the patient's sake and my own."

"Amen!" Madison responded as they arrived at the nurses' station. "We've all had to go through what you are going through. It's a bit of the luck of the draw. But chin up! Get the paperwork done and try to get yourself some sleep! You've got a full day of surgery ahead of you in a matter of hours. If there are any other problems tonight, I'm available if you need me."

"Okay," Mitt managed.

Madison gave Mitt an encouraging tap on his shoulder and a fleeting smile of encouragement before heading down the long, dark corridor toward the bank of elevators.

For a moment, Mitt watched her go. He felt decidedly envious of her experience and apparent sangfroid. Would he ever obtain a similar confidence in such a circumstance? He didn't know, but he hoped so.

CHAPTER 9

Tuesday, July 2, 3:03 A.M.

Mitt's eyes scanned down to the next line on the death certificate form and paused. Up until that moment he'd been
doing reasonably well as he filled in the various blanks with
relative ease despite his pulse still pounding in his temples and his
hand visibly shaking. The pounding had begun the second Benito
Suárez's aorta, or its connection to the graft, had burst—although as
he relived the event, he recognized that his general anxiety had sky-
rocketed the moment he'd entered the man's room. Somehow he had
anticipated the catastrophe.

Mitt's sense of utter panic hadn't eased up for at least a half hour
after the event, not until after Madison Baker had called a halt to any
resuscitation attempts. All in all, the experience had been the worst
twenty or thirty minutes of his life. It had started innocently enough
with confusion in trying to help the man with his pain, but then
rapidly descended into sheer terror. Being literally up to his elbows in

blood during his first night on call was way beyond anything he could have imagined and his worst fears.

Mitt was sitting on one of the wheeled chairs at the central desk. In contrast to the relatively dark corridors illuminated with dim baseboard lighting, the central desk was ablaze with a distinctly white light coming from ceiling-mounted LED fixtures behind translucent panels. Although the light afforded great illumination, Mitt thought it made everyone appear washed out, and as tired as he was, he couldn't imagine how bad he looked.

"Excuse me!" Mitt called to Helena, who was using one of the nearby monitors to file her own report on the episode, which he could tell had disturbed even the nurses. He was interrupting Helena because he was stumped as to how to fill out the next blank on the form. It asked for the time of death, and he had no idea what to put down. In the thick of the ghastly event, noting the time had been the last thing on his mind.

"The patient died when you say he died," Helena said without looking up.

Mitt started. It was hardly the answer he expected. Besides, he was already feeling guilty that he hadn't called for help sooner. He hadn't even been the one who called Madison. On top of that was his continuing uncomfortable feeling of unpreparedness, despite having spent four stressful years in medical school. He was officially a doctor, having received his MD degree at graduation, but he didn't feel like one, especially as alone as he felt in a hospital with a thousand inpatients.

All these thoughts tumbling around in his mind brought back the incident with shocking clarity, and suddenly he remembered something that the stress of the situation had erased: the flickering light and then the popping noises of the skin sutures opening. As he sat there and thought about it, he distinctly remembered gawking at the sutures. It had seemed they were untying in front of his eyes, and he'd worried that he had mistakenly tied granny knots instead of square knots. It was only then that he'd noticed the abdomen was swelling. But now, sitting there at the nurses' station, he had no idea what had come first, the swelling of the abdomen, which caused the sutures to pull open, or the popping open of the sutures, allowing the abdomen to swell.

"Just put down two thirty A.M.," Helena called out, seeing Mitt had stopped filling in the required paperwork. "The exact time doesn't matter. It's merely when the patient was pronounced dead. You get what I'm saying?"

Waking from his momentary trance, Mitt nodded toward Helena and proceeded to write 2:30 A.M. in the appropriate blank. Yet he was still pondering the suture-timing issue. He wanted to take a look to see if the sutures themselves might tell him anything. Glancing back at Helena, he asked: "Do you think the body is still in the room?"

"Yes, most likely. There's always a delay for the medical examiner to send over one of their investigators, unless the body is released during the initial phone call. Their office is practically right next door, so I expect someone will be coming by. They usually do when it involves a death this close to the surgery. And they will probably need to talk with you, so don't rush off."

Mitt nodded. He wasn't planning on rushing off, since he had the rest of the death papers to fill out. But at the moment, he was captivated by the dilemma of what came first: the chicken or the egg. Seeing the first skin-closure sutures he'd ever done mysteriously untie didn't bode well for his surgical career.

Pushing his chair back, he stood up. But then he thought of something else. "Sorry to bother you yet again, but before all hell broke loose, did you notice the lights in the room seemed to flicker or was it my imagination?"

"Now that you mention it, I do remember. It was just for a second or two."

"Has that ever happened before?"

"I'd have to say yes. It happened pretty often when they were renovating the tenth floor a few years ago. We were told they were doing a lot of electrical work."

"Interesting," Mitt commented. *Okay,* he thought. *Apparently flickering lights aren't all that uncommon.* "I'll be right back." He put down his pen on top of the papers he was filling out and then walked out of the nurses' station. On his way he grabbed a package of sterile gloves.

Entering Benito Suárez's room gave him a creepy feeling, enough to make him question why he was there. But he felt motivated since the man's skin sutures had been Mitt's inauguration to what he hoped would be a long surgical career. The question was whether he'd tied square knots. If he could find some of the knots intact, perhaps he could tell. Anyway, he thought it was worth the effort and wouldn't take very long. This was his first death as a resident, and he was struggling with a sense of direct responsibility.

Benito's body was still in the same position: on his back, arms splayed out to the sides. The IV had been stopped but it was still attached to his right forearm. With the overhead lights on, he was as pale as a ghost. Someone had closed his eyes, which Mitt appreciated. The less Mitt thought of him as a person, the easier it was emotionally.

Although the blood on the floor had been mopped up, the blood on the bed had not been touched, nor that on Benito's abdomen or in the gaping abdominal incision. It was now a darker red and no longer fluid. As he had hoped, he could see the tips of at least a few of the black silk sutures lining the sides of the open incision, poking up out of the dried blood.

After pulling on the gloves, he teased out a number of the sutures from the clotted blood. It was immediately apparent that the three topmost sutures had no knots, as if the knots that had been there had completely unraveled, suggesting to Mitt's chagrin they must have been granny knots. But then the rest of the knots were intact, meaning the other skin sutures had broken or had been yanked out of one side of the incision. Holding the knots within inches of his face, Mitt was able to see that they were all indeed square knots, a fact that initially made him more confused. But then he recognized there was a chance that he could have mistakenly made granny knots with the first three stitches before making square knots with the rest.

Mitt shook his head in frustration. He thought he'd tied all the knots the same, but apparently that might not have been the case. What he needed to do was promise himself that he would be more careful in the future. But was that enough to answer the question about what came first, the sutures popping or the swelling? He didn't think so. Yes, the unraveling of the top three sutures could have marginally relieved the intra-abdominal pressure and thereby put stress on the aorta graft attachments, but he didn't think three out of more than twenty were enough to make a difference.

"So much for that idea," Mitt murmured as he removed his gloves and deposited them in an appropriate container. As exhausted as he was, he couldn't think any more about anything. By now his pulse had returned to a semblance of normal and his anxiety had significantly waned from sheer exhaustion. He was closing in on having been awake and busy for almost twenty-four stressful hours.

As Mitt headed for the door, an entire team of housekeeping

personnel arrived to start a definitive cleaning of the room. For a moment he was blocked from exiting as they stopped in the doorway, clearly surprised that the deceased body was still present.

"Excuse me," Mitt said as he tried to push his way through the doorway. In the process, he made fleeting but direct eye contact with a Black woman who seemed to be in charge, and despite his exhaustion, he immediately experienced some mild paresthesia on his chest along with the sense that this woman was strangely enough empathizing with him about his recent experience.

Assuming the surprising and transitory episode was merely another reflection of his mental and physical exhaustion, Mitt didn't stop but continued pushing through the group. Once clear, he quickly made his way back to the nurses' station.

Twenty minutes later, Mitt was finally able to complete the paperwork required following Mr. Suárez's death. By then Helena had apparently finished what she had to do and was elsewhere, most likely taking care of her other patients. At that moment the only other person in the nurses' station was the night-shift head nurse whom he'd not officially met. As tired as he was, he couldn't generate the energy to formally introduce himself.

With shaky legs, he got to his feet. Not knowing what exactly he was supposed to do with the completed forms, he just left them where they were and headed down the long, dark east–west corridor for the distant elevators. The passageway was illuminated only by the dim, nighttime, baseboard lighting system.

He was moving by rote now, placing one foot in front of the other. The only thing on his mind was how wonderful it was going to feel when he finally was able to lie down. Just staying upright required a bit of concentration. But then suddenly he stopped. Ahead, at the intersection of the two equally long corridors coming from 15 North and 15 South, Mitt saw an unexpected sight that shocked him. It was a young, strikingly blond, pale, preadolescent girl who had come from the north hallway seemingly intent on heading down the south one. Apparently seeing Mitt was equally surprising for her, as she also stopped in her tracks, staring intently in his direction.

At first Mitt thought the child had to be a patient who'd snuck out of her room to wander around, something he imagined wasn't all that uncommon although surely discouraged. But then he realized that couldn't be the case because the person he was seeing was definitely a child, whom he guessed was around ten years old. As far as he knew, there were no pediatric patients on the fifteenth floor, and the Department of Pediatrics was way down on the eighth floor, or so he'd been told.

And, Mitt realized, the girl wasn't wearing a typical hospital johnny, the gown all patients were required to wear except for those up on the psychiatric floors. She had on a dress, and even that seemed oddly anachronistic. The child was clothed in a pale off-white shirt-dress with puffy sleeves and a flat, rounded collar that appeared to Mitt, who'd been an old-movie buff as a teenager, to be right out of the 1940s or 1950s.

Mitt's next thought, the clothing notwithstanding, was that perhaps the girl had managed to wander onto one of the elevators and was now lost and needed help to find her way back down to the pediatric floor and to her room. Marshalling a surge of energy motivated by concern for the child, Mitt started forward and was about to call out to her when the horrid cacosmia reoccurred with a vengeance. The smell was as bad or worse than it had been hours earlier in the elevator lobby on the seventeenth floor. It was awful enough to make him stop short and clasp his hand to his face to pinch his nose.

But then almost as rapidly as he'd been assaulted by the terrible odor, it vanished just as it had earlier, leaving him momentarily stunned. At the same instant, the young girl—having caught sight of Mitt—seemed to shrink back in either fright or antipathy, he couldn't tell. Since she was illuminated from below by the baseboard lighting, only her delicate chin and the tip of her nose were apparent. Both eye sockets appeared as black holes beneath her nimbus of radiant blond hair, so blond it seemed almost phosphorescent.

"Wait!" Mitt called out as he again started toward the child. She was now about twenty or thirty feet away, close enough for Mitt to see that something shining in the half-light was protruding from her left eye socket. But the girl didn't heed Mitt's request. Instead, she spun around and disappeared from view back up the north corridor.

Sprinting ahead, Mitt reached the intersection within seconds. Ahead was the bank of elevators, five on a side. Turning the corner, Mitt looked up the north corridor, intending to catch up to the fleeing girl. But again, he abruptly stopped. From where he was now standing, he could see all the way to the hallway's end, where it abutted the corridor that ran along the 15 North patient rooms. Shockingly enough, the corridor was completely empty. There was no young blond patient on a midnight foray. Instead, way at the end, he glimpsed a passing nurses' aide carrying a tray of medications to one of the nearby patient rooms.

Slowly Mitt's jaw dropped open in amazement and concern. He released a long breath and sagged against the wall of the corridor, letting the back of his head rest against the Sheetrock. He closed his eyes. One question burst into the forefront of his mind: *What the hell is happening to me?* He feared he might be losing it. Could the combination of his nonstop anxiety and physical exhaustion take a serious toll on his sanity and cause hallucinations?

Mitt took a deep breath in, held it for a moment, then let it out again through pursed lips. Somehow the fluttering sound and the physical sensation it made were reassuring. For a moment he had no idea of what to think or do. Maybe he was not cut out to be a surgical resident, and the disturbing question of whether that might be true hung unanswered in the air. Did other first-year residents have similar reactions? Had Madison gone through something equivalent a year ago? He had no idea, but her current apparent confidence was encouraging. As agitated as he felt, he wanted to grab onto anything to feel reassured.

Mitt opened his eyes, looking north once again, almost hoping he'd see the blond girl, but he didn't. Instead, he saw what looked like the same nurses' aide again walk past, now going in the opposite direction. She'd apparently dispensed the medication she'd been carrying and was on her way back to the nurses' station. Somehow just seeing such a normal nighttime hospital routine gave Mitt the bit of reassurance he needed to counteract his concern that he was going off the deep end. Olfactory and visual hallucinations were worrisome symptoms, yet it all had to be a combination of stress, anxiety, and exhaustion. What he needed was sleep. It was nearly 4:00 A.M. by his watch, and he'd have to wake up around 6:00 to be prepared for rounds at 6:30, as Dr. Kumar had stressed. It wasn't going to be much rest, but he had to think that was better than none at all.

CHAPTER 10

After more than two hours in operating room #4, one of Belle-vue's newest hybrid ORs, Mitt could not believe how much more interesting his second day was from his first right from the get-go. During much of his first day of surgery, particularly the first several hours, he'd seen little of the operative procedure since his line of sight had been blocked by Dr. Geraldo Rodriguez's torso. On today's open-heart surgery case, which was a mitral valve replace-ment on Ella Thompson, there had been no such problem, even though Dr. Rodriguez was again the first assistant. And good visibility wasn't the only beneficial change for Mitt. Yesterday he'd spent the entire case using both hands to pull up and back on a retractor, which had not been easy, especially for eight hours.

On today's case very little retraction had been needed because the cardiothoracic attending surgeon, Dr. Pamela Harington, who was the associate chief of the department, had employed an instrument called a *sternal retractor*. After using a vibrating bone saw to cut through the sternum vertically, she'd put in the sternal retractor and cranked it open, which fully exposed the fatty pericardium as well as sizable portions of both alternately inflating lungs. Mitt had been spellbound, especially watching the opening of the pericardium to expose the beating heart. As a medical student, Mitt had never seen an open-heart surgical case, although from a technical perspective he knew a considerable amount about the heart-lung machine that made it all possible. He'd been directly exposed to an extracorporeal membrane oxygenation machine, which operated under similar technological principals, during his third-year internal medicine rotation.

To make the situation even more engaging and personal for Mitt, Dr. Harington had taken an early and strong interest in his participation when she'd been told by Dr. Rodriguez at the beginning of the case that it was only Mitt's second full day as a resident. That fact had clearly caught her fancy, as she was quick to say that she, too, had done her surgical training at NYU and mostly at Bellevue, although she'd gone on to do a fellowship at the Cleveland Clinic. It was obvious to Mitt that while she was thinking of him, she was mostly waxing nostalgic.

"You must be thrilled, Dr. Fuller," she added now as she looked across at Mitt during an unexpected delay in the procedure caused by the perfusionist, who wasn't quite prepared to go on bypass. He was still busily in the process of priming the heart-lung machine when Dr. Harington announced she was ready to insert the cannulas to divert the blood away from the heart. Mitt was on the opposite side from Dr. Harington, once again nestled between Geraldo and the anesthesia screen but with a completely open view of the operative site. "I remember my first few days as a resident as if they were yesterday," Dr. Harington continued. "I hope you are aware just how extraordinary and exciting a journey you're beginning. Although I'm sure you had to have worked hard to get here, you are a lucky, lucky man. All I can say is, enjoy it!"

Mitt nodded as if agreeing, but after the previous day and night, he wasn't sure that *enjoy* was the right verb. He was thinking *survive* might be more applicable. Nor did he feel all that lucky. Although he was presently fascinated by the operation, he was exhausted mentally and physically after only one day and one night. The worrisome question of how he'd be feeling after a week or a month dogged him.

Despite how bad he felt physically, he'd somehow gotten through rounds at 6:30 A.M., during which he was introduced to the rest of the surgical residents. Andrea had been particularly eager to learn how his evening had gone, but there hadn't been time for him to explain in any detail. All he said was that he'd fill her in later. During rounds he'd managed to briefly present his three cases, including Ella Thompson, whose surgery he was now witnessing, along with those of Roberto Silva and Bianca Perez, whose surgeries were to follow Ella Thompson's in the same OR.

During rounds, Andrea had presented her cases as well, but no one had told her beforehand to be succinct. Instead, Dr. Kumar had interrupted her first two presentations to speed things up and encourage her to concentrate on just the important facts. By her third, she'd finally gotten the message.

All in all, the morning rounds had gone smoothly, with just a few minutes spent on each case. If there were clinical management problems, like a postoperative fever or lack of bowel sounds after abdominal surgery, the whole group lingered a little longer until a consensus was reached.

At the very end of rounds, there'd also been a brief discussion of the Benito Suárez calamity, but the conversation mostly revolved around the details of the patient's aortic pathology, the difficulties that such pathology caused in suturing the graft, and the associated genetics. To Mitt's chagrin, little was mentioned about the clinical catastrophe that had taken place and whether there was anything that he could have done when he first arrived on the scene to avert what had ultimately happened.

When rounds broke up, Dr. Van Dyke did take Mitt aside to commiserate briefly with him about the Suárez experience. Mitt appreciated her concern and could tell she was genuinely sensitive to his mindset. As a result, he was tempted to bring up his weird olfactory and visual hallucinations to get them off his chest, so to speak, and maybe find out if she had ever had a similar experience. But then at the last moment, he changed his mind. He'd not had time to adequately think through the experiences himself, and besides, he was worried that it might make her question whether he had what it took to be a surgical resident.

Mitt truly didn't know what to make of the experiences, and they seemed crazy in the light of day. He'd always thought of himself as being reasonably creative, but conjuring up out of the blue horrific smells and a mysterious child seemed beyond his capabilities. Actually, now that it was daylight, it was even difficult for him to recall exactly how bad the smell had been and what the child had looked like, both of which lent support to the idea that it had been some aberrant, brief waking-nightmare.

After the rapid rounds, those who were scheduled for 7:30 surgical cases went to the elevators to go down to the eleventh floor, including Mitt and Andrea. As their elevator descended, he at least had an opportunity to tell her exactly how exhausted he was and that he hoped her on-call night would be a hell of a lot easier. Her response was to ask to hear more, specifically about the Suárez case.

"Let's just say it was the worst clinical experience of my life," Mitt had said, knowing that he wouldn't have time to elaborate before Ella Thompson's surgery. At that exact moment, the elevator door had slid open on the eleventh floor, and everyone, including Mitt and Andrea, piled out en masse and headed for their respective ORs.

"While we're waiting to go on bypass, Dr. Fuller, let me share something with you," Dr. Harington suddenly announced with obvious pride, breaking into Mitt's brief reverie. "I happen to be an armchair devotee of Bellevue Hospital history. Maybe that's not quite strong enough. Maybe a 'connoisseur' or 'aficionado' of Bellevue's intriguing history is more accurate. To be honest, I can't get enough of it. It's a fascinating three-hundred-year saga with an astounding list of medical firsts. Let me ask you: Are you aware of the extraordinary history of this hospital, Dr. Fuller?"

"Yes, to an extent." Mitt had no idea where this new discourse was heading, especially in the middle of an open-heart surgery case while waiting for the perfusion machine to be ready.

"One of the most interesting aspects, as you might imagine, is that there's an extraordinary cast of characters involved, any one of whose life stories would make for a great Hollywood movie."

"I'm sure," Mitt said, wanting to be agreeable.

"Why I bring it up is that I recall there were actually a number of Dr. Fullers who served as Bellevue attendings over the years and who were, in their lifetimes, very well-known characters. Are you aware? Could these Fullers have been any relation?"

Mitt tried to look into the depths of Dr. Harington's eyes to get some sense of where she was going with this unexpected topic. Yet it was almost impossible to tell because she was wearing a pair of surgical magnifying eyeglasses with a built-in bright light such that when he looked directly at her, all he saw was a glare. He had very mixed feelings about being associated with past medical and, in particular, surgical greats, which was why he'd never mentioned it during his application process. But at the moment, he didn't see any way to skirt the issue. "Yes," he said after a brief pause. "I am related."

"Oh, my goodness gracious," Dr. Harington said with obvious pleasure. "Oh, wow! I can't believe it! That's fantastic. As I particularly recall, there were three Fuller nineteenth-century surgeons. Are you related to all three?"

"I am," Mitt said reluctantly.

"Oh my goodness! Isn't this rather incredible, Dr. Rodriguez? We have a direct descendant of three historic Bellevue surgeons currently on our residency staff and helping us on this case. I think that's outstanding."

"Amazing," Dr. Rodriguez agreed.

"I'm also related to Samuel Fuller," Mitt said, attempting to divert attention away from his association with surgery at Bellevue. "He was the physician in the Plymouth Colony."

"Interesting, no doubt," Dr. Harington said. "But I'm more impressed with your connections to the Bellevue Fullers. I remember reading that Dr. Homer Fuller had been clocked doing a mid-thigh amputation in nine seconds. That's skin to skin including sawing through the femur. Can you believe that? I can't!"

"That's incredible," Dr. Rodriguez agreed.

"How close a relative was Homer Fuller?" Dr. Harington asked.

"He was my paternal great-great-great-great-grandfather," Mitt said. "He was born in 1801."

"My word! I think this is beyond fascinating," Dr. Harington carried on. "I really do. Your relative must have been an amazing individual, although quite religious, I understand. Maybe even a bit over the top. But despite that, he and Dr. David Hosack, another famous

Bellevue surgeon, were part of a team that took grave-robbing for dissection corpses to new heights, which, by the way, put Bellevue on the anatomical map. Wow! I mean, we're talking about a very colorful history here. The downside was that Homer Fuller, who was some thirty years younger than David Hosack but significantly more religious, ended up being the leader of the anti-anesthesia group here at Bellevue."

"Good grief," Dr. Rodriguez said. "He was against anesthesia?"

"Yes, as crazy as it sounds today. He believed that the pain that patients experienced was God's work and shouldn't be interfered with, or something weird like that. Anyway, for a while here at Bellevue there was a 'pro-anesthesia' faction and one that was against, led by Homer Fuller. Luckily pro-anesthesia won out, for obvious reasons, yet as I understand it, Homer kept doing his lightning-fast surgery without anesthesia long after it was generally accepted by most everyone else."

"Homer Fuller kept doing surgery without anesthesia?" Mitt questioned incredulously. He'd never heard anything along those lines, or even close. All he'd ever heard about his medical ancestors was unadulterated praise. It was a source of significant familial pride.

"Yes, it seems so," Dr. Harington said. "That's what I read, and I have a reference to an obscure, unpublished article that talks about this, if you're ever interested to learn more. In the 1970s, an NYU bioethicist named Robert Pendleton, who was as fascinated by Bellevue Hospital history as I am, somehow came across some revealing primary sources. Unfortunately, his untimely death from a heart attack intervened and his work was never published. As great as the Fuller surgeons clearly were in terms of operative skill, they did seem to have a penchant for being on the wrong side of what we now know were major medical advances."

"What do you mean?" Mitt asked, taken aback.

"Another Fuller named Dr. Otto Fuller was responsible for a number of important technical surgical advances and was also, strangely enough, on the wrong side of another major advance that was as important in many ways as the introduction of anesthesia. It was the antiseptic movement, which, at the time, was being championed by none other than Dr. William Halsted. I'm assuming you are also related to Dr. Otto Fuller?"

"Yes," Mitt admitted. "He was my great-great-great-grandfather, born in 1835." He'd heard so much about his Bellevue relatives, Mitt had all their associated dates committed to memory.

"My gosh, such fascinating history," Dr. Harington said with an appreciative shake of her head. "Back then, before the Joseph Lister antiseptic crusade took over the world's surgical centers, around half the surgical patients died of sepsis, including here at Bellevue. Since we're so accustomed to strictly adhering to aseptic technique nowadays and take bacteriology for granted, it's difficult for us to realize there was a long time before it was accepted. Back then, surgeons didn't even wash their hands or their instruments or change their clothes before doing surgery, and sometimes they went from doing autopsies directly to the operating room or the delivery room without any preparation in terms of cleanliness whatsoever. It truly boggles the mind.

"What about Dr. Benjamin Fuller and Dr. Clarence Fuller?" Dr. Harington questioned after a short pause. "Are they also direct ancestors?"

"Yes," Mitt answered. He was almost reluctant to admit it after hearing what she'd said about Homer and Otto.

"Two more high-powered Bellevue physicians," Dr. Harington said. "Dr. Benjamin Fuller was the second surgeon in the world to perform a mitral valve fracture in 1925, the same valve we're going to replace today, which they couldn't do back then. Were you aware of that?"

"I was," Mitt said, feeling a bit of relief to be reminded of something positive.

"He was a pioneer, for sure," Dr. Harington said. "And extremely technically talented. But, like his two forebearers, he had his downside. He was a rabid opponent of the concept of informed consent, which was becoming a significant issue at the time. He felt strongly that charity patients, which is what Bellevue has always handled as a public hospital—and still does—had a moral or religious obligation to offer their bodies for medical research as their side of the bargain. From his perspective, since they got free care, he felt they were obligated to contribute, even had a moral responsibility to do so. The trouble was back then there was no limitation to what a surgeon could try, even on a whim, and a few of them tried rather strange therapies, like injecting tobacco juice."

"Tobacco juice?" Dr. Rodriguez questioned with astonishment. "Why tobacco juice?"

"Heaven only knows," Dr. Harington said. "It's part of the reason Bellevue history is so fascinating. Of course, I'm talking about a long time ago, back when bleeding and purging were the primary treatment options."

"I had never heard anything about Dr. Benjamin Fuller being against informed consent," Mitt said when Dr. Harington paused.

"I don't imagine you would have," she said. "Especially because he had so many positive attributes. What about Dr. Clarence Fuller? I imagine he's held in high regard in your family, with his contributions of putting Bellevue Hospital psychiatry on the world map."

"I heard a lot of positive things about Clarence when I was growing up," Mitt said. "I've even read a number of his papers predating behavioral therapy," he added. He was tempted to say he'd briefly thought of psychiatry as a potential specialty but held himself in check.

"Yes, he certainly contributed early on to behavioral therapy," Dr. Harington said. "As well as to psychotherapy. But he had a downside, too. He had been a strong, early advocate of lobotomies and was responsible for many of those done here at Bellevue before the procedure totally fell out of favor and he tried to distance himself from it. As I learned also from Robert Pendleton's papers, he even did a huge number on children because at the time he was competing for the top job as division chief. His main competitor was Dr. Lauretta Bender, a big advocate of electroconvulsive therapy, which was getting her a lot of press. He even advocated lobotomies for behavioral problems of childhood, insisting it was far more effective than ECT, which often had to be repeated up to twenty times to get a lasting effect."

"Okay, ready to commence bypass!" the perfusionist suddenly called out, breaking into Dr. Harington's monologue. "Sorry to keep you all waiting. We're good to go."

"All right!" Dr. Harington said, and clapped her gloved hands excitedly. "Okay! Let's get this show on the road!" She leaned over toward the anesthesiologist, asking if the patient was adequately heparinized.

"She is indeed," the anesthesiologist replied, flashing a thumbs-up.

Mitt took a deep breath and changed his posture, moving most of his weight from one leg to the other. He was shocked to hear that his illustrious surgical forebearers had been on the wrong side of history in relation to anesthesia, antisepsis, and even informed consent. Up until then, he'd only heard how great they'd been, without having any idea their greatness was restricted to technical ability. As for Dr. Clarence Fuller, Mitt had never heard of his supposed support of lobotomy.

"I assume you know what we are doing here," Dr. Harington said to Mitt as she got ready to implant the cannulas, which had already been prepared. The closed-circuit tubing had been severed and the appropriate tips connected.

"Generally, yes," Mitt responded, trying to deal with the disconcerting revelations about his ancestors as well as his exhaustion. He'd read about open-heart surgery as a medical student and had a reasonable understanding of the basics but had never actually seen it done.

As the case proceeded, Mitt became progressively more enthralled. To his delight, Dr. Harington explained step by step how the patient's blood was rerouted away from the heart, how the heart was then cooled to four degrees centigrade by the cardioplegia solution introduced through the coronary arteries, and finally how the patient herself was cooled but to a much lesser degree by the heart-lung machine to lower her metabolic demands.

Even though he was participating only by intermittently helping to maintain the necessary operative field exposure, Mitt was truly taken in by the whole process and for a time forgot how tired he was. He was especially interested in the opening of the left atrium and seeing the damaged mitral valve before it was removed. He then studiously observed exactly how the pig replacement valve was painstakingly positioned and sewed into place.

Mitt also couldn't help but notice that as all of this was happening, the atmosphere in the operating room was congenial, particularly compared with the day before. An instrument, which Mitt was told was a pair of DeBakey forceps, named after the famous cardiac surgeon Michael DeBakey, somehow managed to leave the instrument tray and hit Dr. Harington's right elbow as she was about to place another suture on the replacement valve, similar to the incident with Dr. Washington.

"So sorry," the scrub nurse said apologetically as she quickly took the forceps from Dr. Harington's hand. "How on earth did that happen?"

"I'm sure it was my fault for blocking your view of the operative field," Dr. Harington said. "You were probably trying to see over my arm. I know it makes it difficult for you to predict what I'll be needing if you can't see."

Another incident occurred when Dr. Harington and Dr. Rodriguez were exchanging a needle holder, since placement of a specific group of sutures was going to be easier from Dr. Rodriguez's side. In the process the needle holder dropped. Once again, no ill feelings or attempts to cast blame on the other person.

"Sorry," Dr. Harington said, immediately taking responsibility. "My fault."

"Don't be silly," Dr. Rodriguez said. "I wasn't watching like I should have."

Curiously enough, Mitt had been watching, and he had to blink several times, as it had appeared to him that the needle holder had somehow levitated out of Dr. Harington's hand. Knowing that was impossible, he attributed the impression to his exhaustion, just as he had attributed last night's weird hallucinations. As a medical student, Mitt had been tired before, but he'd never been as tired as he currently was. Nor as anxious.

In due course all the sutures attaching the pig replacement mitral valve had been carefully placed, snugged up, and tied. Then there was the closing of the left atrium, which was carried out comparatively quickly. "How long have we been on bypass?" Dr. Harington asked the anesthesiologist as she straightened up when all was done.

"Forty-eight minutes total," the anesthesiologist said.

"Not bad," Dr. Harington commented to no one in particular. "Okay! Let's start the weaning process and get the patient off the heart-lung machine. Are we good to go, team?"

"Good to go," the anesthesiologist and perfusionist said in unison.

"All vital signs good and stable," the anesthesiologist added. He switched on the ventilator with 100 percent oxygen, and the lungs began their rhythmical inflating and deflating.

"Excellent," Dr. Harington said. And then to the perfusionist she said: "Discontinue the cardioplegia solution, while I begin to unclamp the aorta."

When the clamp was off the aorta, she looked across at Mitt. "What I'm doing now allows normal blood to begin flowing through the heart, rinsing out the cardioplegic solution. That's going to warm the heart up rapidly and get it to begin beating again on its own."

Mitt nodded. It was fascinating to get to watch the whole process in real time. As impressive as it all was, he began to wonder if he shouldn't at least consider a future in cardiovascular surgery as a subspecialty despite the previous day's disaster.

A few minutes later silence fell as everyone watched the heart, waiting for it to begin beating. Unfortunately, long minutes passed but the heart remained motionless. "Hmmm," Dr. Harington voiced under her breath, more to herself than anyone else. "I don't like this. What the hell is going on here?"

Over the next three quarters of an hour, Mitt sensed the atmosphere in the operating room progress from congenial to tense. Ella

Thompson's heart was refusing to cooperate. Instead of immediately returning to its normal beating, it remained stubbornly quiescent. With increasing frustration, Dr. Harington tried a series of shocks using sterile paddles supplied by the circulating nurse. Unfortunately, none of the shocks worked, and the ceiling-mounted heart monitor continued to trace a totally flat line.

Following the unsuccessful shocks, Dr. Harington tried an internal pacemaker at the recommendation of a Cardiology consult conducted over the intercom system. But there was no response whatsoever, even over an extended period. The anesthesiologist sent off an emergency blood electrolyte sample, but the results came back normal.

"Was there anything at all from your end that might have suggested there'd be a problem?" Dr. Harington asked the perfusionist.

"Nothing," the perfusionist responded. "Not a hiccup. Everything has been rock stable and normal."

"My word," Dr. Harington said with obvious despair. "Who would have guessed? Certainly not me. I suppose this ticker was a lot sicker than any of us imagined. But I'm truly amazed. There'd been no hint."

Mitt sensed where the conversation was going and experienced a rising sense of dismay. The previous evening when he'd done Ella's history and physical, he'd felt an emotional attachment to the woman, such that the idea that she was now—less than twenty-four hours later—on the brink of death seemed like an impossible transition. It made him feel complicit, as if he were somehow responsible. He'd had several brushes with death as a medical student, but each of those patients had been in extremis when Mitt had been assigned. The deaths had never involved a functioning, seemingly happy, family-oriented, and connected human being, who had lots of grandchildren and even more great-grandchildren.

"What about using ECMO?" Mitt blurted out without much thought. "Couldn't an extracorporeal membrane oxygenation machine tide her over until her own heart comes back online?" The idea of just giving up seemed totally unreasonable.

Dr. Rodriguez chortled but then admonished himself for doing so. "Sorry," he said. "I don't mean to laugh, but using ECMO at this stage would just be putting off the inevitable and ultimately be a disservice to the family and the patient. The heart's been at body temperature and fully oxygenated for more than an hour. If it was going to restart, it would have done so before now. This is real life. You win some and you lose some."

Mitt felt a pang of panic. He didn't want to stop trying. "Isn't there something else we can do?" There was a sense of desperation in his voice. "What about some kind of ventricular assist device or even a heart transplant?"

"First of all, you can't assist a ventricle that's not beating," Dr. Harington said, sensing and appreciating Mitt's anguish. "And second, do you have any idea of how many patients are currently waiting for a transplantable heart who are considerably younger than Ms. Thompson? Let me tell you: more than seven thousand. No, she's not a candidate for a heart transplant. As hard as it might be, we have to accept our limitations as physicians and surgeons. We've tried our best, and for some as-of-yet-unknown reason, it wasn't enough in this case."

After her minor soliloquy, Dr. Harington abruptly stepped back from the operating table. Reaching behind her neck, she undid her gown, then pulled it off. Next she stripped off her surgical gloves as she turned to face the circulation nurse. "Inform the front desk we've had a fatality in here. They'll know what to do. Meanwhile, everyone just leave everything as is other than turning off the heart-lung machine, stopping the IV, and stopping the ventilator. Don't disconnect anything! Even leave the drapes in place! Everything!" With that said, she left.

A few minutes later Mitt stumbled into the surgical lounge in a kind of exhausted daze, feeling shell-shocked. He couldn't believe it. His first two surgical cases as a resident had resulted in death. Although he hardly felt directly responsible, he did feel complicit. It wasn't a good feeling.

"Dr. Fuller," a voice called out. Mitt turned around to see Dr. Rodriguez coming directly toward him. With his surgical mask dangling below his chin, Mitt got a good look at his full face with its three- or four-day beard. He was a heavyset man with full, round facial features. "Hearing about your night with the Benito Suárez debacle, you must be drained. Is that a fair assumption?"

"Pretty close," Mitt responded, worried he was going to be asked to do something menial.

"As you know, the Roberto Silva pancreatectomy will be in the same OR we've been in for Thompson's valve replacement. Obviously, there's going to be a delay with what's happened and the need to involve the medical examiner's office. Why don't you beat it back to the on-call room and get a little shut-eye? I'll give you a shout when Silva's case is about to start, and you can pop back here and join in. What do you say?"

"I'd say that was a great idea," Mitt admitted. He was taken aback by the fourth-year resident's solicitude. It was unexpected but certainly appreciated. "To be truthful, I am really wrung out."

"I'm not surprised. Go get some rest!"

CHAPTER 11

C ontrary to what Mitt had hoped, almost three hours of sleep didn't make him feel markedly better. Quite the contrary, at least when his phone rang to wake him up and for about fifteen minutes thereafter. But after splashing a bit of cold water on his face and stretching his arms and back muscles, he started to rally. By the time he got out to the elevator lobby, Mitt felt almost human.

Unfortunately, feeling almost human had its downside. As he boarded the elevator, he relived the despair he'd felt when it was determined that Ella Thompson's heart wasn't going to restart and there was nothing to be done. In retrospect the episode ultimately freaked him out almost as badly as when Benito Suárez's aorta blew.

Mitt had rather innocently allowed himself to be talked into studying medicine as a way to help people by making them well, certainly not to cause their deaths. What was bothering him was the nagging realization that if Ella Thompson had refused to get her mitral valve fixed or if he hadn't cleared her for surgery with his admitting history and physical, she'd be alive at that moment, probably home and interacting with her great-grandchildren instead of being stretched out on a slab at the medical examiner's office, where he guessed she was at the moment.

And as if those thoughts weren't bad enough, as he rode in the elevator, he started thinking about his renowned medical forebearers and the surprising revelation that although they'd been highly skilled and respected, ultimately they all had been on the wrong side of history. Could that really have been the case? He didn't know, but he vowed to look into it, especially since Dr. Harington was so certain. He thought he'd start by asking his father, who'd always prided himself on being the family historian. Mitt decided to raise the question that night when he called his parents. He didn't know what he'd learn, but at least he could count on sympathy, especially from his mom.

Arriving at the eleventh floor and heading into the OR suite, he made a beeline toward the surgical lounge and the locker room. Mitt wanted to be sure to dutifully change into a clean pair of scrubs, even if his current scrubs would be covered by the sterile surgical gown. He didn't know if it was required, but it seemed to him to be a good idea. Contrary to his famous relative Otto Fuller, he believed wholeheartedly in the "germ theory."

But as he was traversing the surgical lounge he stopped. Unexpectedly he spotted Dr. Harington talking with someone over at the communal coffeepot. She was in civvies and a long white coat while her companion was in scrubs with a stethoscope slung around his neck and a tourniquet looped around his pants' tie. Making a sudden change of plans, Mitt veered in their direction and approached the pair. He didn't have much time, as Dr. Rodriguez had admitted that he'd waited until the last minute to call and the patient was already in the operating room.

The man Dr. Harington was conversing with was the first to see Mitt approach, and he interrupted Dr. Harington and gestured in Mitt's direction.

"Ah, Dr. Fuller," Dr. Harington said, her face brightening when she caught sight of him. "What a pleasant coincidence. I was just talking about you. Meet Dr. Winthrop, our head of Anesthesia, and, Dan, meet one of our brand-new first-year surgical residents."

Mitt shook hands with the Anesthesia chief but immediately turned to Dr. Harington. "Sorry, I only have a minute since I'm late for my case, but I wanted to ask you for a favor. I'm interested in that unpublished article by Robert Pendleton. Do you think you could email it to me or send a link? To be honest, what you said about my medical ancestors was a surprise, and I'd like to look into it."

"Most certainly," Dr. Harington said. "I'll be happy to do so. Does Communications have your email address?"

"They do," Mitt said.

"Consider it done," Dr. Harington said. "Meanwhile, I have to tell you that Dr. Winthrop is almost as much a Bellevue history devotee as I."

"Yes, indeed," Dr. Winthrop said, jumping into the conversation. "Pamela has told me you are a direct descendant of four of our illustrious Bellevue doctors. I think that is terrific. More than terrific. It's an honor to have a member of such a well-known professional family again among us. Welcome aboard!"

"Thank you," Mitt said, unsure of what else to say. "But after what Dr. Harington told me about their stances on some important issues, I'm not so sure how well it speaks for me."

"Nonsense," Dr. Harington said, breaking into the conversation.

"We can't judge our professional forebearers in hindsight. No way! They were all great in their own time, and all made significant contributions to Bellevue and medicine in general."

"Maybe so," Mitt said. He wasn't going to get into an argument over the issue, especially not until he learned more about the reliability of the source. "I have to get to my case, but it was nice to meet you, Dr. Winthrop."

"The pleasure's mine," Dr. Winthrop said.

"I'm sorry our case this morning didn't have a better outcome," Dr. Harington said. "I hope you scrub in with me again in the near future."

"I do, too," Mitt said, and meant it. Even though he was still upset over how matter-of-factly she'd terminated the case with Ella Thompson, he did appreciate the general atmosphere of her OR in contrast to that of Dr. Washington.

After his minor detour to talk with Dr. Harington, Mitt dashed urgently into the locker room, bursting through the swinging doors. Once inside, he slipped out of his doctor's coat and pulled off his scrub top before grabbing a new scrub set, all on the fly. The coat went into his locker, the clean scrubs on his body, and the soiled scrubs in the appropriate bin before he ran back out of the locker room, across the lounge, and into the inner portion of the OR suite.

Before starting his scrub at the sink outside of OR #4, he quickly glanced through the wire-embedded glass window into the operating room. At that exact moment, Dr. Rodriguez and Dr. Arthur Reston, the attending surgeon, whom he'd yet to meet, were in the process of draping Roberto Silva's scrubbed and antiseptic-painted abdomen. As Mitt feared, he was going to be a bit late, which wasn't the way he wanted to start a relationship with another of the Bellevue attending surgeons.

Although he was eager to get into the OR, Mitt scrupulously followed the scrubbing rules he'd been shown by Dr. Van Dyke the day before. Almost five minutes later, he pushed backward into the OR, holding his hands aloft and accepting a sterile towel from the scrub nurse. To his surprise, she introduced herself as Kathy, which was a first for Mitt. Kathy then helped Mitt don his sterile gown and gloves. In due course, the circulating nurse tied the gown behind his neck while introducing herself as well. Her name was Caroline. Although he was nervous about being late, he felt more relaxed after being welcomed by both nurses. That hadn't happened on his first two cases.

Now completely prepared, Mitt approached the operating table. The patient had been fully draped, with just a small area on the upper part of the abdomen exposed. The attending surgeon was standing on the patient's right side while Dr. Rodriguez was on the left. Both men had their hands crossed and pressed up against their chests, waiting. Mitt wondered if they had been waiting for him.

"I'm sorry I'm late," Mitt said.

"No problem," Dr. Rodriguez said. "As you can probably see, we're in a holding pattern on orders from Anesthesia."

Mitt nodded. When he'd entered, he'd noticed that instead of one anesthesiologist there were two, but at that very moment, Dr. Winthrop, whom Mitt had so recently met, also hurriedly entered the room, tying his face mask over the top of his head as he did so. He joined the others and the three gathered in hushed but tense conversation. Mitt could hear that the pinging of the cardiac monitor was not its usual metronomic rhythm but rather irregular, with short, distinct pauses.

"Dr. Reston, meet Dr. Michael Fuller, one of our first-year residents," Dr. Rodriguez continued.

"Welcome to the program," Dr. Reston said. He was a sizable man, even larger than Dr. Rodriguez, with a deep, gravelly voice. "Why don't you go over to the other side and join Dr. Rodriguez. I think that's where you'll be the most help."

"Certainly," Mitt said. He skirted Kathy and her instrument tray and rounded the foot of the operating table. Dr. Rodriguez moved to the side, creating more space between himself and the anesthesia screen. As Mitt slipped into position directly across from Dr. Reston, he hoped he'd not end up being blocked by Dr. Rodriguez as he'd been on his first case. He'd heard that pancreatic surgery was difficult, and he was eager to be able to see how it progressed. Although the three hours of sleep he'd just gotten had definitely helped his situation, he knew he was still truly tired, and he feared how he'd respond if boredom became an issue.

"Dr. Rodriguez was telling me that you are a direct descendant of a number of Bellevue Hospital luminaries," Dr. Reston said, looking directly across at Mitt. "I'm impressed. It must give you a lot of satisfaction to follow in their footsteps."

"I'm not sure how I feel," Mitt said truthfully. "Just this morning, I was told that they might have been reactionary on some important advances."

"Oh, that's not fair," Dr. Rodriguez said, jumping in to defend Mitt's ancestors. "We can't judge our medical forebearers because of what we now know. They were doing the best they could with the state of science as it was at the time."

"Dr. Harington said something similar about the unfairness of hindsight," Mitt said. He appreciated Dr. Rodriguez's support while at the same time feeling uneasy about his genealogy being out in the open, for good or bad. It was something he'd hoped to avoid. "But for me, it can't help but color my feelings if it is true."

"Dr. Rodriguez told me that one of your ancestors could do a mid-thigh amputation in nine seconds and another was only the second person in the world to perform a mitral valve fracture. Those are some pretty impressive facts, if I do say so myself."

"I suppose," Mitt said to be agreeable. He sensed that Dr. Reston had a very high opinion of himself. In hopes of changing the subject, Mitt added, "What's the problem here? Is Anesthesia having some difficulties?"

"I'll say," Dr. Reston sniped, lowering his voice so as not to be heard over the anesthesia screen. "Somehow anesthesia has managed to create an arrhythmia. The patient's ticker was just fine until they got ahold of him. But what can you do? They're all a bunch of monkeys as far as I'm concerned." He rolled his eyes for emphasis, making Mitt wonder if there were competitive feelings between Bellevue surgeons and anesthesiologists, at least from Dr. Reston's perspective.

Almost as if responding to Dr. Reston's snide comment, suddenly the cardiac alarm went off, replacing the irregular pinging of the cardiac monitor. Thanks to the tile walls and floor, the sound was particularly piercing. Everyone in the room started, nurses and doctors alike.

"My God!" Dr. Winthrop blurted loud enough for everyone to hear. "We've got ventricular fib! Call an arrest! Get the OR crash cart in here!"

While the anesthesiologists snatched off all the operative drapes and tossed them onto the floor, completely exposing the naked and intubated patient, Caroline dashed over to the intercom and depressed the button. "Code red!" she shouted into the speaker grate several times.

Both Dr. Reston and Dr. Rodriguez merely backed away from the OR table against opposite walls while keeping their gloved hands pressed up against their chests. Luckily they had not started the surgery. Mitt was aghast and momentarily paralyzed, with his eyes thrown open to their limits. Quickly recovering, he, too, retreated out of the way and joined Dr. Rodriguez.

The anesthesiologists didn't waste any time. One of them rushed up alongside the OR table, pulling the anesthesia stool along with him. Then, after locking the stool's wheels, he climbed up on it and began closed-chest cardiac massage. The ventilator was still functioning and breathing for the patient. A moment later, the door from the hallway burst open and two more anesthesiologists rushed into the room pushing the crash cart. One of them positioned the cart next to the operating table while the other plugged the defibrillating unit into a wall socket.

With trained efficiency and little need for talk, the defibrillator was prepared. Once it was ready, the anesthesiologist who had been giving the closed-chest cardiac massage stepped off the stool he was standing on and took the paddles. He placed one on the patient's sternum and the other along the patient's left rib cage. "Clear," he called out before pressing the button.

The patient's body convulsed. All eyes looked up at the ceiling-mounted cardiac monitor. The blip, which had been tracing erratic chicken scratches across the screen, disappeared with the defibrillator's discharge. In a reverent silence, all waited for the blip to reappear, which it did almost immediately. Unfortunately, it was just as erratic, meaning the heart was still fibrillating.

The team of anesthesiologists recommenced the cardiac massage while the defibrillator reset itself. Then they repeated the process, but to no avail. The fibrillation continued. Various drugs were tried, and then a cardiologist arrived on an emergency consult. He offered some additional suggestions, but nothing worked. Presently the fibrillation indeed did stop, but what intervened was asystole, meaning no electrical activity whatsoever. At that point an external pacemaker was tried, but it failed to initiate a heartbeat.

"What about an attempt at open-chest cardiac pacing?" Dr. Winthrop finally asked Dr. Reston; both men, along with Dr. Rodriguez and Mitt, were still watching the unfolding drama from the sidelines, maintaining their sterility. Two of the anesthesiologists who had responded to the emergency had left, but not Dr. Winthrop or the two who had originally been in on the case. One of those was back to giving closed-chest massage. The consulting cardiologist was also still in the room.

"I don't know," Dr. Reston said with a shrug. "What does Cardiology think?"

"It couldn't hurt," the cardiologist said, "but I sincerely doubt it will help. I'm astounded we've been unsuccessful in getting any response. It almost seems like something's going on here that I don't understand. It's weird."

"As a G.I. specialist, it's been a long time since I opened up a chest," Dr. Reston said.

"I participated in one just this morning," Dr. Rodriguez chimed in.

"Well, there you go," Dr. Reston said. He gestured toward the patient. "Be my guest."

"Fine by me," Dr. Rodriguez said. He turned to Caroline. "Get us a chest pack, fresh drapes, and we'll give it a go."

Mitt watched the preparations with a growing sense of unreality. He intuitively knew he was witnessing a very unusual series of events on just his second day as a surgical resident.

It took Caroline and Kathy only a few minutes to get everything ready, and while they were busy accomplishing what needed to be done, the closed-chest massage continued unabated, and the ventilator continued to alternately inflate the lungs, maintaining the blood oxygenation at an appropriate level.

"Okay," Dr. Rodriguez said to Dr. Reston and Mitt when all was prepared to his liking. "This has got to be fast. The second the closed-chest massage is stopped, Caroline will quickly paint the chest with chlorhexidine, after which you two quickly drape the patient. Then I'll move in immediately with a scalpel followed by the bone saw. Obviously, there'll be no bleeding with no heartbeat, so that's not going to be a problem. Then, as soon as I expose the heart, Dr. Reston, how about you be prepared to start open-heart massage. While you are doing that, I'll get the pacemaker ready to function. Are we good to go?"

"Good to go," Dr. Reston said.

Mitt, who felt he was completely out of his element, tried to follow Dr. Reston's lead in helping to drape the patient the second Caroline finished with the antiseptic. Luckily the draping was just rudimentary, so Mitt's inexperience wasn't apparent. There was no attempt to bother creating an anesthesia screen.

As he promised, Dr. Rodriguez moved in practically before the drapes had completely settled, slicing open the skin down to the bone in one determined swipe. Next, the bone saw made short work of cutting through the sternum lengthwise, sending tiny bits of flesh flying in all directions. With a pair of dissecting scissors, he opened the pericardium. A second later, Dr. Reston shoved in his gloved hand, grasped the heart, and began to compress and release it. The open-chest massage was effective enough that the patient's skin tone improved a shade even though it had never truly gone pallid thanks to his being respired with 100 percent oxygen.

Unfortunately, it was soon obvious to everyone involved that despite all their efforts, the heart was not about to cooperate and recommence beating.

"I've run out of ideas," the cardiologist said while spreading his hands apart, palms heavenward.

"I'm going to stop the open-chest massage," Dr. Reston announced.

"I would," the cardiologist agreed.

"What actually happened before I got in here?" Dr. Winthrop asked the original assigned anesthesiologist loud enough for everyone to hear as Dr. Reston withdrew his hand. The attending surgeon stepped back from the OR table and began taking off his gown and gloves.

"Nothing that could have predicted this," the anesthesiologist said. "The induction and intubation had been entirely normal, and I was about to give the green light to start the case when there were a couple of premature ventricular contractions. Then there was a series, which made me call in Ralph and then you. You saw how the PVCs led to fibrillation despite the beta-blockers. I'm at a loss," he said, throwing up his hands. "It was as if something cardiotoxic had been suddenly injected into the IV, but obviously nothing had been injected. And there was no history of heart disease and the preop ECG was entirely normal. It's all a mystery to me."

Dr. Rodriguez followed Dr. Reston's lead by pulling off his gown and gloves. But he did it angrily. "I can't believe this," he said to no one in particular. "Good God! This is my second operative death in the same day, and I've never had one before in the entire four years I've been a surgical resident."

"Caroline, let the front desk know what's happened in here," Dr. Reston called out to the circulating nurse. She responded with a thumbs-up.

Dr. Reston, Dr. Rodriguez, the anesthesiologists, and the cardiologist all walked out as a group still loudly carrying on about the case, leaving Mitt and the two nurses in a sudden silence after the

OR door closed. Caroline used the intercom to report to the front desk what had happened. Kathy turned her attention to all the instruments that needed to be separated since those from the abdominal pack and chest pack had become intermixed.

Mitt again felt shell-shocked, like he had after Ella Thompson's case and the Benito Suárez fiasco. Standing there motionlessly, still wearing his sterile gown and gloves, he couldn't stop staring down into Roberto Silva's open chest wound with the man's lifeless heart in plain sight. He was seized by an almost irresistible urge to reach out, grasp the organ, and try his hand at open-chest massage, desperate to see if by any slim chance he could get it to function.

Tormenting him in the background was the realization that he, Mitt Fuller, was the only connection all three cases shared at the moment of their death, other than all being in the same hospital. Such a disturbing thought begged the question of how and why, but he had no answers. Instead, he merely shook his head at having to face a third death in his initial three surgeries as a resident: the first one hours after the surgery, the second near the end of the surgery, and this one before the surgery could even start. Was this the beginning or the end of a very dubious and upsetting record? He would have been totally shocked to hear that any other surgical resident had ever had such an experience.

"Dr. Fuller?" Caroline questioned. "Are you okay?"

"Umm, yes, I'm okay," Mitt managed while forcing a weak smile behind his face mask. Caroline's question had pulled him out of his trance.

"Sorry to be a bother, but would you mind removing your gown and gloves so I can take care of them with all the others?"

"Oh, of course not. I'm sorry," Mitt said. He untied the front as Caroline reached up to do the same with the tie behind his neck. She then helped him pull off the gown. Mitt removed the gloves and handed them over. "Thank you. I'm sorry. I'm a little bummed out."

"We all are," Caroline said.

As Mitt headed for the OR door, he untied his face mask and let it fall onto his chest, as it was still tied behind his neck. Pulling open the heavy door, he stepped out into the main OR hallway. As he headed for the surgical lounge, all he could think about was the upcoming surgery on Bianca Perez. Was she going to die, too?

CHAPTER 12

Mitt pushed through the swinging doors leading into the staff cafeteria and immediately began searching for Andrea. He'd phoned her the moment he got into the surgical lounge to change out of his scrubs following Bianca Perez's colectomy. Since he'd hardly had time to talk to her for some thirty-six hours, he was hoping to meet, even for fifteen or twenty minutes. Although she'd already had her dinner by the time he called, she was eager to sit and catch up with him in the cafeteria provided she wasn't paged for some emergency.

To Mitt's utter relief, the Perez case had gone smoothly, without so much as a hiccup, much less a death. The attending surgeon's name was Dr. Maria Sanchez, and she was pleasant enough, with a personality somewhere between Dr. Washington's narcissism and Dr. Harington's conviviality. Technically Mitt thought she was superb. Since it was his first laparoscopic case, he didn't have much to compare it to, but as he watched the procedure on the TV monitor, he could tell Dr. Sanchez was adept at using the instruments. She worked quickly with no hesitation, and Dr. Rodriguez seemed to be able to anticipate her moves. The case had required five small skin incisions with only one being approximately three inches long and the rest much smaller, a far cry from the normal approximately eight-inch incision needed for an "open" colectomy. From skin to skin, the procedure had taken less than three hours, and with such small incisions, the patient's recovery time would be much faster.

At the end of the case, Mitt had written the postoperative orders in the recovery room under Dr. Rodriguez's supervision, and then, in the surgical lounge, he'd done the dictation with similar assistance. All in all, it had been a positive experience, although as Andrea had said earlier, he needed to spend some time in the surgical simulation lab to gain hands-on experience using laparoscopic tools. Obviously, it was the way of the future, especially when combined with robotic surgery.

Since it was already after 7:00 P.M. and there were not that many people in the cafeteria, Mitt was able to locate Andrea easily—especially as she was waving in his direction. After heading over to her table, he went through the expected cheek-to-cheek routine before questioning: "How are you doing timewise?"

"I'm okay," Andrea said. "No calls yet." She sat back down at the table. In front of her was a cup of coffee she was nursing.

"Same with me at this time last night," Mitt said. "It seems at this hour there are lots of attendings making rounds as well as residents, so we lowlifes are spared until they all leave."

"I was told something similar by Dr. Van Dyke."

"Let me grab some chow, and I'll be right back. You okay with that?"

"Absolutely. I'm looking forward to comparing notes."

Mitt nodded, then beat it back to the beginning of the cafeteria line, taking a tray and quickly selecting some food. Surprisingly enough, he wasn't all that hungry, but he knew he needed to eat and didn't want to wait until he got back to his apartment because he still had three admission workups to do. When he got to the drink selection area, he slowed down and was particularly careful with the cup. He couldn't help but remember what had happened the night before.

"That doesn't look like enough food for a growing boy," Andrea commented when Mitt placed his tray on the table across from her and sat down.

"It's enough," Mitt said. "I need sleep more than I need food."

"So, your first night on call was a problem."

"With the burst abdominal aorta, it couldn't have been worse."

"I can't imagine what that was like," Andrea said with an expression of extreme distaste. "But that disaster aside, how would you rate your night on call from one to ten, ten being unbearable?"

Mitt chewed for a minute, thinking. For a fleeting moment, he thought about bringing up his freaky hallucinations to get Andrea's take, but then he quickly nixed the idea. He was afraid of her response, in the same way he was reluctant to even think much about it himself. It was, in many ways, too weird.

Clearing his throat, he said: "Ignoring the bloodbath episode, I suppose I'd rate the night a five. I was busy from somewhere around eleven until about one thirty, but it was all minor stuff like dosage questions and checking people out who allegedly had fallen out of bed."

"Well, I'm hoping to get a little sleep," Andrea said. "With all the excitement, I didn't even sleep that well last night in my own bed. But moving on, I heard your first two surgeries today were as disastrous as the burst aneurysm. I can't believe your luck, or lack of it. My God!"

"Tell me about it," Mitt responded, briefly looking heavenward before going back to eating. "Two operative deaths, one at the end of a case with a heart that would not restart after a mitral valve replacement and a second one where the heart decided to give up the ghost before the surgery had even begun."

"So I heard. Unbelievably bad luck. I have to say, everybody's bummed out about it. No one can remember anything similar, not only on the same day but in the same operating room. I'm sorry you had to witness it all."

"Thank you," Mitt said. He was tempted to bring up his thoughts about being somehow responsible but quickly changed his mind. Now that he was out of the OR and a bit of time had passed, the idea sounded preposterous even to him. Instead, he added simply, "It's enough to make me paranoid."

"I can imagine," Andrea agreed. "It also makes me hesitate to ask how your final case went today. Don't tell me if it went badly!" She laughed humorlessly.

"Well, I'm happy to report my last case went fine. No problem whatsoever, and since it was laparoscopic, I was able to appreciate what you said about needing to spend time in the simulation lab. As for the patient, she's already left the PACU and is back in her room.

"But enough about me and my troubles," Mitt continued. "How was your day?"

"I can't complain," Andrea said. "My three cases went smoothly. I even got to sew up the skin on the last two, which isn't saying much, but we have to start someplace. Dr. Kevin Singleton, the fourth-year resident I've seemingly been assigned to, is a great teacher, and I've also been equally impressed with the attending surgeons I've dealt with. How about you?"

"I've been similarly impressed by Dr. Rodriguez, who I guess I've been assigned to. As far as the attending surgeons are concerned, I have mixed feelings. Dr. Washington, the vascular surgeon on my first case, seems a shade narcissistic; whereas Dr. Harington, the cardiothoracic surgeon who did the mitral value replacement today, is a bit flaky. Maybe that's too strong. Let's change that to eccentric."

"That's an interesting distinction. What led you to that impression about Pamela Harington? I'd heard from Dr. Singleton when this morning's death was discussed that she's one of the more popular and respected attending surgeons, particularly with the house staff."

"That's why I amended 'flaky' to 'eccentric.' She's very likable and technically she seemed great, no question. But she's an ardent Bellevue Hospital history buff, so much so that this morning when there was a delay in getting the heart-lung machine ready to go with the patient's chest open and the heart exposed, she carried on the entire time about Bellevue Hospital history. To my surprise, she even knew specific anecdotes about my relatives, details that I was totally unaware of."

"She sounds like my kind of surgeon, with a healthy background in liberal arts."

"I suppose that's one way to look at it. It just seemed odd to me under the circumstances. But, as I said, she is very likable, although what she said about my ancestors wasn't all that positive."

"What on earth do you mean?" Andrea was clearly taken aback. "Do you think she was intentionally trying to make you feel uncomfortable?"

"Oh, no, not at all. Quite the contrary. To be truthful, she was ultimately embarrassingly complimentary. But at the same time, she said that my medical relatives had a penchant for being on the wrong side of some important issues—anesthesia, aseptic technique, informed consent, and one even advocated the use of lobotomies."

"Yikes," Andrea exclaimed. "I'm sorry to hear that. Did it upset you?"

"Not really, and you don't have to be sorry. I assure you I didn't take it personally. I found it more surprising than anything, provided it is true, because my family has always been so unquestionably proud of our Bellevue heritage. It's even part of the reason I decided to go to medical school. Anyway, I'm definitely motivated to find out just how true her stories are."

"Well, I'll be interested to hear what you learn."

"I'll be sure to let you know," Mitt said. "And about Dr. Harington: One more thing caught my attention, and that was how nonchalantly she dealt with the situation when the patient's heart refused to restart. I mean, she had pulled out all the stops, I guess. But then when it was obvious it wasn't going to happen she essentially just threw up her hands and said, 'Okay, that's it. Leave everything as is,' and then she walked out."

"What did you expect her to do?"

"I don't know, to be truthful. But somehow more than what she did."

Just then Andrea's phone went off. She quickly answered. Mitt watched as she listened for a moment, nodded, and said: "Okay, I'll be right there. Thank you." After disconnecting she glanced at Mitt. "Well, the evening is starting. Someone's fallen out of bed on Fifteen East." She laughed.

Mitt laughed with her at the absurdity. "Welcome to the club. If you'll wait for me to clear my dishes, I'll come along with you. All of my admissions today are on fifteen as well."

"Of course I'll wait," Andrea said as she put her empty coffee cup on Mitt's tray before he hoisted it up and set off. At the exit, she held up, watching him slide his tray in at the soiled-dishes window. A moment later he caught up with her.

"I feel sorry for you," Andrea said as they headed for the elevators. "It's nearly eight o'clock on your night off, and you still have three workups to do."

"No rest for the weary," Mitt said, and meant it. Doing three more histories and physicals was the last thing he wanted to do. But it could have been worse. At least he'd already learned to slim down the process considerably and essentially just make sure there weren't any contraindications for them having their surgery. Prior to Madison Baker's advice, he would have spent an hour on each at a minimum.

They rode up in a packed elevator full of visitors and didn't try to converse, remembering Dr. Van Dyke's very specific warning to avoid talking in the elevators in front of nonmedical people because it invariably ended up being about patients. Once out on floor fifteen, they waited for the visitors who'd gotten off with them to disperse. At Andrea's insistence before they parted, they went through yet another cheek-touching-air-kissing routine.

"Bonne chance," Mitt said with an exaggerated French accent, playfully mocking Andrea's insistence on the display of affection. "I hope you get more sleep than I did."

"I hope so, too," Andrea said as she set off with a wave over her head, heading east while Mitt turned to the west.

Entering the very busy nurses' station on 15 West, Mitt felt lucky to be able to snare the last available monitor. As efficiently as possible, he read through the extensive electronic health records of his three admissions. There was Elena Aguilar, a forty-six-year-old recent emigrant from Venezuela. Mitt immediately called the translation department and was assured someone would be available in fifteen to twenty minutes. Elena was scheduled for a vein stripping. Mitt had read that the reason it had been decided to do the procedure as an inpatient rather than as an outpatient, which was typical, was because the woman weighed more than three hundred and seventy pounds.

The next patient, Latonya Walker, was a thirty-eight-year-old Black woman in for a breast biopsy and possible mastectomy. Unfortunately, she, too, was overweight, although not as dramatically as Elena. During medical school Mitt had learned that doing physical exams on such patients took longer than on thinner people for a variety of reasons.

The last patient was Diego Ortiz, age forty-four, in for a thyroidectomy for papillary thyroid cancer. He, too, was a recent emigrant, this time from El Salvador. Of mild interest to Mitt was that Mr. Ortiz's rather small cancer had been found because a previous diagnosis of hypothyroidism required rather robust daily thyroxine treatment by mouth, drawing attention to the thyroid gland. Mitt found this interesting because he remembered from his internal medicine rotation during third year that being *hyper* or *hypo* didn't increase the cancer risk. In Mr. Ortiz's case, it was just that his being hypo had made his doctor examine his thyroid particularly closely, finding the small lump that was then diagnosed with a needle biopsy.

"Excuse me," a voice said, interrupting Mitt's thoughts. He looked up into the questioning face of one of the many nurses. "Are you Dr. Fuller?"

"I am," Mitt said, momentarily surprised to be recognized and fearful he was about to be asked a question that he wouldn't be able to answer.

"The translator is here," the nurse said, pointing to a middle-aged woman in a short white coat similar to those the residents wore. She was standing outside of the nurses' station counter.

"Great, thanks," Mitt said with relief that a Spanish translator was available so quickly. He turned off the monitor he'd been using, gathered together his loose notes as well as the combination ophthalmoscope and otoscope he'd borrowed, and headed out of the nurses' station.

Doing the physicals and briefs, what he now called "confirmation histories," did take longer than Mitt had hoped. Once again, the translator was an indispensable help and thankfully very patient, but having to use her significantly lengthened the process. By the time Mitt had finished the three admissions and had returned to the nurses' station to type up all his findings, it was well after 9:00 P.M. But at least there was one benefit to the late hour. At that time, it was far less busy in the nurses' station, meaning there were plenty of monitors available. Earlier he'd been lucky. Now he had his choice.

As quickly as he could, he typed in all the information he'd gathered from interviewing and examining the three patients, emphasizing what he knew was the most significant, namely that all three had no signs or symptoms suggesting their scheduled surgeries needed to be postponed. He made it a point to emphasize for the anesthetist's benefit that Mr. Ortiz was taking a sizable daily dose of thyroid hormone.

When he was finally completely done with the third case, he hit the ENTER button and then rapidly stood with the intention of leaving. Instead, he had to wait for an intense but thankfully brief dizzy spell to subside. The moment it cleared, he noticed by coincidence that there was only one person besides himself in the nurses' station, whom he assumed was the head nurse. Since he'd not yet met her, he was briefly tempted to make the effort to introduce himself, but then he changed his mind. Once again, he'd simply run out of gas. Although his dizziness had passed, its presence suggested to him that he desperately needed sleep.

After tossing his no-longer-needed notes into a wastebasket, he headed out of the nurses' station on slightly wobbly legs, turning right to head down the long, now-empty corridor toward the elevators. But then he suddenly halted in bewildered awe. Ahead of him in the middle of the fully illuminated hallway was the selfsame hallucination he'd seen after the burst aorta incident. And at the instant he'd caught sight of the blond girl, he was also once again assaulted by the horrid cacosmia, making him gasp for air. It was as if the hallucination of the girl and the noxious smell were connected.

By pure reflex, his hand shot to his face to use his thumb and forefinger to pinch shut his nose to keep from retching. Otherwise, he remained frozen in time and space, afraid that if he moved, the apparition would again flee like it had done in the wee hours that morning. For some reason that he couldn't explain, he wasn't as afraid as he probably should have been, just mystified and confused. Why was his mind conjuring up such a strange vision and disgusting odor? Was his brain punishing him for denying it the rest it so sorely needed?

As the seconds ticked by, he became aware that the phantosmia had vanished but the visual hallucination hadn't. Slowly he let his hand fall to his side as he watched the girl closely, appreciating that her expression was one of scorn, her upper lip pulled back in seeming contempt. Otherwise, she appeared the same as she had earlier, just as pale and porcelainlike, although her blond hair was even blonder in full light than it had been in the darkness, and it was now even more apparent that her dress was dated, as if she'd just stepped out of an old movie.

"Who are you?" Mitt called out, but there was no answer from the apparition, nor did he really expect one. Building up his courage to face his own imagination head-on, Mitt tentatively started inching ahead, fully expecting the hallucination would flee as it had on the first occasion, but it didn't. Instead, the girl's sneer turned into a self-satisfied smile, as if daring Mitt to come closer and pleased that he was doing so.

When Mitt was no more than ten feet away, he stopped because he noticed something strange. He could see what appeared to be a gleaming, narrow, slender stainless-steel rod complete with a stainless-steel handle sticking out of the child's left eye socket and angled downward around forty-five degrees from the vertical. Now he remembered glimpsing it earlier that morning. He had no idea what it was or what held it in place, as it seemed to be defying gravity. Also, as close as he was to her now, he could make out what looked like a series of bloodstains running down the front of her bodice. Maintaining her smug expression, she reached up and pulled the stainless-steel rod from where it had been embedded above her eye and pointed it at Mitt as if threatening him with it. To Mitt it looked like a metal ice pick with a slightly flared but narrow tip.

Then suddenly the girl again bolted. But she didn't turn and run back up the corridor like Mitt expected. Instead, she ran sideways toward a nearby door that she was somehow able to open although he didn't see her reach for the door handle.

Mitt didn't think about how to react to this sudden development, he just did. He ran forward, banged open the door through which the girl had just disappeared, and rushed headlong into the darkness.

After just a few steps he stopped, searching vainly in the darkness of what was a fairly large room filled with indistinct shapes. The only light was what little spilled in from the hallway behind him. The door he'd thrown open had now mostly closed. The girl was nowhere to be seen. Instead, there was a sudden high-pitched screeching noise and out of the dark a student chair came right at Mitt, seemingly on its own accord.

Reacting by reflex, he put out both hands, caught the chair as it came skidding across the floor, and stopped it. Twisting around and retreating a few steps to reach the wall switch, he turned on the lights, flooding the room with fluorescent glare. Instantly, Mitt recognized where he was. He was in the surgical conference room where he'd started his residency about thirty-six hours previously. Immediately he questioned whether the location was symbolic or ironic. He had no idea, but he felt it had to be one or the other because the young girl was gone. Had the chair run into him or had he run into it? All of a sudden he wasn't entirely certain. It had all happened so quickly.

Mitt collapsed into the chair that had come at him in the darkness or that he'd stumbled into, bent over, and, with his elbows balanced on his knees, cradled his head. He couldn't believe himself and the flights of fancy he was capable of in his exhaustion. After rubbing his eyes and then glancing around the room one more time to make absolutely certain he was alone, he got up, turned off the light, and walked back out into the hallway. As he did so, an orderly pushing a food truck, presumably bringing some late meals to new medical admissions, passed by. For a moment, as he watched the orderly push the wagon down the hall, Mitt luxuriated in the banality of the activity, a sharp and reassuring contrast to his own madness.

Turning around, he walked to the elevator lobby, where he pressed the DOWN button. He needed to get the hell out of the hospital and get home, and more than anything needed to get into bed. If he didn't manage to get some serious sleep, he feared he might totally lose his grasp on reality, especially with his newly gained respect for his own imagination.

CHAPTER 13

Tuesday, July 2, 9:37 P.M.

A s Mitt passed beneath the marble archway of the old façade into the relatively new Bellevue Hospital lobby-atrium, he glanced at his watch and did a little arithmetic in his head. With a sense of disbelief, he calculated that he'd been in the hospital for just about forty hours with maybe four or so hours of interrupted sleep. It was no wonder he was having "walking" nightmares, especially when he added the anxieties of starting his residency and the emotional shock of having to deal with the deaths of three of his assigned patients.

When he finally reached the street and exited out onto First Avenue, he was surprised by the sultriness of the early-July night. He'd become so acclimated to the low humidity and fully air-conditioned hospital environment that he'd completely forgotten that it was summer. As he walked, there was something comforting about the press of cars, taxis, and buses heading north and the familiar sounds of horns and the low roar of hundreds of automotive engines. He even appreciated gazing at the pedestrians he passed heading in the opposite direction although none would return his stare. For him it was like rejoining the normal world after being in a totally artificial environment.

Quickly he came abreast of the old Bellevue Psychiatric Hospital, and just as he had early Monday morning and despite his exhaustion, he couldn't help but stop and gaze between the pickets of the rusting wrought iron fence at the nearly hundred-year-old edifice's First Avenue entrance. In sharp contrast to all the other buildings in the immediate area, which were ablaze with lights, its hundreds of windows were dark and forbidding. As he stood there with a fresh appreciation of the power of his imagination, he was suddenly fearful that he might start to hear cries of anguish from its thousands of previous inpatients. As if to underline that fear, he began to feel paresthesia, which made him abruptly leave. The last thing he wanted to do at the moment was to encourage any more hallucinations of any variety.

At the nearby corner, he had to wait for the traffic light to turn in his favor to cross busy First Avenue. He then quickly headed west along 30th Street. At his apartment building, he keyed its outer door with a huge sense of relief. Feeling much too tired to check his mailbox, which he normally did, he instead went directly to the tiny, claustrophobic elevator. Under normal circumstances, Mitt much preferred to use the pleasant, nautilus-like, original, open stairway with its decorative railing that wound up the center of the building, as he appreciated the exercise as well as the view. With his exhaustion, none of that mattered on this particular evening.

With even more relief, he keyed open the double locks on his apartment's front door. Once inside, he pulled off his white doctor's coat and draped it over the arm of the couch. As he headed into his bedroom, he undid his tie and pulled off his shirt. Stepping out of his pants, he eyed his bed with relish but knew he had to take a shower, as much to wash away the negatives of the day as to get clean.

Somewhat unexpectedly, when he got out of the shower, he felt almost human, and although 5:30 A.M. would be arriving much sooner than he'd like, he belatedly remembered he'd promised to call his parents. With that thought in mind, he rescued his mobile phone from his pants pocket and dialed his father's phone, knowing his dad would certainly be awake while awaiting the first financial news from Europe. With his towel wrapped around his waist, Mitt went out to sit on his brand-new couch, putting his feet up on the coffee table.

"I was so hoping to hear from you," Benjamin answered without any hello. "Hold on, let me put you on speaker."

Mitt raised his eyes heavenward, as he knew that if his mother joined the conversation, it would take longer. But he didn't complain.

Mitt explained that he was calling as late as he was because he'd just gotten home. He openly emphasized he was justifiably exhausted in hopes of keeping the conversation short.

"I want to hear about your first days as a resident," Benjamin said, completely avoiding the exhaustion issue. He was obviously impatient to hear the details.

Mitt made a sudden decision to gloss over the "bad" and emphasize the "good." It immediately occurred to him that explaining the bad would take significantly more time and effort, neither of which he felt capable of. Accordingly, he went on to say that in just two days and one night he could appreciate what an unbelievably eye-opening experience the residency was going to be and that he'd already learned much more than he could ever have expected.

"I'm not surprised in the slightest," Benjamin said smugly. "I told you so, didn't I?"

"I believe you did," Mitt fibbed. He couldn't remember his father saying anything of the kind, but he wasn't up to an argument.

After a little more back-and-forth, Mitt was about to say good night when his tired mind somehow recalled Dr. Harington's surprising revelations about the Fuller Bellevue doctors. Despite his exhaustion, Mitt described what he'd been told about their relatives' disappointing stances on a number of contemporary issues and even that Homer had been a renowned grave robber for dissection corpses. When Mitt finished, he asked his father if he'd ever heard anything at all in those veins.

"No," Benjamin said definitively, almost angrily. "Absolutely not. That sounds totally out of character from everything I've ever heard. I'm shocked to hear someone would even imply such a thing. I had always heard that, if anything, all four of our physician ancestors were ahead of their times. Who is this Dr. Harington, anyway?"

"She's an attending surgeon and a specialist at that," Mitt said. "She's associate chief of cardiothoracic surgery. As I understand it, she's highly thought of professionally and personally. She's also an ardent aficionado of Bellevue Hospital history, which is how she happened to know about our ancestors."

"Well, I will certainly ask my brother if he's ever heard anything along the lines of our relatives being out of step with medical advances. It's a bit shocking, and it seems rather odd to me that someone like this Dr. Harington would try to tarnish their reputations."

"She wasn't calling into question their reputations," Mitt was quick to correct. "Just the opposite. She was extremely complimentary about all our Bellevue relatives, particularly about the surgeons and their technical skills. She knew that your namesake had been only the second person in the world to fracture, or open up, a damaged mitral valve. And she was specifically aware that Homer had been able to do a mid-thigh amputation in nine seconds."

"Well, there was a reason they called it the 'era of heroic surgery,'" Benjamin said, audibly calming. "It is incredible what they were able to do without anesthesia. To tell you the truth, I cannot even conceive of doing surgery without anesthesia—from both the doctor's and the patient's point of view."

"How much sleep did you end up getting?" Clara asked, interrupting the conversation. Mitt would always be her little boy, and he loved her for it.

"Not much," Mitt said vaguely.

"Then we should let you go, so you can get some rest," Clara said.

"Good idea," Mitt admitted. "I'm beyond tired, and I'll be collapsing into bed the moment we hang up."

After goodbyes and Mitt promising to call again probably sometime Thursday evening, the conversation ended, and he tossed his phone onto the coffee table. He sat there for a moment intending to get right up, head into the bedroom, and climb into bed as he'd said, but he didn't. Instead, he went back over the call with his parents, particularly revisiting his father's surprise and umbrage. That thought led to his remembering Dr. Harington's promise to email the reference she'd described. Mitt leaned forward and opened up his laptop, which happened to be sitting on the coffee table right in front of him. After a few keystrokes to get into his email inbox, he let his eyes run down the list of thirty to forty that had not been opened. Almost immediately he focused on one from HaringtonMD and clicked it open. After a brief explanatory note from the doctor in the body of the email, there was an attachment, which he opened in turn.

Quickly he scrolled through the attachment, recognizing it to be an unpublished article that had been submitted to a journal called *The History of Medicine Review* but returned to the author, Robert Pendleton of NYU medical school. It had been rejected by the journal's editorial board with a letter dated October 10, 1975, containing criticisms and suggestions. Mitt had never heard of this particular journal, but it didn't surprise him. As a medical student, he'd learned there were upward of thirty thousand medical journals, most of which were totally off his radar. The only publications he was familiar with were the main clinical journals, like *The New England Journal of Medicine, JAMA,* and *The Lancet.*

The article was titled "Eight Renowned Bellevue Hospital Physicians: Those on the Right Side of History and Those on the Wrong Side." Glancing at the letter sent by the journal's editorial board, he noticed that they first took issue with the title, saying it was much too long. He then read that it was the board's unanimous opinion that the article itself was also *too wordy* and that if the author wanted it to be published, it should be *significantly tightened up.* The main criticism, however, was directed at the author's failure to mention Dr. William Halsted's disastrous addiction to cocaine despite his being on the right side of germ theory. They felt that such an omission should be rectified.

But as Mitt read on, he saw that the editorial board's response wasn't all negative. They had a very positive response to the author's newly discovered sources as revealed in the article's appendix. The board went on to suggest that he consider publishing them in their entirety as an additional piece. They added that it was the board's strong opinion that such material would be of enormous use for future medical historians.

Despite his numbing weariness, Mitt was intrigued, wondering what could have constituted *newly discovered* sources that apparently involved his ancestors. As he put off climbing into his beckoning bed, Mitt's intention was to leaf quickly through the article with the idea of finding the appendix and at least get some inkling of these newly discovered sources. As for the article itself, he vowed to find the time to read it the following day. But as he tried to scan the article, a name on the very first page caught his eye: *Dr. Homer Paul Fuller.* As Mitt skimmed through the section, he was immediately intrigued. He read that his ancestor had studied under Dr. David Hosack, actively aided him in procuring bodies for anatomical dissection, and then teamed up with him to help move Bellevue, which had been a relatively small almshouse in lower Manhattan, up to a newly constructed, very large establishment in its current location on the East River.

On the next page he read that Homer had eventually worked closely with Dr. Valentine Mott, who was considered the best surgeon in the world at the time, and Homer's technical skills had been favorably compared to Mott's. But then he read how he and Mott had nearly come to blows over the issue of anesthesia. With mounting disbelief, Mitt read that Dr. Homer Fuller believed that the pain people experienced served a specific purpose as a punishment from God and that anesthesia was the *work of the devil* in denying it.

"Good God!" Mitt voiced out loud. For a moment he stared up at the ceiling in disbelief. He was shocked and even embarrassed that he was related to someone who could think something so anti-scientific.

After a shake of his head, he went back to skimming the article. The very next page confirmed what Dr. Harington had said about Dr. Otto Fuller. Robert Pendleton wrote that Otto, who had worked with Dr. William Halsted and was considered his equal in surgical skill, had specifically and openly mocked germ theory during one of his Bellevue Hospital amphitheater operations in front of hundreds of student doctors and nurses. He was quoted as saying that the concept of germ theory was based on the craziest idea he'd ever heard, namely that hundreds of invisible particles mysteriously swarmed around in the air. *Ridiculous,* he was quoted as saying.

"Ridiculous is right!" Mitt said out loud. Although Mitt knew that people shouldn't be judged in hindsight, at the same time he was embarrassed to be directly related to such a scientific philistine and to have held him up as a medical inspiration for his entire life.

Almost afraid to have the worst confirmed about Benjamin and Clarence, Mitt went back to skimming Pendleton's unpublished article. On the very next page, he read that Dr. Benjamin Fuller—as Dr. Harington had said—was indeed vehemently against the informed consent movement, firm in his unswerving belief that charity patients had an obligation to offer up their bodies for the benefit of medical research. Benjamin had even gone to the extent of advocating absolutely no constraints on physicians in terms of their research projects and even whims, and he specifically was against any kind of research review boards, believing such restrictions were *anti-science* and a *drag* to the advancement of medical knowledge.

Before he went on to the section about Clarence Fuller, Mitt took the time to again glance up at the ceiling with unseeing eyes. Did he want to share the article with his father or not? As much as what he was learning was upsetting to him, he sensed it would be more distressing to his father, who constantly made positive references to their forebearers' legacy. With a shrug and without a conclusion, Mitt went on to the final pages.

As he feared, learning about Clarence's early advocacy of lobotomies was perhaps the most distressing aspect of the entire article, particularly as it was suggested that Clarence's motivations for doing so revolved around his own personal career aspirations. Mitt read that Clarence wanted to be chief of Bellevue's Psychiatric Division, which he felt he deserved as recognition for all the work he'd expended helping the then-psychiatry chief, Dr. Menas S. Gregory, get the new Bellevue Psychopathic Hospital funded and constructed.

Mitt was aghast to read that Clarence performed over two

ROBIN COOK

hundred lobotomies before stopping them and then trying to hide his initial advocacy. Even more disturbing, Mitt learned he'd done over forty on children, some as young as four. Apparently Clarence believed he was in direct competition for the departmental chiefdom with Dr. Lauretta Bender. Bender was head of Pediatric Psychiatry and was gathering worldwide renown from doing electroconvulsive therapy on children with moderate success.

Mitt clicked to the last page of the article, the appendix, where he hoped to find an explanation of what constituted the newly discovered sources that provided so much information about his relatives. Unfortunately, it wasn't much. All Robert Pendleton wrote was that he had uncovered a vast trove of heretofore unknown Bellevue Hospital patient records going back to the end of the eighteenth century and extending well into the twentieth that had been collected by Dr. Clarence Fuller.

"That's it?" Mitt questioned aloud with disappointment. The terse statement begged the important questions of where these records had been found and where were they now. With a bit of disgust, he snapped closed his laptop. He'd had quite enough of the article and quite enough of the day. With some effort, he got to his feet and padded into his bedroom, ready to turn out the lights literally and figuratively. He was desperate for rest.

While he was brushing his teeth, he paused. In the background he thought he heard something—he could just make out the indistinct sound of a crowd of people crying out in pain and distress, possibly undergoing surgery without anesthesia. He shook his head in amazement, dismissing yet another demonstration of the suggestive power of his imagination.

CHAPTER 14

When his phone alarm went off, Mitt could hardly believe that seven hours had passed since he'd turned off his light—it felt like only an hour or two at best.

With great effort, he swung his legs out over the side of the bed and sat up to allow the cobwebs in his mind to clear. Unfortunately, it had not been the rejuvenating night's sleep he'd counted on; he'd been beset with the same disturbing, inexplicable, and exhausting dream he'd had two nights ago. Again, he'd been chased down endless, two-toned yellow-tan corridors with curious rounded pilasters and arched ceilings, the likes of which he'd never seen in real life. To make the experience more disturbing, he never did get to see who or what was chasing him, so he had no idea of what he was running from.

Immediately recognizing that he didn't have the luxury of pondering the meaning of his recurrent anxiety dream, he stood up, allowed a wave of dizziness to pass, and hurried into his bathroom. There was no time to spare, as he'd purposefully set his alarm for as late as possible. In the future, allowing himself to sleep till 5:30 would be a rare pleasure. Dr. Kumar had specifically said that he and Andrea were expected to have seen all their assigned patients prior to the beginning of surgical rounds at 6:30. The reason Mitt thought he could get away with sleeping so late this morning was that he currently had only one postoperative patient, Bianca Perez, and checking on her progress would take only a minute or two, he assumed, since her surgery and immediate postoperative course had gone so smoothly.

As Mitt rapidly shaved, he indulged in a bit of black humor, a defense mechanism he'd learned as a medical student: The good side of having three out of four patients die meant that his personal rounds were going to be remarkably easy and brief.

Mitt glared into the mirror and silently reprimanded himself for such a thought. Black humor notwithstanding, that the idea of a "good" side to three deaths had even occurred to him was an embarrassment that made him wonder if he was losing his humanity. A second later, Mitt shook his head to acknowledge he didn't have time for such philosophical ramblings and went back to shaving. What he preferred to believe was that the first two days of his surgical residency had to have been a totally aberrant set of circumstances, pure chance, a kind of trial by fire, and that the current day, and indeed the entire rest of his residency experience, would be completely different. With that reassuring thought in mind, he finished his morning preparations, dressed rapidly while eating a banana, and five minutes later was out his apartment door, pulling on his white coat as he descended the open central stairs.

Outside, it was light but barely, and the air was still heavy and misty with summertime humidity. While Mitt hurried east there were no warm rays on his face like there had been on Monday morning, as the sun had yet to top the buildings lining First Avenue.

Mitt sprinted the last fifty feet or so to make the traffic light on First Avenue. As he crossed, he could see that the avenue was already full of traffic. But when he got to the east side of First Avenue and turned south, he slowed. Once again, he eyed the sad and decidedly spooky Bellevue Psychopathic Hospital building. It was like a huge, haunted house smack-dab in the middle of New York City. He wondered with an ironic chuckle if the building had some paranormal power that resisted the wrecking ball. Eyeing the building also reminded him of what he had read the night before in Pendleton's article about Dr. Clarence Fuller being a lobotomy advocate. Somehow Mitt knew he had to find out if that was true. He didn't know how he would do it, but he was intent. If it was true, he'd have to find a different box in his brain for Clarence to occupy.

Despite being pressed for time, Mitt couldn't help but stop yet again at the chain-locked front gate to stare at the decorative but dilapidated entrance. The moment he did so, the same wave of paresthesia he'd felt Monday morning came back in a rush, particularly the hairs standing up on the back of his neck, which made him shiver despite the warm morning. At the same time, he again imagined he'd heard the very distant sound of crowds of people crying out in distress. He heard these voices despite the competing sound of the traffic behind him, recognizing it as the same auditory hallucination he'd had while brushing his teeth the night before, only on this occasion he assumed it was from forced incarceration and not the pain of surgery without anesthesia.

"Oh, come on!" Mitt murmured out loud, angrily addressing his own imagination. "Give me a break and turn the hell off!"

With force of will, Mitt pulled his attention away from the derelict building and rejoined the swelling number of fellow pedestrians. Hospital row was a busy place. As he hurried toward the Bellevue Hospital entrance, he ordered his imagination to stand down. He was determined to have what he would consider a normal day—nothing at all like his first two days.

It was a little after 6:00 A.M. when Mitt entered through the outer door of Bellevue Hospital along with a sizable press of other people coming and going. He was surprised at the crowd just as he'd been Monday morning, particularly when he got into the lobby-atrium that also served as the hospital's busy outpatient clinic. He assumed most of the people were part of the five-thousand-plus employees who allowed the hospital to function, but there was also a healthy mixture of patients and what he guessed were homeless people taking advantage of the public bathrooms and perhaps even the air-conditioning.

Mitt's intent was to hurry across the multistory expanse toward the marble archway and on to the bank of elevators, when he suddenly stopped in shock. Thirty or forty feet away, off to his left in the middle of the throng of people moving in both directions, he caught a glimpse of the young blond girl dressed in the off-white shirtdress he'd seen twice before up on the fifteenth floor. In contrast to everyone around her, she was stationary, so she went in and out of Mitt's line of sight. But it was the same girl with the same clothing for certain. The only thing different from his previous sightings was that there was no accompanying debilitatingly horrid smell. It was also daytime with other people around.

Recovering from his shock at seeing her, Mitt immediately changed direction and started toward her. He was intent on talking with her to find out who she was and whether or not she was an inpatient. But reaching her was not as easy as he would have liked.

"Excuse me, excuse me," Mitt was forced to repeat as he tried to navigate through the crowd in her direction. To make matters worse, the young girl, upon seeing Mitt's approach, turned and fled away from him as she'd done previously. To his surprise and perhaps due to her diminutive size, she seemed able to make more progress than he; instead of the distance between them closing, it widened. Then, when Mitt finally emerged from the seething crowd, she'd vanished just like she had the previous two times he'd seen her.

For a moment Mitt stood there dumbfounded, allowing his eyes to sweep back and forth around the immediate area, searching for the child. Not seeing her and totally confused, he looked back over the amorphous crowd, trying to figure out how he could have missed her. But then he wondered if he'd even really seen her, making him worry that this day wasn't going to be all that different from the first two days. Perhaps he was more stressed than he realized, especially if he was already hallucinating.

Returning to the center of the lobby-atrium, he joined the crowd surging toward the archway entrance while keeping his eyes peeled. As he passed beneath the arch, he experienced the same pins and needles he'd felt the other day. Once again, he didn't know what to make of it, but he didn't stop on this occasion, and by the time he got to the elevators it had passed.

Although Mitt was particularly eager to meet up with Andrea to find out how her first night had gone in comparison to his, he didn't try to locate or even text her. Instead, he went directly up to the fifteenth floor to do a rapid check on Bianca Perez prior to rounds. He thought he'd be able to rendezvous with Andrea in the surgical conference room a little before 6:30. In contrast to his usual time-efficient modus operandi—he made it a point to arrive at meetings exactly on time—Andrea was always early, so he hoped to spend a few moments with her before rounds began.

When Mitt got off the elevator on the fifteenth floor, he remembered the terror he'd experienced with the Benito Suárez disaster and shivered, making him wonder if that was always going to be the case throughout his five-year residency. As traumatic as the episode had been, he thought the chances were good.

After hesitating for a few moments to regain his emotional equilibrium, Mitt set off at a quick gait toward Bianca Perez's room. His plan was to chat with her briefly and check her incisions, which he knew would be easy since each was merely covered with semitransparent paper tape. Following that, he'd head to the nurses' station and use a monitor to skim through the night-shift nurses' notes and check the patient's vital signs that had been recorded during the night. Of course, he could have accomplished the same thing the other way around, which made more sense from a medical perspective, but he didn't care. He was eager to see the patient eye to eye just to reassure himself that she was doing fine. Either way would provide the information he'd need to present the case at surgical rounds.

At that time in the morning, the whole hospital seemed asleep, and as Mitt passed the various patient rooms, he saw the curtains on the windows and around the beds were drawn. Breakfast wouldn't be served until after 7:30. Bianca Perez's room was the next to the last on the north end of the east hallway, and Mitt headed to it without slowing or stopping. He passed a few tired-looking nurses near the end of their shifts. He still felt out of place and vulnerable, so he avoided eye contact as he went by, concerned that one might stop him and ask a question he couldn't answer.

The door to Perez's room was ajar, and Mitt walked straight in. His patient's bed was on the left in the middle. He remembered it well because it was where he'd done her admission history and physical Monday night. But when Mitt pulled back the privacy curtains, Perez's bed was empty.

For a few beats, Mitt stared at the made-up but vacant bed with mounting concern, trying to fathom why she had been moved and where. He even glanced in at all the other occupied beds in the room to be sure she wasn't in one of them. She wasn't.

With growing unease because of what had happened to his other patients, he turned around with the intention of heading to the nurses' station to find out where Bianca Perez was. But as he reached the hallway, he remembered that a few single rooms near the nurses' station were reserved for patients who might need closer attention. Mitt immediately felt better and thought there was a reasonable chance she'd been put in one of them since her surgery had been so late in the afternoon.

Just around the corner, he ran into a nurse heading in the opposite direction. He stopped her and asked if she knew where Bianca Perez was.

"Oh, yes," she said. "I certainly do. She's down on ten in the surgical intensive care unit."

"What?" Mitt stammered. "Why the ICU? What happened?"

"As far as I know, she apparently bled out into her abdomen. No one had any idea until her blood pressure suddenly went to zero. We called the on-call doctor, who immediately called the second-year resident. The patient ended up being rushed down to surgery. Then we heard she was going to the ICU after she left the recovery room."

"Good God," Mitt voiced.

"I wasn't the nurse on the case. That was Elenore Williams. She's back at the nurses' station at the moment, and I recommend you speak directly with her if you want more details."

"That's okay," Mitt said, suddenly feeling weak. Although he certainly wanted to find out more about what happened last night, he specifically needed to learn what Perez's current status was so he could present the case at the upcoming morning rounds. As a major complication, it was obviously going to be one of the most important cases to be discussed. Without another word, he turned on his heels and hurried back toward the elevators. As he ran, he felt an overwhelming sense of unreality, as if he were in a dream. This was his fourth patient, and it sounded as if she might be in extremis. The nurse had said *bled out*. Could that be possible? He didn't know, but he needed desperately to find out.

CHAPTER 15

M itt got off the elevator on the tenth floor and with great trep-
idation walked into the ICU. Just across the threshold, he
felt overwhelmed. He'd visited it briefly on the rapid Monday-
morning tour with Andrea and Dr. Van Dyke, but that was different.
Now he was alone and dressed like the doctor he was supposed to be,
but he was inwardly terrified that someone would ask him a critical
question or, worse yet, to actually do something. Not only would he
invariably not be able to respond but how little he knew would
be exposed to the world at large. In truth he felt like a total charlatan
in his white resident's outfit and wished he were invisible.

His plan was to check on Bianca Perez as quickly as possible and
then get the hell away. But first he had to find out where she was. The
layout of the ICU was similar to the inpatient floors, eighty or so patient rooms located around the periphery, with windows and natural
light, while all the support services were sited in the core of the floor.
Here, though, the nurses' stations weren't centralized but rather dis-

persed, small discrete stations that served only the two adjacent patient rooms or patient slots. He didn't even know if they called them
nurses' stations.

Mitt found the ICU intimidating because not only were all the
patients in a critical clinical state, but it was also an UpToDate
medical-technological wonderland that had already gone through a
total renovation since the Bellevue high-rise had opened. Mitt had
only a vague idea of the function and details of some of the important
equipment, like the ventilators that were breathing for those patients
who couldn't adequately breathe on their own. If a nurse were to ask
him even a simple question about one of them, he'd be lost.

The ICU was also an inordinately busy place with numerous
technicians, other support staff, and nurses for each patient such that
the whole floor was in a kind of anxious frenzy, with people coming and going in constant activity. Also unique, most everyone was
dressed in surgical scrubs, making the place visually very egalitarian.
On the positive side, Mitt knew there were a number of intensivist
residents and attendings mixed in with everyone else since Critical
Care was a medical specialty in its own right.

Building up his courage, Mitt stopped a woman carrying some
blood tubes, apparently on her way to the laboratory. "Excuse me," he
said. "How do I find a specific patient?"

She pointed off to Mitt's left toward a central station of sorts
where there were a number of monitors. "The easiest way is just type
in the name and hospital number. It should pop up."

Mitt thanked the woman and wondered why he hadn't thought
of the idea himself. Although most of the monitors were in use, he
found one that was free. He didn't bother sitting down. He typed in
Bianca Perez, and even without the need to add the hospital number,
her ICU room number, 10 South, appeared. Immediately he turned

off the monitor and headed toward the designated room, even though he knew he could probably find out what had happened to her from the EHR. As upsetting as it might be, he needed to see Bianca Perez so he could say he'd done so at morning rounds. He couldn't quite believe that his sole patient had had a major postoperative complication.

Just getting to 10 South was a little like broken-field running in football with all the people he confronted. It seemed that every bed was surrounded with caregivers, and as Mitt passed down the row of patient rooms, he was beset with a continued low cacophony of monitors beeping and ventilators functioning, like the soundtrack of a science fiction movie.

Mitt stopped at the entrance to 10 South, and at first glance, it did not look good. Bianca was intubated and a ventilator was cycling through positive and negative pressure like an auditory seesaw. Multiple IV bags were hung on poles at the head of the bed. Even from the doorway, he could see that her eyes were taped shut. A woman, presumably a nurse, dressed in scrubs including a surgical cap was on the left side of the bed using a blood pressure cuff. A bank of monitors hung from the ceiling with one tracing an ECG across its screen and beeping with each heartbeat. At least that appeared normal. Mitt took in a deep breath to try to prepare himself and walked in along the empty right side of the bed. The nurse glanced up at him and nodded a greeting but didn't say anything, as she had the earpieces of a stethoscope in her ears and was obviously listening.

While he waited for the nurse to finish taking the blood pressure, Mitt lifted the sheet covering the patient enough to gaze at her abdomen. A new, large midline incision was covered by a narrow dressing. From the bottom of the dressing a drain emerged that was connected to a container that hung under the bed on Mitt's side. There was a small amount of blood visible in the clear tubing and the container.

The five small incisions that had been made during the colectomy that Mitt had helped on all looked fine under their simple transparent paper-tape coverings.

"Can I help you?" the nurse asked in a no-nonsense but friendly tone as she took the stethoscope's earpieces from her ears.

"I hope so," Mitt said before introducing himself as a first-year surgical resident. He then confessed it was only his third day. He now could see her name tag, GABRIELA MARTINEZ. "I'm sorry to bother you, but what happened to Ms. Perez? I helped with her surgery yesterday afternoon, which went entirely smoothly. When I went to visit her in her room, I was shocked to hear she was down here in the ICU."

"Not a happy story. My understanding is that she bled out from one of her mesenteric arteries. She was rushed to surgery and transfused, but I'm afraid she suffered significant brain hypoxia in the interim. At least that's what I was told by the anesthesiologist. Presently she's in a coma, and as you can see, she's not breathing on her own, ergo the ventilator. Otherwise, her vitals are good. We'll have to see if she comes around. The anesthesiologist and the Neurology consult didn't sound optimistic, but there's always a miracle. It's up to the good Lord now."

"Thank you," Mitt managed in a scratchy voice, not knowing what else to say. He swallowed in an attempt to ease his suddenly dry throat. At the same time, his predictive powers, accompanied by a slight tingling on the insides of his arms, informed him the patient was not going to "come around," which was more than disturbing. It meant that the lives of every one of his assigned patients had ended, even if one was technically still living. Bianca Perez wasn't even breathing on her own.

Of course, all four patients were also Dr. Geraldo Rodriguez's recent patients, too, and Mitt wondered if that realization had crossed

Dr. Rodriguez's mind. Actually, Mitt doubted it because Dr. Rodriguez had the benefit of hundreds if not thousands of patients during his years as a resident and could easily explain these recent losses as happening just by chance, which Mitt was struggling to do.

In a daze, Mitt left Ms. Perez to hurriedly rethread his way back through the ICU to return to the bank of elevators. Despite the disturbing news, at least he had gotten out of the unit without having been embarrassed. He pressed the UP button, wondering if during morning rounds anyone would bring up the issue of his bad luck—a wild understatement. If someone did bring it up, what would he say? What could he say? And more important, what might Dr. Kumar say?

When the elevator arrived, it was packed, and Mitt had to literally squeeze in. Although no one said anything, he could tell from their expressions that some of the people aboard were mildly put out they had to make room for yet another passenger when the car was already packed. As the elevator rose to the next floor, Mitt found himself wondering if the architects and designers of the present Bellevue Hospital high-rise had thought in the 1970s that ten passenger elevators and six service elevators would be adequate. It sounded like a lot of elevators, but to him it was already apparent that there weren't nearly enough, and he had only been a resident for two days.

On the fifteenth floor, as he approached the door to the surgical conference room, Mitt couldn't help but be reminded of the mysterious blond girl disappearing through the same door, especially after seeing her again that very morning. What particularly mystified him was why and even how his imagination was conjuring up this same illusion, if that's what it was. As far as he knew, he'd never met or even seen anyone who resembled the child, so why would the vison always be so consistent? And why the curious period dress? And were those bloodstains on her bodice or did they just look like bloodstains?

And what was the instrument she'd pulled from her eye socket? He had no answers to any of these questions, and he wondered if he ever would. More than anything, Mitt hoped he'd seen the last of her, yet when he asked himself the question, his predictive powers and a minor accompanying sensation of pins and needles told him that he had not.

"Will wonders never cease," Andrea quipped when Mitt came into the surgical conference room. She was alone in the room, sitting in one of the student desk chairs. "I don't believe it. You're almost ten minutes early." She made an exaggerated expression of disbelief after checking the time on her phone.

"Okay, okay, let's not create a scene," Mitt said. He took the chair next to hers, and as he did so, he noticed, contrary to him, how "put together" she appeared, just like always, with her bobbed hair perfectly in place. Her only concession to her new status was that she was wearing scrubs under her white coat and not one of her colorful dresses. "To be honest, I made an effort to get here in time to find out how your night was. I know it can't have been good with what happened with my only patient, Bianca Perez. You had to have been involved."

"Obviously," Andrea said. "When I was called to her room just after two A.M. and heard what was happening, I was horrified to learn her name. I knew her having major complications was going to be a serious downer for you."

"'Downer' isn't nearly a strong enough word," Mitt said. "'Devastating' is closer to the truth. She was my only patient. I'm starting to feel directly responsible."

"Oh, come on! Let's not be melodramatic. You and I are totally green as first-year residents. Hell, it's only our third day. You are not responsible. No way. I'm sorry, but that's being way too paranoid."

"I know that rationally. At the same time how can I not feel some responsibility? Except for Dr. Geraldo Rodriguez, I'm the only connection between all four patients."

Andrea looked askance at Mitt. "Are you being serious? Come on!"

"I don't know if I'm being serious or not," Mitt admitted. He nervously ran both hands through his hair, shook his head, and then looked directly at Andrea. For a split second, he was tempted to bring up the hallucinations he'd been having to get her take and have a sympathetic ear. As they had been talking, he'd progressively realized it was the combination of the hallucinations and the deaths that was really getting to him. If it had only been one or the other, he probably would have been able to take it in stride. But the two simultaneously was something else entirely. Yet now that he'd broached the idea of responsibility, he felt he had to justify it. "Let me put it this way: It's a combination of the deaths and my insecurities about being a resident, with one magnifying the other," he added, as it was true. "I don't know about you, but I'm constantly on edge, terrified I'm going to be asked a question or to do something I'm incapable of doing. A few minutes ago, I was in the ICU to check on Perez, and I was a nervous wreck. I couldn't wait to get the hell out."

For a moment, he stared at his co-resident to gauge if she bought his explanation. He wasn't willing to admit to the hallucinations. If it had been the other way around and she told him she was experiencing recurring hallucinations of a blond preadolescent girl and suffering fleeting phantosmias, he'd be seriously concerned about her, maybe even questioning if she should be a surgical resident.

"I'm with you in relation to the anxieties of feeling unprepared," Andrea said. "But I'm certainly not with you in feeling responsible for what's happened to your patients. To be honest, listening to you makes me think you're suffering from a touch of 'illusory superiority.'"

Andrea added the last part with a half laugh, obviously trying to inject a bit of humor into the conversation.

"Okay, I get it. You're teasing me now," Mitt said. He took a deep breath, then forced a smile. There was some truth to what she was saying. There really was no way he could be responsible. He was, as she'd suggested, giving himself too much credit.

"Of course I'm teasing," Andrea said. "You deserve to be teased, saying something so ridiculous. I can assure you that Dr. Rodriguez doesn't feel in the least bit responsible despite his being on the same cases as you."

"Okay, okay," Mitt said. "Enough about me. What about you? How was your night, besides having to deal with the mental trauma and sleep deprivation caused by my patient?"

"Truthfully, your patient didn't cause me any grief other than the first moments of panic when I arrived in her room. I had the presence of mind to realize I was in way over my head when faced with a patient with no blood pressure, a weak pulse, pale as a ghost, and a tense, swollen abdomen. I had Dr. Wu immediately paged. Seeing all the blood in the drain container, I ordered a transfusion, but that was all I did, meaning I was just standing there wringing my hands. Luckily for me, Dr. Wu arrived within minutes, took over, and arranged for the patient to be rushed into surgery. She also contacted Dr. Rodriguez and the attending, Dr. Sanchez. Most important, she got Dr. Rodriguez on his way into the hospital."

"What was found at surgery?"

"I don't really know."

"Why not? Weren't you there? Didn't you have to scrub in, too?"

"No, I didn't. Dr. Wu did. She and Dr. Rodriguez operated and wanted me to be available to handle any problems that might pop up with the other inpatients while they were tied up doing the case. Luckily for me, nothing did, although I was worried something might. Anyway, I just went back to the on-call room and fell asleep. I ended up getting a total of about six hours, which was more than I expected, especially after hearing about your night."

"Whoa, I'm jealous," Mitt admitted. "But I suppose I'm also encouraged. Maybe my first night was an outlier and tonight won't be so bad."

"Let's hope so," Andrea said.

At that moment, the door opened and in came a large group of residents and Dr. Van Dyke, all noisily chatting. Some were carrying paper coffee cups. The moment Dr. Van Dyke saw Andrea and Mitt, she came directly over to talk to them.

"How was your first night?" Dr. Van Dyke asked Andrea.

"It was fine," Andrea said.

"Wonderful," Dr. Van Dyke said. "And I heard there was some excitement with a postop patient hemorrhaging, but I understand you handled it well. Kudos, Dr. Intiso."

"Thank you, but I didn't do much. Dr. Wu handled it."

"You did what you needed to do. But that was then and this is now. Today you both have three surgeries. I should also mention that there is a Journal Club in this room at three P.M., and you are encouraged to come if your surgery schedule permits. Well, you're more than encouraged. If you are free, it is a command performance. Okay?"

Both Mitt and Andrea nodded in unison.

"Now I wanted to talk briefly about tomorrow. I trust that you both are aware it is the Fourth of July, meaning the hospital will be in holiday mode. There will be no scheduled surgery, only emergencies. As for you two, the on-call schedule determines your coverage.

Dr. Fuller, you are on call tonight, so that means you will be officially off tomorrow. Dr. Intiso, holiday coverage will fall to you. Understood?"

Both Mitt and Andrea again nodded. Mitt was mildly surprised. He'd completely forgotten about the Fourth of July although he shouldn't have. During his childhood it had always been a high point, marking the beginning of summer. With everything that had been going on, the idea of being off for a day and a night seemed tantalizingly welcome, like a sudden, unexpected cease-fire in the middle of a pitched battle.

"As for the surgery schedule on Friday," Dr. Van Dyke continued, "I will be assigning you three cases each as per usual. Although most of the USA thinks of Friday as part of the Fourth of July weekend, we here at Bellevue do not. That means that admission histories and physicals will need to be done tomorrow. For you, Dr. Intiso, that will be easy since you will be here. For you, Dr. Fuller, you'll have to decide what you want to do, meaning whether you want to come in and do the H&Ps or have Dr. Intiso do them. Various first-year residents handle holidays differently. It's up to you guys."

Once again, Mitt and Andrea nodded.

"Okay, that's it," Dr. Van Dyke said. "Enjoy your surgeries today, and I'll hope to see you at Journal Club this afternoon." She then moved off, immediately engaging in conversation with some of her resident colleagues.

"I'm happy to do the H&Ps," Andrea graciously said.

"Thank you, but I live around the corner. I'll come in. I don't want to add to your burden of having to cover for the holiday."

At that moment, exactly 6:30 A.M., the door to the hallway burst open and in swept Dr. Vivek Kumar in his inimitable, commanding style. He was, as usual, impeccably dressed in his whites, with his thick, black hair combed to a tee. He was trailed by Dr. Geraldo Rodriguez and the other fourth-year surgical resident, Dr. Kevin Singleton. Dr. Kumar went directly to the podium and commanded: "Okay, everybody, let's get down to business!"

Once started, morning surgical rounds were carried out in an efficient style. First Dr. Vivek called out the name of an inpatient, then the more junior resident involved in the case gave a rapid synopsis and the current up-to-the-minute status. This was immediately followed by comments from a more senior resident also connected to the case. If there was a complication, the team thoroughly but quickly discussed the issue and decided whether the patient should be rapidly seen by the team. When Bianca Perez was brought up, Mitt swallowed his nervousness and gave a rapid review including her present status of being comatose in the ICU.

"This is a strange but interesting case," Dr. Rodriguez said, taking over after Mitt's brief summary. "During the re-op early this morning, something rather odd was discovered. The polypropylene ligature on the inferior mesenteric artery had seemingly become untied. There it was, loose in the abdomen. I've never seen anything like it. I'd tied it and secured it myself."

"That is curious," Dr. Kumar agreed. "Has the attending been notified?"

"Yes, for sure," Dr. Rodriguez said. "She's equally mystified, as she, too, had checked the ligature."

"What about the issue that the patient's deteriorating status wasn't recognized until the blood pressure had fallen to near zero?" Dr. Kumar asked.

"That is an important consideration," Dr. Rodriguez agreed. "I'm scheduled to meet with Helen Straus, head of nursing, this afternoon to figure out what happened. The patient was under the usual postop protocols. Seemingly, the event was remarkably precipitous, as the patient had been documented doing well minutes before the blood pressure alarm sounded."

"You'll let us know what you learn?" Dr. Kumar asked.

"Absolutely," Dr. Rodriguez said.

"All right, let's move on," Dr. Kumar said. He called out the next patient's name.

So progressed morning surgical rounds. Mitt got a chance to present the three cases he was assigned to for surgery that morning, as did Andrea with her cases. Other residents did the same for an extremely rapid review of the day's upcoming surgeries. A brief mention was made of the previous days' surprising deaths of Mitt's two patients, causing him to stiffen, fearing he'd be called upon to say a few words, but he wasn't, to his great relief.

At that point morning rounds were terminated and the whole group marched off to visit the few patients where there was any type of controversy involving future treatment options. When those rapid visits were over, the residents scheduled for the first cases, which included Mitt and Andrea, headed off en masse to the surgical suite on the eleventh floor.

As Mitt watched the elevator's digital floor indicator during the descent, he found himself hoping that the cases he'd been assigned today would go smoothly in contrast to what had happened the day before. But then he made the mistake of actually asking himself the question directly, and the moment he did, he sensed that there was going to be trouble of some sort. But at least the paresthesia sensations were mild, so he hoped that whatever was going to happen wouldn't be anything like yesterday.

CHAPTER 16

M itt surreptitiously arched his back and hunched his shoulders to try to help his stiff muscles, which were mildly complaining about his lack of movement over the last hour. He
was a second assistant for an attending surgeon named Dr. Abraham
Goldstein on his second case of the morning, the breast biopsy of
Latonya Walker. The first assistant was Dr. Kevin Singleton, the
other fourth-year resident besides Dr. Geraldo Rodriguez. So far the
case had progressed perfectly smoothly.

Mitt had done a small amount of retraction assistance in the beginning of the case for the lumpectomy portion, meaning the removal
of the questionable tissue from the patient's breast, but the little help
that had been needed had been mostly provided by Dr. Singleton.
Later, after Surgical Pathology had reported the biopsy to be positive
for grade 1 breast cancer, Mitt was required to provide a bit more
help when several sentinel lymph nodes were removed from the

woman's armpit. These nodes had been sent off to Surgical Pathology to see if there was any microscopic evidence of cancer spread. The results would determine just how much more surgery was necessary.

"Dr. Fuller is one of our very new first-year residents," Dr. Singleton announced to Dr. Goldstein as they waited for the second biopsy results. "Today is his third day."

Mitt had had a favorable opinion of Dr. Singleton from the moment the man took it upon himself to approach him in the surgical locker room and introduce himself. He was a tall, thin man in his early thirties with a boney face but warm eyes and pleasant demeanor. Andrea had obviously been equally impressed with him. She'd worked with him the first two days just as Mitt had worked with Dr. Rodriguez. Now they'd switched. Andrea was helping Dr. Rodriguez and Mitt was scheduled to be with Dr. Singleton for all three of his cases that day.

"Well! Welcome to Bellevue," Dr. Goldstein said. He eyed Mitt, who was on the other side of the patient, standing between Dr. Singleton and the anesthesia screen since the operation was on the left breast. "You must have done rather well in medical school. It's not easy getting accepted into our program."

"I did okay," Mitt admitted vaguely when it became obvious that Dr. Goldstein was waiting for a reply even though he'd not specifically asked a question.

"I'm sure you did more than okay," Dr. Goldstein added with a knowing nod. "I did my residency here, as you might have guessed, and I was in the top ten percent in my class. I had to be. Maybe it was the top five percent. I don't remember exactly."

Mitt nodded in return, as he didn't know how else to respond. He was getting the impression that practicing surgeons, at least the male attending surgeons at Bellevue Hospital, were on the positive side of the narcissistic spectrum.

"What do you know about oncological breast surgery?" Dr. Goldstein asked.

"Not a lot," Mitt admitted. He'd had several lectures on breast surgery in his third-year surgery course and had done well on the final exam, so he wasn't completely devoid of resources, but he'd also learned in medical school that it was far safer to encourage a lecture than try to answer questions when dealing with an attending.

"Do you know who is considered the father of breast surgery for cancer? I'll give you a hint: It was someone who operated here at Bellevue."

Mitt was tempted to say *Dr. Otto Fuller* because that was what he'd been told by his father, but he knew that history reserved the credit for Dr. William Halsted, whose life was significantly more colorful than Mitt's ancestor's, especially after Halsted's very public move from Bellevue to Johns Hopkins, where he became one of the four founding fathers of the medical school and hospital.

"Was it Dr. Halsted?" Mitt said, careful to put his answer in the form of a question. When that was done properly, it, too, invariably stimulated a lecture rather than another question that you might not be able to answer.

"You got that right," Dr. Goldstein said. And true to form he added: "And I'll tell you what else he advocated. First of all, he insisted on strict antisepsis similar to what we adhere to in this day and age. Second, he encouraged very delicate handling of tissue just like we've been doing today. And third, he urged careful hemostasis, which we've also done."

Mitt was tempted to ask Dr. Goldstein if he'd ever heard of

Dr. Otto Fuller, but he was reluctant for obvious reasons. Luckily, Mitt didn't have to wrestle with the urge very long. At that exact moment, the circulating nurse reappeared to say that one of the sentinel lymph nodes was positive.

"Okay, team, let's go to work!" Dr. Goldstein ordered. "But before we do, I have one more question for our first-year resident. Does finding cancer in a sentinel node mean we need to do a Halsted radical mastectomy?"

Mitt struggled to think of a way to answer the final question with a question, but nothing came to mind. Fortunately, he did remember the lectures. "I believe nowadays we can get the same prognosis and a significantly better cosmetic result with less surgery."

"Right on!" Dr. Goldstein said, flashing Mitt a quick thumbs-up. "I'm getting the impression you were indeed high in your class, similar to me. As for this current operation, we'll be doing a rather extensive lymphatic dissection, but we aren't going to remove any pectoralis muscles, so the result will be far less disfiguring. In fact, it will be damn good, if I say so myself." Then, turning to the scrub nurse, he said: "Scalpel, please!"

From that point on, Mitt did do a significant amount of retracting as Dr. Goldstein created a large skin flap and proceeded with the lymphatic dissection on the left chest wall and up in the axilla. The surgeon also concentrated on what he was doing, which ended his mild efforts at teaching, if that was what it had been. Mitt was uncertain.

After fifteen or twenty minutes had passed, Mitt began to wonder why Dr. Singleton was even there since, as a fourth-year resident, he was almost finished with his training, and currently he wasn't doing much beyond anticipating Dr. Goldstein's actions and helping when he could. The only conclusion that occurred to Mitt was that perhaps

Dr. Singleton, like Dr. Rodriguez for the first two days, was there really for his benefit, to make sure his experience during the first week of surgery was as it should be. It made sense from a pedagogical standpoint. The problem with that plan, if it was the plan, was that Mitt's patients hadn't been chosen very well, with all four so far turning out to be clinical disasters.

After another ten minutes of the tedious lymphatic dissection and silence in the operating room, where the only noise was the metronomic sound of the respirator, Mitt's general fatigue began to weigh him down. Seven hours of sleep marred by a recurring restless nightmare had not been nearly as rejuvenating as he'd hoped. Multiple alterations of his posture and tensing his spinal muscles helped, but only for short bursts of time. The very last thing he wanted to do on his third day of surgery was fall asleep and then jerk when he awakened, which had happened to him during first-year anatomy lab after staying up the night prior studying.

To keep himself awake, Mitt replayed in his mind his first case that morning, the vein stripping on Elena Aguilar. In contrast to all the other surgeries that Mitt had witnessed so far at Bellevue, Elena's surgery itself went relatively smoothly despite her close-to-four-hundred-pound body, which presented a care challenge in getting her from the gurney onto the operating table. The challenge she presented to anesthesia had been another story.

Initially Elena's case had been scheduled to be done under spinal with the thinking that it would be safer than general anesthesia, but getting the spinal in place turned out to be nearly impossible. Since Mitt had never done a spinal tap, he couldn't really appreciate the problems the patient presented besides watching the difficulty of getting her positioned on her side on the narrow operating table.

Although several anesthesiologists had given it their best effort, even one nurse anesthetist who was reputedly the best in the department at placing spinal needles, no one was able to do it, and eventually they decided to use general anesthesia. Once that decision had been made and the patient put to sleep, the operation was able to commence.

The patient's size made Mitt feel that he'd truly been needed to provide exposure to the veins, particularly in the woman's groin. The attending physician's name was Dr. Winona Benally—a particularly talkative and diminutive woman who needed a stool like the scrub nurse. During the forty-five minutes the actual operation took, Mitt learned more about vein stripping than he ever realized there was to learn, meaning from his perspective the operation was probably the best so far of his Bellevue career. The only blip in the procedure was another strange forceps incident. Just when Dr. Benally was about to tie off the saphenous vein on the right side, a pair of forceps fell directly into the incision that Mitt and Dr. Singleton were struggling to keep open.

"Hmmm," Dr. Benally voiced questioningly but calmly. She put down the needle holder she held on the drapes and rescued the forceps. Holding them up, she turned to the scrub nurse. "Where did this come from?" she asked in a pleasant but obviously confused tone.

The scrub nurse, who'd been busy opening additional suture packets she'd just gotten from the circulating nurse, leaned toward the surgeon, looked at the forceps, and said: "I have no idea." She took the instrument, examined it more closely, and, with a shrug, returned it to the instrument tray.

Dr. Benally directed her attention across the patient to look at Mitt and Dr. Singleton. "Did either of you see where those forceps came from?"

Dr. Singleton said no. Mitt merely shook his head. He was tempted to describe similar forceps anomalies that had occurred in surgery the day before and the day before that, but he hesitated. It sounded too weird, so weird he wondered if he'd imagined it. Yet, wasn't this another similar event?

"No matter," Dr. Benally said with a gesture of indifference. "Let's get on with this." She picked up her needle holder and went back to work. About twenty minutes later, the operation was completed. After the drapes had been removed, everyone helped wrap the woman's legs in Ace bandages while the anesthesiologist began to revive the patient, but a problem quickly developed. The anesthesiologist wasn't able to wean the patient off the ventilator, seemingly because the patient wasn't able to adequately breathe on her own, presumably because the weight of the adipose tissue of her breasts and upper chest prevented her from doing so.

The moment Mitt became aware of this situation, he began to feel progressively nervous. Elena Aguilar was his fifth surgical patient, and it now seemed she was having difficulties, certainly not as bad as the others, but worrisome nonetheless. The disturbing question in his mind was whether something bad was going to happen to her. When he asked the anesthesiologist what she thought, he was relieved to hear she fully expected it was not going to be a problem. She thought the patient might have to stay in the PACU a little longer than usual, but otherwise everything would be fine.

"All right, that's that!" Dr. Goldstein said, breaking into Mitt's reverie. The surgeon handed off the instruments he'd been using to the scrub nurse and stretched his back after having been bent over doing the lymph node dissection up in the patient's axilla. "Obviously, we've cleaned everything out superbly. Now it will be up to the radiologists and oncologists. One thing I've definitely learned in my career is that treating breast cancer is truly a multidisciplinary activity."

Mitt relaxed the hold he had on the retractor, and Dr. Singleton took it out of his hand. Mitt stretched his own back and then his neck muscles.

"Okay, let's begin the breast reconstruction!" Dr. Goldstein said as much to himself as to the others. But then he added for their benefit: "The last thing I want for any of my breast cancer patients is for them to suffer needless psychological morbidity."

Mitt was impressed with the job Dr. Goldstein did reconstituting the breast's contours with the closure of the flap he'd created for the axillary lymphadenectomy—although he could have done without Goldstein bragging about his year's fellowship in plastic surgery. At that point and with Dr. Singleton's encouragement, Mitt was included in placing and tying some of the subcutaneous sutures as well as some of the skin sutures under Dr. Goldstein's watchful eye.

When the case was done, the drapes removed, and a pressure bandage had been applied, Dr. Goldstein stepped back from the operating table to remove his gown and gloves. "Well done, gentlemen," he said. "I trust that you two will see to the postop orders and the dictation."

"Dr. Fuller and I will see to it together," Dr. Singleton assured him.

"Thank you, everyone," Dr. Goldstein called while waving goodbye over his shoulder as he pushed out into the hall and disappeared.

To Mitt's relief, Latonya Walker recovered from her anesthesia quickly. She was even lucid enough to cooperate in moving her from the operating table onto a gurney.

As Mitt walked along the hospital corridor with Dr. Singleton, following Latonya's gurney to the recovery room, or PACU, he felt better than he had when he'd followed Elena Aguilar. At least Latonya was doing okay and her surgery—despite being significantly longer—had gone smoothly. Yet Mitt still felt nervous, remembering that Bianca Perez's surgery the previous day had also gone without a hitch. If something truly bad was to befall either of today's patients, and unfortunately Elena was already knocking on that door, his sense of responsibility was going to skyrocket.

"Your knot tying isn't bad for it being your first week," Dr. Singleton said graciously.

"Thank you, but it needs a lot of work," Mitt responded. He thought the fourth-year resident was just being kind, because from Mitt's own perspective he'd been all thumbs under the attending's attentive gaze.

"There's some knot-tying setups in the simulation lab," Dr. Singleton said. "It's good practice for someone just starting out like yourself."

"That's a good suggestion," Mitt said. What he didn't say was, *When the hell am I going to find the time?* Then he remembered he was scheduled to be off the following day and realized coming in to utilize the simulation lab might be a good way to spend at least part of the day. He could also do the admissions for his Friday surgeries then.

Once in the PACU, Mitt and Dr. Singleton sat behind the counter of the central desk to use one of the monitors. With the fourth-year resident looking over his shoulder and making suggestions, Mitt wrote out Latonya Walker's postoperative orders just as he'd done for Elena Aguilar earlier that morning. While they were busy doing that, the PACU nurses went through the admitting procedure for Walker with the help of the anesthesiologist. Mitt had learned that the PACU was organized in a similar fashion to the ICU, with separate nurses for each patient, at least until the patients were stable and ready to be transported back to their hospital rooms.

When the postoperative orders were completed to Dr. Singleton's satisfaction, Mitt used a recording line to dictate the details of Walker's operation, again with Dr. Singleton's guidance.

"Okay," Dr. Singleton said, standing and stretching once they were done. "We have a good fifteen or twenty minutes before Diego Ortiz's thyroidectomy, which might turn out to be a relatively long procedure. With that in mind, I recommend you make a pit stop if you are at all inclined."

"Thanks for the suggestion," Mitt said. "I certainly will. But I'd first like to ask a question, if I may."

"Of course," Dr. Singleton said. "What's on your mind?" He sat back down.

"I'm a little confused, Dr. Singleton," Mitt began hesitantly. "I'm wondering if Andrea Intiso and myself are being purposefully teamed up with either you or Dr. Rodriguez for some specific reason. Particularly today, it didn't seem necessary for an experienced fourth-year resident like yourself to be assisting on a vein stripping or a breast biopsy."

Dr. Singleton smiled. "First of all, you can call me Kevin. Second of all, yes, it was Dr. Kumar's idea that at least for your first week, Geraldo and I would make sure you were introduced to your surgical residency appropriately, with a wide variety of cases and attendings, some of whom are better than others when it comes to teaching. We were also tasked with evaluating your technical skills, since residents arrive here with a wide variety of experience."

"I see," Mitt said. It did make pedagogical sense. He then glanced across the room at Elena Aguilar. He could see there hadn't been any change. To his chagrin, she was still intubated and on a ventilator. He'd hoped she'd be off by now and the longer she stayed on, the more worried he became, as much for his own peace of mind as for the patient. At that point, she'd been in the PACU for more than two hours. "What are your thoughts about our first patient? Are you concerned?"

Kevin glanced across the room. "I guess," he said somewhat vaguely. "Why don't we go over and have a chat with the nurse? The PACU nurses know their stuff. Let's get her take."

Relieved that Kevin was taking an interest, Mitt eagerly followed him over to Elena's bed. As they arrived, the assigned nurse was making a slight adjustment to the ventilator.

"What's the good word?" Kevin asked.

"Not so good, unfortunately," the nurse responded. "She's not fighting the ventilator like she was earlier."

"Uh-oh! That's not what we'd like to hear," Kevin said. "Has the anesthesiologist been by?"

"Certainly, a number of times. She also called for a Pulmonary consult because the patient's oxygen saturation started to inch downward. And there was also a Cardiology consult."

"Cardiology? Why Cardiology?"

"She started having episodes of premature ventricular contractions. Cardiology started a beta-blocker and ordered a stat electrolyte test. Surprisingly, her electrolytes were totally out of whack, which required immediate adjustments. At the moment they are all fine, but I tell you, it's been an ongoing challenge."

Mitt felt a general chill as well as some pins and needles on the insides of his arms while he listened to what the nurse was saying. As he looked down at the patient, he sensed that a worst-case scenario was relentlessly underway. The patient was mysteriously going downhill and it would continue, all of which made his concern that he was in some way responsible rocket skyward. He felt all this despite his rational sense trying to convince him of the opposite, namely that everything was happening by chance and chance alone.

CHAPTER 17

Wednesday, July 3, 1:22 P.M.

Mitt stood at the stainless-steel scrub sink outside of OR #4. He was in the process of using a disposable, blue plastic nail file to clean the subungual area of each finger. Dr. Kevin Singleton was to his right. To his left was Dr. Taylor Smith, Bellevue's chief of Head and Neck Surgery. All three men were scrubbing for the upcoming thyroidectomy on Diego Ortiz. Mitt was attempting to concentrate on what he was doing to proactively avoid thoughts about Elena Aguilar in the PACU and his possible role in her seemingly downhill clinical course. He specifically didn't want to wonder how her electrolytes could have gotten so screwed up.

Kevin had introduced Mitt to Dr. Smith out in the surgical lounge but the introduction had been cursory, as Dr. Smith had simultaneously become preoccupied by an incoming call on his mobile.

To Mitt's eye, Dr. Taylor Smith was a man of indeterminate genealogy, probably in his early fifties. He was darkly complected, rather hirsute, and slender with a scraggly, graying goatee and mustache, which Mitt thought might be to compensate for scant hair on his head. Mitt mused that he'd rarely come across *Taylor* as a male given name although he knew several women, including the popular singer. As these arbitrary mental gymnastics about Dr. Smith passed through his mind, Mitt recognized it was merely an attempt to keep from thinking about Elena Aguilar.

"Dr. Smith," Kevin called, interrupting Mitt's thoughts. "When I introduced Dr. Fuller out in the surgical lounge, I didn't get a chance to tell you that he is one of our brand-new NYU surgical residents."

"You don't say?" Dr. Smith questioned with a slight English accent that confused Mitt even more. "Welcome, young man. How are you finding it so far?"

"Challenging," Mitt responded, which certainly was the case.

"Well, then, we'll have to make this interesting for you," Dr. Smith added. "I was wondering why I was getting two assistants, and a fourth-year resident at that. How much do you know about thyroid surgery?"

"I know approximately where the thyroid gland is located," Mitt said.

"Ha, ha, I like your sense of humor!" Dr. Smith responded. "To start off, do you know why this is being handled as an inpatient rather than an outpatient procedure, which is the way I've been doing most of my thyroidectomies these days?"

"I'm not sure," Mitt said.

"The patient has a history of severe hypothyroidism requiring thyroxine replacement. Post-surgery, he'll need to be covered intravenously for a short time until he can take it orally. It is safer as an inpatient."

"That makes sense," Mitt said. He remembered the patient's history from doing the admission workup.

When the three had finished scrubbing, they entered the OR in descending order of status. Once inside, Dr. Smith introduced Mitt to the two nurses, Marianna, the scrub nurse, and Juana, the circulating nurse. During the gowning-and-gloving routine, the same order was followed with Dr. Smith first, Dr. Singleton second, and Mitt last. During the process Dr. Smith maintained an explanation of what had already been done to facilitate the surgery, namely that the patient had been intubated with a special endotracheal tube that incorporated a monitoring device to protect the function of the recurrent laryngeal nerve. He went on to explain that damage to that particular nerve was one of the complications of the surgery and needed to be scrupulously avoided by continuously monitoring the nerve's function. Additionally, at his request the patient had been positioned with his head nestled in a donut to maintain its position and a roll had been placed under the patient's shoulders to hyperextend the neck, all to facilitate the surgery. Dr. Smith gave credit to the anesthesiologist and Juana for carrying out all these preparations.

Mitt was impressed by Dr. Smith's pedagogical inclinations and was now genuinely interested in the upcoming procedure. He believed it might turn out to be the best teaching experience he'd had so far in the operating room. At the moment he wasn't even feeling tired, and more important, he wasn't obsessing about Elena.

"Which side do you want to be on?" Dr. Smith asked Mitt after the patient had been draped, and Marianna, the scrub nurse, moved the instrument tray over the patient's legs to be close enough to hand the surgeon what he needed. When Mitt glanced at the instrument tray, he couldn't help but notice there was a fairly large instrument he didn't recognize that looked like it belonged in a plumber's toolbox. It seemed that there were lots of new aspects to the case. Earlier Dr. Smith had used a marking pencil to indicate where he would be making the incision while explaining to Mitt that careful planning of the exact location of the incision would improve the cosmetic result, hiding the scar within a neck fold.

Straining under a bit of informational overload, Mitt struggled to answer which side of the operating table he wanted to be on, as he'd not been asked before. "I don't know if I have a preference," he said ultimately, shrugging his shoulders. "What side do you think I should be on?"

"I don't have a preference, either," Dr. Smith said. "I'll be using a small five- or six-centimeter incision, as you can see by my marker. I want you to be where you will see as much as possible."

"I think he should be over here," Kevin said, speaking up. He was already standing on the other side.

"Fine by me," Dr. Smith said agreeably. He gestured for Mitt to head over there by rounding the foot of the operating table.

Mitt quickly did as he was told and ended up in his usual location between the first assistant, Kevin, and the anesthesia screen. Encouraged by Dr. Smith's general attitude, Mitt asked about the strange instrument on the tray, which looked like a cordless soldering gun.

"That's a harmonic scalpel," Dr. Smith said with a chuckle. He picked up the instrument and held it closer to Mitt so he could appreciate it close up. "It's a marvelous piece of technology that cuts and cauterizes at the same time using ultrasonic energy. The thyroid is a heavily vascularized gland, and hemostasis is of particular importance. I like the harmonic scalpel particularly because it has minimal thermal spread, so it can be used near critical tissues, like the recurrent laryngeal nerve and the lower parathyroid glands, when we have to dissect out the inferior thyroid artery."

"Interesting," Mitt said, and meant it. He was wracking his brain at the moment to remember anatomical details about the thyroid gland from his first-year medical school cadaver. He wished he'd reviewed the details the night before with one of the anatomy books he had in his apartment, but then he remembered how tired he'd been.

"Okay," Dr. Smith said. He looked over the anesthesia screen at the anesthesiologist. "Everything ready? Is the nerve monitor functioning okay?"

"Everything is ready," the anesthesiologist said.

"Regular scalpel, please, Marianna."

Marianna slapped the scalpel into Dr. Smith's waiting hand. Using it, he made an incision down through the skin, subcutaneous tissue, and the superficial muscle layer along the line he'd made with the marking pen. "Do you know what this muscle is called?" he asked Mitt as he quickly worked.

"Platysma?" Mitt was nearly certain of the name but still posed it as a question for the usual reasons.

"Right you are," Dr. Smith said. "Now, as you can see, I'm going to create skin flaps deep to the platysma but superficial to the sternohyoid and sternothyroid muscles, being very careful to avoid the anterior jugular vein as well as the superficial veins that lie under the platysma." He continued to seemingly revel in the teaching.

Mitt didn't respond audibly but nodded several times as he watched Dr. Smith carefully undermine the skin flaps on either side of the neck. When the flaps were done, the surgeon then used the scalpel to cut vertically through what he called the *median raphe* between the two major neck muscles. It was at that point that Mitt was handed several retractors. These were tiny compared to the retractors he'd been using during all his previous surgeries. With them in place he could see everything clearly, especially as Dr. Smith continued to point out all the appropriate landmarks while using the harmonic scalpel to expose the thyroid gland, first its left lobe and then its right. Mitt even got to see the pulsating carotid sheaths on both sides. The most critical parts of the procedure were the isolation of the major arteries and veins, particularly from the nerves and inferior parathyroid glands, and then their ligation and severance, all of which was described in detail to Mitt and performed right under his nose. All in all, as the surgery progressed, it became the most engaging anatomy lesson he'd ever had, and for the first time in three days Mitt was totally absorbed, finally feeling that being a first-year surgical resident wasn't all bad.

"Okay, Juana," Dr. Smith said, getting the circulating nurse's attention. She'd been reading a paperback book while sitting on a stool in the corner. "We're going to want frozen sections on these lymph nodes just to be a hundred percent certain they are cancer free." He had dissected them from beneath the left lobe of the thyroid gland directly under the location of the small cancer nodule. He then handed them off to Marianna, and Marianna, in turn, put them in a sample container, which she dropped into Juana's waiting hand.

"I'll be right back," Juana announced before disappearing out through the operating room door into the hall. She could have called down to the front desk to have someone come by to get the sample, but it was much quicker to do it herself. Surgical Pathology was just a few doors down the hallway.

At the same time Juana was on her short mission and the anesthesiologist was busy manually checking the patient's blood pressure, Dr. Smith and Dr. Singleton became engaged in a mini debate over a particularly esoteric operative detail. Momentarily on his own, Mitt straightened up from having been slightly bent over to get the best view possible through the tiny incision. As he lifted his shoulders and stretched his neck muscles, he raised his eyes toward Dr. Smith, who was wearing a pair of magnifying optical loops. But then over the surgeon's shoulder, Mitt's attention was drawn to the door near the circulating nurse's built-in desk, which connected to the sterilizer room, as it began to open.

At first the door's opening hardly registered in Mitt's brain since he naturally assumed it was Juana returning on an alternate route from her short errand. Besides, his mind was still totally occupied in marveling at how interesting Dr. Smith had made the thyroidectomy case. But then to his shock, he was jolted to see the person who threatened to enter wasn't Juana, but rather the blond girl in the bloodstained dress. She had the same pencil-like stainless-steel instrument in her hand that she'd had before and she was again pointing it at him, either to show it to him or threaten him, he didn't know. And as an added horror, she wasn't alone. Pushing against her back, seemingly trying to break out of imprisonment in the sterilizer room, was a silent but angry band of hideously injured people in all manner of period dress and undress, some carrying their severed and bloody limbs or intestines. Intuitively Mitt knew that all of them had been operated on at Bellevue Hospital in the distant past.

"Oh my God! No!" Mitt gasped under his breath.

CHAPTER 18

Are you all right?" Dr. Smith demanded of Mitt in a concerned voice with his head cocked to the side. He and Dr. Singleton were staring at Mitt in shocked surprise. The attending surgeon had been interrupted in midsentence by Mitt's sudden mumbled outburst.

Mitt's line of sight shot over to Dr. Smith for a millisecond and then back to the girl and the crowd that he feared were about to storm into the operating room. But to his astonishment, the girl and her grisly cohorts had miraculously disappeared in literally the blink of an eye. In their place, the door seemed to be slowly but calmly settling back into its jamb, or was it? Mitt jumped as the door then did burst open in the next fraction of a second, and on this occasion, it banged open with a thud as its interior door handle hit up against the operating room's tile wall.

"Surg-Path promised me we'll have the results ASAP," Juana called out to the team as she breezed into the OR from the sterilizer room, heading directly over to Marianna. Brandishing a package, she then added for Marianna's benefit: "Here's the three-zero Vicryl suture you asked for before I ran down to Pathology." Being scrupulously careful to use sterile technique, she tore open the package and made certain the contained suture packet dropped untouched into Marianna's open hand.

"What's the matter, young fellow?" Dr. Smith prodded when Mitt didn't immediately respond. The surgeon had not taken his eyes off Mitt.

"I don't know," Mitt stammered, trying to mentally orient himself after the shock. His mind was in a momentary jumble, questioning what he had truly seen. Once again, the question loomed: Was the fleeting and disturbing visual a product of his tired, overstimulated mind or had he briefly fallen asleep and experienced some kind of an instantaneous nightmare, all while standing up and otherwise functioning? He had no answers, nor did he have the time for any internal debate. Dr. Smith was expectantly staring directly at him, waiting for an answer.

"I'm sorry," Mitt said, believing an apology was the way to start. He stuttered a bit, then pulled himself together, shaking his head. "I don't know what came over me. Maybe I fell asleep for a second. I apologize. I've been under a bit of stress these first few days."

"I know exactly what you mean," Dr. Smith said in a fatherly tone. "I think all of us can relate to what you are saying about just starting out as a resident. Am I right, Dr. Singleton?"

"No doubt," Dr. Singleton responded.

"Have you already been on call?"

"Yes," Mitt said. "Monday night. It was my first night."

"Well, there you go," Dr. Smith said knowingly. "Did you get much rest?"

"Not a lot," Mitt admitted.

"I can remember falling asleep in surgery my first week," Dr. Smith said with a self-deprecating chuckle. "The night before I had gotten called in the wee hours of the morning to help with an emergency surgery where the surgeons were trying to save this guy's leg that had been crushed by a garbage truck. My job was to stand down at the end of the operating table and hold the foot aloft while they tried to connect the vessels behind the knee. It went on for God knows how long, and I fell asleep standing up. I remember that incident to this day, especially because the two attending surgeons got really pissed."

"Something similar happened to me," Dr. Singleton said with a chuckle. He went on to describe his experience, but Mitt tuned him out. He'd gone back to agonizing about the hallucination he'd just experienced. Since he'd seen the girl before, she was at least familiar, even if scary. But that wasn't the case with the others, which begged the question of why on earth his mind had conjured up such a horrid, disgusting ragtag group. It was as though patients who had been surgerized at Bellevue sometime in the distant past were returning en masse to exact revenge for what they had experienced and suffered.

Mitt inwardly shuddered when he recalled the image, some men and women holding amputated limbs while others held even more disgusting bloody organs. Could the whole idea have somehow originated from his skim-reading Pendleton's unpublished article the night before? After all, it had been a shock to learn that his own medical forebearers had inexplicably eschewed anesthesia and antisepsis when the benefits were so glaringly obvious.

"Good news, everyone," Juana called out, putting down her phone and interrupting Dr. Smith and Dr. Singleton, who had continued trading war stories, with each trying to outdo the other in how much they'd been overworked as a point of pride when they had been first-year surgical residents. "Frozen sections are all clean. No malignancy."

"Perfect," Dr. Smith said. He straightened up, pulling himself together. "Okay, let's close up. But before we do, I want you to notice, Dr. Fuller, that our operative field is completely bloodless. I can't emphasize enough that hemostasis is vitally important in thyroid surgery. That said, how would you rank yourself with suturing ability?"

"Amateur," Mitt admitted.

"Well, I guess we'll see," Dr. Smith said. "Marianna, hand Dr. Fuller the three-oh Vicryl so he can close the strap muscles for us."

To Mitt's surprise, Marianna did hand him the loaded needle holder along with a pair of forceps while Dr. Smith removed all the retractors before approximating the strap muscles to the midline with a pair of forceps.

"Try to grab just the connective tissue of the two sides of the median raphe," Dr. Smith instructed. He used the point of another pair of forceps to indicate exactly where he meant.

Mitt tried to concentrate, pushing the shock of the hallucination out of his mind with some difficulty. He was able to handle the needle holder as Dr. Wu had suggested, rolling his wrist to follow the curve of the needle point. He did the same on the opposite side of the median raphe.

"Not bad," Dr. Smith said. "Now tie it so the tissue edges just touch."

Mitt felt like all thumbs as he tried to tie the suture, and by the time he'd placed the second knot, the suture itself was loose. In a flash, a pair of scissors appeared and the mis-tied suture was gone.

"Try it again, but this time maintain adequate tension on the ends of the suture to maintain the position of the tissue edges, particularly as you run down the second knot."

"I've advised him to spend some time in the simulation lab," Dr. Singleton said.

"Very good advice," Dr. Smith agreed. "Suturing is the bedrock of surgery."

Mitt tried again, and the result was better. Then, after having placed three sutures, he began to feel a progressive confidence. Not long after, the strap muscles were back to the same position they had been in at the beginning of the case.

The skin closure took Mitt a bit longer, as he found the fine silk that was used more difficult to handle. Also, following the advice of Dr. Wu, he took the time to make sure that the skin edges didn't roll in or pucker out. While that was being done, Dr. Smith gave a mini-lecture on why he didn't use a drain with his thyroidectomies despite a number of surgeons doing so. Mitt listened with half an ear, concentrating on his suturing.

When the case was finished, Mitt thanked Dr. Smith with great sincerity. Except for the brief but disturbing hallucination episode, it had been the most positive experience he'd had in the operating room so far. There had been real teaching, the atmosphere had remained cordial and cooperative, and the instruments didn't do any gymnastics. Mitt gave full credit to the attending, who seemed to take Mitt's compliments to heart, and thanked him in return. He then made sure Dr. Singleton would see to the postoperative orders and the dictation, and left the OR.

Mitt and Dr. Singleton helped move Diego Ortiz from the operating table onto the gurney and then angle the gurney out into the hallway. With the anesthesiologist, Dr. Lenora Carpenter, at the head of the gurney and Mitt and Dr. Singleton at the foot, they began heading toward the PACU. "Thanks for the help, guys," Dr. Carpenter said. "This gives me a chance to give you a heads-up when you write up the post-op orders. I did something a little out of the ordinary on this case. As a bit of background, I'd learned that this patient had been severely hypothyroid for some time and was taking a rather large daily dose of thyroxine. Since I've personally had a couple of bad anesthesia experiences with cases of severe hypothyroidism that resulted in a cardiac arrest made even worse by being difficult to resuscitate, I've hung a micro drip with a specific concentration of levothyroxine to piggyback his IV at ten drops a minute to avoid such a situation." While she was pulling the gurney with one hand, she used the other to gesture toward the smaller IV setup next to the normal-sized one that hung from the IV pole at the head of the gurney. "My point is that the levothyroxine should be maintained at the rate I set until he can take it orally. To be doubly sure, I did check the TSH level, and it was normal. If you have a problem with this strategy, you could get a medical consult. But let me warn you: During the case he did throw a few extra heartbeats to keep my attention, so all this is not a hypothetical concern."

"Sounds like a good plan to me," Dr. Singleton said. "And this is certainly your area of expertise, not ours."

They arrived at the PACU and pushed in through the double swinging doors. Mitt immediately hazarded a glance over to Elena Aguilar's bed, and his heart missed a beat. She was gone! With everything else that had been happening, he took her absence as a very bad sign. Things were looking better when he looked in Latonya Walker's direction. She was sitting up in bed sipping ice water through a straw. Her color was good. Mitt imagined she'd soon be heading back to 15 West.

While Dr. Singleton headed to the central desk, Mitt stayed with

Mr. Ortiz along with Dr. Carpenter and the assigned PACU nurse to get the patient situated. Although fearful of what he was going to hear, the moment Mitt had an appropriate opportunity, he asked the nurse if she had any idea what had become of Elena Aguilar.

"Yes, I do," the nurse said. "A bed opened up in the ICU, so she was transferred."

"Was she doing better?" Mitt asked.

"I wouldn't say better," the nurse said. "Let's just say not worse."

"Okay, thanks," Mitt said. He was partially relieved. Although he would have preferred to hear she'd been sent back to her room, at least she was still alive. The ICU wasn't auspicious, especially since he found going in there so damn stressful, but as he already needed to go in there because of Bianca Perez, he tried to reassure himself it wasn't all that bad.

A few minutes later, Mitt said a quick hello to Latonya Walker before joining Dr. Singleton at the central desk. Just as he'd done for the previous two patients, Mitt, with Dr. Singleton's aid, typed Ortiz's postoperative orders into the EHR. When he got to the end and was about to press ENTER, Dr. Singleton tugged on his arm and reminded him about the levothyroxine.

"Oh, right!" Mitt said. "Sorry! What exactly should I put in here about that?"

"Just type in what Dr. Carpenter told us."

Mitt did as he was told. When he was completely finished and they both stood up, he mentioned to Dr. Singleton that Elena Aguilar had been moved to the ICU.

"Good to know," he said. "I'll make it a point to check her out sometime this afternoon. Let's hope the pulmonary and medical people can do some magic. At least she doesn't have varicose veins any longer." He gave a half laugh at his own stab at black humor.

Mitt tried to force a laugh but couldn't quite manage it.

"I've got a pile of work, but before I take off," Dr. Singleton said, lowering his voice and assuming a more serious tone, "did you want to say anything more about that little episode of yours back in the OR when we were waiting for the frozen section results? For a second there you appeared . . . I don't know how to describe it, but maybe 'terrified' is the right word or something in that vein."

Mitt stared at the fourth-year resident as his mind processed this surprising question. He intuitively liked this man and trusted him, and despite his suggesting he be addressed by his given name, Mitt saw him as a definite authority figure. So he hesitated. As much as he would have liked an experienced person to offer his opinion about what Mitt's mind was conjuring up on occasion, he intuitively worried more about what Dr. Singleton might think, whether he might decide that Mitt was losing it and was a potential handicap for the program. Mitt was fully committed to becoming a surgeon, and he knew enough about the system to understand that if he got asked to leave NYU for having weird hallucinations, he'd probably not be able to get in elsewhere. All in all, it was too big a risk.

"All I can think of is that I momentarily fell asleep," Mitt said, reiterating his previous explanation and trying to sound convincing. "There'd been a pause in the procedure, and maybe I kind of let myself relax too much or something along those lines."

"Okay! You're probably right," Dr. Singleton said with a shrug. "And at least you didn't violently jerk like I did when I fell asleep in surgery my first year. To make matters worse, at the time I was holding a retractor, which I ended up yanking out of the incision. Anyway, it's water over the dam. Tell me! Are you on call tonight?"

"I am," Mitt admitted.

"Well, I recommend you try to get as much rest as you can. Really!

Get yourself to the on-call room early on and relax. If you are able to get some sleep in the beginning of the evening, it won't be so bad if you end up being called to the floor in the wee hours. That was the trick that was so hard for me to get through my thick skull back when I was in your shoes. Too often I was out in the evening trying to scare up trouble. Well, not really trouble, but you know what I mean. I did spend a lot of time in the simulation lab when I should have been sleeping."

"Good point! I'll take your advice and try to get some sleep early on," Mitt said, and meant it. The one helpful circumstance was that he wasn't facing three admission H&Ps like he'd had on the first night he was on call. "And even if it is a busy night, at least I'll be off tomorrow on the Fourth!"

"Oh, that's right. It's a holiday. Good for you. Enjoy it! Sleep all day if you can."

"I will," Mitt said, which was a lie. He fully intended to come into the hospital.

"We will have another day of surgery together on Friday," Dr. Singleton continued. "You'll be assigned three more cases, which I'm certain will be different from the cases you've had so far, since Dr. Van Dyke is making a concerted effort to give you a taste of the breadth of general surgery during your first week. As for today, let me compliment you. Your suturing technique is good for a beginner, but your knot tying needs some serious attention. I'm sure you know this, which is why I suggested you spend some time in the simulation lab.

"And one more thing: If you have any difficult management conundrums about the patients we operated on today while you are on call tonight, you're welcome to call me directly no matter the hour. Walker and Ortiz should do perfectly fine, but Elena Aguilar is another story. I don't know what it is with her, but there's something going on we don't understand. But medicine in general and surgery in particular can be like that. You do everything right and do it the same way you've done it successfully in the past, and some patients go south no matter what you try. Anyway, enough philosophizing. Good luck tonight and see you again on Friday."

To Mitt's surprise, Dr. Singleton stuck out his hand, and Mitt shook it. Dr. Singleton then tapped his surgical hat with the tips of his right-hand fingers in a kind of abbreviated form of a salute before heading toward the swinging doors. In the next moment he was gone.

Mitt turned and headed back toward Diego Ortiz's bed as he was expected to, to make sure the attending nurse didn't have any questions about or possible addendums to the postop orders. If all was copasetic, then Mitt would be able to get to the surgical locker room and prepare himself for the night on call. As he thought about the coming evening and night, his prognostic abilities sent him the unwelcome message that it was not going to be a picnic by any stretch of the imagination, especially as he could feel the hairs on the back of his neck rise as he thought it. What that meant, he had no idea and was pretty sure he didn't want to guess.

CHAPTER 19

Wednesday, July 3, 4:15 P.M.

M itt entered the surgical lounge with the intention of heading directly into the locker room, but then he caught a glimpse of Andrea sitting near the communal coffeepot, using her phone. Pleased to run into her, he immediately changed directions and walked over. She acknowledged him with a nod and a smile but continued her conversation. Mitt could tell it was a personal call, so he took the chair directly opposite hers. While he waited, he took out his own phone to check for any messages and, pleased that there weren't any, turned off DO NOT DISTURB mode. A moment later Andrea concluded her call and pocketed her phone. They exchanged a knowing glance. She was back to her fashionista mode, wearing her white coat over an arresting blue dress. As usual she looked a lot more put together than Mitt felt.

"I guess we both missed Journal Club," Andrea said with a sly smile and a glance at her watch to be certain it wouldn't be worth heading up to the fifteenth floor. After morning rounds they'd both admitted that with everything else going on the last thing they wanted to do was attend Journal Club, especially since they hadn't had an opportunity to read any of the designated articles.

"I'd completely forgotten about Journal Club," Mitt admitted. "How on earth did you remember? Was seeing me a reminder?"

Andrea's smile morphed into an actual laugh as she hunched her shoulders in a shrug. "Maybe so. Who's to know?"

"How was your day of surgery?"

"So-so," Andrea said, holding her hand aloft, palm down, and letting it flutter.

"Don't tell me you had a bad outcome."

"Nothing that serious," Andrea said. "The last case was a Whipple procedure, and I was holding a retractor for almost the entire interminable operation, and like you described with your aneurysm case, for too much of it all I got to see was Dr. Rodriguez's back. In that sense it was miserable. On the good side, my first two cases were fine, and I did get to do more suturing on all three cases. But enough about me, what about you? How were your cases, and how did you get along with Dr. Singleton?"

"Dr. Singleton is a delight," Mitt said. "How did you find Dr. Rodriguez?"

"Fine," Andrea said. "He's obviously more than competent, but I did get a little spoiled with Dr. Singleton. He's so much more personable."

"I know exactly what you mean," Mitt said, succumbing to a kind of psychogenic blackout. Andrea's comment had made him revisit Dr. Singleton's concern about his hallucination in the operating room, which brought back the hallucination itself in shocking detail. Right there in the front of his mind and momentarily blocking out his view of Andrea and the surgical lounge was the taunting blond girl, viciously gesturing toward him with some kind of surgical instrument as she'd done earlier. Behind her and threatening to push past was the bloodied horde of surgerized, tortured souls.

"Mitt, are you all right?" Andrea questioned with a touch of urgency.

Mitt looked down at his knee as he became aware that Andrea had reached out and grasped his leg, awakening him from his disturbing but fleeting trance.

"Yeah, of course," Mitt responded with a slight shake of his head to clear his mind. "I'm sorry. I just drifted off there for a second."

"What were you thinking about? You suddenly had this dazed expression."

"I was just agreeing with what you said about Dr. Singleton," Mitt said, hunching his shoulders as if to say it was as simple as that. At the same time, he again wrestled with the idea of telling Andrea about his hallucinatory experiences, especially this most recent one, but just as he had on the previous occasion and with Dr. Singleton, he hesitated. Despite the fact that he thought of her as a true, close personal friend and fellow resident going through the same emotionally traumatic experience, he had no idea how she'd take such strange information. The question was whether her loyalty would ultimately be to him or the residency program if she thought he was losing it. As he'd reasoned previously, he wasn't even sure how he'd respond if the situation were the other way around.

"What's with these sudden pauses?" Andrea questioned. "You're acting a bit weird, like you are having a premature senior moment." She looked at him askance, brows knitted. "Are you sure you're okay?"

"I'm fine. Really, I'm fine."

"Okay, I'll accept that, I suppose." She rolled her eyes. "Let's move on! You haven't mentioned anything about your cases today. Did everything go okay in that department? You didn't have any more strange deaths that I didn't hear about, did you?"

"No, no deaths. My cases went okay. Well, that's not exactly true. There was a problem with the first one. After a vein stripping on a nearly four-hundred-pound woman that went reasonably well, other than not being able to use a planned epidural, the patient wouldn't start breathing on her own. And then while she was in the PACU, somehow her electrolytes got totally out of whack and she started having extra heartbeats. As far as I know, she's still on a ventilator six or seven hours after her surgery. Since I did her admission history and physical, I know she had no history of pulmonary disease, and her lungs were perfectly clear last night and presumably this morning. Weird, for sure. Dr. Singleton did say that there are some patients who just go south and there's nothing to be done. He actually used that specific phrase. Unfortunately for all concerned, the patient is now in the ICU, meaning I have two cases in there."

"That's not good."

"Tell me about it!" Mitt said, rolling his own eyes.

"What about the other two cases you had? Are they okay?"

"Yes. They seem to be doing fine, fingers crossed." Mitt held up his intertwined fingers for emphasis.

"What were they? Were they the kinds of cases that can have a rocky postop course like my Whipple procedure? I think she's going to be a challenge for me for the next few days, but I hope she doesn't cause you any trouble tonight. It's amazing how much the digestive system is rearranged during a Whipple."

"I don't think my two cases are going to be a problem, at least I hope not. They were pretty standard general surgical cases: a breast biopsy with a lymph node dissection and a thyroidectomy for a cancerous nodule. From my perspective in terms of learning surgery, the first procedure was okay, but the second one was a joy, better than any anatomy lesson by a long shot. In fact . . ."

All of a sudden the memory of the girl and ugly crowd again flashed into Mitt's mind like a psychic thunderstorm. Only with significant mental effort and another even more obvious shake of his head was he able to dispel it this time.

"In fact, what?" Andrea questioned. She leaned forward, staring into Mitt's eyes with a questioning expression. "Am I losing you again? What is it with you? Are you okay? Come on, something is bothering you, I can tell."

"No, no! I'm fine! Really, I'm okay," Mitt assured her, but he could see she wasn't convinced. "All right, to be honest, I am still tired, maybe even a bit more so. And I'm definitely still on the anxious side with all these deaths. And to top it all off, I haven't eaten anything all day. So, after I force myself to descend a floor to the ICU, our least favorite place in the hospital, to look in on both Elena Aguilar and Bianca Perez, I plan to take myself directly to the cafeteria for an early dinner. How about joining me? Are you game?"

"Hell no!" Andrea said but with a smile. "After I check all my postops including today's, I'm getting the hell out of this hospital. I was just on the phone with a friend. We're going to have an early but real dinner in a real restaurant. But finish your thought. You were talking about your thyroidectomy, and you started a sentence with 'in fact' . . . in fact what?"

"Good for you to get yourself out of this hospital for a few hours," Mitt said. "That's a healthy idea, and I'll try to do the same tomorrow. What I was going to say was . . . in fact, my thyroidectomy case was a superb anatomy lesson in a living, breathing human being. And that's by far the best type of anatomy lesson.

"The attending surgeon's name was Dr. Taylor Smith, and he was excellent. I got the definite sense he loves teaching. I hope I get to scrub with him often, and I hope you do, too. The only thing mildly unusual about the whole experience was the attending's rather curious name. I've never met another male 'Taylor,' whereas his family name is one of the most common. Anyway, the combination caught my attention."

"What are you talking about?" Andrea said with an exaggerated questioning expression. "Taylor is a fairly common name for both men and women. I know several."

"Regardless," Mitt said with a wave of dismissal. "The commonality of the name isn't important. The point I'd like to emphasize is that this Dr. Taylor Smith is a born teacher. I learned more during this thyroidectomy today than in all my other surgeries put together. You're going to love him if you get to work with him. Believe me!" Mitt heaved himself out of the rather low chair and got to his feet. As he did so, he experienced a fleeting touch of dizziness, which he attributed to low blood sugar. With that thought in mind, he noticed a bowl of individually wrapped peanut butter crackers over Andrea's shoulder by the coffeepot and was momentarily tempted, but then he thought he could hold out another half hour or so for a real meal.

"Thanks for the heads-up about Dr. Smith," Andrea said, getting to her feet as well. "I'll look forward to scrubbing in with him. Before you go, let's talk about tomorrow morning. What time do you want me to show up? My guess is it's up to us, since there are no formal rounds."

"Good question," Mitt said. "I hadn't given it any thought, to be truthful." He'd had a premonition that the night ahead was not going to be pleasant, but he didn't know how bad or at what point during the night it might be bad—late in the evening or early in the morning or both. But he did know that the worse the night turned out to be, the earlier he'd want to be relieved.

"Here's my offer," Andrea said. "If you are willing to hand off the baton as late as nine A.M., I'll do your histories and physicals. That way you won't have to come in to do them."

"That's very generous," Mitt said. "But I don't think it's fair to burden you with my responsibilities just because I lucked out having the day off. As I said, I literally live around the corner. I don't mind coming in. But nine A.M. is fine."

"Are you sure?"

"No, I'm not sure. If it's a bad night, I'll kick myself for saying nine. But there's no way to know, so let's say nine."

"Okay," Andrea said. "Fair enough! I'm not going to fight you, that's for sure." She moved toward Mitt, offering first one cheek, then the other, in her usual warmhearted fashion.

After the gesture, Mitt glanced around the surgical lounge, feeling self-conscious. He couldn't help it, but public displays of affection made him feel uncomfortable. He was relieved to see that no one paid them the slightest heed. Besides, there weren't that many people in the surgical lounge at that moment.

Together they walked out to the elevator lobby as Andrea described in enthusiastic detail the restaurant she would soon visit. An up elevator came before a down, and Mitt waved to her as she boarded. "Good luck tonight," she called out as the door began to close.

"Enjoy your dinner date," Mitt responded, still waving. For a brief moment standing in the elevator lobby with Andrea gone, he experienced a strange sense of loneliness, as though he was being abandoned. He couldn't explain his feeling, especially with several other people around him waiting for a down elevator. A moment later he was able to board and the feeling vanished. In its place was the more understandable and worrisome concern about his upcoming visit to the ICU.

Minutes later, Mitt pushed into the ICU and immediately felt a sense of déjà vu. He experienced the exact same anxiety over the threat of potential clinical catastrophe as he had that morning, although maybe it was a little more intense now that he had two patients. As he penetrated deeper, it got worse, and Mitt paused to decide if he should head immediately to 10 South and check on Perez or if he should stop and find out Aguilar's location. Coming abreast of the bank of monitors made the decision for him.

Several of the people using the monitors nodded a greeting to him, and he nodded back, feeling a bit more welcome. Again, without sitting down, he typed in *Elena Aguilar* and was immediately rewarded with her location, 8 North.

Leaving the central desk, he made a snap decision to check on Perez first since he knew where that specific room was located and it happened to be physically closer to where he currently was. As he approached 10 South, he began to formulate what he'd like to see if it were up to him, namely that the woman was off the ventilator and conscious. He knew it was wishful thinking, but he indulged himself anyway. Since it was already after four in the afternoon, he knew the chances of Gabriela Martinez still being the nurse on duty were slim, so he planned on again admitting his newbie resident status up front.

Coming to the door of 10 South, he stopped short. Not only was Gabriela Martinez not there, but the patient wasn't Bianca Perez. In the bed was an elderly Black man with white hair and a short white beard who was sitting up and sipping a cup of ice water. A second later, a nurse popped out of the connecting nurses' station. Like everyone else in the ICU, she was dressed in surgical scrubs. She, too, was Black and didn't look much older than Mitt's twenty-three years, if that.

"What's up?" the nurse questioned with a friendly smile. "Have you come for Mr. Henderson? He's ready to go."

"No," Mitt said. Instinctively he leaned to the side to make absolutely certain he was in the correct room. He was. "I'm a first-year surgical resident," he quickly added while trying not to believe what his mind was telling him. "I was coming to check on Bianca Perez, who was in here this morning. Has she been sent back to her regular assigned room?"

Without so much as a slight hesitation, the nurse approached Mitt, latched onto his right arm above the elbow, and drew him a couple of steps away from the room's doorway and out of earshot of her current patient.

"Bianca Perez passed away this morning," the nurse said quietly. "She had a cardiac arrest and was a DNR."

For Mitt the information was like a slap in the face, and he recoiled. "No," he said as if he had the power to alter reality, but then quickly added: "When did this happen?"

"Ten A.M. or thereabouts. You can find it on the record if need be."

"Okay, yes, of course," Mitt said. "Thank you for letting me know."

"You're welcome," the nurse said. She raised her eyebrows as if asking if Mitt had any more questions.

Mitt spun around and headed toward the north-facing ICU patient rooms. As he walked, skirting various hustling people and passing a multitude of rooms, each with a very sick patient and at least one nurse, he felt numb, like he was in a nightmare and couldn't wake up. What he was having to face was yet another patient death, meaning that all four of the initial cases that had been assigned to him had died: first Suárez, then Thompson and Silva, and now Perez.

Can that have happened by chance? Mitt silently wondered. Knowing something about statistics, he was well aware the odds were very small indeed, and when he added in the fact that Elena Aguilar was doing poorly, it seemed almost beyond statistical probability.

Mitt turned the corner and started along the north-facing ICU rooms. As he got closer to 8 North, he found himself purposefully slowing, as if by doing so he could influence reality. But it didn't work. The moment he reached the door and looked in #8, his hopes of a positive clinical turnaround were dashed—Elena Aguilar was still on the ventilator and obviously not breathing on her own. Her eyes were taped shut. And she was completely motionless save for the slight rise and fall of her chest with each mechanical respiration. The assigned nurse was busy on the right side of the bed, adjusting the flow from a cluster of intravenous containers hanging from the IV pole.

"Can I help you?" the nurse asked, catching sight of Mitt standing frozen in the doorway.

Mitt went through the same explanation he'd given to Perez's nurse that morning to emphasize his status as a three-day-old surgical resident. He then asked how the patient was doing since her arrival in the ICU.

"She's been reasonably stable, yet that's not much to write home about," the nurse said with a series of nods as if agreeing with herself. Mitt tried to see the woman's name tag, but it was partially covered up by a surgical gown she was wearing backward over her scrubs. The ICU was kept at a lower temperature than the rest of the hospital, and Mitt had noticed most of the nurses wore a variety of such cover-ups over their scrubs. "Her pupils, although reactive, are sluggish in my book, but that hasn't changed," the nurse continued. "Of particular importance, she had some premature beats a few minutes ago. The second it happened, I let the Cardiology fellow know. Other than that, she's been stable in terms of BP and oxygen saturation. I'd been told that the O_2 had dropped in the PACU, but down here it's been fine provided the ventilator volume and pressure are maintained."

"Has the Cardiology fellow come to see her?"

"No, but he said he'd be by shortly. He did up her beta-blocker and told me to call him back if there are any more PVCs."

"I see," Mitt said. He recognized that he didn't even know enough about the ventilator to ask any pertinent questions. "What about the electrolytes? Up in the PACU, I'd been told by the nurse they'd gotten out of whack and had to be adjusted."

"Yeah, we heard about that," the nurse said. "So, we ran electrolytes the minute she got here. They came back reasonable, maybe a tad low on potassium, but otherwise within normal limits. We also did a chest X-ray, and it was clear."

"I'm on call tonight, so I'll be around," Mitt said, silently gritting his teeth. The last thing he wanted was to be called to the ICU, yet he felt responsible for Elena, especially since he didn't have a good feeling about the woman's near future.

"What's your name again?" the nurse asked. She tried to make out Mitt's name on his ID tag but couldn't.

"Fuller," Mitt said, purposefully leaving out the doctor title. "Michael Fuller."

"Okay, I got it, Dr. Fuller. I'll give you a shout if there's any marked change. Because she's making absolutely no attempts to fight the ventilator, I'm not feeling optimistic there's going to be a lot of change. The only thing that seems to keep changing is this damn IV." She'd been watching the drip chamber as she'd been talking to Mitt, and now she went back to adjusting the IV. "If you want to call me at any time until I leave at eleven, just dial ICU bed 8 North," she said over her shoulder. "I'll pick up if I can. If I can't, leave a message, and I'll call you right back."

"Okay, will do," Mitt said. He liked that. It meant he had the option of checking on Elena without having to come into the intensive care unit, and that sounded like music to his ears. Turning on his heels, he hurried back toward the relative safety of the hospital proper. Thinking of the news he'd just gotten, he realized the ICU was certainly living up to his worst fears, with Bianca Perez dead and Elena Aguilar hanging onto the edge of the precipice with just the tips of her fingers.

Reaching the elevator lobby, he knew he had to think about something other than death and statistics. Luckily his gnawing hunger provided a distraction, and he started wondering exactly what he was going to have for his upcoming dinner.

CHAPTER 20

Mitt's phone jolted him out of a dead, dreamless sleep, and he bolted upright. For a brief moment he was disoriented, but he quickly acclimatized to his surroundings. With a bit of a struggle, he got his strident phone out of his jacket pocket, and before he connected the incoming call, he checked the time. It was a quarter to eleven, meaning he'd gotten a bit more than three hours of uninterrupted sleep, more than he had expected but not nearly enough. It took him a moment to even focus on the phone.

When he'd come back to the on-call area just after seven, he'd gone directly into his room, purposefully avoiding going into the lounge area to join other on-call residents who were sitting around socializing. Following Dr. Singleton's advice, he wanted to try to maximize sleep opportunities early in the evening. Again, like Monday night, once he was in his room, he didn't shower or do anything else that might have given him a second wind. All he did was stretch out on the bed in his scrubs and white coat and attempted to think about nothing. Apparently it had worked like a charm.

"Hello?" he said, hoping the call might be some minor issue such as a dosage question or the need for a sleep-medication order, both of which he was becoming progressively adept at handling over the phone. But it wasn't to be. The caller sounded hurried, even frantic. "Is this Dr. Fuller?" she questioned.

"It is," Mitt responded, throwing his feet onto the floor. His flight-or-fight reaction had now been fully awakened by the sound of the urgency in the woman's voice.

"I'm calling about Latonya Walker. She is your patient, is she not?"

"She is," Mitt said, feeling an added jolt. "What's the problem?"

"She's had an arrest," the nurse barked. "The crash team is here on Fifteen West, but I thought you'd want to know."

"Good grief," Mitt said. In the next instant he was holding a dead phone. Pocketing it and leaping to his feet, he had to momentarily put his hand against the wall to steady himself to weather a fleeting spell of dizziness. He then shoved his feet into his loafers, quickly exited the room, ran through the now-empty lounge area, and headed out into the elevator lobby.

After his early dinner, Mitt had made it a point to visit all six nurses' stations on floors fifteen, sixteen, and seventeen, saying hello specifically to the head nurses but other nurses as well. His goal was to generally make his presence known in an attempt to head off having to deal with pesky issues like laxative requests later. All the surgical inpatient floors had been exceptionally busy, presumably due to the holiday the following day. Not only were there lots of visitors but also plenty of residents and attendings making rounds. But most important, he'd confirmed that there were no looming clinical problems. During his meet-and-greet, he'd run into Dr. Madison Baker, who was rounding on her own patients. She gave him the excellent news that from her perspective things were looking good for the night. She said the sickies she'd worried about Monday night had all dramatically improved.

During his walk-around Mitt had also made a point of stopping in to see the two ward patients he had, Diego Ortiz and Latonya Walker. Both had been doing fine, particularly Ms. Walker, who had eaten a decent meal and didn't seem to have much pain. Her drain showed almost no drainage and her incision looked fine beneath the paper tape. As well as she'd been doing, a cardiac arrest now seemed hard to believe. As far as he could remember, she'd had no personal or family history of any cardiac issues whatsoever.

Mitt hit the elevator call button multiple times despite knowing full well that it wouldn't bring the car any faster. Now that he was on his way, his sleep-deprived brain had cleared considerably, bringing with it a definite case of the jitters. The idea that another one of his assigned patients, who had been doing well, was now struggling for her life was an issue he didn't even want to contemplate. Although he was realistic about not being needed with the crash team on-site, he felt a responsibility to be present. And there was a slight possibility he could help because he'd had a bit of experience with cardiac arrests as a medical student. He'd participated in a handful during his third-year internal medicine rotation and had made it a point to read the most recent medical literature on the subject.

"Where the hell is the goddamned elevator?" Mitt growled under his breath while slapping an open palm against the nearest elevator door and mentally cursing whoever it was who had come up with the idea of siting a hospital in a high-rise. As he stood there waiting, he marveled that it was Latonya Walker who was in trouble. Earlier, he'd worried that there was a good chance he might be called on an emergency with Elena Aguilar, considering how precarious her clinical state was. He'd even forced himself back to the ICU to check on her before heading to the on-call room, in a kind of superstitious hope that making the effort might forestall it from happening.

The moment the elevator arrived, he jumped into the empty car, pressing the 15 button almost a dozen times. He wracked his brain, trying to imagine what could have caused Latonya Walker to have a cardiac arrest. The only possibility that came to his mind was her obesity, since he knew that there was a direct correlation between being overweight and heart disease. Yet why would it happen now, when she'd not shown any signs suggesting that she was developing a problem? Could it have been merely from having had anesthesia, even if there hadn't been any problems whatsoever during her procedure? Mitt had no idea, especially since he knew next to nothing about anesthesia other than it was a medical specialty in its own right.

As the elevator door finally opened on fifteen, Mitt charged out and turned toward the west rooms. But he didn't get far beyond the elevator lobby when he came to an abrupt halt. About twenty feet down the nighttime-darkened hallway stood the blond girl, arms akimbo, seemingly laughing at him soundlessly. Thankfully there wasn't any accompanying terrible odor.

Mitt closed his eyes tightly for a moment, hoping the hallucination would vanish like it had that afternoon in the operating room when he'd momentarily averted his gaze. But it didn't work on this occasion. When he looked back, she was still there and still silently giggling, giving Mitt the sense that she was making fun of him. Then the girl stopped laughing, and when she did, she raised her arm and extended her hand, which was gripping the same stainless-steel, pencil-like instrument he'd seen before.

Overcoming his shock, Mitt started forward, intent on getting to

Latonya Walker's cardiac arrest despite this distraction set up by his overactive imagination. The hallucination's response to his approach was seemingly glee, as her smile broadened. And similar to the previous night, as Mitt neared she again disappeared into the surgical conference room. It had happened so quickly—one minute there, the next minute gone—that Mitt wasn't even certain if the door had been opened or if the girl simply passed through it.

Mere seconds later, Mitt himself was abreast of the door, and despite his being on an emergency call, he thrust it open, lunged in, and flipped on the lights all in one continuous motion. His thought was that the bright, fluorescent light would dispel the hallucination, as it had the night before. But on this occasion, it didn't. Instead, he saw not only the blond girl but the horde of apparently surgerized people who had been behind her in the operating room. As close as they were, Mitt could see they were in all manner of period dress and undress and varying levels of cleanliness and filth, some carrying their missing limbs or organs. And to add to the horror, swirling around their feet and climbing up their legs were hundreds if not thousands of rats. Then, on top of the almost incomprehensibly repulsive scene, the cacosmia returned with a vengeance, making Mitt stagger back from both the stench as well as the sight.

As the young girl and the crowd surged forward, Mitt leaped back out of the room, noisily yanking the door shut behind him. Terrified that the blond girl, the mob, and the seething mass of rats would in the next instant pass through the door and come at him, he flattened up against the opposite wall, preparing to defend himself as best he could.

But then nothing happened. A few seconds passed. To his left down the hall, he heard someone shout a question, although he couldn't make out what it was. A moment later he heard someone else respond, again unintelligibly. But the reassuring sounds of normal people doing normal things meant he was in the real world and not an imaginary one.

Building up his courage, Mitt took a step back across the hallway to the door and grasped the knob. He waited for a moment, listening, sure that there was no way the horde could be silent—although now he couldn't remember if he'd heard anything when he'd confronted them or not. It had all taken place so quickly.

When Mitt didn't hear anything from the room beyond, he pushed open the door suddenly while anticipating he might have to close it in a flash. But he didn't have to. The room was empty of people and rats and spotlessly clean despite what he'd seen just a few moments earlier. And the stench had also mercifully evaporated.

Quickly, Mitt leaned back out of the room, pulling the door closed behind him. He took a deep breath to fortify himself. He couldn't believe what his imagination was apparently capable of doing. It boggled him. At the same time, he knew he didn't have time to ponder the issue.

With renewed urgency, Mitt rushed the rest of the way down the hallway from the elevator lobby to the corridor that ran along the west-facing patient rooms. Latonya Walker's room was a six-bed ward to the left, and as Mitt turned the corner, he saw a small group of nurses and residents clustered at its doorway. As quickly as he could, he joined this group.

"How's it going?" Mitt asked the first nurse who turned in his direction. Despite being stressed from his most recent hallucinatory experience, he tried to act normal.

"I don't think they are having much luck," the woman responded. "But it's not been going on for that long."

Mitt nodded. He pushed into the room. Latonya Walker's bed was the first one on the left, near the door to the en suite lavatory. The privacy curtain was drawn shut, leaving about four feet of space between the curtain and the bed. The crash cart was on the bed's right side with the curtain partially draped around it.

There were four residents obviously in charge of the resuscitation, and Mitt assumed they were the on-call cardiac unit. Teaching hospitals, like Bellevue, all had standing, highly trained resuscitation teams available 24/7. It was a service that was too important to be left to chance. Currently the team was three woman and one man, all dressed in full whites, and they were busily engaged. A female resident was at the head of the bed using an Ambu bag to respire the patient, another was up on her knees on the bed doing closed-chest cardiac massage, while the lone male was operating the defibrillator. The final resident, who was obviously the most senior and in charge, was watching the blip of the cardiac monitor as it traced a flat line across the screen. She appeared frustrated and confused, slowly shaking her head with her lips pressed tightly together.

Mitt quickly saw someone whom he recognized: Madison Baker. She was intently watching the monitor over the senior medical resident's shoulder. Relieved to see his surgical backup was already there, meaning he wouldn't have to call her if he was asked to do something he wasn't capable of, which was just about anything at all, he moved over behind her. "Hello, Madison," Mitt said to get her attention.

Madison turned around upon hearing her name. "Mitt," she said, acting surprised. "What are you doing here? I was hoping you were in never-never land."

"I was but I got a call saying my patient had an arrest. I got here as soon as I could." Mitt was aware of being less than truthful, but hallucinations were the last thing he'd be willing to admit to Madison.

"Oh, for goodness' sake," Madison complained. "I told the nurses specifically not to call you because I was already here. Well, I was not exactly here in this room, just a couple of doors down with one of my patients. The nurse who'd been assigned to Ms. Walker ran in and got me. It's a strange story. She said the patient had been perfectly stable all evening, even ate a full liquid diet, and had only been using her PRN IV analgesic sparingly. The next thing she knew, the patient had no heartbeat. None. Zero. It's weird. And the resuscitation team can't figure it out, either. They've tried multiple shocks and even an external pacer and can't get any electrical response. I know you scrubbed on the case this morning. Was there any problem with the anesthesia that you remember? Anything at all?"

"No," Mitt said. "The anesthesia went perfectly fine. It was the earlier case where there was a problem with anesthesia."

"Oh, yeah, I heard about that one. She's in the ICU, correct?"

"Correct. The name is Elena Aguilar."

"I looked in on her earlier in the evening. That's another weird situation. I understand she never started breathing after her succinyl-choline was stopped."

"Unfortunately, that's true. And then later on, she even stopped fighting the ventilator."

"What did the anesthesiologist think was going on?"

"I asked but didn't really get an answer. Later it was discovered her electrolytes were abnormal, and she started having cardiac issues as well."

"You mean the electrolytes became abnormal while she was in the PACU?"

"Apparently. That's what the nurse suggested to Dr. Singleton and me."

"Somebody mustn't have been watching the IV," Madison hypothesized with a disapproving shake of her head. "That's even stranger, because the PACU nurses are a terrific bunch and extraordinarily competent."

"I got the impression the PACU nurse herself was confused."

"Well, enough about Aguilar. What's the story with this patient? I haven't had an opportunity to check the EHR. Any personal history of cardiac issues that might explain this episode?"

"There wasn't," Mitt said. "None at all. No family history, either."

At that moment a nurse pushed by Mitt and Madison, forcing them to step out of the way. The nurse handed the medical resident in charge of the resuscitation a slip of paper.

"Holy shit!" the medical resident exclaimed the second she glanced at what the nurse had handed her. "The freakin' potassium's 14.95! I've never heard of that. That's impossible! My God! No wonder there's no electrical activity." She then barked a series of orders to the male resident to prepare bicarbonate, calcium gluconate, hypertonic glucose, and insulin, all of which she immediately began to administer as soon as it was available. While she was busy doing so, she asked Madison over her shoulder if the patient had a history of kidney failure, adrenal insufficiency, diabetes, or HIV, all of which can be associated with high blood potassium.

Madison looked at Mitt, and Mitt responded with a definitive no.

"This is ridiculous," the resident complained to no one in particular. "A 14.95 potassium level has to be a world's record, and if we don't get it down ASAP, there's no chance of success here." She then turned to the nurse who'd handed her the slip of paper. "Call the medical resident on call and say we need emergency dialysis stat!" Then she turned to Madison. "Since you surgery guys are here, can we get you to insert a tunneled dialysis catheter for us? I'm sure you're better at it than we are."

"That's to be debated," Madison said. "But sure. We're happy to help."

At that point things moved into high gear, and in the rush of activity, Mitt was even able to forget about his recent hallucination and his fatigue. With Latonya Walker's right groin prepped, Madison insisted that Mitt insert the dialysis catheter at her direction while she held back the abdominal adipose tissue with a small retractor. The catheter itself was sizable, containing a double lumen, one for the blood to be taken from the vein to be processed in the dialysis machine and another for the cleansed blood to be returned to the patient's circulation.

"You remember the inguinal canal anatomy, I presume?" Madison asked in a joking fashion. It was an area of the body all medical students remembered from a popular mnemonic device, NAVEL, meaning nerve, artery, vein, and empty space with lymphatics.

"I do," Mitt replied. He could feel the pulsating femoral artery and knew that the femoral vein, his target, was immediately adjacent medially. Taking in his breath and holding it, he plunged the pointed catheter tip through the skin, angled upward toward the patient's head.

"Great," Madison encouraged. "Now, advance it slowly until you feel it break through the vein wall."

As a medical student, Mitt had become relatively proficient at drawing blood, and what he was currently doing was similar, just in a unique anatomical location and under far different circumstances. As Madison suggested, he felt the catheter break through an unseen boundary as he advanced the tip. When he drew back on the attached syringe, it filled with blood.

"Perfect," Madison said. Then after instructing Mitt to thread the catheter up into the vein a short distance and tape it securely to the skin, she called out to the dialysis team that the catheter was good to go.

Mitt enjoyed a rare feeling of accomplishment after he'd stepped back to give the newly arrived on-call medical residents room to attach the catheter to their dialysis machine.

For the next hour and fifteen minutes, the resuscitation team kept up their frantic activities with the person doing the closed-chest massage changing every five to ten minutes. The group of people observing thinned considerably, although Mitt and Madison stayed. After about an hour, the medical resident in charge ordered a repeat potassium level, and when it returned at still over ten, she'd become discouraged, admitting that despite all that had been done, the potassium level remained much too high to expect a return of the heart's electrical function.

"Okay," the senior medical resident of the resuscitation team called out. "We gave it our best shot. The key point here is that the patient's pupils, which were widely dilatated when we first arrived, have never come down. I'm afraid this is a lost cause. Let's stop."

As the resuscitation group began to dismantle all their equipment, Mitt and Madison walked back toward the nurses' station.

"Well, at least that was a good effort," Madison said. "I was impressed. They pulled out all the stops, but it's still a mystery to me what the hell could have happened to make the patient's potassium level go through the roof. I've never seen or heard anything like it."

"It is surprising," Mitt agreed. Now that the excitement was over, the reality of the situation was sinking in. Another patient he'd been assigned had died under what seemed to be inexplicable circumstances. Latonya Walker had had no history of cardiac disease, and her obesity notwithstanding, there'd been no reason to suspect she'd have cardiac problems despite having undergone general anesthesia and a reasonably extensive operation.

"I'm assuming you'll handle the paperwork," Madison said. Her usually crystalline voice had lost some of its sparkle. Like Mitt, she was feeling drained after the excitement and the less-than-optimal result on top of a long day.

"I will," Mitt responded, although he wasn't looking forward to it.

"Try to get it done ASAP," Madison said. "And then get yourself back to the on-call room. Let's hope that's all the excitement for tonight."

"I'll do my best," Mitt said. "Thanks for encouraging me to put in the dialysis catheter and then talking me through actually doing it. I appreciate it."

"You did a superb job and nailed it first try. Bravo!"

When they reached the nurses' station, Madison said a quick good night before waving and heading down the darkened corridor toward the elevators. For a few beats, Mitt watched her recede, half-wishing that the blond girl would make an appearance ahead of her so that Madison would see her, too. But it wasn't to be.

Taking a deep breath to give himself a new semi-burst of energy, Mitt went behind the counter. There he was greeted by the head night nurse who, without being asked, handed him the paperwork required for the death. With a sigh of resignation and now armed with the appropriate forms, he took a seat at the counter. He then unclipped a pen from his jacket pocket and got down to work. But as he worked, he couldn't stop thinking about the blond girl and wondering why the apparition was hounding him and whether he'd have to again confront her and the others on his way back to his on-call room. And the rats: That was something new. All in all, it was one hell of a nerve-wracking situation having his own imagination haunt him, especially considering the stress he was under starting a surgical residency.

CHAPTER 21

Thursday, July 4, 12:35 A.M.

When his phone rang, Mitt wasn't even certain he'd had the opportunity to fall asleep, especially since he was holding his phone and the last thing he could remember was debating whether to put it on the night table next to the head of the bed or to slip it into his jacket pocket. When he'd gotten back from Latonya Walker's cardiac arrest a few minutes earlier, relieved to have done so without any repeat hallucinations, he'd immediately stretched out on the bed fully clothed without even kicking off his loafers. It seemed like the next second the phone rang.

"Yes?" Mitt said into the phone after connecting the call. He sensed he wasn't fully awake, so he must have been asleep.

"This is Carl Higgens, the ICU ward clerk. I'm calling about Elena Aguilar to let you know that she's just had a cardiac arrest and the resuscitation team is on its way."

"Thank you," Mitt said by reflex, and immediately sat up. He could tell the clerk had hung up, so he pocketed his phone. Although it wasn't surprising that Elena Aguilar had had a cardiac arrest since her course had been steadily downhill since her surgery, it was still a blow, particularly after just returning from Latonya Walker's even more surprising arrest and death.

Mitt got to his feet and waited a beat for his cardiovascular system to adjust. He knew that of all places in the hospital, the ICU was the most attuned to handling a cardiac arrest and that the resuscitation team was on its way, so he didn't feel the need to break a speed record getting there. There was no doubt in his mind that, as with Latonya Walker, he'd be more of an observer than a participant, so he took a moment to duck into his bathroom and splash some cold water on his face. The shock of it did wonders, and he felt much more capable of facing the reality that Elena Aguilar might be yet another death, which seemed almost inevitable considering her progressively downward course. After also taking the time to push his hair into a semblance of order to try to counterbalance appearing like "death warmed over," with his dark circles and pale complexion, Mitt left the on-call room.

As he passed through the deserted on-call lounge area, he didn't run, but he didn't take his time, either. He needed an opportunity to think more about Elena Aguilar's potential passing, remembering his thoughts that afternoon after Bianca Perez's death. As incredible as it might seem, if there was another death that night, then six out of the first seven patients he'd been assigned would have passed away. It was an incredibly high percentage, and as he had agonized that afternoon, the chances of it happening simply by bad luck were incredibly small, nearly untenable. And if the deaths weren't being caused by chance, what could possibly be the explanation? Mitt had no idea . . . none, even though in the back of his mind his sixth sense was suggesting there was.

Upon reaching the empty elevator lobby, Mitt pressed the call button and positioned himself in the middle of the room to wait for whichever of the ten elevators might arrive. While he waited, he struggled to stop agonizing over his apparent personal patient-death rate, vaguely imagining that if future patients had any idea of his atrocious record, he'd be shunned for certain. No one would want him to be involved with their case in any capacity.

With a warning chime from the elevator that was about to arrive, Mitt hustled over and positioned himself inches from the appropriate door. His plan was to jump on even before the door completely opened and quickly hit the button for the tenth floor as well as the close button. The sooner he did, the sooner the door would reverse direction, and he'd be on his way.

As the elevator door began to open, Mitt moved even nearer, his nose now practically resting against the cream-colored metal as it slid past in front of him. The actual moment the door cleared his face on its way to collapse into the wall, he started forward as he'd planned. But in the blink of the eye, he froze. To his horror, he found himself within inches of a ghostly pale man with bloodshot eyes and wild hair who was balancing on a single leg and dressed in what looked like a colonial costume. In his arms was his amputated leg with its bloody, severed thigh muscles, blood vessels, nerves, and sawed-off femur in plain sight.

As Mitt reeled back, he saw that this pitiful person was not alone. The entire elevator was thronged with similar wretched figures, everyone appearing as if they were in agonizing pain although no one cried out and total silence reigned. Completely taken aback, Mitt froze, unable to move a single muscle. For the first time with any of his hallucinations he was close enough to reach out and touch one of the miserable human beings or be touched by them. Thankfully, no one moved. And the people weren't the only ghastly occupants. The entire floor of the elevator was a writhing mass of rats in constant motion, climbing all over one another and trying to clamber up the legs of the surgerized people.

For what seemed like an eternity although it must have been only seconds, the elevator door remained open. Finally, it began to close, and as it did so, the image of the crowd of sorry human beings progressively disappeared until it was gone, and Mitt found himself staring at a closed elevator door.

Then, before he could recover from the shock, another elevator arrived. As its door collapsed back into the wall, Mitt hesitantly checked its interior and, with tremendous relief, saw that it was empty.

With great strength of will and needing more time than he would have liked, Mitt finally managed to break free from his shocked paralysis. By then he had to lunge for the empty elevator and bang against the closing door to get it to reverse itself.

Once inside, Mitt pressed the button for ten, and then let himself lean his back and head against the elevator wall. Desperately, he tried to make sense of what he'd just witnessed. He had no idea if it was the same group of sad people that he'd seen in the OR and the surgical conference room, but they appeared similar. Regardless, in his mind they certainly represented the same pitiful constituency that Mitt imagined had been operated on at Bellevue Hospital in the distant past. How his mind was capable of mentally imagining such a crowd, he had absolutely no idea. Nor why, which seemed an important question, his hallucinations were coming more frequently and with increasingly realistic details. The vision of the young girl had been shocking enough, but these crowds of tortured souls were far worse. And what about the rats? A few years ago, when he'd read a book about the history of Bellevue Hospital, he'd learned that rats coming in through the sewers had been a major problem in the hospital over many, many years, partially due to its location along the East River. He'd been appalled that the vermin had been known to climb over bedridden patients at night, possibly gnawing people and even infants. As awful as that sounded, why was his creative mind adding those creatures to his hallucinations? It certainly hadn't been something he'd spent a lot of time thinking about.

The elevator door opened on the tenth floor, and Mitt exited. He'd mostly recovered from the fright of his hallucination, even wondering anew what would have happened had he simply ignored what he'd seen and just boarded the elevator despite it appearing jammed full. Would they have physically blocked his way or just instantly disappeared? It was an interesting thought, but he doubted he'd have the courage to put it to the test.

When Mitt pushed into the ICU proper, he felt significantly better than he had on his previous visits. He imagined the resuscitation team was already present, so he was confident he wouldn't be expected to do something beyond his abilities. He was also just becoming more acclimated purely by repetition.

As he approached Elena Aguilar's ICU room, he again saw a clutch of people observing just outside the door, but it was a significantly smaller number than had been outside Latonya Walker's room. When he got close enough to see within the bay, he could tell it was the same team that had responded to Walker's arrest. He wasn't surprised, as he imagined there was only one resuscitation team on during the night, but he didn't know that for sure.

First he looked for Dr. Madison Baker either inside the room or in the hallway, even though he didn't expect her to be there. He knew she'd been at Walker's arrest by chance. Although he wished she was there for the support she offered, he didn't want to call her if he didn't have to.

"How is the resuscitation going?" Mitt asked one of the few ICU nurses observing the action from the hallway. She was a youthful Hispanic woman who was about Mitt's age. He was impressed she was working in the ICU, where most of the other nurses appeared older and more seasoned.

"Not well," the woman said. She briefly eyed Mitt, making him suspect she was thinking the same thoughts about his age. "I think they are about to call it quits."

"So soon?" he questioned. He tried to see this youthful nurse's name tag, but it was covered by the surgical gown she was wearing over her scrubs like Elena's earlier nurse.

"I understand there'd been some disappointing new developments in the patient's condition," she added. "And that's in addition to her reverting back into ventricular fib after every defib attempt."

"Oh?" Mitt questioned. "Like what kind of new developments?" Elena Aguilar not breathing on her own for more than twelve hours was certainly serious enough. He couldn't imagine what could have been more "disappointing" than that. He noticed some of the ICU staff who had been watching the proceedings were turning to leave.

"I heard she's been exhibiting some decerebrate posturing," the nurse said. "And that's serious stuff, especially when it's progressive as it's been. It certainly goes a long way to explain why she hasn't made any attempts to breathe on her own the whole time she's been here."

"I'm not familiar with decerebrate posturing," Mitt admitted. "What is it exactly?" He tried to rally his tired brain, but it was difficult. He vaguely remembered the term from his medical school neurology rotation, but all that came to his mind was it being seriously bad news and generally incompatible with life.

"You don't know what decerebrate posturing is?" The nurse eyed Mitt with surprise, but then her expression changed, ushering in a smile of sudden understanding. "Wait a second! Are you perchance a new resident? I mean, it is the beginning of July."

Mitt raised his hands in mock surrender. "Third-day surgical resident," he confessed. He was happy to admit it, particularly there in the ICU.

"Of course! Well, welcome to the team! To answer your question, decerebrate posturing is a hyperextension reflex. Usually, the arms are tensed with the palms rotated outward and wrists flexed, which you can see some of if you look in at this patient. What it probably means is that she'd had a major stroke that involved the brain stem."

"Good grief," Mitt said, wondering if Elena Aguilar had had a stroke during her surgery, which no one suspected, particularly Anesthesia.

"Are you following this patient, or are you here just being curious, like me?"

"I assisted with her vein stripping this morning."

"Well, that's nice to hear. At least she no longer has any varices."

Mitt regarded her. He was mildly taken aback by what seemed like an insensitive comment, but he saw a slight rise to her eyebrow, suggesting she was indulging in a bit of "insider" black humor.

"Well, nice chatting," the nurse said. "I have to get back to my patient who luckily is doing a lot better than this poor woman. Sorry about your patient, but good luck in your residency!"

"Thank you," Mitt said. As the nurse walked away, he moved into the relatively crowded room and found a place to stand off to the side behind the medical resident, who was clearly the captain of the resuscitation team. Since the ventilator was respiring Elena Aguilar, no one needed to be manning an Ambu bag, and everyone was watching the monitor except the medical resident, who was kneeling on the bed and doing the chest compressions. By moving slightly side to side, Mitt was able to get a reasonable view of Elena's body and confirm what the nurse he'd been talking to outside the room had told him, Elena's arms were rigidly held along her sides with her wrists flexed and palms directed outward. Also, from his perspective, it appeared as if her back was slightly arched. Her legs, still covered with Ace bandages, were definitely straight out, with the toes extended and pointing medially. Mitt made a mental note that what he was looking at was an example of decerebrate rigidity, suggesting that Elena Aguilar had suffered a major stroke, or maybe even a series of major strokes that had been missed.

"All right, everyone, clear," the captain of the resuscitation team called out. "Let's try one last defibrillation attempt." In either hand, she was holding up the charged paddles of the defibrillator. As soon as everyone backed away, she placed the paddles against Elena's chest and discharged the defibrillator. Elena's body reacted stiffly, very different from Latonya Walker's when she'd been shocked.

At that point everyone in the room, now including Mitt, watched the overhead monitor to see the result. Within seconds the blip reappeared, tracing a wildly abnormal pattern as it moved across the screen.

"Is there a pulse?" the captain asked while keeping her eyes glued to the monitor.

"No, there's no pulse," one of the team said, feeling against Elena's neck.

"Okay, that's it," the captain said, throwing up her hands. "We're done. I think this should have been a DNR from the word 'go' with this amount of decerebrate symptomatology. But who's to say? Let's close up shop and get out of here in case we get another call."

Almost the moment the woman finished her little speech, the cardiac alarm went off, indicating that Elena Aguilar had yet again fallen back into fibrillation. Several of the resuscitation team members reacted to the alarm, but the captain raised her hands to stop them. "Hold up! As I said, we're done here."

As the resuscitation team packed up their equipment, which mostly involved tending to the defibrillator and its paddles, the monitor alarm kept sounding until one of the ICU nurses turned it off. Not too long after the resuscitation team had pushed the crash cart out of the room and away down the hall, Mitt noticed that the monitor's blip changed from its chicken scratch–like tracing to a perfectly flat line. Elena Aguilar was now dead by definition.

Mitt watched the straight-lined monitor for several beats until one of the ICU nurses turned it off along with the ventilator, which had mechanically continued respiring the patient despite her heart having stopped. Then everyone but Mitt left the room. He remained rooted to his spot, staring at his assigned patient's motionless body.

Although he'd expected for a number of hours that Elena Aguilar was going to die, now that she had, it weighed on him anew that six out of his seven initially assigned patients had passed away. Once again, his mathematically oriented mind struggled to deal with the reality of such a statistic, especially now that he couldn't get any potential traction out of the Dr. Geraldo Rodriguez connection since Latonya Walker and Elena Aguilar had been with Dr. Kevin Singleton. Now, as far as Mitt knew, he was the only person or circumstance that connected the deaths together, and he struggled to try to understand what, if anything, that could possibly mean. The only idea that came to his mind was rather preposterous: Maybe a medical serial killer was on the loose in Bellevue Hospital and was plotting for Mitt to take the fall if he or she were to be discovered.

Yet almost the moment Mitt entertained the implausible idea of a medical serial killer being somehow involved, he dismissed it out of hand. In his mind such an unlikely explanation was evidence of his desperation. There was no way the idea made sense, as the patients were too disparate, with no association other than being Bellevue patients. If these deaths were related, it had to be by something else. But what, he had absolutely no inkling whatsoever.

"Excuse me!" a voice said. "Can I help you?"

Mitt took a breath as if coming out of a trance and turned to see a nurse enter the room carrying a fresh bedsheet. He'd noticed her earlier during the resuscitation attempt and now assumed she'd been originally assigned as the night nurse for Elena Aguilar.

"No, I was just leaving," Mitt said, finding his voice. But he didn't leave. Instead, he watched the nurse cover the body with the sheet and otherwise prepare the room for the arrival of housekeeping. "I was the surgical resident assigned to Ms. Aguilar and assisted with her surgery," Mitt added. "Tell me, do I need to fill out the death certificate or anything like that here in the ICU?" Since Critical Care had its own physicians and residents, Mitt wasn't sure.

"No, I'm certain that's being taken care of. I can assure you that everything is under control and you are free to go. Sorry about the outcome with your patient, but it had never looked good from the moment she arrived here in the ICU from the PACU."

"She never was able to breathe on her own after her surgery," Mitt said.

"So I heard," the nurse said. She had now moved to the head of the bed and was detaching the intravenous line.

After a further brief conversation to be personable, Mitt set out back through the ICU on his way to his on-call room. As he walked, he felt numb, still mulling over the disturbing issue of trying to explain six out of seven patient deaths, but falling short. Yet by the time he'd passed through the swinging doors out into the empty elevator lobby, he'd come to accept that the situation had to have been chance despite its very low probability. After all, he reasoned, in the course of human history there'd been many unexpected and surprising events of extraordinarily low probability that had nonetheless happened. He also found himself thinking about his one remaining patient, Diego Ortiz. Mitt was briefly tempted to stop by the fifteenth floor just to make certain he was okay but then changed his mind. The patient would undoubtedly be asleep, and Mitt would be understandably reluctant to wake him. Besides, Mitt would have heard from the nurses if everything wasn't copacetic.

As he pressed the elevator button his mind instantly switched from thinking about statistics to the horrid image of the ragtag surgerized people he'd been confronted by on his way to the ICU. He tried to prepare himself if there was a repeat, again wondering if he should or could ignore the apparitions as fanciful constructs and just pretend they weren't there. Mitt couldn't decide, nor did he have much chance because a moment later, the chime sounded at one of the elevator doors, indicating the car was about to arrive.

Quickly moving down to the appropriate spot, Mitt positioned himself about three feet back and tried to brace himself in case there was a repeat episode. As the door began to slide open, he tensed despite not having decided exactly what he was going to do if the hallucination of the disgusting crowd and rats returned. But then he let out a sigh of relief. The elevator was empty.

Within minutes, he was walking through the deserted on-call lounge area and, a moment later, keying his room. Once inside, he took off his jacket and draped it over the lone reading chair. Before collapsing on the bed, he needed to use the toilet.

Already fantasizing about what it was going to feel like to lie down and allow himself to fall asleep, he turned on his bathroom light with the wall switch, opened the bathroom door, and went to step inside. But then he froze with his foot suspended in the air and his hand still holding the doorknob. Inside the bathroom, hundreds of rats were emerging from the toilet and crawling all over one another, filling the entire floor, the shower, and even the sink with a seething mass of vermin.

With a shudder Mitt frantically yanked the door shut and reflexively stepped back, momentarily terrified that the rapidly expanding army of rats was about to break through and swarm the room. But then he quickly recovered. Remembering how his hallucinations had a tendency to disappear, he forced himself to step forward and re-grasp the bathroom door handle.

After a brief hesitation to build up his courage, he cracked open the door. Seeing no vermin whatsoever, he pushed the door completely open. As he'd hoped, the room was free of the disgusting creatures. Allowing himself to enter, and despite significant unease, he quickly relieved himself. As he did so, it occurred to him that the more exhausted he became, the more frequently the hallucinations seemed to be appearing. They were now even invading his personal space. Whatever that meant, he had no idea, but he didn't like it nor did it bode well for the future.

CHAPTER 22

Thursday, July 4, 2:02 A.M.

Like an exquisite torture, Mitt's phone again rang seemingly the
moment he'd fallen asleep. And on this occasion, it was particularly loud, as he'd put his phone on the bedside table instead
of leaving it in his white jacket pocket. With the jacket draped over
the reading chair and out of reach, he'd purposefully taken out the
phone to have it within his reach. His hope was that if he was called
yet again that night, he might be able to handle the issue remaining
recumbent, without even getting to his feet. The downside was that
it took a moment of frantic fumbling in the dark to find the damn
thing and bring it up to his ear. By then his pulse was up over a hundred beats per minute.

"Yes?" Mitt managed scratchily but urgently. He could feel his
pulse hammering away in his temples.

"Dr. Fuller, this is Sheila Ferguson. Your patient, Mr. Diego Ortiz,
is acting strangely."

"Oh?" Mitt questioned. Half expecting something significantly worse, his flight-or-fight reaction mellowed a few degrees. "Acting strangely" was a far cry from being informed his patient was having an arrest, like he'd been told about Latonya Walker and Elena Aguilar. "What exactly do you mean by 'acting strangely'?"

"He's agitated, speaking Spanish a million miles a minute, and waking up all his suite-mates. One of the nurses who speaks Spanish says he's not making any sense, which is strange because he'd been so calm all afternoon and evening according to the report when I came on duty. And he's been asleep the whole time I've been here."

"Are you suggesting we give him something like a tranquilizer or just double down on his sleep medication?" Mitt asked. He was trying to think of something specific to offer. The last thing he wanted to do was go to the fifteenth floor just because someone was anxious. "Or do you have something else in mind?"

"I think you need to come and see him," Sheila said. "My intuition tells me that his sudden change in attitude is worrisome. It's bizarre in my experience, and I don't like it."

"What about his incision?" Mitt asked. He was still fighting against the need to pay a visit to the patient in person. Mr. Ortiz's dressing was just a piece of paper tape, so any developing problems like bleeding or swelling would be immediately apparent.

"The incision looks fine. I don't think you understand. The man is beside himself. You need to come!" With that final comment, the nurse disconnected the line.

Reaching over in the darkness, Mitt turned on the bedside lamp. Then, for a minute filled with a slew of barely audible curse words, he lay back against the pillow and lamented his fate, wondering why he hadn't been attracted to a future in finance, following in his father's footsteps, where you could at least sleep through the night. But then, recognizing the inevitability of the situation, he put his feet over the side of the bed, sat up, and slipped on his loafers. Getting to his feet, he waited a few beats for his circulation to catch up to the changing demands. When it did, he picked up his white jacket and slipped it on.

As he walked through the on-call lounge, he didn't rush. It sounded to Mitt more like a behavioral problem than a medical problem, which the nurses should have been able to handle. At the same time, he did recognize that Diego Ortiz was his only living patient and that he should be inordinately thankful he wasn't being called for a cardiac arrest or some other medical emergency. In comparison, handling a behavioral issue should be relatively easy.

When Mitt arrived at the elevator lobby, he found himself speculating whether or not he would be seeing a hallucination in the elevator. The thought made him smile ironically at his nonchalance, and he wondered if it was because he'd become numb from lack of sleep, or because the increasing frequency was just making him expect one. Whatever the reason, when the elevator arrived and the door slid open to reveal an empty car, he merely shrugged and boarded without giving it much thought.

He felt the same way when the elevator discharged him on the fifteenth floor, wondering if he'd have to endure the bad smell or see the blond girl in the darkened hallway on the way to the west side of the building. As it happened, he didn't smell or see anything, but he did hear his patient screaming in Spanish while still in the hallway and not even abreast of the nurses' station.

Picking up his speed, Mitt hurried the rest of the way down to Mr. Ortiz's room. Inside, all the overhead lights were on. Mr. Ortiz's bed was next to the window with the curtain pulled out. All five of the other beds were occupied and all the patients were awake and wide-eyed, with their covers pulled up around their necks. There were two nurses trying to deal with Mr. Ortiz, who was sitting cross-legged in the middle of his bed and loudly carrying on in Spanish. At that moment the nurses were trying to take his blood pressure, but he was resisting. He was totally naked with his short dark hair spiked up wildly like a cartoon character who'd stuck his fingers into an electrical outlet. Another woman dressed in a white coat over a dark pants suit was near the head of the bed. Mitt later learned she was a Spanish translator who'd been called to assist. Her expression was one of confused alarm.

Already wondering what the hell he was going to do as the supposed "savior" doctor, Mitt approached the foot of Mr. Ortiz's bed, rapidly taking in the scene. The patient's body was flushed a bright crimson, and he was sweating profusely as if he'd just run a marathon. Even more alarming, his bloodshot eyes were bulging like they were going to pop out of his head. His IV was still in place, running into his left arm.

"My God!" Mitt croaked under his breath. As green as he was, he knew instantly this was no simple behavioral problem and that once again he was in way over his head. Aware that the patient had had thyroid surgery, Mitt surmised he was seeing something he'd only read about, namely acute thyrotoxicosis, or worse yet, a thyroid storm, which could be fatal. "Somebody please get Dr. Baker here stat!" Mitt yelled as he pushed up alongside the bed so that he could slap his hand against the patient's forehead. Mr. Ortiz fought back, but Mitt persisted, and when he got his hand against the man's forehead, his fears were corroborated in spades. The man was burning up.

"Tell Dr. Baker we've got a patient in thyroid storm!" Mitt yelled after the nurse who'd broken away to call her. At that moment, Mr. Ortiz suddenly stilled with a confused expression, but then blew out his cheeks before exploding with a bout of projectile vomiting. The episode was so forceful that most of the vomitus cleared the foot of the bed and sprayed out onto the floor.

"Good Lord," Sheila Ferguson, the other nurse, exclaimed. She'd just managed to dodge the icky deluge.

As if vomiting had exhausted him, Mr. Ortiz's eyes suddenly rolled back as much as they were able, and he collapsed onto the bed unconscious.

"What's the blood pressure?" Mitt demanded. Sheila already had a blood pressure cuff partially around the man's right arm and a stethoscope in her ears, as she'd been struggling to take his blood pressure even before Mitt arrived.

While Sheila repositioned the blood pressure cuff and blew it up, Mitt felt the man's pulse at the wrist and quickly guessed it was galloping along somewhere between 150 and 200 beats a minute. Concerned at the tachycardia, he looked across at Sheila as she removed the stethoscope's earpieces. "It's way up there," she said urgently. "It's in the neighborhood of 180 over 135!"

"Holy shit," Mitt murmured with alarm. Despite being a newbie, he intuitively knew that kind of blood pressure and pulse had to be cardiotoxic and unsustainable. With a sense of desperation, he looked back down at the patient, trying to come up with something he might do before Madison arrived. Although he knew he was in way, way over his head, he was sure there had to be something that could start to reverse the process. Then his mind latched onto an idea that he knew had to be important: Try to get the man's body temperature down. The sky-high body temperature had to be feeding both his pulse and his blood pressure and turning his body into a kind of pressure cooker.

"How can we cool him?" Mitt demanded frantically. "He's burning up."

"We have ice," Sheila said.

"Get it!" Mitt yelled. "Get as much as you can."

Sheila disappeared, leaving Mitt alone with Mr. Ortiz, who was like a piece of glowing charcoal, cooking all his internal organs. Seeing the stethoscope that Sheila had dropped on the bed after taking the blood pressure, Mitt reached across, put the earpieces in his ears, and listened to Mr. Ortiz's chest. The man was breathing fast and shallowly, and Mitt heard all sorts of additional sounds that he knew he wasn't supposed to hear, all of which made sense if the man was not long for this world. He was frying his lungs, as well as his kidneys, liver, and brain.

Sheila was back in a flash along with a number of other nurses. Word traveled quickly around the ward that an unusual problem had developed, and everyone was curious and willing to help if they could. Sheila had brought back a bucket of ice as well as a bunch of towels. Soon everyone was putting ice cubes onto towels, folding them up, and then placing them all over Mr. Ortiz's body. One of the nurses thought to bring a remote thermometer. When she used it, everyone was both shocked and horrified. It registered 111 degrees.

A few minutes later and to Mitt's utter relief, Madison showed up. "Do you really think it's a thyroid storm?" she demanded, out of breath, while pushing in against Mr. Ortiz's bed across from Mitt.

"It has to be," Mitt said. He described what he found when he first arrived. "The guy's literally burning up. Even with the ice packs, his remote temperature was over 110 a minute or two ago!"

"Whoa," Madison commented. "Yikes! That's not good. Anyway, I took your word about the diagnosis and immediately called for an emergency Internal Medicine consult. They should be here momentarily. I've never handled a thyroid storm. Have you?"

"Are you joking?" Mitt asked. He looked across at Madison to see if she was being serious.

"No, I'm not joking. I'm impressed you made the diagnosis and so quickly."

"When I saw him sweating and felt his temperature, I knew there weren't too many medical explanations for what was going on. Besides, he'd had thyroid surgery today, which I suppose is a giveaway. But then again, his past history is of hypothyroidism rather than hyperthyroidism, which is what a thyroid storm is. Well, to be honest, I can't explain it, but here we are. What are we going to do?"

"We're waiting for the medical guys," Madison said. "Handling a case of thyroid storm is out of my league. I'm assuming all is okay on the surgery end?"

"See for yourself," Mitt said. He lifted the ice-filled towel draped over Mr. Ortiz's neck to reveal the paper tape covering the incision.

"Well, at least that appears to be fine. What's his blood pressure?"

As soon as Madison asked the question, Sheila nudged her out of the way and retook the blood pressure. As she was busy doing that, Mitt felt the pulse. Another nurse lifted an ice pack and again used the remote thermometer.

"His pulse is still way up there around 150," Mitt said.

"Blood pressure about the same," Sheila said. "I'm getting about 170 over 130."

"Temperature still reads 108 despite the ice packs," the nurse with the thermometer said.

"Good grief," Madison said. "That's not good. Such numbers are incompatible with life, at least in my book."

At that moment a team of three on-call medical residents came rushing into the room out of breath. There were two males and one female, all dressed in whites. Many of the nurses who'd grouped around the bedside gave way to the newcomers.

"I'm Dr. Deion Phillips, senior medical resident on call," the lead resident said breathlessly as he pressed in against the bed. He was a strapping young Black man with imposing but restrained dreadlocks. "I've been told you have a case of thyroid storm. Is that true?"

"That's what we believe," Madison said. "He'd had a thyroidectomy this morning."

"Any idea of the BP, pulse, and temp?" the medical resident asked hurriedly as his eyes took in the entire scene, particularly noting the patient's dramatically flushed color, his copious perspiration, and the vomit on the floor. He snatched up Mr. Ortiz's wrist to feel the pulse.

Madison rattled off the results. "We'd just taken them before you arrived."

Dr. Phillips whistled in appreciation at hearing the numbers. "Whoa, this is one sick dude." Quickly pulling his stethoscope from around his neck, he listened briefly to Mr. Ortiz's chest, first his heart for a couple of beats and then his lung fields for several breaths. "Shit, man!" he said, straightening up. "This does look like a thyroid storm! Amazing! He's already got serious pulmonary edema! No wonder he's breathing so rapidly. Not good! Let's get an O_2 monitor on him and get an idea of his saturation. I bet it's in the toilet." He then turned to his compatriots, and in keeping with Bellevue being a teaching hospital, he asked them what they thought the guy needed and needed stat.

"Methylprednisolone, metoprolol, methimazole, and propranolol," the two more junior residents rattled off in unison.

"Right on!" Dr. Phillips said, flashing them a thumbs-up. Then he turned to Sheila Ferguson. "Do you have these meds here on the floor?"

"I'm sure we do," Sheila said. She immediately left to head down to the floor's pharmacy room.

Dr. Phillips stepped up to the head of the bed and checked what the IV bags contained. Only one had fluid remaining and it was saline. Grasping the tubing that snaked down into Mr. Ortiz's arm, he called out: "Who put in this IV line?"

"Anesthesia did this morning at the beginning of his surgery," Mitt responded.

"Okay, good," Dr. Phillips said. "That means we can count on it. Now, let's get more ice!" He handed off the empty bucket to one of the nurses, who quickly disappeared. At that moment, the patient's rapid, rather noisy breathing came to a sudden stop. Immediately Dr. Phillips again snatched up Mr. Ortiz's wrist to feel for a pulse. When he couldn't feel one, he let go and then tried again. When he still didn't feel one on the second attempt, he shouted: "Good God! We've got an arrest here! Someone call the resuscitation team and let's start CPR!"

Dr. Phillips himself climbed up onto the bed, kneeled next to Mr. Ortiz, and started the closed-chest massage. He also called out for an Ambu bag, and another nurse ran to get it. Next he questioned loudly if the resuscitation team had been called. One of the nurses responded positively. Dr. Phillips then told one of his fellow medical residents to get a syringe and draw some blood for stat electrolytes.

"Looks like we have been appropriately preempted," Madison said as she drew Mitt a few steps away from the bed to give everyone who was actively engaged more room. "This is another unique experience for me, and I have to give you credit for appropriately calling this one. Seems your diagnosis of a thyroid storm was right on. I'm impressed. I'm also impressed that you seem to be a magnet for what I'd call rather unique clinical cases, considering this thyroid storm and the aneurysm blowout on Monday night."

"Maybe I am a magnet," Mitt admitted. "This case is making me seriously paranoid."

"What on earth do you mean? How can a case of thyroid storm make you paranoid?"

"It's simple," Mitt said, looking back at the frantic activity around Mr. Ortiz. "This is another of my assigned cases. I assisted on his surgery this morning."

"Okay! A couple of cases of bad luck, but you certainly didn't have any role in causing the thyroid storm or the abdominal aorta bursting."

"It makes me paranoid because I'm getting the distinct feeling he's not going to make it. And if he doesn't, I'm batting a thousand."

"Batting a thousand?" Madison questioned, staring directly at Mitt with confusion. "What on earth are you talking about?"

"Maybe you don't know this yet, but Bianca Perez also had an arrest and died tonight in the ICU. And with Latonya Walker's earlier arrest, this fellow, Diego Ortiz, is my only living patient after three days of surgery, and I think you'll admit, he's on the edge of the precipice."

Madison's mouth slowly dropped open as her tired mind came to understand exactly what Mitt was saying. She shook her head in disbelief. "All right, I'm getting your point. That is big-time weird. How many patients are we talking about?"

"So far, six out of seven are dead," Mitt said. "And this one ain't looking so good."

At that moment the resuscitation team came flying into the room, pushing their noisy crash cart, forcing Madison and Mitt to move farther out of the way to give them access. Then after a quick conversation with Dr. Phillips to get the details, they took over the resuscitation from the medical residents. Mitt watched with interest, hoping against hope that such an experienced, first-class team might be successful on this attempt, but in his heart of hearts he knew it wasn't going to happen. Like it or not, he was going to be forced to deal with a shocking 100 percent mortality statistic.

For a few minutes, both Mitt and Madison silently watched the frantic activity as the resuscitation team determined that the heart was in ventricular fibrillation, and as soon as the defibrillator was set up and charged, it was used, but it wasn't successful. Before they tried again, they started epinephrine and lidocaine. They also intubated the patient and switched to 100 percent oxygen to improve his respiration, which was critical, as his saturation was below 50 percent.

"Okay," Madison said, looking back at Mitt to resume their conversation. "I can understand you feeling a little weird and maybe even victimized by chance with what's happened to the patients you've been arbitrarily assigned, but I certainly don't understand you feeling paranoid and thinking that it is any way your fault. To me that smacks of a bit of megalomania since you happen to be low man on the totem pole.

"Listen! You are obviously doing your best, and from my vantage point, you are doing extremely well. If anyone is guilty of setting you up, it would have to be Dr. Van Dyke because she's the one assigning the cases, but that's an absurd notion. So, for goodness' sake, ease up on yourself! I know the first days of residency are hard until you get the swing of things, but I can assure you that you are almost there. All of us have gone through what you are going through, namely a period of questioning our capacity to handle what is a very difficult job, especially when first starting out. Believe me, it's going to get better. In fact, it is going to get a lot better a lot quicker than you imagine from where you are standing right now. Trust me!"

"Thank you for the pep talk," Mitt said sincerely.

"You're welcome," Madison said emphatically. "With that said, what do you have in mind to do at the moment?"

Mitt looked at her questioningly. "What do you mean?"

"I mean, are you going to hang here while the medical guys and the resuscitation people try to handle this problem, which, like you said, is probably doomed to failure with a body temperature of 111 degrees? Me, I'm going to head back to the on-call room and get some shut-eye. Selfishly enough, I have a beach barbecue scheduled out on Long Island tomorrow, and I'd prefer not to be a zombie. Maybe you should do the same, meaning go get some sleep. They can always call you back to do the paperwork if need be. If perchance the medical people are successful, which I sincerely doubt, they'll be responsible for following the case and undoubtedly transferring the patient to the medical ICU."

For a moment, Mitt studied Madison's face. Her apparent insouciance in the face of Ortiz's real-time life-or-death struggle surprised him, and he wondered if after a single year he might develop the same nonchalance. From his present perspective, it seemed like a rather large transition. "I'm going to hang," he said finally, borrowing her particular word choice.

"Suit yourself," Madison said. "But do me a favor and skip any more ridiculous paranoid ideation. Deal?"

"I'll try," Mitt said.

"That's all I ask," Madison responded. She gave Mitt's shoulder a reassuring squeeze before heading for the hallway.

Mitt watched her leave before turning his attention back to the resuscitation attempt. Building up his courage, he advanced to the foot of the bed, avoiding the vomit on the floor. After multiple bouts of ventricular fibrillation and defibrillation, the resuscitation team was now dealing with no cardiac electrical activity at all. The monitor was monotonously tracing a straight line and nothing seemed to be working. Mitt wasn't surprised.

A few minutes later, the clearly frustrated resuscitation team leader happened to cast a distracted glance in Mitt's direction and then did a double take. "Hey," she said, staring directly into his face. "You look familiar. Haven't I seen you on several unsuccessful cases tonight?"

"You have," Mitt admitted. "One on this same floor and another in the ICU. I'm a first-year surgical resident, and unfortunately I assisted on all three of these patients' surgeries."

"Whoa!" she voiced. "All three? Well, thank you for thinking of us. We appreciate the business, but maybe it would be best if you slowed down a tad. Either that or at least provide us with a case that we can cheer about. The amount of cardiopulmonary failure involved with this one didn't give us much to work with. Without doubt it's the worst case of thyroid storm I've ever seen. Of course, that's not saying much since it is only my second case, but it's so much worse than the first to seem like a completely different physiological phenomenon."

"It was totally unexpected," Mitt said. "Especially since the patient's history was hypothyroid not hyper."

"I guess he'd been saving up," she said, attempting a bit of dry humor. Then turning back to the group, she called out: "That's it, guys! Hold up on everything. We're done here, and we need to move on!" She handed the defibrillator paddles she'd been holding back to the resident manning the machine.

Once again ignored, Mitt stepped away from the bed and watched the resuscitation team and the three on-call medical resident consults work together to start packing up the crash cart and other paraphernalia and clear the debris they'd caused. As they worked, there was a fair amount of general camaraderie and even joking despite the presence of the recently deceased. It surprised Mitt to a degree, just as Madison's indifference had, and he wondered again if he was destined to respond similarly when he became more acclimated to being a resident. At the moment, it seemed doubtful, but what did he know.

In a kind of daze, Mitt left the patient room and walked back to the nurses' station, where he requested and was given the appropriate death papers to fill out. Since he was having so much practice with the forms, it took him no time at all to get started, at least compared to his first experience. While he was working, he also made it a point to avoid thinking about his patient-mortality track record as Madison had recommended. Besides, he reasoned, he'd have plenty of time to mull it over during the upcoming holiday that was now just a few hours away.

Some forty minutes later Mitt had finished the forms and was about to head back to his on-call room when it popped into his mind to return to Diego Ortiz's room one more time to try to come to peace with the situation and deal with the residual feelings of guilt and responsibility that were hounding him despite Madison's lecture. As he headed back in that direction, he wondered if he was doing the right thing or just being masochistic. There was no way to know.

Entering the six-bedded room, he appreciated that it was now dark and peaceful, with Ortiz's suite-mates asleep after all the excitement. The curtain at Ortiz's bed was still pulled out and the reading light was still turned on. Mitt walked up along the bed's left side, looking down at Ortiz's sheet-covered corpse. He wasn't surprised the body was still there. He suspected its removal had to be held up until the death was cleared by the medical examiner.

Although he meant to lift the edge of the sheet to allow him to look directly at Diego Ortiz's face, his attention was drawn to the IV tubing that snaked out from beneath the sheet. What he was looking at was a second IV line joining the main one. He then looked up at the top of the IV pole where the IV source bags were hung, and as he did so, he recalled the anesthesiologist's description of having added a micro drip setup to allow a constant, slow infusion of synthetic thyroid hormone not only during the operation but also for days afterward until it was certain the patient could take the necessary medication by mouth.

"What the hell?" Mitt questioned softly as he looked at the micro drip's source. It was completely empty. To be absolutely certain, he even reached up and felt the empty plastic container. There was no doubt. That meant the patient had gotten many days' worth of thyroxine all at once, perhaps enough to cause a severe thyroid storm.

Suddenly Mitt was no longer tired as he stared off into the middle distance trying to reconcile what he'd just learned. How could this have happened? Was it a mechanical issue, meaning the micro drip malfunctioned, or had someone purposefully turned up the rate of flow? If so, was it done on purpose or by accident?

Mitt shook his head slowly, wondering what he should do—if anything—and whether he should mention what he'd learned to anyone. Madison was the first person who came to mind, but he certainly wasn't going to call at that moment and wake her up. Maybe there was a simple explanation for what he'd found that was just eluding him at the moment. Maybe one of the nurses mistakenly turned on the micro drip full blast when they turned off the main IV after Mr. Ortiz's death. Mitt shrugged. Maybe a lot of things, but it was something he would definitely need to think about, and at that time in the morning after such a busy day he wasn't at his rational best by any stretch of the imagination.

With an obviously false burst of energy, Mitt power walked out of

Diego Ortiz's room. The situation with the micro drip troubled him. As he turned into the night-darkened hallway, passing the nurses on his way to the elevator lobby, the thoughts about the micro drip were chased out of his mind by concern he might again be confronted by the blond girl, and he slowed his pace. The first time he'd seen her had been in similar circumstances of time and place. But to his relief, there was no blond girl, nor a crowd of surgerized people, nor any rats.

Suddenly Mitt found himself wondering if he might have some control over the hallucinations. Was it possible that the mental process of anticipating them could keep them at bay? He didn't know, but he thought the idea had to have a certain amount of validity since hallucinations were mental phenomena. At least that was how he explained their absence at the moment. Feeling somewhat reassured he wasn't going to be hounded, he quickened his step.

When he arrived at the elevator lobby, he checked his phone for the time. It was 3:20 in the morning, but as wide awake as he felt, he rashly decided to go to the cafeteria. He felt suddenly more hungry than tired. Besides, the last thing he wanted to do was go back to the on-call room and potentially end up staring at the ceiling in the dark with no answers to any of his current questions, particularly about all his patients dying. In a few hours, he was going to be off duty for the Fourth of July, meaning he could sleep all day if he so desired. On top of that, he'd heard through the hospital grapevine that the night shift's "midrats" were some of the best food of the day.

CHAPTER 23

The cafeteria was far more crowded in the wee hours of the morning than Mitt had expected. He even had to wait in a short line just to get a tray before joining the queue moving along in front of the steam table. And the food selection was impressive, as good or better than when he'd eaten his early-evening meal more than ten hours previously. On this occasion, he selected a roast chicken breast with mashed potatoes. At the drink dispenser, he was again very careful not to fill the cup to the brim, and when he placed it on his tray, he did so with great care. He wasn't about to suffer that ignominy again.

Thinking about the number of people required to keep a state-of-the-art, nearly thousand-bed modern hospital running 24/7 to provide general care as well as maintain sophisticated treatments, Mitt pondered the difference between the current, modern Bellevue Hospital and the old Bellevue Hospital almost two hundred years ago when his ancestor Dr. Homer Fuller had joined the staff. At that time, the hospital had just moved from its almshouse location in downtown Manhattan up to its current location on the East River and had assumed the name Bellevue, taking it from the title of the property itself. Here, in what was then countryside, it was able to expand, eventually reaching upward of two thousand beds. Still Mitt hazarded a guess that the night staff back in those days was probably minimal in sharp contrast with current day, meaning the patients most likely had had to fend for themselves.

Mitt had made it a point to read an engrossing history of the hospital during the early part of June before his residency started. He'd been particularly interested in the hundred-plus years his ancestors were on the staff. Because the field of medicine in those times, particularly when Homer was professionally active, had very few curative treatments to offer patients and much of what it did do—such as bloodletting and the use of powerful purgatives—only added to patients' distress, the hospital served more as a kind of storage bin for the sick, injured, and mentally compromised poor than as a treatment center. Mitt had even read that during pandemics, particularly those involving yellow fever, typhus, and cholera, there had sometimes been more than one patient per bed and even people sleeping on the floors and in the hallways. Because Mitt had some appreciation for the distressing symptoms of these infectious diseases, particularly propulsive diarrhea with cholera, it was difficult for him to imagine what the conditions had been like.

Holding his tray of food and drink, Mitt paused to let his eyes roam the room, hoping to see a couple of fellow residents to join. Maybe he could engage in conversation to avoid thinking about his patient situation, or more accurately, the lack thereof. But he didn't see a single person who fit the bill. The vast majority of diners were nurses, along with a fewer number of orderlies, janitors, and mainte-nance men. The level of chitchat was intense.

Abandoning the idea of finding residents, Mitt looked for a seat where he wouldn't be intrusive, yet most tables were either full or nearly so. Sensing he would not be able to add to any of the ongoing conversations, he opted for a table with only a single person that looked promising. It wasn't the best table in the house, as it was over near the soiled-dishes intake window, but he couldn't have cared less. The sole occupant was an older Black woman, dressed in a long white coat over a conservative dress, making Mitt believe she might be an attending. Why an attending would be eating in the middle of the night was a mystery, but he was encouraged, thinking that it would be easy to initiate a conversation just by asking her about her spe-cialty. As an added incentive, she was at the moment steadily and invitingly staring at him despite being in the middle of her meal.

As Mitt approached, he had a strange sensation he knew this woman, but from where or how he had no idea. His first thought was maybe he'd met her during the week of orientation before his resi-dency officially started, but if that was the case, he couldn't recall the circumstances. And then as he drew closer he felt his familiar tactile sensations, particularly on the back of his neck and along the inside of his arms. He sensed that this woman was sharing his thoughts and mirroring his, believing she was acquainted with him.

"Excuse me," Mitt said as he came abreast of the table. "Do you mind if I join you?"

"I was hoping you would," the woman said in a clear and relatively deep voice. She gestured to the seat opposite herself at the four-top table. Her expression was serious but welcoming, as if she had been expecting him.

As Mitt placed his tray down, he studied the woman, who was

continuing to stare back at him after putting down her flatware. Confirming his initial impression, up close she looked to be in her sixties, which seemed moderately aged from his twenty-three-year-old point of view. She was a healthy-looking woman with a broad face and smooth light brown skin with a sprinkling of freckles across her nose. Her hair appeared to be naturally gray, dense, and curly. Her eyes were dark and penetrating behind rather large and stylish red-rimmed glasses.

Feeling mildly uneasy under the woman's intense scrutiny, Mitt made a point of looking down at the chair as he pulled it out from the table and sat down. He then moved himself and the chair closer to the table in a hopping and rather noisy fashion. Only then did he again raise his eyes to look up at the woman. He was mildly unnerved to see that she was continuing to stare at him rather than returning to her meal. He noticed that she, too, had chosen the roast chicken and had only just begun to eat. He also noticed that she did not have a stethoscope in the pockets of her long white coat, making him wonder what her specialty was. Yet now that he was close to her, he sensed she was not a doctor, without knowing why.

"I don't mean to interrupt your meal," Mitt said. He gestured toward her plate. "Please! Continue."

"I will in a moment," she said. "I'm glad to meet you, Dr. Fuller. I was wondering how I was going to arrange it. I was very surprised to see you here at the cafeteria in the middle of the night shift but also happy. It makes my task of getting to talk with you so much easier."

Mildly shocked that she knew his name, he suddenly realized that he knew hers as well—Lashonda Scott—but without knowing how. "Did we meet last week during my orientation?"

"No," Lashonda said simply. "I'm never invited to meet the new residents, medical or surgical or any other specialty for that matter.

Myself and my team work behind the scenes throughout the hospital. The staff, including you residents, are only aware of our contribution when we slip up and don't do our job or we're busy elsewhere and you have to wait for us."

"What is your job?" Mitt asked. He was confused by knowing her name and yet not knowing her hospital function or why she felt the need to talk with him.

"I'm the night-shift housekeeping supervisor," Lashonda said. "My team cleans and prepares patient rooms throughout the medical center. It's a vitally important role that's underappreciated. You helped add to our workload very early Tuesday morning on the fifteenth floor. I saw you then, and I recognized exactly who you are when our eyes met. And knowing who you are meant that I very much needed to talk with you to ask you a particular question, which you might find shocking or bizarre or both."

"What do you mean, you recognized who I am?" Mitt questioned, totally confused. He had absolutely no idea what Lashonda was talking about. At the same time, he had to admit that as a doctor-in-training, he'd never given the role of housekeeping much thought or appreciation. Remembering the dramatic burst aneurysm and the god-awful mess it created, he had to give credit where credit was due.

"I recognized that your name is Michael Fuller and that you are directly related to all the Fullers who have been members of the Bellevue Hospital staff going back more than a hundred years. You, like me, Dr. Fuller, bear a special burden being here, and yours is more worrisome than mine because your relatives were doctors and not support staff."

For several disbelieving beats, Mitt stared at Lashonda with his mouth slightly ajar. She sounded more like a mental health professional than who she was. It seemed extraordinary and difficult to believe that the night-shift housekeeping supervisor not only knew him but was also aware of his legacy and on top of that wanted to talk with him. Thinking there was only one reasonable explanation, he asked: "Let me guess: Have you been talking with Dr. Harington about me, by any chance?"

"No, I haven't been talking with Dr. Harington," Lashonda said. "She knows a lot about Bellevue history, that is certainly true, and she and I have talked on multiple occasions about Bellevue's past. But her source of information, other than myself, are books and articles written by medical historians. As good as such sources can be, I have a better one."

"Oh?" Mitt questioned when Lashonda paused. "Like what exactly?"

"Family," Lashonda said. "Similar to you, I am a direct relative of Bellevue Hospital employees who were either in housekeeping like I am, and my mother was, or in maintenance, like my father and most of my previous relatives going back seven generations. My family has been very committed to Bellevue's cause over several hundred years, and I have to say, the relationship has been mutually supportive. My great-great-great-grandfather joined the Bellevue staff just about the same time as your relative Dr. Homer Fuller, but I know for a fact that they never got to know each other."

My God, Mitt thought. He couldn't believe that not only did Lashonda know he had Bellevue Hospital physician relatives, but she also knew their names. But how and why?

"I felt the need to ask you a strange question," Lashonda continued when Mitt didn't immediately respond about her family's close ties to Bellevue Hospital. "But I'm afraid there has to be a ground rule. If you answer my question in the negative, you can't then ask me why I felt obligated to ask it. If you answer yes, we will very much need to discuss the issue in more detail, particularly for your benefit. Do I have your agreement?"

"I suppose," Mitt said without enthusiasm. With his curiosity aroused, he didn't like having restrictions on this conversation. At the same time, he was keenly interested in hearing her question as he assumed it had something to do with his forebearers. Little did he know it was going to be much more shocking than that.

CHAPTER 24

Lashonda briefly glanced around the immediate area to make certain that no one was paying her and Mitt any heed. Quickly confirming that to be the case, she returned her attention to Mitt, and as she did so, she adjusted her eyeglasses, leaned forward, and lowered her voice, magnifying Mitt's burgeoning curiosity. He, too, leaned forward.

"Here's my question," she began. "Have you by any chance and particularly at night seen what I'll call an 'apparition' of a blond eight-year-old girl who looks a bit older? She'd be outfitted in a pale old-fashioned dress and carrying what looks like a surgical instrument."

The question so startled Mitt that his first response was to place both hands on the table palms-down as a way to support himself, as though he'd been buffeted by a shock wave. He'd wanted so much to talk to someone about his hallucinations, particularly Andrea or Madison or Dr. Van Dyke, or even Dr. Singleton, yet he'd been reluctant to do so from fear of the possible consequences. And here was someone asking him.

Mitt swallowed with a mild degree of difficulty, as his mouth had gone suddenly dry. While his mind went into overdrive, he stared back at this rather extraordinary housekeeping supervisor, who was not only preternaturally poised, but also seemed clairvoyant. How did she know what she knew about his ancestry, and even more astounding, how did she guess he'd been seeing a young blond girl?

"You seem shocked," Lashonda said when Mitt remained silent and frozen like a deer caught in headlights. "Such a response suggests to me that you have indeed seen this particular phantasm, because if you hadn't, I believe you would have responded with simple surprise and a 'no' rather than with the confusion you are projecting. Am I correct?"

"Yes, you are correct. I've seen that hallucination," Mitt said hesitantly. It was difficult to find his voice.

"So, I would imagine that your first question will be how it is that I even suspected you might have seen this specter. Am I correct?"

"Yes," he managed again.

"Before I answer your question let me explain something to you that I realized when our eyes briefly met up on the fifteenth floor. You and I share certain unique traits and abilities, which can be seen as either a burden or a benefit depending on your point of view. As young as you are, you might not totally appreciate your unique capabilities, but I would be shocked if you didn't have some idea. I know I didn't fully recognize mine until I was well into my thirties, and even then it took someone else similarly endowed to clue me in, which I mean to do to you. Are you with me?"

"I guess," Mitt said with continued confusion.

"What I imagine is that you are already aware you can occasionally predict the future, not all the time, but at least often enough to recognize it when it happens. Am I correct?"

Mitt merely nodded. Once again, he was taken aback by Lashonda's insight. He'd never discussed his prognostic abilities with anyone.

"And more important, you can sense now and then what people are generally thinking. Or at least you have an idea of what they are thinking, and when it happens you experience a kind of tingling. Is this true?"

"It is true."

"And what do you sense I'm thinking right now?"

"I sense that you're worried I am somehow in danger."

"Bravo! Exactly. And that is true, which is my real motivation for wanting to talk with you. Now, the answer to your question is simple. I, too, see her, not often but often enough. I see other visions, too, but most consistently the girl."

Mitt sat up straighter in his chair. It seemed incredible! He'd been wondering if anyone else had seen the girl and now he knew. But then the problem was that if she could also see the child, could he still call it a hallucination? From his general understanding, a hallucination was a product of an individual's mind and certainly not the product of several minds.

"Do you think we are seeing the same girl?" Mitt asked.

"Without doubt," Lashonda said with absolute assuredness. "You didn't challenge any of my descriptions."

"True," Mitt admitted. She had a point.

"And I could describe the dress with even more accuracy if it will convince you. I said an old-fashioned dress. What I meant is what they used to call a shirtwaist dress, with puffy sleeves and a Peter Pan collar."

"I'm not sure what a Peter Pan collar is."

"It's a flat collar, fairly broad, mostly with rounded ends. It's still used today but it was even more common back in the 1940s, as I learned when I looked it up."

"That sounds like what I remember, although I have to admit, each time I've seen her I wasn't so concerned about her dress. I was completely taken aback by seeing her at all."

"That's understandable. The first time I saw her, I'm sure I didn't notice much detail. But what about the surgical instrument? It's a critical observation."

"I did notice the instrument," Mitt said. "In fact, she pointed it at me."

"She actually pointed it at you? Are you sure?"

"I don't know if I'm sure. That was my impression at the time," Mitt said with a shrug. "But maybe she was just trying to show it to me. How can I know? Again, I was overwhelmed by just seeing her. I'm sure there were other details that I missed entirely from shock. What's impressed me the times I've seen her is how consistent the apparition is."

"The reason she is consistent is that she is a real ghost."

"What on earth do you mean, a 'real ghost'? Isn't that an oxy-moron?"

"No, I don't think so," Lashonda said with conviction. "A 'real ghost' is the soul or spirit of a specific dead person, not just an illusory likeness of a human being."

"Let me understand you," Mitt said, trying to organize his thoughts. "So you believe this blond girl apparition was a living, breathing person at one time?"

"I don't just believe it, I know it," Lashonda said. But then she looked down at Mitt's plate and nodded toward it. "I see you are not eating. I don't mean to interrupt your meal."

Mitt glanced down at his roast chicken. He'd almost forgotten it was there.

"Please eat!" Lashonda said. "You must be hungry or you wouldn't be here. We can continue our discussion while you do, as I have a lot more that I need to say to you."

"All right," Mitt said. He was flustered but wanted to be agreeable, as he was desperate to hear more. "But you aren't eating, either. I'll eat if you eat."

"Fair enough," Lashonda said.

They both picked up their respective knives and forks and began to eat. While Mitt did so, he found himself overwhelmed by everything Lashonda had already said and was brimming with questions, most important about the blond girl having been a real person and not just a random phantasm. After just a couple of bites, which he swallowed with observable difficulty, he put his utensils down and sat back in his chair.

"I'm not as hungry as I thought I was," he said. "Would you mind if we continued our discussion?"

"Not at all! Whatever suits you, but I'm going to continue to eat if that's okay."

"Of course," Mitt said. "But before we get back to it, let me ask you a personal question. I don't mean to sound condescending, so I apologize if I do, but by your manner of speaking and word choice, you sound like a mental health professional rather than a housekeeping supervisor. Are you both?"

Lashonda smiled as she took a bite of chicken and chewed it thoughtfully. "I don't think of your question as condescending in the slightest. Thanks to both my parents being long-term employees of Bellevue Hospital, I was able to go to City College on scholarship. My major was psychology, which I enjoyed and undoubtedly colors my speech. After finishing college, I still followed my family's tradition and came back here to work at Bellevue Hospital. My mother had been the night-shift housekeeping supervisor for many years. I ended up taking over from her, bless her soul."

"Does that mean she is no longer with us?"

"It does. She passed away four years ago."

"I'm sorry."

"Thank you, but life goes on."

"Which brings me back to the blond girl," Mitt said. "You said that you know she was a real person. How do you know that?"

"Not only do I know she was a real person, I even know what her name was. It was Charlene Wagner."

Once again, Lashonda had startled Mitt enough to cause him to lose his train of thought. He'd had in mind to challenge whatever it was that she was going to say, never suspecting she'd come up with an actual name.

"Not only do I know her name, but I also know the day she died as well as the circumstance. The date was November 15, 1949."

"Okay," Mitt said as an appeasement, holding up his hands in a surrendering gesture while struggling to organize his thoughts yet again. Every time he had in mind that there was no way that Lashonda could surprise him any more than she already had, she went ahead and did, and the surprises seemed to be coming with increasing frequency. "How on earth do you know all that?" he managed, slowly enunciating each word.

"Before I go into an explanation of how, I want to go back to the issue of the special abilities you and I and a few other people command, namely being able on occasion to predict the future and sense what other people are thinking. Are you okay with that?"

"I suppose," Mitt said. "But you are killing me with suspense."

"I would prefer you use a different metaphor."

"Whatever," Mitt said with mild irritation. It seemed to him she was dragging out their conversation unnecessarily.

"Having the abilities I just named is in reality a function of another trait, which I sense you might not be aware you possess. You, my friend, are a living, breathing 'portal.' Are you familiar with the term?"

"In the sense of being a metaphorical gateway?" Mitt stared at his new acquaintance, wondering if she was now being serious or whether she was intellectually toying with him.

"Yes, exactly. A gateway into what we call another dimension for lack of any better term. Some people have mistakenly assumed portals are only physical objects such as an old mirror or an old house and the like. Such places and objects can be portals, there's no doubt, and I have definitely experienced one such portal. But more to the point, certain people can be portals, too, like you and me. The fact that you are a portal is the reason you are seeing the blond girl who haunts these Bellevue Hospital buildings. You, my friend, are a gateway to the paranormal."

Mitt continued to study Lashonda's face, thinking that maybe she was going to smile and say that she was only teasing. But she didn't. She was staring back at him with a serious expression, waiting for his reply.

"I don't know what to say," Mitt offered at length.

"You don't have to say anything," Lashonda said. "But it's a reality that you need to recognize so you will take to heart what I am ultimately going to tell you. Before I do, let's revisit the instrument that Charlene pointed at you. You saw it as a surgical instrument, correct?"

"That was my impression," Mitt agreed. "But I wasn't sure."

"I'm convinced it is a surgical instrument, and each time I've seen

Charlene, she's always carrying it. Although she's never pointed it at me, I naturally concluded it had to have some significance, wouldn't you agree?"

"I suppose," Mitt said.

"When I looked into it with the unique sources I have available, I came to the conclusion that it's an outdated instrument called an 'orbital-lobotomy knife,' or an 'orbitoclast,' which resembles an old-fashioned ice pick but with a slightly flattened tip. It was designed by a mid-nineteenth-century physician named Walter Freeman. He was a staunch advocate of lobotomies and tried to popularize the procedure by creating a way for it to be done at the bedside rather than requiring a full operating room and anesthesia."

The moment Lashonda mentioned the word *lobotomy*, Mitt's mind flashed back to the Pendleton article, where he'd learned that Clarence Fuller had done as many as forty lobotomies on children. With the remembrance came the concern that maybe Clarence had performed a lobotomy on Charlene Wagner.

"I can tell what you are thinking," Lashonda said. "And I'm afraid that you are entirely correct. Your ancestor Dr. Clarence Fuller attempted to do a bedside lobotomy on Charlene, but it went horribly wrong, killing her."

"Good God," Mitt managed. In his mind's eye he could see Charlene's scornful expression when looking at him. And if everything that Lashonda was saying was true, he could understand why. "I did notice what appeared to be bloodstains on the front of her dress."

"Yes, I've noticed that as well, and they're there for good reason. The orbitoclast inadvertently cut through a major brain artery, causing a massive fatal stroke. Charlene was obviously wearing that particular dress when she was, in a sense, murdered."

Mitt took a deep breath and let it out noisily. He spread his hands. "I don't know what to say."

"You don't have to say anything at the moment," Lashonda said. "But you must give what we have been talking about some very serious thought. The reality, I'm afraid, is that Bellevue Hospital might not be where you should do your training as a surgeon."

"What?" Mitt questioned with sudden angst and even some anger. "Why?"

"Simply because I believe you are in danger of retribution as a direct descendant of the previous Dr. Fullers, all of whom were responsible for many deaths and measureless suffering, which unfortunately accompanied their positive contributions. Now, it is not that I believe the ghosts of Bellevue, of which there are countless numbers, can do you harm directly, as they cannot. But they can effect change through inanimate objects and generally harass you in that fashion. Have you noticed anything that might qualify in that realm during these few days you've been here?"

Once again, Mitt was back to staring at Lashonda, again clearly taken aback by what she had just said. What had immediately come to his mind were the curious forceps incidents in the operating room, the popping of Benito Suárez's sutures, and even the spilled drink episode in the cafeteria, and he wondered if they might qualify. But then he had an even scarier thought that made his heart metaphorically skip a beat. What if the deaths of his patients were due to transcendental, inanimate workings?

"I can tell that I have once again struck a chord with your emotions, and I'm getting the message that there have been other deaths. I'm sorry to learn that. Am I sensing that correctly?"

"Yes, all my patients," Mitt said reluctantly. He'd worried that he bore some responsibility, but he'd kept dismissing the idea. Now, from what Lashonda was saying, it came back in a rush. If his patients had been assigned to Andrea instead of to him, would they still be alive and well? The possibility alone, true or not, filled him with anguish.

"Was there anything about the deaths that might suggest a paranormal influence?"

"Yes, I'm afraid so," Mitt said without hesitation. "Three of my patients died tonight, and when I think about them, I have to say there was something I'd felt was strange involving all three. Particularly with the last patient, who suffered a thyroid storm just hours ago after having his thyroid removed yesterday morning."

"A thyroid storm? What is that?"

"It's when a person's metabolism goes into overdrive by too much stimulus. The point I want to make is that there was an intravenous source of thyroid hormone set up to give a slow drip over as many days as needed until he could take the medication by mouth. After he died, I happened to notice that the drip had somehow been opened such that the entire container was empty, meaning he'd gotten perhaps a week's worth of thyroid hormone all at once."

"I think I understand what you are saying, and yes, I'd say that could definitely fall in the paranormal realm. What about the other two?"

"Both were somewhat similar. Both patients were also on intravenous support and both experienced sudden severe electrolyte abnormalities that affected their heart function, leading to their deaths."

"How many patients have you been assigned so far?"

"Seven total."

"And they have all died?"

"Unfortunately, yes."

"In my mind, the chances of seven out of seven patients dying under questionable circumstances is a rather convincing argument for the point I'm trying to make here. Do you not see it in those terms?"

"I suppose I do," Mitt reluctantly agreed. He'd been arguing the same point with himself.

"Earlier when I asked you if you'd seen the blond girl, you answered yes, but you used the term 'hallucination.' I prefer 'ghost' or 'specter' or 'phantasm,' as they are more substantive to me. A hallucination is a product of the mind, so I can't see your hallucinations and vice versa. But be that as it may, have you had other 'hallucinations' over the few days you have been a resident?"

"I have," Mitt said. "I've seen a pitiful crowd of post-surgical patients with many of the people carrying amputated limbs or excised organs. I've also seen hordes of rats. On top of that, I've also been assaulted with some of the worst odors I've ever confronted as well as the sounds of distant cries of anguish."

"I'm not surprised. I would have guessed as much. Bellevue's ghosts have a lot to complain about. During its long history it was described as the place where the groans of the dying met the stink of disease. The hospital did serve the poor of New York, but at the unimaginable cost of overcrowding and lack of sanitation. Its patients were also considered fair game for doctors, particularly surgeons, to hone their skills and also try whatever their imagination might suggest, which nowadays is considered a major ethical lapse. What this all underlines is that Bellevue Hospital and you are uniquely mismatched because of your direct link to Homer Fuller, Otto Fuller, Benjamin Fuller, and Clarence Fuller. I hope you will give serious thought to everything I have said tonight. Obviously, I am not going anywhere, as Bellevue is my life, so if you want to talk to me some more or have some specific questions, just call the main housekeeping number anytime, day or night. Between eleven P.M. and seven A.M. I will answer. Otherwise just leave a message for me, and I will get back to you. My days off this week will be Sunday and Monday, so you can put that in your memory bank."

"Am I being dismissed?" Mitt asked.

"Heavens no," Lashonda said. "I just assumed you'd want to leave since it appears that you don't want to eat any more."

"I lost my appetite," Mitt said. "My mind is racing around in circles. I don't quite know what to think. I've wanted to share the phantasms, the noxious odor, the pitiful, distant cries, with someone but I've been reluctant. I was afraid of what people would think of me. Hell, I didn't even know what to think of myself. And then, out of the blue you not only bring them up but provide an explanation.

"To be entirely honest, I've never given the supernatural much thought. Well, that's not true. What I mean to say is that I've never given the supernatural much credence. I think of myself as scientifically oriented, yet everything that you have said makes sense, and I'm blown away by it. Still, I don't know quite what to think."

"I'm glad you're being open with me. To be equally honest, I wrestled with the idea of talking with you or not, which is why I didn't approach you Tuesday morning when our eyes met and I realized we shared the gift or burden of being portals. My concern was that you wouldn't believe me or, worse, would think I was deranged and possibly cause me trouble with the administration. I hadn't really decided whether to approach you or not until you unexpectedly showed up here at the cafeteria during my middle-of-the-night lunch break. The moment I saw you I decided it was fate. If you had not come to my table, I would have come to yours."

"It certainly sounds as if fate played a significant role," Mitt said. "After my patient with the thyroid storm died, I was suddenly not tired, which is weird because of how little sleep I've had all this week. Instead, I decided I was hungry, which was also weird. I can't remember that ever happening to me before."

"It seems destiny was involved," Lashonda agreed. She then paused before adding: "Is there anything specific you'd like to ask me before we part?"

"Actually, there is," Mitt said. "When you described in detail the instrument Charlene Wagner apparently holds every time she appears, you said you learned it from your unique sources. What did you mean by that?"

Lashonda's eyes did a quick detour around the room before settling back on Mitt. She leaned forward again and lowered her voice. "I have access to a cache of patient records, thanks to my mother, bless her soul, that have not seen the light of day and probably never will, at least in my lifetime."

"What kind of patient records?" Mitt asked. Sensing Lashonda's interest in being secretive, he also leaned forward. His curiosity was piqued.

"Not very flattering ones," Lashonda said. "At least that is my take. Apparently they were purposefully gathered and then hidden away by your ancestor Dr. Clarence Fuller. Of the ones I've looked at, they include a lot of the records of unsuccessful or outlandish medical and surgical procedures carried out over several hundred years at the whim of the involved doctors, including a number performed by your ancestors. More important and related to Charlene Wagner, they include most of Dr. Clarence Fuller's lobotomy records. He did a lot more lobotomies than what has generally been attributed to him, which apparently he didn't want the world to know after the procedure fell out of favor."

Suddenly Lashonda paused and for a few beats stared directly at Mitt. "I'm sorry. Is this upsetting for you to hear?"

"Moderately," Mitt admitted. He was shocked and horrified to hear about Clarence. It was so contrary to what he'd been raised to believe, yet it was consistent with what he'd read in the Pendleton paper.

"Do you want to hear more, or have you heard enough?"

"Definitely I want to hear more. Please!"

"I read through many of Dr. Clarence Fuller's records, and doing so, I learned that he'd lobotomized quite a few young patients where the indication was marginal. In Charlene's case, although she was for a time housed on the 'distressed ward'—the locked ward, where restraints were occasionally needed—her diagnosis was 'age-related behavioral disorder' and certainly not something more serious. Such a diagnosis, which is a condition children often outgrow, makes her death that much more tragic. It also makes the decision to lobotomize her an inexcusable mistake."

"I would like to see these records personally," Mitt said. "Can you get them for me? Or at least some of them, particularly records of my ancestors?"

"I'm sorry, but that's not possible."

"Oh?" Mitt questioned with obvious disappointment. "Why not?"

"Because of a promise I made to my mother."

"How is your mother involved?" Mitt asked with confusion. Lashonda's evocation of her late mother might have been the absolute last thing he expected.

"Well, it's a rather long story, and it most definitely has something to do with how long our family has been associated with Bellevue Hospital. Are you sure you want to hear it?"

"Absolutely," Mitt said.

"The records we're talking about have been hidden away for more than a half century, most likely initiated by your ancestor Dr. Clarence Fuller's wish to hide his advocacy of lobotomy. But it became more than that. He'd also gathered other records he wanted to hide, some of your earlier ancestors' files as well as their surgeon colleagues', presumably because their operative survival rate was so low, and it reflected badly on them, as well as on the hospital. At least this is my educated guess. Before Clarence Fuller retired back in 1975, he turned the care of this cache of hospital records over to one of the hospital hospitality administrators, who happened to be my mother's boss. Before this administrator could decide what to do with them, as they were still in your ancestor's vacated office, they were inadvertently found by an NYU researcher named Robert Pendleton, who then threatened to publish them."

Mitt straightened upon hearing the name *Robert Pendleton*. It seemed that Pendleton's sources and Lashonda's were one and the same, which only fanned his interest.

"Somehow the hospital administrator thwarted the publication of the records, but the episode underlined the need to deal with them, at least in the short term. To do so, he turned to my mother with whom he was particularly close. He asked her to hide them along with a promise she would never give them to anyone, ever."

"Why on earth did a hospital administrator turn to your mother?"

"Exactly why, I have no idea other than their mutual respect. I guess there was some confusion about what to do with them, as they were probably seen as a potential public relations nightmare, although I suppose he was reluctant to take the responsibility of destroying

them. Ultimately it was also a reflection of the long relationship between my family and the hospital administration, particularly this
specific administrator."

"Where did she hide them? Can you tell me that?"

"Of course. She hid them in the housekeeping storeroom with all
the cleaning supplies in the basement of the Psychopathic Hospital.
At that time the Psychopathic Hospital was still very much in use."

"You mean the Bellevue Psychiatric Hospital, the one that's still
standing essentially empty next door?"

"Yes. And the entire trove of records is still there. They have been
there since 1975, when your ancestor retired. It was my mother who
moved them out of his office during the night. At that time, she was
the night-shift housekeeping supervisor just like I am today."

"And these records have never been moved?"

"Only once, and that was when Hurricane Sandy happened. It
was then that my mother told me about them. Up until that moment,
I had no idea of their existence. She asked me to help her move them
to avoid the flooding, which we did. At that time, she made me promise I would honor her pledge to leave them where they were and not
to give them to anyone unless told by the administration to do otherwise. She was a woman of her word, as am I."

"What about the hospital administrator that originally asked her
to hide them? Is he still on the hospital staff?"

"Oh no, he's long gone. He passed away before my mother."

"And you still feel obligated to honor your mother's vow?"

"Of course. Vows are not time dependent."

"When you moved the records for the hurricane, where did you
take them?"

"Just a few floors up, locking them in an empty hospitality office
on the third floor."

"Are they still there?"

"No. When we could, maybe a month later, we returned them down to the basement. It was my mother's idea. They'd been safe there since she'd hidden them, and she felt strongly they should be returned."

"Does anyone in administration today know about their existence?"

"I don't have any idea. I only found out about them just hours before the hurricane in 2012. After we returned them to their original hiding place, we never talked about them again. I had the distinct feeling my mother wished to leave the subject alone, so I never brought it up."

"If someone was to go into the old psychiatric building today, might they stumble across these records?" The more he thought about this mysterious stash, the more he wanted to read through them and find out for certain what kind of doctors his relatives had been and whether they warranted the kudos extended to them by his family. And equally as important, especially if he was a "portal" as Lashonda suggested, Mitt wanted to know whether any Bellevue paranormal beings might have reason to harass him, which unfortunately seemed to be the case. What ultimately convinced him he had to see these records was the disturbing death of all seven of his assigned patients, particularly the most recent death of Diego Ortiz. Such a bevy of strange occurrences lent credence to everything Lashonda was saying, most significantly the possibility that Bellevue was not where he should be for his surgical training.

"It's doubtful someone would come across them unless they were specifically looking for them," Lashonda was saying. "First of all, there'd be no reason for anyone to suspect they are there, as the building had been emptied of all records years ago even though a lot of its old furniture and outdated equipment are still there. Besides,

access to the building itself is restricted other than to the small portion that is being used as a homeless shelter. Even getting into the
main portion of the building isn't easy, as it is secured under lock and
key, as you can imagine, especially of late with the concern raised
about the enormous amount of toxic asbestos used in its construction. And the basement is probably the last place someone would go.
Like any basement, it is hardly inviting. So, to answer your question,
I'd have to say no."

"What about the building being repurposed and renovated? I
know it hasn't happened yet, but that can't go on forever. Wouldn't it
be better to move the documents to a safer location to honor your
commitment to your mother? I'm certain between the two of us, we
could find another place, say in a housekeeping storage area of your
choosing here in the high-rise." Mitt knew his motive was devious,
but he had in mind to offer to help Lashonda move the records to a
new location, which would give him access.

"It's passed through my mind," Lashonda admitted. "But the
building seems to have a remarkable staying power, including avoiding a planned conversion into a luxury hotel and medical conference
center just two or three years ago."

"I'd heard something about that idea," Mitt said. "It is prime real
estate right here in the middle of hospital row. Doesn't the risk support my idea of moving the records?"

"Yes and no," Lashonda said. "The hotel conversion was a good
idea, and most everyone agreed it was a good idea. So why didn't it
happen?"

"I certainly don't know why, but it sounds to me that you have an
idea."

"I do indeed," Lashonda said. "It's the last major building of the
old Bellevue Hospital complex left standing. All the others have seen

the wrecking ball to make way for the high-rise. What that has meant is that all the ghosts, demons, and phantoms born out of the hospital's three-hundred-year history have moved into the old psychiatric building to take up permanent residence, and they are obviously a force to be reckoned with. I wouldn't have said this to anyone else, but I'll say it to you. I believe they have succeeded in thwarting past proposals."

Again, Mitt studied Lashonda's face for a few beats, looking for a slight smile or some other indication that she was teasing him. But he saw no trace. It was obvious she was being perfectly serious. Since he had been specifically questioning the building's abandoned state whenever he'd passed the structure and had come up with zero explanation, he felt he had to give the paranormal idea significant weight.

"It's my feeling that the records couldn't be in a safer place than where they currently are," Lashonda said. "If that changes in the future, I'll make adjustments."

Mitt nodded, still staring at Lashonda while his mind wrestled with how he was going to manage to see these hidden records. If worse came to worst, he considered just trying to break into the place and searching the basement that afternoon when he was off for the July 4 holiday. But he could think of lots of reasons why that was a bad idea, starting with possibly being caught by hospital security, who undoubtedly kept the building under surveillance. Besides, the basement was obviously a huge space with lots of nooks and crannies. That meant he could make the risky effort of getting into the building and never find the records. Then, all at once, he had another, better idea.

"I really need to see some of these records if you want me to take all this seriously," Mitt said, deciding suddenly to be completely up-front. "Specifically, I would like to see Charlene Wagner's record."

"I'm sorry, but as I already mentioned, I can't give them to you, even one record."

"Okay, I understand," Mitt said. "And I respect your promise to your mother. What I'd like to propose is that you simply show me the record and let me read it."

"You mean we both go into the psychiatric building? You'd be willing to do that?"

"I would," Mitt said. "It's not that I doubt what you are saying because I don't—I believe you. At the same time, what you are telling me seriously challenges what I've believed all my life. Seeing this record and holding it in my hand will go a long way toward convincing me about the role of my ancestors and the existence of the paranormal. I hope you understand. I need this kind of corroboration."

"You're willing to go in there despite what I told you about all the Bellevue ghosts from its three-hundred-year history pretty much having taken over the building?"

"What are you implying?" Mitt asked. "Is that where you've seen apparitions like I've described?"

"Absolutely," Lashonda said. "I see them every time I've gone in there to check on the papers and particularly when my mother and I moved them because of the hurricane."

"Did your mother see them as well?"

"No, she didn't. She wasn't a portal."

"But they didn't bother you or your mother?"

"No, they had no cause with us. Our family has only been service personnel."

"I think I can deal with seeing them," Mitt said. "I've almost gotten accustomed to it."

"If we were to make such a visit, it would have to be at night," Lashonda said, warming to the idea if it was going to help Mitt understand his peril. "Whenever I've gone inside, it was always at night. During the day hospital security keeps an eye on the building and makes regular tours around the grounds. As far as I know, the last time someone was allowed in during the day was when a mandatory test for asbestos was ordered by the city."

"I'm fine with going in at night," Mitt said. "In fact, why not tonight? Why not right now and get it over with? Do you have the key or keys with you?"

"No, but they are in my office," Lashonda said as she glanced at her watch to check the time.

"What do you say?"

"How long would you need for us to be there?"

"Not long. How many pages is Charlene's record?"

"Just two pages. The earlier records going back into the early nineteenth century are even shorter. Most of those are a single page or just a couple of paragraphs. Back then recordkeeping was hardly what it is now."

"Ten to fifteen minutes would probably be adequate," Mitt said. "I'd like to see her record and maybe a few of my earlier ancestors'." Once he knew exactly where the records were, he figured, he could return at some point in the near future and do them justice.

"All right, why not!" Lashonda said, suddenly making up her mind. "It is important for you to understand the seriousness of what is happening, especially considering the deaths of your seven patients. That can't have been by chance, and unfortunately, it's bound to continue. And, to be honest, I'm seriously worried about your own safety. Bellevue Hospital is simply not where you should be, for everyone concerned."

"I'm getting that message," Mitt agreed.

"Let me first check with the operator to make sure there isn't a housekeeping issue brewing." Lashonda picked up her phone, which was lying on the table next to her plate. Her conversation with the operator was rapid and to the point. She quickly ascertained there were no current problems requiring her presence.

"All is quiet," she said, pocketing her phone. "I'll get the necessary keys and a couple of flashlights from my office. There's no power in most of the psychiatric building, just the tiny section being used as the homeless shelter. I'll meet you downstairs in the elevator lobby. We'll get over there by going out through the laundry building. Okay?"

"Okay," Mitt said. "I trust that you know the way."

"I should hope so, after all these years. My department did the housekeeping in the psychiatric building until all the patients were moved over here to the high-rise in 1984."

They both lifted their trays with their mostly uneaten food and headed toward the soiled-dishes window. No one in the cafeteria paid them any heed as they departed together.

CHAPTER 25

Thursday, July 4, 4:32 A.M.

Mitt was waiting on the first floor when Lashonda got off the elevator. She was carrying a relatively large, nondescript brown paper bag. She motioned for Mitt to follow her. As befitting the city that never sleeps, the first floor of the Bellevue Hospital was more crowded than he expected, which he imagined had mostly to do with the emergency room. Even the outpatient pharmacy was open although no one was currently at its counter.

"Just follow me," Lashonda said as she waved over her shoulder before heading first west, then north. To keep up, Mitt had to pick up speed.

"You are motivated," Mitt said once they were on their own in an otherwise empty corridor.

"I want to get this over with well before the shift change," she said without slowing her pace. "And as fast as possible because either one of us could get called at any minute."

Mitt nodded to acknowledge she was correct. Although there was a possibility he could be called, he felt justified in doing what he was doing because he wasn't leaving the hospital grounds, and it was hospital business in a way. Besides, he trusted that if there was a real emergency and not something like a falling-out-of-bed episode, Madison would be called.

They passed through the laundry building and then out into the night. Once again, Mitt was mildly taken aback by the warm sultriness of the night air after spending nearly twenty-four hours in the hospital air-conditioning. But he wasn't surprised, knowing full well that New York City acted like an enormous heat sink composed of millions upon millions of tons of concrete and macadam that absorbed all the summer sunlight energy during the day and then gave it off continuously during the night.

They crossed a hospital service road that at one time in the distant past had been part of East 28th Street and skirted another mostly dark building. "What's in the bag?" Mitt called ahead toward Lashonda. He was curious and had been meaning to ask, but she was not slowing to make it easy. "Flashlights?"

"Yes," she said without slowing. "There are security cameras all over the entire first floor of the hospital, including the outpatient atrium, that are watched day and night by the Security people. I didn't want to advertise that we were heading someplace where we'd need flashlights."

"Good point," Mitt said. A moment later, upon reaching the 29th Street extension, the old Bellevue Psychiatric Hospital loomed ahead, soaring up into the night sky like a totally dark, forgotten landmark from the past. From this vantage point, it was strikingly huge. The sight of it caused Mitt to catch his breath, especially since the instant its ten stories came into view, he simultaneously experienced a particularly strong flash of the same paresthesias he'd felt early that

Monday morning when he'd passed the structure on his way to start his residency and again when he headed home Tuesday evening. Then, as now, the tingling sensations evoked an involuntary shudder.

Mitt sensed that the sudden sighting of the deserted building had had a similar effect on Lashonda despite her familiarity with it because she abruptly stopped to stare up at it. He had to put out his hands to cushion the collision. "I beg your pardon," he said, lifting his hands off her back and stepping to the side.

"My fault," she said, still staring up at the hulking black edifice with all its architectural details appearing ghoulish in the darkness. Adding to the drama was the high wrought iron fence interspersed with granite stanchions that surrounded the building. In the darkness the imposing barricade had a particularly menacing quality, especially with every other baluster having a stylized spear point.

To the left, Mitt could see the unending traffic on First Avenue heading northward while to the right the street dead-ended. Directly ahead of them was a decorative but locked double gate as part of the surrounding wrought iron fence. It was topped with symmetrical, curvilinear elements and secured with a rusting chain and a hefty padlock. Beyond the gate was an overgrown walkway leading up to an ornate two-to-three-story entrance structure, which stood proud from the building's central façade with a pedimented top, decorative concrete urns on plinths on either side, and a large arched niche containing what appeared to be an ornamental state seal. Below that were two Corinthian columns supporting a full doorway entablature and framing an oversized double door. Incised into the frieze area and just barely visible in reflected light were the words PSYCHIATRIC HOSPITAL.

"I hope you also have a key for the gate," Mitt said, trying for a bit of humor. They certainly weren't about to climb over a barricade of that size.

"Of course," Lashonda said while continuing to gaze up at the black, massive red-brick structure. Unlike all the other more modern buildings in the neighborhood, the psychiatric building was totally dark: Every one of the windows was pitch-black. "The numerous times I'd gone in and out of this place, especially when I worked here on a nightly basis before all the patients were moved out, I never stopped to look at it critically. Now that I have, I can see why it would give anyone pause." She laughed humorlessly. "I have to say, it definitely looks spooky, almost like a set for a horror movie."

"You are right about that," Mitt said, but in his estimation it was more than "spooky." To him, it was a huge anomaly, a quintessential haunted house smack-dab in one of the busiest parts of one of the busiest cities in the world. As the thought occurred to him, he felt a definite chill, wondering what it was going to be like inside. Was he going to see the apparitions that supposedly had taken up residence, and if so, would he and Lashonda be seeing them simultaneously? And if they did, would the visions be exactly the same or would the eye of the beholder influence what was perceived?

Mitt had no answers to these questions, but for the first time he felt a tug of reluctance to follow through with the plan, wondering if there was any risk involved. If the building was actually haunted as Lashonda claimed, it would be a world in which he had absolutely no understanding or experience. At the very least it promised to be a disturbing, scary experience and possibly disgusting if it included the surgerized people, the rats, and the horrid cacosmia.

At the same time these thoughts and questions arose, his motivations for going ahead with the plan quickly reasserted themselves. He was more than motivated, he was compelled to make the visit. With his family legacy at stake, he had to see this stash of hospital records. And there was another reason as well. He had an inkling that the visit had the potential to provide answers as to how and why all his patients had died, which would add credence to Lashonda's warning about Bellevue not being safe for him or his future patients.

Encouragingly enough, Lashonda obviously had no qualms about entering the building, and from Mitt's perspective, she definitely seemed to know what she was talking about. Of particular importance, she was confident that the spirits or ghosts or whatever couldn't touch them directly but could only make their presence known by manipulating inanimate objects. As reassuring as that idea sounded, what if Lashonda was right about the ghosts but wrong about their capabilities? What if they had more earthly power in their own domain than, say, in the high-rise hospital building?

Mitt broke off staring up at the empty psychiatric building and looked back at Lashonda. She, on the other hand, was still totally mesmerized. "Are you rethinking whether you want to go inside?" Mitt questioned. "I have to say, it is forbidding-looking, particularly in the darkness. Maybe it would be better to do this tomorrow during the daylight hours."

"No! Absolutely not," Lashonda remarked definitively. "As I said earlier, if we are going to do this, it has to be at night, and this is as good a time as any. I'm hesitating because I never appreciated how truly unique this building is. I'm amazed at all the fancy ornamental details like the columns, the urns, the plaques, and even those fake balconies on some of the upper-floor windows. It's almost like a parody of itself or, like I said, a set for a horror movie."

"I read that it was designed to be in what's called the Renaissance style," Mitt said. "All those embellishments are taken from classical architecture, like the columns on the side of the entrance door. I have to say, it is a particularly decorative entranceway. I thought the building's main entrance was on First Avenue, where there is also an impressive door."

"This was always functionally the main entrance," Lashonda said. "The one facing First Avenue was purely decorative and was never used."

"Really?" Mitt questioned. He'd never heard of a building having a purely decorative entrance. "That's all very interesting, but maybe we should get on with this visit. If we're going to spend a lot of time on this errand, I'd rather spend it reading the old records than just standing out here."

"You're right," Lashonda agreed. She quickly handed her brown paper bag to Mitt while getting out a key from her side pocket. A moment later, she had the padlock open and proceeded to slip the chain out of the double gate. As she pushed one side open with some effort, its hinges complained loudly with a grating squeal. She then gestured for Mitt to precede her onto the psychiatric hospital grounds.

Once inside, Lashonda took the time to pull the gate closed behind them despite its equivalent strident rasp. She even looped the chain back through the frame and re-engaged the padlock but without locking it. "I prefer not to take any chances someone might see this lock and chain open," she explained even though Mitt assumed as much. She took the bag back from him and extracted the two flashlights. They were of a significant size with large lenses and square battery packs. After giving him one but telling him not to turn it on, she put the empty bag behind one of the granite fence stanchions for their return to the hospital high-rise.

From there they faced a short stretch of sidewalk to the front steps and the impressive, oversized double doors. As they hurried forward, Lashonda used the opportunity to exchange the gate key for the key to the building. A narrow lawn extending along the entire length of the building was a riot of overgrowth. Several small trees and shrubbery were completely enveloped in vines and even a bit of poison ivy.

Now that they were close, Mitt noticed something else that had escaped him as it was covered by the overgrowth, namely that the building's entire first floor was sheathed in decorative granite and crowned with a narrow cornice separating it from the brick. "My word," he said as he mounted the front steps behind Lashonda, glancing up and down the structure's façade. "This place must have been quite impressive in its heyday."

Lashonda nodded, preoccupied. She had to struggle a bit to insert the key in the lock and get it to turn. When it finally did, there was a loud mechanical click. But then before pulling the door open, she hesitated and turned back to look directly at Mitt. "Are you sure you are ready for this?" she asked. She was still holding on to the key.

"I don't know," Mitt admitted. "I was wondering the same thing back when we were eyeing the place from a safe distance. Let me ask you this: What do you think the chances are we're going to be seeing some of the . . . resident spirits?" He'd hesitated asking his question and was reluctant to use the term *ghosts*. He still wasn't convinced ghosts existed in the real world, and saying the word out loud seemed like too much of an acknowledgment.

"My guess would be about a hundred percent," Lashonda said. "At least that's been my experience. I've always seen them when I've come in here after all the patients had been moved out and the building was empty. But I've never done that with anyone other than my mother just before and after Hurricane Sandy. You'll be the first."

"Did she see them?"

"No, she didn't, as I told you in the cafeteria. But remember, she was not a portal like I believe you and I are. I expect to see a lot of them tonight as I normally do, and I'll be shocked if you don't as well."

"Fair enough," Mitt said. He was encouraged that she was taking the experience so much in stride. "I guess the important thing is that you're convinced that they can't interact with us directly, correct?"

"Correct, that has been my experience. What I've learned to do is to ignore them, which can be difficult, as they can be visually distressing if not revolting. It's hard to imagine how much these patients suffered when the major medical treatments for just about any ailment were to be bled or made to vomit and have propulsive diarrhea. It defies current-day imagination, especially with the little or no sanitation that was available back then and the horrendous overcrowding. I understand that at one point Bellevue had two thousand beds, which is hard enough to grasp, but then during epidemics, like cholera outbreaks, the patients had to share beds and even the floor and the halls. On top of that, patients were regularly experimented on, even subjected to surgery with no anesthesia and no antisepsis in front of an amphitheater full of students."

"Good God," Mitt voiced. Just thinking about what Lashonda was saying made him squirm anew. He'd always wanted to believe a hospital was a place for people to go to be relieved of suffering and not vice versa.

"And those poor people labeled as insane were even worse off," Lashonda said. "Before this psychiatric hospital was built and the specialty reformed, a lot of such patients were treated with chains, various other kinds of restraints, and truncheons. On top of that, with the restraints there'd probably been even worse sanitation."

"Okay, okay," Mitt repeated, raising his hands in submission. "I get the picture. There's more than enough reason for the place to be haunted. Fine! All I want is to be assured that we'll be able to walk back out with life and limb intact when we are finished with our visit."

"That I can guarantee," Lashonda said. "It's not physical injury that I'm concerned about in the slightest, but rather your state of mind. Please gird yourself because your senses are going to be assaulted. Since you told me you have already experienced the apparitions, heard the cries, and suffered the odors, I assume you'll be able to tolerate it. My advice is to ignore it all as best as you can. That's what I've learned to do, and it works—the visuals, sounds, and odors usually just disappear if they are ignored. Do you think you can do it?"

"I haven't been able to do it yet," Mitt said. "But then again, I haven't tried. I do have to admit, each time I've been confronted with what I've called hallucinations, I've been a bit less taken aback."

"I assumed as much," Lashonda said, "which is part of the reason I agreed to take you inside. Are you ready?"

"I guess I'm as ready as I'm ever going to be."

"Okay, but stay close!"

Mitt laughed hollowly. "Don't worry about that."

Lashonda turned her attention back to the oversized double doors and gave the one on the right a significant tug. The door reluctantly let itself be opened, creaking in protest just as the outer gate had. Immediately a stale smell wafted out of the abandoned building.

"Here we go," Lashonda announced, gesturing inside. "You first, but don't turn your light on until I close the door behind us. And keep your beam mostly covered with your free hand and trained downward. We don't want any lights to flash in any of the windows. But we won't have to worry about it for long, as we'll be taking the central stairway directly down to the basement, where the lack of windows means we won't have to worry about our lights."

"Got it," Mitt responded as he hesitantly preceded Lashonda into the building's foyer. As he did so, he experienced another passing wave of paresthesia, which added to his mounting jitters.

CHAPTER 26

Thursday, July 4, 4:46 A.M.

As soon as Lashonda had stepped inside and pulled the heavy door closed behind them, Mitt switched on his flashlight. As he'd been advised, he carefully made certain the beam was mostly shielded with the palm of his left hand and angled downward. Lashonda quickly moved past him, turning on her flashlight and covering it in a similar fashion. With a wave over her shoulder for him to follow, she passed an empty reception desk and headed into the central hall. From there two main corridors ran east and west along the long axis of the building. On both sides of the central hall were multiple out-of-service elevators, and in the middle was a Da Vinci–like open, spiral stairway with an ornate metal railing.

As Mitt followed Lashonda, he allowed his flashlight to illuminate a bit more of the surrounding central hall. He also briefly shined his light down each of the corridors, but both were longer than his flashlight beam's reach. In keeping with the Renaissance embellishments on the exterior, both the main corridors' interiors were remarkably decorative, with a series of half-round pilasters with Doric capitals supporting faux rib vaulting. Each of the many doors leading off the corridors had decorative jambs and miniature entablatures. A few of the doors in the immediate vicinity were open, and in several Mitt was surprised to catch a glimpse of remaining but outdated office furniture, as if the people had left for the night and would be back in the morning.

But what was the most striking to Mitt was the color. The walls of the two lengthy hallways extending east and west were a two-toned yellow-tan with the more yellow color starting about five feet off the tile floor to include the barrel-vaulted ceiling. The lower portion of the walls were the darker tan. The baseboard was a five-inch strip of glossy black, rubberized artificial material. Why Mitt found the color scheme so eye-catching was that it uncannily resembled the walls in the nightmares he'd experienced just prior to waking up Monday and Tuesday morning. In both instances he'd been chased down similarly colored, endless hallways by an unknown assailant or assailants, and the association gave him yet another chill. Was the dream some sort of harbinger of this visit? He didn't know, but he certainly hoped not.

"How are you faring?" Lashonda questioned as Mitt reached her. To give him time to catch up, she'd hesitated at the top of the downward flight of the circular stairs.

"So far so good," Mitt announced, although he was tempted to mention the similarities of the unique wall color and his disturbing dream.

"Do you hear what sounds like low-pitched distant cries of people in anguish?" Lashonda questioned.

"I haven't," Mitt said, as he had yet to stop and listen, making him momentarily forget about his nightmare. The moment he did, he could just barely make out a distant wailing. It was of a very low but gradually increasing amplitude as if the wailers were slowly approaching. "I hear them now. I suppose you do, too?"

"Obviously," Lashonda said. "Since it's getting louder, you'd best brace yourself."

Before Mitt could respond, the terrible cacosmia that he'd experienced in the high-rise hit as a powerful olfactory assault, making them both involuntarily slap their hands to their faces to squeeze their noses against the foul smell. At the same time, the cacophony increased dramatically, and in the distance down the west-facing corridor a mob of people began to emerge out of the darkness, heading in their direction. Similar to the grisly, surgerized people Mitt had seen in his apparitions in the high-rise, these individuals were all partially clothed in historical garb. Many of them were also covered in what appeared to be filth. Perhaps worst of all, many of their faces and portions of their bodies had been dissected away as if they were living, anatomical specimens meant to show interior muscles or organs.

"Come on!" Lashonda said, suddenly grabbing Mitt's arm and attempting to pull him forcibly down the stairway. "Ignore them!"

Horrified yet intrigued, Mitt initially resisted being pulled away from the oncoming group. He was totally mystified by what they represented, but his curiosity was quickly overwhelmed. The closer they got, the worse the cacosmia became, and now he recognized the odor's character was a little different. On the previous occasions, he'd thought of the smell as being mostly of excrement, but now it was more of putrefaction and even more repulsive.

Finally, Mitt allowed himself to be pulled onto the stairway. To his utter relief, as soon as they started down, the odor inexplicably vanished. Halfway down, Mitt hazarded a quick look back up over his shoulder toward the first floor, expecting to see the ghoulish mob massing at the top of the stairs or, worse yet, starting down. But he didn't see them at all.

"Don't look for them!" Lashonda commanded. "I'm telling you, you'll encourage them if you do."

"What are they?" Mitt questioned. "They're different than the people I've seen before, who looked post-surgical."

"I believe you are right," Lashonda said as she reached the basement level and turned around to face Mitt as he continued to descend. "I was mystified when I saw that group for the first time. With a bit more reading about the history, I've come to believe they're the spirits of the thousands of dead bodies dug up by Bellevue physicians and physicians in training to be used for anatomical dissection. Apparently your ancestor Dr. Homer Fuller had been an avid grave robber. Before the Bone Bill was passed in the mid-nineteenth century, no grave in New York was considered off-limits."

"What was the Bone Bill?" he asked, reaching the basement level. He vaguely recalled reading something about the legislation back in June, but in the pressure of the moment he couldn't remember.

"It was a law passed in the 1850s which expanded the cadavers that could be used for dissection. Previously it had only been executed criminals but after it included unclaimed bodies from prisons and almshouses. The Bone Bill dramatically increased the supply to meet the demand and decreased the need for grave robbing."

"No wonder they appear so hideous," Mitt said. By reflex he glanced back up the stairs over his shoulder, but Lashonda reached out and forcibly tugged on his arm.

"Control yourself!" she loudly warned. "As I said, paying them attention encourages them. Please!"

"Okay, okay," Mitt repeated. He had to consciously restrain himself. With his fleeting glance, he hadn't seen the dissected corpses, but he did see something else. He'd caught sight of a more familiar apparition coming down the stairs, the blond girl. And now, knowing she was behind them presented Mitt with an almost irresistible temptation to defy Lashonda's warning. "I didn't see the corpses," he quickly admitted, "but I did catch a glimpse of Charlene Wagner!"

"I'm not surprised," Lashonda said. "I see her every time I come in here. But ignore her, too! Come on! Follow me! We have a bit of a walk ahead of us." With a wave over her shoulder, Lashonda set out across the rather large space lined with cabinetry and shelving at the foot of the stairs. She headed toward an archway that led into the main corridor heading west.

Mitt followed but with his skin crawling, particularly along the back of his neck, from knowing they were not alone. To keep from turning around to glance at Charlene, he had to utilize every ounce of restraint he could muster. The one good thing, since they were now in the basement where there were no windows, was that they didn't have to concern themselves at all with the light from their flashlights. Mitt could use his flashlight however he saw fit as Lashonda was clearly doing. Ahead, her beam was dancing around in front of her as she passed under the archway and entered the central corridor. Trying to catch up, he increased his walking speed.

From Mitt's perspective, the basement appeared pretty much as he imagined it would. Upstairs had been a surprise with the embellished architectural details and coloration, totally unexpected for a psychiatric hospital. None of that existed in the basement. Also, the upstairs had appeared surprisingly normal for a hospital building deserted for some forty years, meaning more organized and even cleaner than expected, albeit dusty on horizontal surfaces like the reception desk or the handrail of the circular stairway. In contrast, the basement, although whitewashed in the distant past, was obviously dirty and the hallway was lined with debris of all sorts—rags, broken tools, old paint cans, empty boxes. Along the ceiling was a tangle of piping, some areas with rotting insulation hanging down, as well as masses of exposed, aged electric wiring. Strung through the tangle was a fair number of cobwebs. The hallway was also lined with doors, most of which were closed. The few that were ajar revealed stacks of stored junk, even old, disused furniture.

"This is a different world down here," Mitt called ahead to Lashonda. He was nervous and just wanted to maintain contact. From the moment they'd entered the building, the place gave him the creeps and that was even without apparitions.

"It always was," she said without stopping or even slowing.

Although Mitt was still sorely tempted to turn around because he assumed they were being followed by at least Charlene, he resisted, willing to follow Lashonda's advice. As nervous as he was in the environment, he tried to make light of it by mentally noting that every reasonably intelligent person knew that the last place you were supposed to go in a haunted house was the basement, yet here he was.

Presently they came to an intersection, and without a second's hesitation, Lashonda turned right. After about twenty-five feet she turned left, with Mitt close behind. He sensed they were now in the northwest wing of the building, parallel with 30th Street and approaching First Avenue, near where he had stopped to gaze at the building early Monday morning. Once again, he was glad he'd not tried to come on his own to look for the records. He never would have found them.

"Okay, here we are," Lashonda finally said, stopping at a door with an actual label in contrast to most of the others. The sign was small and at eye level. It read simply: HOUSEKEEPING SUPPLY. Then she turned to the door immediately opposite and felt along the top rail until she found a key. Facing back around, she brandished it. "We always had to keep the supply door locked. Ever since I've worked here at Bellevue, employee thievery has been a problem. It's amazing. We even have to keep the toilet paper locked up." She unlocked the door, put the key back, and then entered the supply room, leaving its door ajar.

Mitt started forward but paused on the threshold. He couldn't resist a quick glance back down the corridor from which they'd come. Although it was only for a fraction of a second, the fleeting image his eyes caught startled him. He'd expected to see Charlene, but instead, he caught a glimpse of the surgerized crowd. They were silent, standing stock-still with venomous, angry expressions and holding their removed limbs or organs, all still bloody. With the closest spirits a mere twenty feet away, Mitt guessed that the gruesome crowd had been behind them for a good part of the long walk, and he shuddered. He'd sensed he and Lashonda were being followed by something but certainly not by such a horde and not so closely.

Mitt quickly entered and shut the supply room door behind him even though he suspected it wasn't a barrier to such ghostly spirits. He then turned and let his flashlight beam circle the room. In contrast to the cluttered basement rooms Mitt had glanced into, the housekeeping supply room was almost totally empty. A number of open bottles and cans of cleaner lined the shelves along one wall. There was also a rack for mops and brooms, which contained a half dozen or so.

"The records are back here in a closet off the lavatory," Lashonda called out, waving for Mitt. She'd retreated to the very rear of the storeroom and was standing next to an opened interior door. Her flashlight was on the floor in the main part of the storeroom with its lens angled upward. By the time Mitt got back there, she had stepped into a small toilet room and opened an interior closet. Inside, in plain sight and stacked chest-high, were five cardboard bankers boxes.

"Here they are," Lashonda announced while giving the top box a tap. "Here are the records presumably collected by your ancestor Dr. Clarence Fuller."

"Are all the boxes full?" Mitt questioned. It appeared to be more material than he'd expected.

"Pretty much," Lashonda said. "Your ancestors were very busy people. I'd guess each box has fifty to a hundred records or thereabouts." She then bent down and pointed to the box on the bottom. "This one has records that go back all the way to the 1820s and range up until around the 1860s or thereabouts. As near as I could determine, they were mostly Dr. Homer Fuller's patients. But don't count on that. I certainly didn't go through all of them, just read a few here and there. On the top of each box there is a range of dates of the contained records."

"So, the higher you go in the stack, the more recent the records?" Mitt asked. He was amazed at the sheer number of records seemingly involved and could imagine the excitement Robert Pendleton must have felt when he'd stumbled onto them.

"That's correct. The lowest down is mostly for Homer, next up Otto, then Benjamin, and these on the top are Dr. Clarence Fuller's lobotomy records." Lashonda ended by patting the box on the very top.

"I know we don't have a lot of time," Mitt said as he put his flashlight on the floor next to Lashonda's and also made a point of angling the lens upward as much as it would go but in the opposite direction, making the ambient light in the room more evenly disbursed. "And I appreciate your promise to your mother that the records mustn't leave here, but I'd like to get an idea of them with the time we have. Do you mind if I check out the lower box first? I might as well do it in chronological order."

"We're here for you, so of course I don't mind. In fact, let me help you." With that said, Lashonda began handing the uppermost boxes out to Mitt, who stacked them in reverse order next to their flashlights. As he did so, he noticed the dates written on the top.

"Here's the last one," Lashonda said, handing it to Mitt, "which I believe contains mostly Homer's cases."

"Perfect," Mitt said. He put the box on top of the others and lifted off its lid. Inside was a stack of patient records that seemed to be written in a rather flamboyant but mostly readable cursive style on yellowed paper. Being particularly careful and respectful, he reached in and lifted out a short stack. Randomly, he picked one from the middle. The others he carefully placed face down on the top of the opened box. The record he was holding was a single page, and he had to angle it carefully in the meager light to be able to read it, as the ink had faded.

The date on the record was August 8, 1854, and at the bottom was Homer's impressive signature, which gave Mitt a real sense he was looking into his family's past. The patient's name was John Mercer, age forty-three, described as a one-eyed farrier. Mitt had no idea what that meant until he learned a little later in the narrative that John had been attempting to shoe a horse when the animal collapsed on him, severely damaging his right leg from just above the knee down to the ankle, which caused unremitting pain. The above narrative was all under a heading: *Problem*. There were three more sections under the headings: *Operation*, *Procedure*, and *Outcome*.

Mitt looked up at Lashonda, who was peering over his shoulder at the record. "It's like a miniature time machine," he said.

Lashonda nodded. "I know what you mean. It must be especially so for you since it involves a relative."

"It is amazing reading it, knowing he wrote this with his hand."

"Maybe even moments after he'd done the operation," Lashonda added.

"Perhaps," Mitt said. He had no idea of the timing, but it didn't matter. Going back to the record, he continued reading with difficulty as the ink intensity varied significantly: *After bringing Mr. Mercer into the operating theatre filled with attentive students and asking him in front of all the witnesses if he wished to go ahead and have his damaged leg off or if he wished not to have it off, he responded to have it off, and four stout men took ahold of him and held him fast.*

Suddenly Mitt stopped reading. Instead, his eyes snapped back to the top of the page to ascertain that the date was indeed 1854, and it was. Like every medical student, he was aware that anesthesia was first used at Massachusetts General Hospital in Boston in 1846, so he was certain it was available at Bellevue in 1854. The fact that Homer chose not to use it, as Robert Pendleton had written, horrified Mitt, even as he recognized the role played by hindsight. He felt strongly that his relative's rejection of the benefits of anesthesia, spurred by his supposed belief that denying natural pain was the devil's work, bordered on the insanely delusional. It was also brutal, cruel, and remarkably cold-blooded even if the amputation could be done in a mere nine seconds.

"What's the matter?" Lashonda questioned. She sensed Mitt's emotional reaction.

"I'm embarrassed to tell you," he said. "But this is a case of my ancestor doing a leg amputation without anesthesia eight years after anesthesia had been introduced. And remember, amputation of this kind required sawing through the largest bone in the human body."

"Lordy!" Lashonda commented with a distinctly dismayed expression along with a disbelieving shake of her head.

"That's my reaction, too," Mitt said. "It's perplexing as well as shameful." With a shake of his own head, he went back to reading John Mercer's short medical record. Unfortunately, the rest was just as bad. The man died of overwhelming sepsis after suffering through three post-surgical days in what had to have been indescribable pain. The last sentence explained that just before death, the leg wound spontaneously split open and discharged "a vast amount of pus."

"Ay ay ay," Mitt muttered under his breath. He assumed that Homer probably hadn't washed his hands or his instruments or even changed his clothes before operating on poor John Mercer, even if he'd been doing something like an autopsy in the morgue. Back in those days, Mitt knew that as many as half the people suffering through surgery died of sepsis within days.

He raised his eyes and looked at Lashonda, who was still watching him. Since all the light in the room was coming from two flashlights sitting on the floor, he couldn't see her eyes, and her sockets looked like black holes. "What a sad story," he said. He waved the document in her direction. "Were all the records you looked at similar to this?"

"I'm afraid so," Lashonda said. "But remember, I didn't look at that many, so don't jump to conclusions. Although the ones I did read were similar. Well, let me clarify. When I looked at Otto's and Benjamin's records, there were significant differences, but it seemed that the outcomes, meaning frequent deaths, were the same."

"That's not encouraging."

"I'm sure not. What I'm hoping is that by seeing even this one record, you'll take my warning and my advice to heart."

"You mean leave Bellevue."

"Yes."

Mitt struggled to organize his thoughts. Although he'd been

rather successfully fighting his exhaustion, it was starting to truly influence his ability to think. He'd also noticed the record was fluttering in his hand—he'd developed a mild tremor that he couldn't control.

"What would you like to do?" Lashonda questioned. She gestured toward the stack of boxes. "We've a bit more time. Would you like to see more of the records? Here they all are."

"I don't know," Mitt managed. He felt momentarily incapable of making up his mind. To give himself something to do while he organized his thoughts, he carefully returned John Mercer's record to its place within the short stack of documents he'd originally removed and then replaced them all back into the bankers box. When he was finished, he straightened up and looked directly over at Lashonda.

"I'm having trouble dealing with all this," he admitted.

"That's entirely understandable," Lashonda said. "We can come back at some future date, but I recommend we do it sooner rather than later, even tomorrow night. No, sorry. I'm off tomorrow because of the holiday. We could come back Friday night, about this same time. I'm truly distressed to hear about all your patients dying. Although we can't be certain, it suggests to me that my fears are well grounded. This many angry ghosts, from the three-hundred-year history of this hospital, are a force that has to be respected and reckoned with. It's not only for your safety, but it's also for all your future patients' safety."

"I'm certainly getting the message that the Bellevue paranormal forces have to be respected," Mitt said. He thought for a moment and then added: "Here's what I'd like to do tonight before we leave. I'd like to see Charlene Wagner's record. Would you be able to put your finger on it with reasonable ease?"

"Of course! I can find that after we return all the boxes to the lavatory closet. Charlene's is in the top box, which unfortunately at the moment is on the bottom."

"Fine, let's do it," Mitt said with newly found resolve.

With Lashonda restacking the boxes and Mitt bringing them to her, all the records were returned to their original resting place in short order. When it was done, Lashonda opened the last box after taking it from Mitt and, as promised, quickly produced Charlene Wagner's record.

"I'm impressed," Mitt said, taking it. "How did you find it so quickly?"

"I've seen her so many times and had referred to the record often enough that I ended up flagging it."

"A wise move," Mitt said as he rapidly leafed through the stapled, eight-page record. Although it was typed and not handwritten, the font size was small, making it very difficult to read in the available light, but at least it was a hundred years newer than Homer's hand-written record, and it was in the format of a modern inpatient medical record. He skimmed the last page, which tersely described that the bedside lobotomy had resulted in death. Below that there was an equally brief summary of the autopsy findings, with the cause of death listed as exsanguination and intracerebral hemorrhage. The final sentence of the report, which had been underlined with red ink, noted that the patient had been found to have an aberrantly positioned anterior cerebral artery. Mitt looked at the underlining and wondered if Clarence had done it in an attempt to absolve himself of the child's untimely demise, as it was probably true that if there hadn't been an anatomical anomaly, the child might not have died. But the same was true for the lobotomy itself—even more so.

When he was finished with his quick scan and feeling more enticed than satisfied, Mitt looked up at Lashonda and said: "Do we have time for me to read this with a bit more care? It won't take long."

"Of course," Lashonda said, but Mitt saw her look at her watch. "That's what we're here for, but time is marching on."

"I appreciate it," Mitt said. "I'll be very quick." He flipped back to the first page but paused.

What suddenly flashed through his mind was Robert Pendleton and how ecstatic the man must have been when he'd first stumbled across this trove of old Bellevue Hospital records. For a bioethicist, it would have been nothing short of a gold mine. Mitt now knew that the discovery had happened right after Clarence's retirement but before the hospital administrator had been able to deal with these records. Perhaps Pendleton's discovery forced the administrator to panic and coopt Lashonda's mother into hiding them in the housekeeping supply room in the basement. For the administrator, Pendleton's discovery and threat to publish must have been a nerve-wrackingly close call.

On his second read-through, Mitt squatted down to make better use of the meager light. He was hoping to find a reasonable and understandable explanation for why a lobotomy—of all things—had been done on eight-year-old Charlene Wagner, considering the procedure's irrevocability. He quickly confirmed that the child's diagnosis had indeed been in the realm of a behavioral disorder, probably what was now called an oppositional defiant disorder, but then nowhere in the relatively lengthy chart was the issue of whether or not to do a lobotomy even raised. Since it was generally known, even back then, that such behavioral disorders often resolved as the child aged, especially in girls, this drastic treatment option was the last thing that should have been done. Yet as the issue was not addressed in the file, Mitt had nothing to refute Pendleton's claim that Clarence Fuller had been advocating the use of lobotomies for his own personal reasons and not in the patients' best interests. Mitt felt the selfsame letdown and even anger that he'd experienced reading that Homer had chosen not to use anesthesia when he amputated John Mercer's leg.

Mitt let out an agonized sigh along with another disappointed shake of his head. He then extended Charlene's record toward Lashonda as if he didn't even want to hold it any longer.

"Not good?" she questioned as she took the record.

"Not good," Mitt repeated. "Not good at all. I'm thinking I want to disown some of my ancestors."

"Unfortunately, even if you do, it's not going to do you much good. It's certainly not going to improve your reputation with the Bellevue ghost community."

"At the moment, I'm thinking more about my own state of mind."

"Fair enough," Lashonda said. She again looked at her watch. "It's five after five and sunrise is fast approaching. We have to leave before it gets light outside. Are you ready?"

"I suppose," Mitt said. He was having more and more difficulty thinking clearly. He needed sleep and he needed it badly.

Lashonda quickly returned Charlene's medical record to its appropriate position in the top box and replaced the lid. She then closed the closet door and stepped out of the lavatory. She looked at Mitt as she picked up her flashlight. "You don't look so good."

"I don't feel so good," Mitt admitted. He picked up his flashlight, too.

"Okay, let's get you out of here so you can get some sleep."

"Good idea," Mitt managed. He followed her over to the door to the hall, but just as Lashonda went to open it, he raised his arm and put his hand against the door to keep it closed. It was the same hand that was holding the flashlight. "Hold up for a second!" he said. "Before I followed you in here when we first arrived, I couldn't help myself from glancing back up the hall from whence we'd come. I know you told me not to, but I did, and the entire corridor was jam-packed with surgerized patients carrying their limbs or organs. Isn't that going to be a major problem?"

"No, as I told you, if they are still there, they should just be ignored."

"How can I ignore them if they are staring me in the face?"

"You just do! You merely pretend they are not there because, in a way, they are not there. You are seeing them because you are a portal. I can't explain it better than that. Do you understand?"

"No, I don't," Mitt admitted.

"Okay, fine," Lashonda said with a roll of her eyes. It was obvious she was getting progressively more tense and impatient as dawn approached. "Listen! Just follow me! Close your eyes if you have to."

"Are you serious? Walk with my eyes closed? I'm not sure I can."

"If it comes to that, put your hand on my shoulder." To demonstrate she reached out and grasped Mitt's free hand and placed it on her shoulder, giving it a final pat. "Just like this, okay?"

"Okay," Mitt said, retrieving his hand and removing the other from the door to the hallway.

"Okay, brace yourself!" Lashonda said as she reached for the door handle.

CHAPTER 27

Thursday, July 4, 5:06 A.M.

Although Mitt did try to prepare himself, he was still startled as Lashonda pulled the door wide open. Pressing up against the outside of the door was the horde of patients he had glimpsed earlier. The angry but silent crowd had not vanished, as he'd hoped, but rather completely filled the entire corridor in both directions. Front and center were two individuals Mitt recognized. To the left was a one-eyed man teetering on one leg while holding his other mangled leg, which had been amputated mid-thigh. The amputated ends were bloody, as if the operation had just occurred. He was dressed in homespun clothing. His facial expression was of pure fury. Instantly, Mitt knew the one-eyed man had to be John Mercer.

Immediately to the right of John was Charlene Wagner. Although she'd been only eight years old, she was almost as tall as John. Her pale, otherwise cherubic face was twisted into an expression of anger, and she was again holding an orbitoclast, presumably the one that killed her.

"Dr. Fuller!" Lashonda yelled. She was staring at him, seeing his shock. She reached out and grabbed his free hand and slapped it back onto her shoulder, maintaining a grip on his fingers. "Shut your eyes! We're leaving here now!"

Although Mitt meant to comply, he didn't do it instantly, and to his utter astonishment, he saw Lashonda step forward despite the doorway and the entire hallway being completely blocked. In the next instant, as if defying belief, he saw Lashonda glide out through the crowd like a hot knife through butter. At that point Mitt did manage to shut his eyes, and with his hand firmly clasped onto Lashonda's shoulder, he, too, moved into the hallway without impediment.

In the next instant, he felt himself being turned around and heard the door to the housekeeping storeroom close and click shut. "Keep your eyes closed," Lashonda repeated hotly. He felt her hand clamp down even tighter on his fingers as they turned around yet again and began to move along the corridor.

"Is the hallway clear?" Mitt asked after twenty or so steps.

"Mostly," Lashonda answered. "But keep your eyes shut, otherwise you'll bring them all back."

"Okay," Mitt said, although he had to fight against opening his eyes. The concrete basement floor was not completely uniform, and he was stumbling over occasional debris as he walked.

"We're making a right-hand turn," Lashonda warned.

"Okay," Mitt said. "Thanks." He was surprised it was so difficult to follow someone this closely while keeping his eyes shut. On several occasions, their feet and legs ended up making contact. He was glad that Lashonda was keeping hold of his hand on her shoulder.

"Okay, now a left-hand turn," Lashonda said.

"Got it," Mitt responded. He knew they were now on the relatively long stretch of hallway leading to the circular stairs, meaning they were making significant progress. As he lurched ahead, Mitt found himself again marveling at how they had been able to walk through the crowd that appeared to be so substantive but clearly wasn't. Obviously, he had a lot to learn about being a portal, if that truly was the case.

"We're now approaching the circular stairway," Lashonda said.

"Good, can I open my eyes now?"

"I prefer you wait if you don't mind."

"I suppose not," Mitt said as he felt the floor change from bare concrete to tile. In his mind's eye, he could see the circular helix-style stair curving up in the darkness. Then he felt Lashonda stop and he followed suit. "How about now with the eyes?"

"Yes, I think we should be okay," Lashonda said. "And it will make going up the stairs a good bit easier."

Mitt opened his eyes and directed his flashlight along his line of sight. He immediately glanced around the area and then up the circular stairs. It was a relief to see no apparitions. Twisting around, he shined his light down the central corridor from which they'd come. Again, there was nothing, at least as far as the light penetrated.

"Come on!" Lashonda urged. She'd already started up the stairs. "I'm afraid it's going to be lighter outside than I'd like as it is."

Gaining the stairs, Mitt rose rapidly, catching up to Lashonda so that they both reached the ground floor in tandem. Without hesitation, she headed directly across the lobby area and into the foyer, toward the oversized double doors. Mitt followed but just before he entered the foyer, he glanced at the arched opening of the west main corridor. Standing there alone in the darkness was Charlene, her blond hair and pale shirtdress nearly luminescent.

Mitt slowed but didn't stop, nor did he shine his light in Charlene's direction. And in the instant that she remained in view, he had the distinct impression she was frantically motioning for him not to leave but to come toward her. But that was the last thing he wanted to do, and her gesture gave him one last chill up and down his spine. In the next instant, Charlene was blocked by the intervening foyer's wall, and Mitt joined Lashonda, who was already outside holding open one of the oversized double doors. He immediately passed her, glad to get out of his first haunted house none the worse for wear. Outside it was already getting light even though sunrise wouldn't occur for another fifteen to twenty minutes.

While waiting for her to lock the door, he glanced up at the building's ornamented façade, truly amazed that such a ghostly menagerie could exist in the middle of such a vibrant city. Once again, he was struck that the building had not been razed or converted despite its central location and despite having been empty for almost forty years. Its mere continued existence afforded a degree of credibility to Lashonda's claim that it was supernatural power that kept the wrecking ball at bay.

"Come on!" Lashonda urged as she now passed him in a leap-frog fashion, hurrying out to the gate to deal with the padlock. "Grab the paper bag for me!" she called over her shoulder as she fumbled with the heavy chain.

Following orders, Mitt stooped to retrieve the folded bag from the side of the gate's granite stanchion, and by the time he had it in hand, Lashonda had the gate open. Now it was time for him to pass her, and as he did so, he collected her flashlight. While she pulled the gate closed, replaced the chain, and relocked the padlock, he put both flashlights away inside the bag.

"Perfect," she said, taking the bag from him before passing him yet again and rapidly crossing the old section of 29th Street.

Dutifully he caught up with her as they retraced their steps back toward the high-rise, but then he forced himself to stop for a moment, turn around, and give the psychiatric building one more quick glance before it passed out of sight. Now that it was getting light, it was significantly less forbidding. Having overcome his fears in the dead of night and confronted its ghosts or spirits or whatever they were, he felt a significant lessening of the sense of the unknown. Besides, thanks to Lashonda, he now knew he could handle the phantoms by ignoring them, so he knew he could return, and he thought he would, with or without her.

"Penny for your thoughts," Lashonda said, surprising Mitt. He'd been certain she'd continued on without him.

"I'm not really thinking very much," Mitt blurted out guiltily. "I'm just relieved to have weathered the experience and come out safe and sound."

"You did brilliantly," Lashonda complimented, making Mitt feel even more guilty.

"I hardly think that's the case," he said. "You're the one who has done brilliantly by somehow learning how to deal with the spirits of Bellevue." Despite what he'd just been through, he was still reluctant to use the term *ghosts*.

"I never had to face the animosity your presence obviously arouses in them," Lashonda said.

"I'm afraid I'm learning it is justified hostility," Mitt added.

"I'm glad you recognize it. That was the goal, but now you need sleep, a lot of sleep. And after you rest, I hope you take to heart what you've learned tonight. Remember, I'll be back on duty Friday night, Saturday night, too. Let's meet up when it suits you. As I said, it is for your own good and for the good of your future patients. But enough for now! Come on! Let's get inside before someone questions what we're doing out here."

"You're right," Mitt agreed. They headed for the door to the laundry building. "I'll certainly be in touch with you, most likely sometime during your shift on Friday night. Since I'm off today, I can sleep the entire day."

"That's good. You need it."

Once they were inside the laundry building, Lashonda said that there was someone she needed to see in the laundry department, so they took their leave of each other. Mitt thanked her sincerely for her concern about his safety and for taking so much time on his behalf and even seeking him out. She modestly downplayed the effort and instead brought up the issue of her own family legacy and allegiance to Bellevue.

"Whatever the motivations," Mitt said, "I'm immensely appreciative. I'll look forward to seeing you probably tomorrow night. By then, after digesting all I've learned tonight, I'll have a lot more questions for you."

"I will look forward to it as well," Lashonda said before heading into the laundry offices.

For a moment Mitt watched her go, duly impressed with her and thinking how lucky Bellevue Hospital was to have her and her family as part of its history.

Less than five minutes later, Mitt keyed open his on-call room door and stepped inside. He first eyed the bed and then looked toward the bathroom with the idea of possibly taking a quick shower. He didn't debate long. The bed won out hands down, and without even taking off his white coat, he stretched out, crossed his legs, and let his tense body begin to relax.

For a moment, he stared up at the ceiling as his exhausted mind replayed the extraordinary experience of visiting the deserted psychiatric hospital, especially the anxiety and then the terror it had evoked.

It had been an ordeal, there was no question, yet he knew he had to return. The cache of old hospital records was just too tempting a draw, especially since the vast majority of them were presumably written by his ancestors. In many ways he felt he had no choice. It was incumbent on him to go through them. Would they all be as damning to his family legacy as the first two? Although he didn't know for certain, he feared it was likely, but he had to be certain. The critical decision of whether or not to remain a resident at Bellevue hung in the balance.

"Good God!" Mitt voiced out loud. It seemed so unbelievably incredible that a bunch of ghosts, which he still wasn't entirely sure he believed existed, were forcing him to make the most important decision of his life. If he did resign from his NYU surgical residency, what could he possibly offer as the reason? He'd have to come up with something other than blaming it on ghosts! The thought alone brought a wry smile to his face as he pictured saying such an outlandish thing to the director of the Surgical Residency Program. And even if he came up with a reasonable explanation, what would it do to his chances of finding another residency, especially considering how difficult it was to get a surgical residency slot in an academic medical center? Resigning from the program without something like a significant health issue was going to be career suicide, at least as far as being a surgeon was concerned.

"Shit!" Mitt called out in utter frustration. It seemed he was caught between the proverbial rock and a hard place. Yet he had to decide. If Lashonda's concerns were correct, all his future patients were in danger even if he himself wasn't.

As he fretted, one thing was certain. He couldn't put the decision off, meaning he had to go back into the psychiatric hospital, and it had to be sooner rather than later. Luckily there were two significant things he hadn't shared with the night-shift housekeeping supervisor despite how much he respected and appreciated her. The first was that he didn't particularly care about possibly being caught in the building by Bellevue Security as she obviously did. After all, it had been empty for an interminably long time, his ancestor had been one of the institution's higher-ups, and it was owned by Bellevue Hospital, where he was currently a surgical resident. If he was to be caught visiting it, which he doubted would happen since he planned on being careful, the powers that be would probably tell him it was off-limits and that would be that.

The second thing he didn't share with Lashonda was her determination not to move the records. What Mitt had in mind was to find his own way into the psychiatric hospital so he could merely borrow a box or two and bring them back to his apartment. There he'd be able to give them the attention they deserved, rather than trying to read them standing up in the basement of a filthy, hundred-year-old, haunted building while holding a flashlight. When he finished with the first set of boxes, he would return them and exchange them for others. In the end, he planned to read as many of the records as he could without ultimately violating Lashonda's or her mother's promises.

Mitt sighed. With at least the backbone of a plan, he felt considerably better, and with that decided, he exhaled and finally allowed his eyes to close. A second later, he was asleep.

CHAPTER 28

Thursday, July 4, 9:05 A.M.

The next thing Mitt became aware of was the sound of knocking on his on-call room door. It was soft knocking, which was why it took a relatively long time to rouse him from his coma-like sleep. "Just a second," he managed, finding his voice and then having to clear his throat. He uncrossed his legs, which apparently had been crossed for the nearly four hours he'd been comatose, and threw them over the side of the bed to help him sit up. Immediately he could tell his right leg remained "asleep" from having its circulation compromised. As he massaged the involved calf, he called out: "Hang on! I'm coming."

"No problem," came back through the door.

Mitt instantly recognized Andrea's voice and assumed she was responsibly checking in with him to start her on-call status. When Mitt felt his leg was capable of bearing weight and would be reasonably responsive to commands, he stood up. He then had to weather a short-lived spate of dizziness. When that passed, he staggered a few steps on a leg that still felt wooden and opened the door.

"Oh my gosh, you look like you've been through the wringer," Andrea said, but her tone was cheerful. She then followed up with a teasing verbal once-over as she stood in the doorway, pointing out his bloodshot eyes, his rumpled white coat, and his hair, which stuck out at odd angles the way terrified cartoon characters were drawn.

"Thanks for all the compliments," Mitt said. In sharp contrast to his own appearance, as per usual she looked rather chic, as if she were heading out on a date rather than starting what might turn out to be a grueling twenty-four-hour on-call stint as a first-year surgical resident. He couldn't help but notice she was back to wearing her trendy, bright red dress under a clean and starched white coat. On top of that, her dark, bobbed hair had been scrupulously attended to, and she was even wearing a small amount of makeup. Despite feeling decidedly outclassed, he added: "Do you want to come in for a few minutes and chat?"

"I'd like to hear about your night," Andrea said. "But only if it won't bother you. You do look exhausted. Maybe you should just go back to sleep, and we can talk later?"

"No, it's okay! I want to get up," Mitt said. "I prefer to get out of here, go back to my apartment, and get some real sleep."

"Fair enough," Andrea said as she stepped into the room.

Mitt let the door go, and it closed on its own accord. While Andrea sat in the lone reading chair, he went back to the bed and sat down.

"I'm sorry to have awakened you," Andrea said. "The way you look, it seems cruel in retrospect. In my defense, I did debate with myself for a few minutes. Ultimately I thought it behooved me to find out if there was anything particular that I should know as part of a responsible handoff."

"It's okay," Mitt said. He ran both hands through his hair, trying to tame it to a degree. "Seriously! I'm glad you woke me. As I said, I'll appreciate getting home. As for the current inpatients, 'All's Quiet on the Western Front,' at least at the moment."

"That's good to hear, which reminds me: I haven't had anything to eat yet. Want to grab a bit of breakfast together?"

"Thanks for the invite, but to be honest, I'm not hungry in the slightest."

"Fair enough," Andrea said. "Sounds like you didn't get much sleep. Otherwise, how was your night?"

"Pretty terrible," Mitt said, nodding as he spoke.

"Bummer," Andrea said. "What made it bad? Did you have emergency surgery in the middle of the night?"

"No surgery. I wouldn't have minded that. Instead, all three of my remaining patients died."

"What?" Andrea loudly blurted. She was plainly shocked. "Oh, come on! I hope you are trying to make what would be the world's most tasteless joke."

"I wish I were," Mitt said. "Elena Aguilar had a cardiac arrest in the ICU, which I suppose wasn't so startling as she had been doing poorly since her surgery. But just before that happened, Latonya Walker, my breast biopsy, also had an arrest, which was a huge surprise for everyone because she'd been doing perfectly fine and had no cardiac history whatsoever."

"Unbelievable! What about the last one? Was that the thyroidectomy you were so hyped about?"

"Exactly," Mitt said. "In some respects, the third one was the most disconcerting of all. His name was Diego Ortiz. He'd been doing fine, too, but then out of the blue he suffered an off-the-charts thyroid storm."

"Whoa! I'm not sure I've even heard of a thyroid storm, but I guess it's self-explanatory."

"It is self-explanatory. The body's metabolism just goes berserk, and the patient kind of burns himself up from the inside."

"Good God! I'm blown away! This means that every single one of the patients you'd been assigned so far has died."

"I'm afraid so."

For a few beats, the two friends just stared at each other. Mitt longed to bring up the extraordinary idea that he was being targeted by the ghosts of Bellevue because of the sins of his forebearers, but he couldn't get himself to do it. Once again, if the situation were the other way around, and Andrea was trying to tell him that malevolent spirits were targeting her patients because of her ancestors' behavior, he'd think she'd gone off the deep end. At the same time, he was desperate to talk with her and feel a connection with a friend and colleague to help him deal with a difficult emotional situation. If nothing else, he wanted reassurance that his plan to return to the psychiatric hospital to borrow the records behind Lashonda Scott's back wasn't taking advantage of her good graces and personal generosity.

"How are you handling this amazing coincidence?" Andrea asked with obvious concern. "I hope you are not taking it personally?"

"It's difficult not to," Mitt said as his shoulders visibly sank. "Seven out of seven is just pushing the limits of probability."

"But you are only a first-year resident," Andrea exclaimed. "We talked about this. You haven't made any of the decisions nor done the surgeries. It can't be your fault. There's no way."

Mitt shrugged his shoulders. Once again, he wanted to talk about the apparitions he'd been seeing, especially now that he'd visited the psychiatric hospital where they all apparently resided, but he dared not. "Something else very disturbing happened last night," he said, thinking about where he could take the conversation and remain on reasonably safe subjects.

"As bad as three of your patients dying?"

"I suppose not, but pretty bad just the same."

"Okay, lay it on me."

"I got specific confirmation from two actual cases that Dr. Harington was correct about my Bellevue ancestors being on the wrong side of history."

"I'm not sure what you mean?"

"Exactly what I said. My ancestor Homer Fuller amputated a leg in mid-thigh in 1854 and chose not to use anesthesia, which was obviously available at the time. And Clarence Fuller, the psychiatrist, attempted to do a lobotomy in 1949 on an eight-year-old girl with what was probably a behavioral disorder, which she probably would have outgrown, and killed her in the process supposedly because of an aberrant cerebral artery."

"Holy crap! That is pretty bad. And how is it you got confirmation of all this in the middle of the night?"

"It's a moderately long story. Do you really want to hear?"

"Yes, of course, but if it is a moderately long story, I'd like to revisit the breakfast idea. Are you sure you're not game?"

"You know, now that I've been upright and conscious for a few minutes, I do feel a bit hungry. Let's do it."

After Mitt had splashed some cold water on his face and tamed his hair a tad with a brush, he and Andrea left the on-call room. Out in the lounge, he also took the time to exchange his soiled and seriously wrinkled white coat for a clean, starched one. This effort improved his appearance enough for Andrea to joke that she now wasn't all that embarrassed to be seen with him.

Twenty minutes later, they were in the cafeteria seated at a table for two with breakfasts in front of them. Although Andrea had the works—scrambled eggs, bacon, and toast—Mitt was content with juice, cold cereal, and skim milk.

"Okay, enough of the suspense," Andrea said. "Out with it! How on earth did you learn such specific details about your relatives in the middle of the night?"

"What happened was . . . I was introduced to a trove of old Bellevue Hospital records going back several hundred years. It's somewhat of a long story that happened by a strange sequence of events. I'll try to explain it all provided I can count on your strict confidence."

"Of course," Andrea said. "Don't be silly. That's a given."

"I don't know exactly how many records are involved, but it's a lot. I'm guessing in the hundreds. They'd been collected by my great-grandfather Clarence Fuller, the psychiatrist, and hidden away out of circulation back in 1975 by a hospital administrator after Clarence retired. Although I've only had a chance to quickly skim two of them so far, I understand most, if not all, of them are records of patients treated by my relatives. The key thing is that they are not flattering, to say the very least."

Andrea, who had been eating with gusto, stopped and put down her flatware. Leaning forward, she stared at Mitt with unblinking eyes. "Wait a second! Are you suggesting that these records have never seen the light of day?"

"That's exactly what I am saying."

"I'm fascinated. And they go back to the nineteenth century?"

"Early nineteenth century."

"Okay," Andrea remarked mostly to herself, ostensibly to reorient her brain. She took a deep breath, leaned back in her chair, then looked directly at Mitt. "Out with it! Let me hear this long story."

Mitt proceeded to tell her about his sudden unexpected hunger after Ortiz's thyroid storm, his chance meeting with Lashonda Scott in the cafeteria, her telling him about the records hidden by her mother in the basement of the now-deserted psychiatric building, and what the records represented.

"Okay," Andrea suddenly repeated, interrupting Mitt's monologue. "Hold up for a freaking second! Are you suggesting that this supposed night-shift housekeeping supervisor just offered all this to you essentially out of the blue?"

"Yes, that's exactly what I'm saying. She'd seen me earlier after Suárez's death and was aware of my family's association with Bellevue because her family has an even closer association with the institution. She thought that I should know about the records." Mitt didn't tell Andrea anything about Lashonda and him being portals.

"Wow!" Andrea commented, rolling her eyes as she was wont to do. "This is one strange story."

"I agree," Mitt said. "And it gets stranger. What she had told me had certainly fanned my curiosity. I felt I had to see these records, and she offered to take me to see them. Well, maybe I asked. Anyway, that's what we ended up doing around four A.M. Since her mother and she had worked in the building back when it was a functioning psychiatric hospital, she still has the key. Luckily she also had a key for a padlock on the outer gate."

"You guys went into the deserted psychiatric building last night?" Andrea asked incredulously.

"We did. With flashlights, and it wasn't for very long, mind you, but long enough for me to scan the two records."

"What's the place like after being closed up for decades?"

"It's pretty weird," Mitt said, knowing that was a gross understatement. "Even after all this time, it's not completely cleaned out. I saw some old furniture in a couple of the first-floor offices as if people expected to return. But what really caught my attention was that the interior has weirdly decorative architectural details, reminiscent of its exterior and certainly unlike any hospital I've ever been in." In his mind's eye he could again see the unique yellow barrel vaulting in the first-floor hallways.

"What an absolutely crazy night for you," Andrea commented. She rolled her eyes yet again. "No wonder you looked as frazzled as you did when I woke you."

"It was one of the worst and weirdest nights in my life," Mitt admitted. "But, again, all this is for your ears only. Okay?"

"Yeah, sure, okay," Andrea responded.

"And there is a reason I'm particularly interested in telling you all this," Mitt continued. "I'd like to get your opinion and even your reassurance about something I plan to do."

"Oh?" Andrea questioned.

"Yes. I feel compelled to read more of these records but not while I'm standing up in the dark with a flashlight. It doesn't do them justice. The problem is that they're all located in the back closet of a distant storeroom down in the building's basement, and there's no electricity. My plan is to somehow find a way back into the building on my own this afternoon, which shouldn't be that difficult, and bring a box or two of the records back to my apartment. They're all stored in a half dozen or so cardboard bankers boxes. When I'm finished going over them properly, maybe even photographing a few, I will return them and possibly exchange them for more. I'll cross that bridge when I get to it."

"How are you going to get into the building?"

"That I don't know yet, but I can't imagine it will be too difficult. A very small section involving a couple of floors of one wing along Thirtieth Street down near the East River is being used as a homeless shelter. It has its own entrance from Thirtieth. I'll check that out first. I'd be surprised if there wasn't a way to get into the building proper through there since it's all the same building."

"Why not just borrow the keys from Lashonda and go in the same way you did last night?"

"That would be the easiest," Mitt admitted. "But there's a rub. When Lashonda's mother was originally tasked to hide the records, she made a binding promise that she would not give the records to anyone, and she in turn made Lashonda agree to the same, and this is a family that takes such promises to heart. To obviate making Lashonda feel like she's violated her vow, I've decided not to tell her my plans. But I feel a little guilty since I truly respect her and am genuinely thankful for her efforts on my behalf. What's your take?"

"I see your point, but if you are just borrowing some of the records for a few hours and will return them, it seems okay to me, particularly since your interest is personal, and she already showed you the files."

"Thank you," Mitt said. "That's what I thought, but it's nice to have reassurance." He finished the last spoonful of cereal, then lifted the bowl to drink the remaining milk. Replacing the bowl, he stood. "And now I have to get home and clock some serious shut-eye. Thanks for listening to me, and I hope your day and evening aren't too bad."

"I hope so, too," Andrea said. "Good luck this afternoon."

"Thank you. I'll give you a call later and let you know how I've made out if you'd like." He picked up his tray.

"I'd definitely like," Andrea said. "I'll be wondering what's up with you all day!"

"Okay, I'll keep you informed of my progress. I promise."

"What about those three patients you have been assigned for surgery tomorrow? Do you want me to do the admission histories and physicals?"

"Oh damn, I forgot all about them, but thanks for reminding me," Mitt said. He put his tray back down to think for a moment, recognizing it would be best not to be associated with any patients for their own safety, at least until he decided what he was going to do vis-à-vis the residency. "You know, under the circumstances, I would really appreciate if you do them provided you are not too busy. One way or the other, let's be sure to talk as the day progresses."

"Sounds like a plan," Andrea said. "I really don't mind since I have to be here anyway."

"You are a true friend," Mitt said with all sincerity.

Andrea stood up and offered one cheek and then the other. Mitt was more than willing to comply. He then carried his tray over to the soiled-dish window before heading out of the cafeteria. Just before leaving, he waved back at Andrea and she returned the gesture. He felt lucky to have her as a friend.

Mitt was eager to get back to his apartment. As wired as he was after his conversation with Andrea, he worried he might have a problem falling back to sleep even though he was exhausted and mentally strung out. As he hurried through the hospital atrium on his way out, he couldn't help but search for Charlene since he'd seen her there the previous morning. He didn't see her, although surprisingly there seemed to be just about the same number of people coming and going and milling about as yesterday, despite it being the Fourth of July, a national holiday. It was living proof that Bellevue Hospital was a magnet for all types, no matter the date or time of day.

When he emerged onto the street and turned north, he was struck by how much warmer it felt than it had a few hours earlier just before dawn when Lashonda and he had hurried back from the psychiatric hospital. And when he walked out of the shadow of the Bellevue high-rise, the sun beat down on the back of his neck with such surprising intensity that he picked up speed by reflex.

Coming abreast of the psychiatric building's padlocked gate on First Avenue, he couldn't resist the temptation to stop and peer in at what he now knew was a faux entrance to the old hospital. Doing so brought back with disturbing clarity all the moments of surprise and terror he'd experienced on his recent visit. Despite how unnerving that had been, merely thinking about it had the benefit of forcing him to more seriously consider how he was going to get back inside that afternoon.

As he told Andrea, he was more or less counting on the homeless shelter to provide the route, but now he wasn't as confident as he had been. He'd assumed there'd be a passable connection into the building proper just because it was the same structure, but now that he thought about the idea, he questioned what possible function such an access would have. On the contrary, he could think of a lot of reasons why it would be better to have none, considering the population the homeless shelter was serving.

With a rather sudden sense of disappointment, Mitt stepped back from the padlocked gate and looked up and down the wrought iron fence. Even it was a formidable obstruction, meaning there was no easy way for him to get over the fence, much less into a disused building that had been locked and boarded up for forty years. But then he thought again about the homeless shelter, but in a new way. The fact that the shelter existed and had for a number of years told him something else. It needed heat and power. He was also confident that the psychiatric hospital did not have its own furnace. Like any building in a major complex like Bellevue, the heat and other utilities had to come from a central source, and since the homeless shelter needed heat, the connection had to be still active and, more important, still open.

With a sudden sense of excitement, Mitt remembered something else that he'd learned somewhat by accident while he was in medical school at Columbia's College of Physicians and Surgeons. That entire complex of multiple hospitals, academic buildings, and residences was connected underground by a maze of passageways and tunnels, which carried all the utilities, and when he thought about it, he couldn't imagine that Bellevue would be any different. Suddenly it seemed to him that perhaps the best way to get into the mostly empty psychiatric hospital would be to meet a friendly but knowledgeable member of the engineering or maintenance staff and flatter him or her into giving up the info needed.

With a revived sense of resolve, and even a bit of newly found optimism, Mitt broke away from the psychiatric hospital and its imposing fence. Out of the corner of his eye, he'd caught the traffic light at 30th Street and First Avenue changing in his favor, so he took the opportunity to dash across the busy avenue. Reaching the other side, he kept up the power-walk momentum. From there, he only had another half block to go. Suddenly the idea of slipping into his bed naked after a quick shower completely engulfed his tired brain.

CHAPTER 29

Thursday, July 4, 2:47 P.M.

Mitt felt his pulse pick up both speed and intensity as he paused outside a heavy fire door with the designation BUILD-ING 16 displayed in prominent block letters. He already knew from the Bellevue Hospital Engineering and Maintenance Department's supervisor, Tomás Delgado, that building #16 was the departmental designation for the mostly vacated psychiatric hospital building. He also knew that the door could not be locked by law because it was a designated fire door.

For Mitt, it had been a busy but very productive early afternoon. When he'd finally gotten into bed a bit after 10:00 A.M., he'd set his phone alarm for 1:30 P.M. He knew he'd probably still feel exhausted after only a few additional hours of sleep, but he was eager to get the most out of his day off and that didn't include languishing in bed. True to form, when the alarm went off, he'd felt as miserable as expected until he had shaved and taken another shower. By then, he was charged up and eager to face the day, as it was his goal to make a sincere attempt to learn and face his family's true legacy.

The first thing he'd done was walk the two blocks to Third Avenue and visit the nearest hardware store. There he'd been able to purchase a flashlight similar to Lashonda's such that it could be placed on the floor and the beam directed appropriately. He'd also obtained a sizable but inexpensive backpack that was capable of accommodating possibly two of the bankers boxes. He hadn't planned on getting a backpack but happened to see it while waiting in the checkout line. On the way back to his apartment to grab his white doctor's coat and hospital ID, he'd ducked into the neighborhood Kips Bay Deli for a takeout sandwich.

When he did return to the hospital, he went directly to the information booth in the lobby-atrium, where he had to wait in line. Despite the holiday, or perhaps because of it, the booth was a beehive of activity. Mitt's question was about the exact location of the Engineering and Maintenance Department. Interestingly enough, the volunteer Mitt asked didn't have any idea and had to make a call to inquire. Mitt and the volunteer both learned the department office was in the sub-basement, reachable by one of the high-rise's service elevators.

As it turned out, finding the department and then finding a person took more effort than Mitt had anticipated, but it was well worth it. The department office was appropriately located in the subterranean engineering spaces, but the supervisor's private office was not occupied when Mitt finally was directed to it. He had to enlist the help of one of the department workers before meeting the shift head, Tomás Delgado, who was in the furnace room dealing with a problem relating to hot water.

Mitt had introduced himself as Dr. Fuller and explained that he wasn't on duty but wanted to come into the hospital on his day off to learn a bit of what it was like to keep the place functioning and see some of the behind-the-scenes infrastructure. Mitt made it a point to specifically emphasize his appreciation for all the work that Tomás and his team did to make Mitt's doctoring possible.

As Mitt had imagined, his interest and flattery were particularly well received, and Tomás was more than eager to satisfy Mitt's professed curiosity. To that end, the supervisor had carried on nonstop for a good half hour, and Mitt did learn much more than he expected. What he found particularly interesting were the intricate details of the complicated HVAC system involving HEPA filters and a continuous monitoring of the ambient pressures in various parts of the hospital to guarantee proper airflow. It was something Mitt had had absolutely no knowledge about yet knew was obviously of vital importance, particularly keeping constant negative pressure within "infectious" isolation rooms so that the "bad bugs" could not escape into the hospital proper.

When Tomás had come to the end of his monologue, Mitt said that where he'd gone to medical school all the buildings in the complex were connected by passageways, which he had occasionally used in inclement weather. He then asked if that was the case at Bellevue.

"Absolutely," Tomás had exclaimed, as if he needed to defend Bellevue.

"So, you can essentially walk to any of the buildings in the complex underground?"

"Of course," Tomás had said as if it had been a ridiculous question. "We have to provide utilities and the tunnels provide access."

At that point Mitt had switched the conversation to the most distant building, namely the old psychiatric hospital, which Tomás immediately referred to as building #16. As if taking the cue, Tomás spontaneously went on to say that although building #16 was now mostly empty, a small portion of its northeast wing remained in use, so the tunnel connection was still functional to provide the section with power, water, and HVAC. After a bit more banter and a few pointed questions, Mitt had found himself in the tunnel system following a map hastily drawn by Tomás that brought him face-to-face with building #16's fire door.

In preparation to pass beyond the door, Mitt first pocketed the map. He then peeled off the backpack that he'd slung over his shoulder and took out his flashlight. Although the rather dingy Bellevue tunnel system was fully illuminated by a series of bare bulbs in ceiling-mounted sockets above all the piping, he knew from Tomás's explanation that on the other side of the fire door, it was going to be pitch-black the moment the door closed. Mitt also knew that his point of entry was going to be the psychiatric hospital's southwestern wing, which meant he would have to walk around to the northwestern wing to reach the housekeeping storeroom. To do that, he certainly needed the light.

With the backpack returned to his shoulder and the flashlight in hand, Mitt faced the door. Now he just needed to boost his confidence. To that end he was mightily thankful that Lashonda had brought him in earlier and shown him how to deal with the slew of Bellevue ghosts who haunted the building. The key was to make a conscious effort not to look at them, even briefly. But perhaps even more important, if they seemed to block the way, he needed to pretend they were not there and merely walk through them, thereby denying their existence. This latter injunction had been the most difficult lesson for Mitt, but he was confident he could handle it from having experienced Lashonda having so effectively done it that very morning. What he had to remind himself repeatedly was that the spirits were unable to interact with him physically and could only do so indirectly via intermediary objects.

When Mitt thought he was mentally prepared, he audibly counted down from ten to zero. He then reached out, grasped the fire door's vertical handle, and began to pull. At first the door resisted, so he increased the pressure. Finally, it cracked open, and once it did, it swung open easily. The closing mechanism mounted on the top mildly squeaked. Out of the inky darkness ahead wafted chilled, damp air. Switching on his flashlight, Mitt stepped over the threshold and let the door swing shut behind him with a hushed thump.

For a few minutes, Mitt stood where he was in a short side corridor. Ahead his flashlight beam hit up against the whitewashed wall of the psychiatric hospital's basement corridor that extended the length of the southwest wing. He listened intently, as he fully expected to hear distant wailing or other sounds of torment from either the surgerized masses or the souls of the corpses who had been dug up from their graves, just as he and Lashonda had heard when they first entered on their recent visit. But there was none. There was no sound whatsoever. It was as if he'd suddenly been cut off from the rest of the world even though he was in New York City in the middle of a busy summer holiday afternoon. Aboveground, maybe as little as a hundred or so feet to the west, he knew that heavy traffic worked its way north on First Avenue. But where he was standing a heavy silence reigned, almost oppressively so.

Surprised but also ultimately relieved, Mitt started forward and turned to the right down the main corridor. After a short walk, he followed the hallway to the left and came to where the main basement corridor joined those of the two west wings. There he stopped again to listen as he directed his flashlight beam down the main corridor. It was then that he realized just how much more powerful his flashlight was compared with Lashonda's. From where he was presently standing, he could see all the way down to the ornamental central stairway.

Once again, he strained his ears for sounds, but there was nothing, making him wonder if the time of day had any bearing on the Bellevue phantoms' activity. It suddenly occurred to him that perhaps they only came out at night, but then he quickly nixed the idea, remembering he'd seen both Charlene and the surgerized group in daylight hours in the high-rise building.

Progressively encouraged that his current visit was going to be even easier than he'd envisioned, Mitt pushed on. He made one more turn to the left and then soon arrived at the housekeeping supply room. Turning his attention to the door opposite, he got the key from the upper rail. A moment later, he had the supply door open. After returning the key and before entering the room, he shined his light back up the hallway, half expecting to see a bevy of ghosts, or at least Charlene or John. But again there was nothing. He listened intently, even holding his breath for a moment, but he still heard nothing. Although he was pleased, he was also mystified as to why he was being spared. With a shrug, he entered the storeroom. He didn't bother to close the door to the hallway, as he intended to make this a short visit.

After putting his flashlight on the floor of the main part of the storeroom, Mitt first opened the toilet-room door and then the closet. He then spent a minute gazing at the stack of records. His original plan had been to take at least one box and maybe two back to his apartment. But since his visit inside the psychiatric hospital was turning out so different from what he'd expected, he reconsidered his plans. There was a definite downside to going all the way back to his apartment as part of a multiple-visit plan, including traveling

ROBIN COOK

back and forth. There was also the risk of raising suspicions by appearing on multiple occasions in the engineering spaces to access the tunnel system. Suddenly it seemed much more sensible to remain in the psychiatric hospital. He could simply take the boxes he wanted to study upstairs to the first floor. He distinctly remembered seeing some furniture in one or two of the offices. He also assumed there would be more than enough ambient light coming in through the windows even though most, if not all, were boarded up.

"Let's do it," Mitt said out loud to encourage himself. He knew if the circumstances changed and a problem arose, he could always go back to plan A. With that decided, he moved quickly. First he took one of the top boxes, which he assumed were mostly Clarence's lobotomy cases, and put it aside. He then separated out the three lowest boxes to evenly represent the one-hundred-year interval when Homer, Otto, and Benjamin were professionally active.

Since he now planned to remain in the building, he figured he could manage four boxes without difficulty by squeezing two boxes in the backpack and carrying two with one arm, leaving his free hand for the flashlight. All he had to do was walk the length of the basement corridor and up one flight of stairs, hardly an impediment.

Five minutes later, he was ready to go, and he slung the now-full backpack over his shoulder and put his arms through the straps, cinching them snugly. He then picked up the last boxes and held them against his chest with one hand and the flashlight in the other. Moving to the door, he hesitantly leaned out into the hallway, shining the light first in one direction and then the other. Seeing nothing amiss, he listened intently. Hearing nothing, he was reassured. He then started out for the central circular staircase, leaving the storeroom door ajar. After only a few steps, he jumped in fright and sucked in a lungful of air when he detected sudden movement out of the corner of his eye. Quickly redirecting the flashlight beam, he caught sight of the source and relaxed. It was a rat, a real rat, which swiftly scampered out of sight into a side room. After taking a reassuringly deep breath and acknowledging how tense he was for obvious reasons, he continued on.

The moment Mitt reached the main basement corridor, he was able to see a bit of welcome daylight ahead, which was flooding down the circular staircase. Encouraged, he quickened his pace, and the closer he got, the brighter it became. When he finally entered the tiled, cabinet-lined area at the base of the stairway, he turned off his flashlight. Moving to the center of the space, he looked up and could see all the way up ten stories to a skylight that was bright enough with direct sunlight to make him squint. When he held his breath and listened, he could now hear a slight variable hum, which he interpreted as traffic out on First Avenue. Most important, there were no distant cries of anguish or distress. Nor was there any horrid, sickening smell. At that moment, the psychiatric hospital was just an empty, sad, derelict building with a long and involved history of troubled residents, nothing more.

Without the need for the flashlight, Mitt readjusted the two bankers boxes he was carrying and started up the stairs. He was feeling progressively at ease with ever-increasing confidence that the sizable Bellevue Hospital spirit population was taking the Fourth of July holiday off, for which he was decidedly thankful. When he reached the ground floor, he even stopped for a moment to appreciate the high-ceilinged, architecturally decorated lobby, all of which was significantly more impressive in daylight. He also noticed something he'd not seen on his previous visit, namely an information booth off to his left behind the reception desk. Within the booth he could make out a glass-fronted directory hanging on the wall, which he assumed listed the various professional and departmental office locations, as if the building were still in use.

Drawn to the building's directory and wondering if he'd recognize any of the names, Mitt stepped over to it by skirting the reception desk. To his amazement, Dr. Clarence Fuller's name was still on the board, listing his office as 303! At first it didn't make any sense, since he knew the Psychiatric Department didn't move completely into the high-rise until 1985 and his great-grandfather had retired in 1975. But then, giving the issue a bit more thought, Mitt assumed that during that decade, the staff knew they were moving and were probably doing so on a piecemeal basis because the high-rise was available beginning in the early 1970s. During that interim transition period, the building's directory was probably just ignored and forgotten.

Mitt pondered the coincidence of discovering his great-grandfather's office number and that thought led to another. Since he needed a place to look at the records, including Clarence's records, what better spot than Clarence's office? It seemed to him as if a bit of poetic justice was involved, especially considering the stress he was under. In fact, the surprising circumstances so moved him that he put the boxes of records he was holding on to the information booth counter along with his flashlight and took out his phone. He had a sudden urge to share the unexpected discovery with Andrea, if she was available.

As the call went through, he leaned against the information booth, letting his eyes take in more of the hospital lobby's details, including gazing up the west corridor. As he did so, its unique yellow-and-tan coloration was an unpleasant reminder of his recurrent nightmare.

"What's up?" Andrea answered with no preamble.

"Are you busy?" Mitt asked.

"Not at the moment," she said. "I'm in the on-call lounge schmooz-ing with some of the other residents. Where are you?"

"Don't tell anybody, but I'm in the old psychiatric hospital as we speak, standing in its lobby."

She lowered her voice. "So, you made it in?"

"I did."

"How did you manage it? Through the homeless shelter?"

"No, something better. Remember how we used the tunnels at Columbia on occasion in bad weather? They have the same tunnels here at Bellevue, and it brought me into the basement, no problem."

"What are you doing up in the lobby? I thought the records were down in the basement."

"They are, but I've had a change in plans. Instead of going back and forth between here and my apartment, I'm going to do my read-ing here."

"I don't like that. I think you should get the hell out of there. I'm worried about you."

"Oh, come on! You don't need to worry. I'll be fine. It's a perfect place to read old Bellevue records. For one thing, I can assure you that it is understandably quieter than any library."

"Very funny," Andrea said insincerely. "Excuse me for not laugh-ing, and I suppose I should be pleased for you getting in and all, but I'm not. I don't like you being in there, period. Don't get caught!"

"I'm not going to get caught," Mitt said with mild irritation. The conversation was starting to remind him of talking to his mother. "But listen! Let me tell you something rather amazing that I just learned." He went on to describe how his ancestor's office was still listed on the building's directory and that he was planning on using it to read through the man's records.

"That's interesting," Andrea said, but hardly with the surprise or excitement Mitt was expecting.

"I'm getting the impression you don't think this coincidence is quite as interesting as I do."

"That's not the point. I don't like you in that building for a host of reasons. I thought you were going to be taking the records home."

"Going back and forth from here to my apartment would take too much time and effort," Mitt said simply, since he couldn't tell her about the surprising apparition situation.

"All right, get to it and then leave! But listen! Call me the moment you get out of that place. Okay?"

"Okay," Mitt agreed. "I'll call you when I leave, but don't hold your breath. It might take me an hour or two. There're a lot of records, although I'm guessing there's going to be a lot of repetition."

"Whatever," Andrea said. "Just get your butt out of there ASAP, and I want to hear from you the minute you do."

"You got it," Mitt said, and he disconnected. He couldn't believe that Andrea didn't share his amazement about Clarence's office. With a disappointed shake of his head, he readjusted his backpack and picked up the boxes and his flashlight. He then returned to the grand circular staircase and started up.

Mitt didn't waste time. He took the stairs in twos all the way to the third floor. There, he quickly determined which direction was 303 and then found the office. In the process he was again reminded of his recurrent nightmare, since the main east–west corridor had the exact same unique coloration and architectural details as the main corridor on the first floor.

Visually there was nothing special about 303. It was a nondescript office that was still furnished with very basic, old office furniture. It comprised an outer office for a secretary, where there were a number of aged side chairs and a metal desk, and an inner office for Clarence, with a larger, wooden desk and an ancient, black faux-leather executive desk chair. There were absolutely no personal objects whatsoever in either room, although there were pale rectangles on the walls as evidence of pictures having hung in the past. The inner office had two good-sized but dirty windows looking south, both of which afforded a direct line of sight out over the Bellevue Hospital complex, which was now dominated by the high-rise tower soaring twenty-five stories into the hazy summer sky. Mitt pulled out several of the desk drawers. All were empty, save for a few errant paper clips.

Taking Andrea's advice, Mitt got right to work. He took the boxes out of the backpack and, along with the two he'd carried by hand, he arranged them chronologically on the desktop. He then sat down in the old-fashioned desk chair, which faced the door to the outer office. From not having been used for decades, it loudly squealed in protest, momentarily shattering the heavy silence of the abandoned building. For a fleeting moment, Mitt marveled at the idea that he was occupying the very same desk and chair as Clarence Fuller, a man who'd been his idol since Mitt was a teenager.

The first box Mitt opened was Clarence's. As soon as he looked at the stack of medical records, he could see how Lashonda had found Charlene's so quickly. It was tagged with a yellow Post-it note. Although he'd already skimmed the record once and then attempted to read it more carefully, he took it out again to go over it once more with adequate light. He wanted to be absolutely certain he hadn't missed even a brief medical explanation of why the child had been lobotomized. But the moment he started the very first paragraph, he sensed a presence emanating from the direction of the outer office that raised the hackles on his neck. Glancing up, he jolted and caught his breath.

Standing in the doorway to the outer office no more than about eight feet away was Charlene Wagner. The shocking aspect of her sudden appearance was twofold. The first was that from where he was sitting, he had an unobstructed view through the outer office all the way out into the central corridor, making him wonder why he hadn't seen her coming. The second was that she radiated a totally different vibe, despite being clothed in the same dress with the same bloodstains and with her hair being as blond as ever and her skin as pale as Mitt remembered. Contrary to all the other times he'd been confronted by her, she wasn't exuding the all-consuming anger and resentment she had in the past. In point of fact, although she was holding the orbitoclast, she wasn't pointing it menacingly at Mitt as if it were a weapon. Instead, she was merely holding it in her left hand while, with her right hand, she was actively gesturing Mitt to follow her. Perhaps even more compelling from Mitt's perspective was that she was smiling as if she were deliriously happy. In fact, Mitt sensed she might even be happily laughing even though she was emitting no sound.

Immediately intrigued at what might possibly be making Charlene's spirit so contented, Mitt stood up. Although he could hear in the back of his mind Lashonda's warning about ignoring the ghosts, he couldn't think of any reason he shouldn't at least see what Charlene had in mind. Stepping around the desk, he watched her reaction. She was visibly pleased and began backing up toward the door to the hall, all the while gesturing for Mitt to follow.

Ever more intrigued, Mitt first ended up out in the main corridor and then at the circular stairs. There Charlene started up, and as Mitt approached the first step, he saw something he thought was both fascinating and, in retrospect, predictable. When Charlene moved through a ray of sunlight streaming in a north-facing window, it passed through her unencumbered, attesting to her immaterialism.

Mitt followed Charlene up to the fifth floor as she continued to urge him on. Once on the fifth floor, he followed her all the way down the east portion of the building's central corridor and finally almost to the end of the southeast wing. There she gave him a particularly broad smile and gestured for him to follow her into what Mitt guessed had been a VIP patient room with an open but lockable door. Mitt hesitated at the threshold. From where he was standing, he could see that the room had a single window with a view that included a small slice of the East River as well as the Bellevue high-rise building. The furniture consisted of a single bed with a thin, heavily stained mattress and nothing more.

With Charlene's continued encouragement, Mitt hesitantly entered the room but stopped a few steps from the door. At that moment, Charlene was standing alongside the bed, pointing down to it repeatedly. Mitt was confused, not understanding what she was doing. "What is it?" he asked. He shrugged his shoulders and spread his hands, palms up, to indicate his bewilderment. Suddenly he had a flash of insight and immediately spoke up. "Is this the room where you were lobotomized?"

Charlene nodded yes and her happy expression faded. But she continued gesturing down at the bed, even more intensely. It was at that point that Mitt gathered that she wanted him to lie down on the bed, which he had absolutely no intention of doing. Instead, he took a step back, deciding it was time to ignore Charlene and get the hell out of the room. But before he could, she quickly rounded the end of the bed and approached him. Although his mind was shouting at him to turn around and flee, he somehow couldn't do it, as he was momentarily transfixed by her unblinking, intensely blue eyes.

And then the worst possible thing happened. Without warning, she reached out and grasped his arm to pull him back toward the bed—worse still, he shockingly, terrifyingly felt it! There was actual physical contact and a tug, which was impossible with her being an apparition without physical presence. After all, he'd just seen sunlight pass right through her! How could she touch him? But she did!

With a sudden overwhelming sense of panic, Mitt yanked his arm free from Charlene's grasp, spun around, and fled from the room. Once in the hall, he began running full tilt back toward the central stairway. As he did so, it occurred to him that he was at that moment living his recurrent nightmare. He was being chased down an arched, two-toned yellow-tan corridor by unknown forces whose presence had been announced by the shocking reality of physical contact with Charlene's ghost.

With his breath coming in gasps, Mitt first turned right and then left. He was now in the building's central corridor, racing toward the circular stairs. His plan was to rapidly descend the central stairway to the first floor and then dash out the door that he and Lashonda had used. At this point, he didn't care if he was apprehended by Security. In fact, he hoped he would be.

But he didn't quite make it to the central stairway. All at once, he came to an abrupt stop. Suddenly appearing directly ahead of him was a dense crowd of surgerized ghosts. But this gruesome horde was not carrying amputated limbs or excised tumors and organs. Instead, they were carrying all manner of old-fashioned hay forks, knives, and axes that appeared to be all too real, and they were coming toward him.

Unwilling to test whether these ghosts and their weapons could touch him or not, he changed direction, and in an utter panic fled back the way he'd come. After the first turn, he saw Charlene directly ahead, obviously pursuing him. But as he rapidly closed on her, he didn't stop. Instead, at the last second he closed his eyes and kept running, unsure of what was about to happen when he collided with her. An instant later and still running, he reopened his eyes. She was no longer there.

Running to the very end of the southeast wing, he rushed into what had been a locked, disturbed ward housing violent mental patients. Once inside, he spun around and slammed the heavy metal door shut. He then took several steps backward while staring at the door, praying it would be a barrier to the swarm of nightmarish phantoms chasing him.

He didn't have long to wait. The entire horde including Charlene came through the door as if it wasn't there. And once they had, the awful cacosmia Mitt had suffered previously enveloped him like an olfactory shock wave. For a few seconds, the angry mob halted with all of them staring daggers at Mitt. But then they quickly recommenced bearing down on him, threateningly brandishing their weapons, including Charlene with her orbitoclast. Mitt backed up, feeling terrified. When his back hit against the far wall, he closed his eyes and desperately tried to think of something else, something decidedly more pleasant, like walking in Central Park or riding a bike along the Hudson River. Anything! But the mental ploy of actively trying to ignore the apparitions didn't work. Nor did it affect the cacosmia. A moment later he felt a hundred hands seize him and lift him off his feet.

EPILOGUE

Monday, July 8, 11:15 A.M.

T he doctor can see you now," the secretary said to Benjamin and
Clara Fuller. They had come to the office of Dr. Claes Lundström in the NYU Department of Neurology in hopes of getting some good news, but they weren't optimistic. Since the late-night
call on the Fourth of July, their lives had taken a sudden and remarkable turn for the worse. It had been then that they learned that their
only son, Michael Fuller, whose life had held so much promise as a
surgeon-to-be, had suffered an inexplicable trauma with severe mental ramifications.

Benjamin and Clara got to their feet. Then Benjamin turned to
Mitt, who was quietly sitting between them, and took the young
man's hand, urging him to stand as well. Mitt did as he was told and
did it agreeably. He'd been shaved, bathed, and dressed in a white
shirt, tie, and jacket early that morning and looked entirely present-
able, although at that moment the tie was slightly awry. Benjamin
adjusted it, gave Mitt a reassuring pat on the shoulder, and then again

took his hand to lead him into Dr. Lundström's inner office. Mitt complied silently without any change of his blank, apathetic expression.

The doctor had gotten up from his desk to come to the door to welcome them. He was tall and thin with a pale, almost sallow complexion. He spoke with a pleasant, slight Swedish accent. "Please," he said while graciously gesturing toward three chairs he'd arranged to face his desk. His expression was serious and empathetic.

Both parents helped to guide their compliant son to the middle chair, then took the chairs on either side.

When the doctor was certain his guests were comfortably seated, he retreated behind his desk. A large, flat-screen monitor was built into the wall behind him. Currently displayed was a black-and-white, sagittal, cutaway image of a human cranium.

"Thank you for coming in," Claes said. "And thank you for bringing your son into the hospital this morning to have his MRI."

"We are here to do whatever needs to be done," Clara said. Benjamin nodded. "Has the MRI been helpful? Has it provided any explanations?"

"Yes and no," Claes said. "Let me show you what the MRI tells us." He picked up a remote from the desk and turned half around so that he could gaze up at the screen. He also picked up a pencil-like laser pointer, which he turned on. It projected a small white arrow. "It's this area that I'd like you to look at," he said as he moved the arrow around in a tight circle in the left-hand portion of the image just behind the forehead. "Now, let me run through a number of slices and have you concentrate on this same area of the forebrain."

The image changed a number of times in succession, and each time Claes indicated the area he wanted his visitors to observe. Unfortunately, to Benjamin and Clara, all the images looked exactly the same. Surreptitiously, as Claes continued speaking, they exchanged a bewildered glance.

"Tell me, are you able to appreciate the murkiness of these areas in the various slices that I'm indicating here in the forebrain?"

"I'm afraid neither of us are able to notice much of a difference," Benjamin admitted. Clara nodded in agreement.

"Okay, sorry," Claes said. "Forgive me! I do tend to forget that laypersons are not accustomed to interpreting MRI images. Well, take my word for it. There is definite murkiness in these areas, which confirms for us something rather surprising, even shocking."

"Oh?" Benjamin murmured. "Exactly what does it confirm?"

"It confirms for me, as well as for the consulting radiologists, that your son has been surgically lobotomized."

Benjamin and Clara simultaneously sucked in a lungful of air, as both were aware that such a diagnosis meant Mitt's current troubles weren't transient, stress-related psychological issues, as they had been vainly hoping, but rather a permanent state. Benjamin was the first to find his voice and it shook with shock and anger: "Lobotomized? But wasn't that procedure totally discredited decades ago?"

"You are absolutely correct," Claes said soothingly. "It was discredited more than a half century ago, to be more exact."

"But then how could this have happened?" Benjamin sputtered.

"That is the question of the hour," Claes continued. He maintained a calm tone of voice, which tended to emphasize his slight accent. "Everyone is making every effort to find the answer, particularly those people in charge of the NYU Surgical Residency Program and the Bellevue Hospital Security Services. I'm sure we will soon know more than we do now, as there is an active investigation underway."

While Benjamin, obviously fuming, continued to stare at Dr.

Lundström, Clara turned to her son to see if he had responded to this disturbing news. But he hadn't. Mitt's blank expression was unchanged, reminding Clara of the saying "the lights are on but no one's home." Feeling particularly pained at this new information, Clara couldn't help herself; she reached out, rested her hand on her child's motionless knee, and asked him if he was all right.

Mitt's response was to focus on Clara, at least for a moment, and say he was fine. But the response was so emotionally blunted that it sounded like a recording. In the next instant, his eyes re-clouded over, and he slipped back to wherever he'd been moments before. As blank as his expression was, he seemed to Clara to be in another universe.

"Your saying 'we'll soon know more' implies we know something already," Benjamin blurted out after a moment of pained silence. He was desperately trying to rein in his emotions and organize his thoughts. The news that his son had been lobotomized was a crushing blow.

"I'm sorry, but what have you been told so far?" Claes questioned.

"Almost nothing," Benjamin snapped. "When we got here early Friday morning, our boy was an inpatient in the ICU and we were informed only that he was stable and in that sense doing well. Yesterday we got to take him home to his apartment, where we are currently staying with him. We didn't see any doctors when he was discharged. From the nurses, we'd been told that the consensus was that he'd suffered a severe emotional shock and that he was scheduled for the MRI this morning."

"I'm sorry," Claes said sympathetically. "I apologize for the hospital and the university. I suppose everyone assumed someone else had spoken with you, which I, too, have been guilty of. Be that as it may, let me fill you in. Your son was discovered wandering around in the darkness of the locked and deserted Bellevue Psychiatric Hospital. It's been empty since 1985.

"A call had been made to Bellevue Security by his surgical resident colleague Dr. Andrea Intiso, who'd received a call earlier in the afternoon from your son telling her where he was—supposedly in the closed-up building reading hospital records. Of course, that was entirely fictitious, as the hospital had long since been emptied of all its records. According to her, she'd insisted that he call her the moment he left, which never happened, nor did he respond to her attempts to get in touch with him, ergo her eventual call to Security. What she did tell Security when she called was that your son had been under great psychological stress because a number of his assigned inpatients had passed away unexpectedly, and she thought he was taking it personally."

Claes paused for a moment to allow Benjamin and Clara time to absorb what he'd told them. "Had you heard any of this?" he questioned after a few beats.

"No," Benjamin and Clara echoed.

"Then let me continue. When Security did locate your son, which didn't happen until around ten P.M. since the building is rather large, he was in a stupor with bloodstains on the front of his white doctor's coat. He was also carrying an outdated surgical instrument called an orbitoclast, which had been used in the old days to do bedside lobotomies and which he had apparently found in the deserted building. At that point he was immediately taken to the emergency room, where the source of the blood was determined to be the upper conjunctival vortexes of each eye, which at least raised the possibility, as unbelievable as it seemed to everyone, that he had had a transorbital lobotomy. At that point he was admitted to the ICU to be stabilized and a non-emergency MRI was scheduled for this morning."

"How in God's name could he have suffered a lobotomy in a vacant hospital?" Benjamin demanded, his anger returning in a rush.

"I can appreciate your frustration," Claes said. "Believe me, we all feel it, as there is only one possible way for it to have happened."

"I'm listening," Benjamin snapped.

"Self-inflicted," Claes stated. "Your son had to have done it to himself."

AUTHOR'S NOTE

For those readers with a newly generated interest in the history of the legendary Bellevue Hospital, I cannot recommend more highly the fascinating *Bellevue: Three Centuries of Medicine and Mayhem at America's Most Storied Hospital*, by David Oshinsky (New York: Anchor Books, 2017). In many ways it reads like a novel, complete with larger-than-life characters and a fascinating narrative, revealing all the warts as well as the triumphs. After having personally had the experience of being a sub-intern at Bellevue Hospital in the early 1960s on Columbia Division 1, an experience that was both intellectually stimulating and horrifying at the same time, I've always wanted to include this storied hospital in one of my novels, and David Oshinsky's book helped make that happen.